THE MAN SHE LOVED TO HATE

Deric's green eyes darkened with fury. "Damn it, woman," he swore, "don't push my patience too far!"

In the face of his rage, Juliette knew it was unwise, but she had never been able to control her tongue. The words were out before she could stop them.

"Or what?" she taunted.

Two strides brought Deric around the table to her side. Her eyes widening when she saw he was serious, she started to dodge to one side, but he was far too swift for her. He swept her up into his arms, and though she struggled, his strength made it seem an effortless gesture. He strode to the bed and paused.

Deric's face was close to hers, and those furious green eyes bored into her frightened ones. He seemed about to drop her angrily on the bed when she saw his gaze change.

Juliette had had enough suitors to know what the change meant: the sharp intake of breath, the darkening eyes, the heated skin. She steeled herself grimly for the hated kiss that was surely to follow . . . but discovered that the longer he delayed, the more she was eager to feel his touch!

ZEBRA BOOKS
KENSINGTON PUBLISHING CORP.

ZEBRA BOOKS

are published by

Kensington Publishing Corp.
475 Park Avenue South
New York, NY 10016

First printing: May, 1989

Printed in the United States of America

Part One

Ah Love! could thou and I with Fate conspire
To grasp this sorry Scheme of Things entire,
Would we not shatter it to bits—and then
Re-mold it nearer to the Heart's Desire!

Omar Khayyám, *Rubáiyát of Omar Khayyám*

Chapter One

North Africa, June 27, 1804

The sun shone mercilessly on the expanse of desert. To the north were the dim shadows of the hills behind which stood Derna; an hour's ride to the south were the palm trees and buildings of the oasis of Jalo. But this stretch of desert was empty except for the small knot of figures; there was no help in sight.

They were fierce Bedouin raiders, and their leader sheathed his bloody scimitar with a grin and turned to the girl cowering behind the tumbled rocks. Four bodies lay broken and bloody at his feet. The girl's escort had put up a fierce fight, but they were no match for the six Bedouins who now surrounded the girl.

Her dark eyes flicked with hopeless terror at the men. Their swarthy faces were cruel under their headcloths. The leader was a giant of a man with a black beard and a hooked nose, his bulk seemingly larger because of the flowing robes he wore.

His eyes gleamed with pleasure as he looked at her cowering terrified behind the rocks. She was beautiful, young. Her long black hair was like a river, her olive skin smooth. She would bring him a fortune, for she was the daughter of a wealthy desert sheik who would pay a great ransom for her. But first . . . he and his men would have her.

He stood looking at her, savoring her fear, when there was a shout from one of his men. He turned, his eyes narrowing.

The man pointed. There was a small swirling cloud of dust on the rocky hill above. The Bedouin raider knew what the dust meant. Riders.

Two riders swept over the hill and halted, silhouetted against the burning white sky. They were robed as the Bedouins were, in flowing burnooses and headcloths, their faces half-covered. Their steeds were swift Arabians, and the Bedouins caught the glint of rifles and cutlasses that hung at their sides.

For a moment, no one moved, as the riders on the hill took in the tableau below them. But they were as experienced in the desert as the Bedouins were, and the meaning of the scene below them was immediately apparent.

The girl's head swiveled, hope lighting in her eyes as she stared at the riders, then fading. What could two do against six, when her escort of four had been so easily overcome?

With a flash, two rifles were swept out of their scabbards and raised simultaneously to the riders' shoulders. Before the Bedouins could react, the crack of two shots rang out, and two of the Bedouin raiders fell motionless in the dust. Just thirty seconds had passed since the riders appeared over the hill.

With a yell, the riders put their heels to their horses and came charging down the rocky slopes. By now, the four Bedouins left were running for their horses, drawing their cutlasses and shouldering their rifles. Shots rang out but were wide, missing the riders as they thundered down the hill.

The two riders swept into the camp, trampling the fallen bodies under their horses' pounding hooves, catching two of the Bedouins as they scrambled for their horses. But the Bedouins were fighters; turning, they raised their cutlasses and parried the strokes. Still the mounted men had the advantage. The riders' cutlasses whirled in a whistling arc, cutting the air, and the two Bedouins fell almost at once.

A rifle shot rang out as the riders fought to turn their rearing horses, and one spun from the saddle by the force of the bullet plowing through his shoulder. He hit the ground with a jolt, but rose almost at once, a deadly light in his eyes and his cutlass gripped in his right hand.

He faced the huge Bedouin leader, who threw down his spent

rifle with a laugh and drew his scimitar. The Bedouin grinned when he saw the red stain spreading on his opponent's shoulder. But a moment later his grin faded when he saw the man advance on him with a lethal light in his eyes, face grim. The man moved as if he didn't feel the wound.

They circled each other, the huge Bedouin leader measuring the man who faced him. His foe was taller, but lean under his robes, light on his feet and fast . . . but the Bedouin was confident. His own strength would be the greater. With a yell, he leapt at the man, his scimitar flashing.

Cutlass met scimitar and held. For a moment, the men struggled, testing their strength, faces close, every muscle straining. But the Bedouin was the larger, and his opponent was wounded. He felt the man begin to give and, with a triumphant growl, pressed forward violently with all his strength to break the locked swords—

But he had underestimated the man's fighting skill, had gone for the kill too soon. With a lightning-swift move, the man released his locked cutlass and dodged deftly to one side, letting the Bedouin's weight carry him past in a stumble. His left hand, holding a knife, came up. The Bedouin's weight drove him onto the point.

The Bedouin staggered and fell, dropping his sword. He rolled onto his back, his eyes already dimming with death, and looked into the face of his adversary. He would see the man who sent him to Paradise before he died. The face he saw was as bronzed by the desert sun as his own was . . . but the eyes that met his with such an implacable, deadly light were a brilliant shade of green.

The green-eyed man straightened, turning to see how his companion fared. He laughed when he saw him standing over his fallen adversary, grinning at him.

"So you were faster than I was, Farouk," he said.

Farouk's dark face split into a wider smile. "And I would gloat about it except that I see you were wounded. Still, it's not often I have the better of you, Dahkir. By Allah, I will savor this moment as long as I can!" Both men spoke Arabic rather than the Bedouin tongue.

Dahkir grinned back and then turned. He walked to where

the girl still cowered behind the rocks. He stopped and looked down at her frightened face for a moment, then said quietly, "Did they harm you?"

She stood on trembling legs, shaking her head. "I—I was on my way to my father's tents in Jalo from Giarabub. The Bedouins . . . they killed my escort." Her eyes were passionately grateful as she stared up at the man who had rescued her. "You saved my life, but you are wounded!"

He smiled, a smile that took her breath. "It is nothing," he said. "Now, shall we ride for Jalo—and your father's tents?"

The sun was rising the next morning as Dahkir and Farouk rode away from Jalo, their faces once more to the desert. Dahkir's wound had been bound, and both had headaches from the lavish banquet the girl's grateful father had feasted them with.

Farouk grimaced, then glanced at his companion. Dahkir's profile was unreadable, his mouth set in a line, his eyes narrowed under straight dark brows. Obviously his head felt no better than Farouk's. A wicked grin spread over Farouk's face.

"As usual, my friend, you manage to land on your feet," he said. "Who would have guessed the girl would be the daughter of a sheik? But knowing you, I should have guessed. Allah favors you. Though why you refused the gold he wanted to give us—"

Dahkir threw Farouk a quelling look. "Because, as you well know, his future friendship could be handy. This way, he owes us. If we accepted his gold, his debt to us would have been paid."

Farouk laughed. "You are a devious soul! And as I said, fortune smiles on you, though I was surprised to see you decide to do such a chivalrous thing, rescuing that girl. After all your black words about the worthlessness of women, I thought you'd leave her to the raiders."

A dark brow lifted. "I don't take back my words. Most women are worthless—except in bed, of course." A quick smile flashed across his face. "I have yet to meet one who could change my mind . . . but do you really think I would have left her to them?"

Farouk gave his companion a knowing look. "No . . . I know you would not. That is what I am saying. Your words about women are very black, but your heart does not believe these words. You are bitter because you put one of them on a pedestal and then found she did not deserve your worship. So now you say you condemn the whole race, but there is a soft heart under that steel exterior, my friend."

Dahkir scowled blackly. "You speak with the wits of a sand flea," he growled. "I'm no more chivalrous than you are!" Obviously he considered Farouk's words an insult.

Farouk grinned again irrepressibly. "But I am very chivalrous, my friend," he protested, then threw back his head and laughed when Dahkir put his heels to his stallion's side and galloped away.

With a shout, Farouk followed, and the two riders raced into the desert, their robes cracking behind them in the hot wind, raising a cloud of dust that could be seen for many miles.

England, June 27, 1804

Juliette Hawkins slipped around the corner of the great half-timbered Elizabethan house and held her breath as she surveyed the scene before her. The only sound was the warm afternoon breeze rustling the ivy that covered the mellow, centuries-old, red-brick walls, and far away the faint barking of a dog. Everywhere, peace lay like the bright sunlight. The enclosed courtyard and stables in front of her looked deserted, and beyond was a tempting view of woods and fields that beckoned her.

Her eyes sparkled with delighted mischief at the thought that she just *might* manage her escape. If she could only make it to the stable without being seen . . .

She picked up the full, bottle-green skirts of her riding habit and made a dash for the stable door across the courtyard. She had timed her break for freedom with care; all the men were out on a shooting expedition, and the women were resting in their rooms.

Except Juliette. She had donned her riding habit instead of taking a nap, hoping to snatch a few hours of glorious freedom from this dull house-party that seemed like it would never end.

Inside the stable door, she paused, her eyes adjusting to the darkness. She listened, but heard no sound of the grooms and stable boys. No doubt they were resting in their quarters, snatching a few hours before the gentlemen would return.

Quickly and efficiently, she saddled and bridled Cinnabar, a restive gray mare she had ridden before on sedate riding expeditions with the other ladies. She ran her gloved hand down the mare's neck, anticipating that at last she would be able to put her through her paces instead of jogging along at a gentle—and boring!—trot.

She checked Cinnabar at the stable door, taking a last look around. She hoped no one was observing her from the upper windows, but that was a chance she would have to take. If Lionel found out—she sighed. Her guardian Lionel would lecture her about her "improper" behavior, like he had a thousand times before, and tell her her actions could hurt his career in the diplomatic service. . . .

She shook her head, the bronze and green plumes of her hat rustling in the breeze. The trouble was, Lionel thought *everything* she did could hurt his career. He was so stuffy, with so many rules and regulations that chafed her, always dragging her to dull dinners and balls with his conservative friends in the diplomatic service. Or to country weekends like this one. But at least they were more tolerable than the dinner parties, because she had been raised in the country and missed the freedom of riding over the woods and fields. She lived with Lionel in his Kensington town house, and weekend house parties like this one offered the chance to escape society's restrictions for a little while.

She put her heels to Cinnabar's flanks and rode away from the stables at a sedate pace . . . just in case anyone was watching. She wouldn't give Cinnabar her head until she reached the cover of the woodlands, she thought.

*   *   *

Avery Ashburn leaned his rifle against a low stone wall and pulled out a silk handkerchief. He made an ostentatious show of dusting off the weathered gray stones, then sat gracefully. He pulled a silver flask from his pocket and unscrewed the top.

"Time for a rest, gentlemen," he said. "All this riding and walking is most tiresome. I for one don't find much amusement in persecuting these odious birds. I prefer not to have such intimate knowledge of the food on my table." He took a long pull from the flask and regarded his companions with a supercilious smile.

The three other gentlemen gave him a dry look. Avery Ashburn was a fop with a poisonous tongue, and a rake with a bad reputation. But he was the oldest son of Damien Ashburn, a senior diplomat, and so he had to be tolerated. He had a pretty, malicious face, his light brown curls were artfully arranged, and his tweed hunting jacket had a dashing cut too fashionable to be entirely respectable.

"Look here, Ashburn, we've only been out for an hour," said the party's host, Gordon Burns, throwing him a glance of distaste. "I say, can't expect to bag any grouse if you don't stick with it. I don't intend to give up just yet." His portly face was red with annoyance.

"That's right, old chap," agreed Lionel Hawkins, Juliette's guardian. Lionel was stout too, in his thirties, but looked ten years older. His fair hair was thinning; his face, always serious. He had very little sense of humor and couldn't abide a dandy like Ashburn. "'Fraid we aren't ready to stop just yet."

"Then by all means, do go on," said Ashburn, raising a mocking brow at them. "Shoot me one for dinner, won't you?"

William Timberly, the third man, joined Ashburn on the wall. He was also a young dandy, frankly bored with the shooting party and the ponderous discussions of world affairs rather than gossip. "I'll stay here with Ashburn, I believe." He grinned. "I'd rather finish off a flask than some grouse."

The two young men watched Lionel and Gordon walk stiffly off, obviously outraged that their companions had elected to stay behind and drink. It was typical of today's youth, they agreed, even though neither of them was more than ten years older than the two they left behind.

Ashburn laughed and passed his flask to his companion. "Too damned nice a day to ruin it with exercise," he drawled. "This is a shockingly boring house party. If the beautiful Juliette wasn't here, I believe I would have expired of *ennui* the first night."

Timberly laughed, then threw a gleaming look at Ashburn under his brows. "How goes the pursuit, Avery?"

Avery's pretty face hardened. "Not as I would wish, Will. She's as cold and haughty to me as she is with every man who courts her. She's avoided me ever since I cornered her in the butler's pantry and, ah . . . tried to melt her coolness. My head still rings with the slap she gave me."

Timberly snorted with amusement and smoothed his cravat. "Aye, for a wench who looks so fiery, it's damned hard to light a spark in her. Then it looks like you will lose our wager. I doubt you'll get her into your bed after all."

There was a glint of determination in Ashburn's eyes. "If I could ever get her alone, I wager I would. But she's always so damned chaperoned . . . and now time's running out. You know Lionel has accepted a post in Malta? And he's taking La Belle Juliette with him."

"Malta? But that's in the Mediterranean, isn't it? The other side of the world, almost." Timberly's voice registered disbelief. "Why would anyone want to go to a place like that?"

Ashburn's lips curved in a disdainful smile. "Well, for Lionel, it'll be an advancement for his career. Very big stuff for a diplomat, I gather. Some kind of trouble in that part of the world, but don't ask me for details. You know how closely I follow world affairs." Both men laughed at this sarcasm.

"And that damned girl says she can hardly wait to go with him," Ashburn went on, annoyance in his voice. "Thinks it will be an adventure. I tried to tell her being my mistress would be much more exciting, but she was deaf to my pleas. Damn my eyes, I'm so desperate to get her in my bed, I'm even thinking of doing the honorable thing and offering to marry her."

Timberly's brows rose in astonishment. "You—married?" He chuckled, vastly amused.

Ashburn threw him a wry look. "Married, perhaps, but I didn't say I would be *faithful*. It might be worth it to get that delectable girl into my bed."

"And if you don't do it soon, you'll lose our wager." Timberly grinned. "I can use the money just now. I've had a run of bad luck at the tables lately."

Ashburn took another long pull from the flask. Then he whistled softly. "Well, speak of the angel!" he exclaimed. "There she goes."

Timberly looked up in time to see a horse and rider cross the fields and disappear into the woods. "And alone!" Timberly exclaimed. "I'll be damned."

Ashburn rose, smoothing a hand over his curls. There was a lustful gleam in his eyes. "This is a chance I can't afford to miss, Timberly." In a moment, he had mounted his bay gelding, slinging the rifle carelessly into its leather scabbard on the saddle. His grin was devilish. "Wish me luck," he said, and put his heels to his horse's flanks.

Juliette entered the cool green woodland ride with a feeling of bubbling freedom rising inside her. She leaned forward over Cinnabar's neck and urged her into a gallop. The woods flashed by, shafts of sunlight and shade, as they flew along the ride. The wind tugged at Juliette's coppery curls until they escaped from their ribbon and tumbled over her back in disarray. She laughed aloud as her exhilaration grew, hearing Cinnabar's pounding hooves, the wind singing in her ears.

As she jumped a fallen tree with perfect timing, she knew she missed following the hounds like she had as a child, missed the freedom of those days. But thank God, now a change had come in her life. She'd almost given up hope that anything exciting would ever happen to her again, when Lionel told her about the post in Malta. It seemed like a miracle. Life had been lonely and confining since her parents were killed in a coaching accident when she was fifteen. Her cousin Lionel was her only living relative, and he'd become her guardian. Life between fifteen and her nineteenth birthday had been dreary.

But now, that was all over! She was actually going to live in the Mediterranean.

After a good long gallop, she reined Cinnabar to a walk,

cheeks flushed, eyes sparkling. It was a warm day, and she felt the heat. Suddenly she spotted sunlight glimmering on water through the trees.

Dismounting, she led Cinnabar through the bracken and found herself at the verge of a river. The woods were all around, but at this spot, the river curved slightly, widening into an inviting pool. She stood looking at the place for a few moments, then a smile lit her face. On this day of beautiful rebellion, a swim would set the jewel in the crown.

Ashburn dismounted and quietly led his horse toward the river, following the plain hoofmarks in the bracken. In a moment, he saw the gray horse Juliette had been riding, tethered on the bank. And he caught a glimpse of her beyond the horse. He paused, then with utmost care, went forward. He tied his horse next to hers, expecting her to hear him and turn; but her back was to him, and it seemed she didn't hear him over the murmur of the river. All he could see through the screen of leaves was the top of her head; so he decided he'd sneak up on her and see what she was doing before he announced his presence.

Slowly he worked his way to the riverbank and looked out through the bushes. Then he drew in his breath, his eyes widening at the sight before him.

Juliette was standing on the grassy bank. Her gleaming brown leather boots lay on the grass beside her, and she had her skirts lifted above her knees. His throat tightened as he watched her loosen a lacy garter and peel her stocking slowly down her long shapely leg. He felt the blood start to pound in his body at the sight. He was in luck! She must mean to go wading—and he had arrived in time to get a view of her legs!

But he was in more luck than he could have imagined in his wildest dreams. He watched disbelievingly as she started to unbutton her jacket. It fell in a heap on the ground. He held his breath as her hands reached behind her and unclasped her skirt. *My God, is she going to take off all her clothes?*

He couldn't believe his good fortune as she started to unbutton her white blouse. In a moment, it joined her riding habit on the ground. His eyes swept over her feverishly, hoping she would continue. But she stopped and straightened. She stood clad only in a thin white chemise and lacy slip that fell to her ankles. She wore no corset, and he licked his lips at the sight of her so scantily clad. Her figure was slender and curving, half-concealed by the hair falling down her back almost to her waist in loose waves that glowed in the sun like copper. She turned her face up to the sun, and he studied the features that had so haunted him: large, dark-lashed eyes of a blue as deep as the night sky; high cheekbones that swept down to a wide coral mouth with a beckoning cut that maddened him; a dainty, square jaw and a delicate, tip-tilted nose.

She stepped forward and stuck a bare toe in the water, testing its temperature. Then she waded in, lifting her slip so he could once again admire the curve of her ankles, her calves.

And then she paused a moment and dived under the water.

Avery's mouth dropped open, it was so unexpected. A little sedate wading was the most a lady would dare, even on a hot day like today. But swimming! His lips curved in a hot smile. She was in truth an uninhibited, sensuous baggage, just as he'd long suspected! Her cold airs were all an act. . . .

She rose from the water and stood, the river lapping at her thighs.

The sight was almost more than Ashburn could bear. The thin chemise she wore clung to the lines of her body wetly, almost transparent where it touched. He could see the thrust of her coral-tipped breasts, the slim waist and flat lines of her stomach, the curve of her hips, her long, shapely legs— He felt his desire rise, his blood fired to near madness. By God, he'd have her; she was begging for it, standing there dripping in the sunlight, looking like Venus coming out of the sea. . . .

He stepped out of the bushes and stood with his legs braced apart, a lusty glint in his eyes. "You're a sight to drive a man mad, Juliette," he said.

She gasped, turning, startled by his sudden voice. She saw him standing on the bank, his eyes roving over her, hands on his hips, and her eyes narrowed with anger. Avery Ashburn! Of all people to catch her swimming! She followed his eyes and looked down at her indecently clinging chemise, gave another indignant gasp and sank under the water to her shoulders.

"Avery! What are you sneaking up on me for?" she demanded hotly. "Get away from here and leave me alone!"

"Leave you alone?" He laughed, a cocksure look on his face. "Not when you present such an enticing vision, Juliette. I've long dreamed of what you might look like if I could ever get your clothes off . . . and now that I have such a delightful preview, do you really expect me to turn around and meekly walk away?"

He was insufferable! Couldn't he understand she wasn't interested in dallying with him? He should be taught a lesson for his outrageous effrontery. Suddenly her gaze fell on his horse tethered on the bank behind him.

She smiled.

Avery saw it and a hot flame leapt in his eyes. The wench was actually smiling at him! Maybe she would drop her cool games and let him have her. He pictured her lips opening passionately under his, the feel of her breasts under that wet, clinging chemise. He would tear it off her body and take her here on the grass! Desire throbbed through his veins as erotic visions raced through his mind.

Juliette set her lips in an inviting curve and looked at Avery through half-closed lashes, a languorous look. Then she slowly rose again, the water streaming off her gleaming shoulders, dripping down her legs. "Why don't you join me, Avery? It's a gorgeous afternoon for a swim," she suggested, her voice low and seductive.

Avery licked his lips and stared at her in astonishment. He couldn't believe what he'd just heard!

She almost laughed at the look on his face, then added mockingly, "Or are you afraid to join me? Of course . . . you wouldn't want to ruin those elegant hunting clothes. . . ."

It was the only invitation he needed. Not taking his eyes off her, he began feverishly unbuttoning his jacket. He threw it on the ground on top of her piled clothes, and in a moment, his shirt followed. He stood bare-chested, his frame too spindly without the artful padding his tailor sewed into his jackets, and Juliette had to stifle a contemptuous smile at the sight. Really, as if Avery Ashburn thought she would be interested in such a girlish-looking fop as he was! But men were all so conceited. Well, she would teach him a lesson!

"Aren't you going to take off your boots?" she questioned sweetly.

He gave her a hot look, then sat and tore off his boots.

"Come in, Avery. It's deep enough to dive. And if you can catch me . . ." She trailed off, a challenge in her voice.

He waded in, then dived under the water toward her. But the moment he moved, Juliette dived too, shooting away from his underwater form and gaining the bank. His hands closed on nothing where he had expected to find her, and he broke the river's surface, shaking the water out of his eyes, mad to find her and painfully excited by this game of pursuit.

She was standing on the bank above him, holding his rifle. And it was pointed straight at him!

She laughed, but there was a dangerous glint in her eyes. She looked like a young Amazon, and suddenly Avery felt extremely nervous. He remembered that Juliette had always been unpredictable, almost wild sometimes. It was what made her so desirable, but just now it had him wondering what she meant to do with the rifle!

"Checkmate, Avery," she said. "You thought you'd catch me, but it appears I have caught you."

"Put that gun down, Juliette!" His voice was sharp with panic. "You don't know what you're doing! It's loaded—you can't point a loaded gun at someone, you foolish chit!"

She smiled. "I don't know what I'm doing? It so happens I'm a very good shot, Avery." He took a step toward the bank, and she calmly cocked the rifle. "I wouldn't move if I were you. But maybe you don't believe me. I warn you, my father taught me to shoot, and he was an excellent teacher. Shall I demonstrate?"

She pointed to a dead branch overhanging the river on the other side. "See that branch?" Avery's eyes could barely make out the target. Coolly, she raised the rifle, sighted and squeezed the trigger. There was a loud report. Avery paled when he saw the branch was neatly broken in two. Damn it—it was a shot most men couldn't have made!

He turned back to her, plainly nervous now. "So you—so

you can shoot. It's still outrageous to be pointing a rifle at me. Believe it or not—I followed you out here with honorable intentions. I intended to ask you to marry me." His voice had an injured tone.

She laughed again, but the rifle pointed at him didn't waver. "You followed me out here with the same dishonorable intentions you've always had, Avery! Do you think I'm stupid?" Her eyes sparkled mischievously. "Take off your pants," she commanded.

"What?" he gasped.

"You heard what I said. Take them off—and throw them on the bank. Since you saw me undressed, it's only fair I should see you the same way."

His eyes narrowed with suspicion. He stood in the water, not moving.

She added, "I would do as I say, Avery. If you don't, I may decide to shoot you. Just a flesh wound, perhaps. But if you do . . . who knows? I may decide we can be . . . *friendly* after all." She pitched her voice low with tones of seduction again and was pleased when she saw him fall for the bait. The hot light came back into his eyes, and he reached down and unbuttoned his pants. He peeled them off underwater, then held them up. The water lapped around his waist.

"Throw them on the bank, Avery," she said softly. He grinned wolfishly and obeyed her. They landed with a wet slap at her feet. "Are you . . . wearing anything underneath them, Avery?" she asked quietly.

"No," he breathed, a suggestive leer on his lips. "Why don't you come back in and . . . swim, Juliette? The sight of you standing there in that enticing chemise will soon make me forget you hold that rifle, and I'll come after you."

She lowered the rifle and looked at him, considering. "Maybe I will, Avery." He drew in his breath and waited.

Suddenly she grinned a rakish grin and bent, swiftly gathering up the piled clothes at her feet. "And maybe I have a better idea." Before he could react, she untethered her horse and leapt lightly on Cinnabar's back, the clothes and rifle in front of her. His jaw dropped in disbelief as what she was doing penetrated.

"Juliette!" he cried. "Don't you dare—! You can't leave me here alone without my clothes—"

"Can't I, Avery?" she said mockingly, and her light laughter rang out. "But I'm leaving you your horse. You can ride back instead of walking. Maybe this will teach you to leave me alone."

He stared at her in helpless fury, sitting dripping on her horse, laughing down at him. He still didn't believe she meant to leave him there without a stitch of clothing. . . .

But she put her bare heels to Cinnabar's side, wheeled the horse, and sent him a last parting smile before she rode off into the trees.

"Juliette!" His voice came after her in a furious wail. "I swear I will make you pay for this! Come back!"

She rode off, laughing, finding it hard to keep her seat. The look on Avery's face when she rode off with his clothes! And how would he explain his naked state . . . she giggled again, picturing him trying to sneak back into the house without being seen. . . .

Before she came to the edge of the woods, she stopped and dismounted, quickly dressing again in her riding habit, boots and blouse. She twisted her damp hair into a bun, then stuffed it under her hat. She looked the picture of respectability now. She giggled again.

She swept Avery's clothes off the saddle and laid them on the path in clear sight. He would come this way eventually, she knew, because there was a good view of the house from here. Then he'd find his clothes. But first he'd have a nice long period of agonizing about his embarrassing situation.

She jumped lightly on Cinnabar's back again and rode out of the woods, a smile playing on her lips. She couldn't wait to see Avery's face tonight at dinner! He wouldn't be able to say a word to her in front of other people about it . . . without confessing he'd been bested by her and left without a stitch of clothing!

And then she only had to avoid being alone with him for another few weeks.

Because in a few weeks, England would be far behind her.

Chapter Two

Juliette stood at the rail of the *Alexandria* and stared with enchantment at the Mediterranean Sea by moonlight. The moonlight frosted the waves, and the ship's wake glowed luminously behind her. A soft breeze blew off the coast of Sicily and caught at her skirts.

I can't believe I'm actually here, she thought, breathing deeply of the scented air, looking up to the billions of stars that studded the night sky. A sliver of crescent moon hung just above the horizon, looking Eastern and mysterious. Shipboard nights in the Mediterranean were more glamorous than anything she'd imagined back in England.

The wind ruffled her full skirts, causing a flash of silver as the dress of rose-and-silver brocade fluttered. She laughed softly and put a hand to her blowing curls, her heart alight with adventure and an odd feeling that *this* was the kind of life she was meant for.

She laughed again at the thought that Lionel, conventional Lionel, was the one who brought this exciting change into her life. *That just goes to show how strangely fate works,* she thought, shaking her head in wonder.

Tonight the ship was passing through the strait between Tunis and Sicily, and tomorrow or the next day, depending on the wind, they would reach Malta.

And Lionel. She sighed, regretting the journey was coming to an end. The last few weeks had been heaven, travelling with just her maid, Elise. Lionel had left for Malta three weeks before her at the governor's urgent request. She was thrilled at the prospect of making the trip on her own and scoffed at Lionel's fretting that it wasn't proper. At last she had convinced him she could cope, and he had set off, grumbling.

She and Elise had come overland across France by train and coach, staying in charming little inns. She'd been fascinated by her brief stay in Paris, by the little French villages with red roofs and bustling cafes, by the great chateaus glimpsed sometimes between the rolling green hills. At Marseilles, they had boarded the merchant ship *Alexandria,* bound for Malta, and had sailed past Corsica and Sardinia, heading toward the coast of Africa. She had spent hours on deck, entranced by the exotic coastlines they passed, the strange cities with their flat roofs and tall minarets, a world so utterly different from England. Her spare hours had been passed poring over a book of Arabic, studying the language of the country she was travelling to. She'd enjoyed every minute of the journey.

But now her freedom was coming to an end. No doubt the governor's mansion would be as proper as Belgravia Square, and Lionel would be as strict as ever.

She put the thought away, determined not to let the evening be spoiled. After all, tonight she was dining in the captain's cabin!

She looked down at the dress she wore and smiled. It was far too grand for a shipboard dinner, but it was her favorite dress. Impulsively, she'd set down the "suitable" silk she'd picked up and, over Elise's scandalized protests, had chosen this dress instead.

It was a dress she'd loved from the moment the dressmaker first pinned it on her. The sparkling reflection she saw told her it was a dress to make conquests in, a dress to break hearts. Brocade was stately, but this brocade had a softness lent by the rose and a moonlit shimmer from the silver. The colors were flattering to her: The brocade's muted sheen made her skin look creamy and lit her hair with copper threads. It sat low on her shoulders, the deep square neckline emphasizing her breasts, the bodice clinging to her slender waist like a second skin.

In her cramped cabin, she'd stood on tiptoe to peer into the mirror and was pleased with what she saw, tossing her curls so her dangling seed-pearl earrings glittered, smoothing the spills of lace at her elbows. She ignored Elise's frowning disapproval. Elise was a dour woman, silent except when she was admonishing Juliette on what a lady did and didn't wear for different occasions.

As she'd shaken her full skirts out and slipped on her rose suede heels with the silver buckles, she'd given Elise an impish smile. For once she was going to please herself and wear what she wanted! After all, it was her last night of freedom! All too soon, she'd be under Lionel's thumb once again.

Now as she lingered at the rail, she was glad she'd worn the dress. It matched the glamor of the night—and her high spirits. As she took a last breath of the balmy night air before leaving the rail, her mind was on the kindness of fate which was at last sending her on the way to a new life. . . .

But as she left the rail, skirts sparkling in the moonlight, she didn't know yet that Fate was a capricious goddess, and that the smallest thing—even the choice of a dress—could change her fate forever.

"We should reach Malta by sunset tomorrow if the wind holds. Mistress Hawkins, may I offer you a glass of wine?"

Captain James nodded to the steward. His dark eyes dwelt on Juliette with reserve. He disliked having a woman on board his ship at any time—but just now, it was more than an inconvenience, it was a worry.

For the last few months, the waters along the coast of Tripoli hadn't been safe. Those damned Barbary pirates were the trouble. Their low-slung xebecs were fast sailers, and they were getting too bold for comfort. They robbed and killed and did a brisk trade in slaves up and down the coast. It was getting damned dangerous making the run through these waters.

Captain James sighed inwardly, looking at Juliette under frowning brows. A woman had no business in the Mediterranean just now! But at least they would reach Malta tomorrow, and she would be safe enough there.

"That's good news, Malta tomorrow," said Ralph Winston

jovially. He was a bluff, hearty man of forty, an American merchant. He and his clerk were the only other passengers. "Been an easy trip so far. No storms, no wind. But you look like you're a good sailor, Mistress Hawkins."

Captain James noted with disapproval the avid way Winston was eyeing Juliette. She was a damned good-looking woman of course, but that was no reason for men to act like fools and lose their dignity. He looked distastefully at his own first mate, who was gaping at her like a silly sheep, almost falling over himself to bring her a glass of wine. Most undignified.

"I haven't had a moment's uneasiness," she was saying now. "I love being on board a ship. It's such an adventure!"

"Well, I like my trips in this part of the world as boring as possible," Winston said with a coarse laugh. "No storms or encounters with any of the brigands that sail these waters, thank you."

"Brigands?" Juliette's voice was interested. "Oh, you mean the Barbary pirates? But I thought the Navy had them quite under control."

"Don't you believe it! Why, I heard in Palermo—"

"One of the exaggerated tales that spread like wildfire in this part of the world, no doubt," the captain interrupted smoothly. He threw a repressive look at the bluff Winston, trying to convey that this was no conversation for a lady's ears. He didn't want a hysterical female, screaming and fainting, on his hands when she heard some of the hair-raising things that were happening recently.

"Sailors are notorious for tavern rumors," he went on. "You are quite right, Mistress Hawkins. Our Navy has things well in hand. Oh, there's the odd incident now and then, but the waters we are in now are well-patrolled, I assure you."

Juliette sipped her wine and looked at the captain through her lashes. He was lying! Why? Obviously, these waters must not be safe from pirates at all for him to interrupt and take pains to be soothing. *He thinks I'm a weak female who must be sheltered,* she thought disgustedly, disappointed that she wasn't to be allowed to hear all about the Mediterranean pirates. They sounded fascinating.

The captain was leading the conversation into less troubled

waters, asking Mr. Winston all about his business. Juliette sighed. Despite the dress, it looked like this was going to be a boring evening—not an attractive man in sight to dazzle.

There was a knock on the door, but before Captain James could call permission to enter, the door swung open and a young officer stood framed in the doorway.

Captain James stood, setting down his glass of wine. "What is it, Graves?"

"Gunboat, sir! Sighted off the port bow!"

Captain James's lips tightened. He turned and bowed stiffly to his dinner guests. "Pray excuse me, Mistress Hawkins, Mr. Winston. I must see to this. Bond, come with me."

The first mate rose and followed the captain out the cabin door. Juliette turned to Mr. Winston. He looked pale and anxious.

"What is it, Mr. Winston? Is it serious—this gunboat?"

He picked up his wineglass and drained it, then favored her with an unconvincing smile. "Nothing to worry about, I'm sure. Could be a Navy ship—American maybe. Or—" He stopped.

"Or a pirate ship?"

Mr. Winston looked vastly uncomfortable. "Well, no, probably not—but don't you worry, miss. Even if it is, we can outrun the bast—beg your pardon! Just slipped out. We can outrun them, don't you worry. Besides, didn't you hear the captain say there are no pirates in these waters? He'll be back any moment for dinner, you'll see. Nothing to worry about."

Juliette looked at him uncertainly, wondering if he was telling her the truth—or merely trying to shelter her like the captain had. She was just opening her mouth to speak when a shot rang out and shattered the night.

Juliette's head flew up, eyes wide, and met Winston's terrified look across the table. They sat in frozen silence for what seemed an eternity, but was marked by only three swings of the lantern over their heads.

Then the night erupted with an ear-splitting din: volleys of shots, the booming roar of large guns, running feet, shouted orders.

"Mr. Winston—what is it?" Juliette jumped up, her napkin

still clutched in her hand.

"I don't know. We're—we're being attacked!" cried Winston, his face red and sweating. "Get down! Stay—you stay here. I'll look out and see if I can tell what's happening!"

Juliette stood frozen as he ran to the cabin door and opened it, disobeying his order to get down. Her heart beat in jerks, and she clutched the chair next to her so her knees wouldn't give way.

The din from outside was deafening. She could hear orders being shouted hoarsely above the gunshots, could smell powder and smoke. For a moment, Winston's bulky form was framed in the door. Then he suddenly spun and crumpled, falling in a heap in the doorway.

"Mr. Winston!" she screamed, running forward and kneeling at his side.

She grabbed his shoulders and turned him over. A dark red stain was spreading on his chest, and his eyes were open, staring at the ceiling.

"Mr. Winston!" she gasped again, shaking him in horror; then frantically she felt for a pulse. There was none.

He was dead!

Dead so fast! She knelt beside him, staring open-mouthed in horror, not able to take in the fact that moments—just moments—before he had been across the table from her. She was deaf to the din all around her, oblivious to her own danger in the doorway. She didn't smell the smoke or notice his blood staining her dress. She could only kneel in shock, unable to take in what had just happened.

"Elise!" Suddenly she remembered Elise, below decks in her cabin. She had to get to Elise—protect her!

She stood and in a flash of rose and silver ran out onto the deck into a world gone mad. She didn't think of the danger, or of what good finding Elise would do. She just ran like a mad woman.

Down the deck, the ship was burning. The masts were illuminated with a dancing orange glow, and streamers of smoke clouded the night with smudged grayness. She could see the enemy ship lying off the bow. It was the dark, low-slung outline of a xebec—a Tripolitan gunboat.

An arc of fire and a whistling scream cut the night, and a shell hit their bow with a terrifying explosion. The ship tilted slightly, and Juliette staggered, coughing on smoke. She grabbed a rope and kept on her feet with an arm-wrenching effort. She heard pounding footsteps coming down the deck, and she flung herself into the path of a running sailor.

"What in God's name is happening?" she shouted, and he turned, white eyes staring in a smoke-blackened face.

"Get below! We're being boarded, and it will be hand fighting up here!" he shouted, shoving her away and drawing a pistol as he ran.

Juliette backed into the shadow of the quarterdeck and watched in frozen horror as a hand appeared over the rail not ten feet from where she stood. In moments, dark shapes came swarming over the rail, brandishing pistols and cutlasses. She dared not move. They would see her if she tried to get below!

Through the dark and the smoke, she glimpsed nightmare scenes as the turbaned, swarthy men grappled for life with the sailors. The smoke hid the battle from her, and she stood praying the pirates would be defeated, praying she wouldn't be seen.

Suddenly several of the pirates were back at the rail in front of her. They were lowering something over the side. Heavy chests! They were looting the ship. If only they didn't turn and see her concealed in the shadows—

Another booming explosion rent the night, and the ship lurched violently. Her high heels played traitor, pitching her out of the shadows onto the deck. She sprawled, stunned, almost at the feet of one of the Arabs at the rail.

He whirled, raising his cutlass over his head in a whistling circle. She realized in an instantaneous flash of terror that he was going to bring the blade down and kill her!

It was the dress that saved her.

Flames suddenly leapt upward with a fierce light, and the silver threads, so thick in the dress, caught the light and threw it back with a savage sparkle.

The pirate's eyes widened as he started the downward movement of the blade; his shoulders wrenched as he tried desperately to deflect the blow. The glittering blade cut the air and swished past her cheek, glancing off her shoulder. It slashed the dress and grazed her arm.

He stood over her, legs planted wide, chest heaving, dark eyes fathomless beneath his turban. Juliette stared up at him, paralyzed with fear. Then she saw his eyes change. A shiny, appraising look came into them as they roved over her where she lay.

A decision lit his face. He bent down and with a frightening strength grasped her wrist and hauled her to her feet. She didn't even have time to scream as he picked her up, threw her over his shoulder and strode to the rail.

He leaned out and shouted something unintelligible into the night and was answered by shouts from below. A grappling hook snaked up through the air, and he caught it.

Juliette was roughly set on her feet, and she twisted, trying to run. But she was caught and held, and the pirate pulled out a knife and held it to her throat. He grated something in Arabic that was too fast for her to understand and gestured roughly to the rope ladder now hanging over the side.

Wide-eyed, she felt the prick of the knife at her throat and went limp in his arms. She nodded slightly.

Knees shaking, she climbed over the rail and set her foot on the ladder. With a last despairing glance at the burning deck, she climbed slowly down into the longboat waiting below.

Rough hands settled her, and in moments, more Arabs were swarming down the ladder into the longboat. The one who had captured her sat down at her side and showed her the knife again with a grin. Then he turned to his comrades and said something that brought a shout of laughter.

Shivering, she looked up at the ship as the longboat was rowed away from its shadow. It was in flames! Fire swept the deck from end to end, staining the sea with a dreadful red light.

As she watched, the ship began to list to one side. There were no more shots, no grappling shapes on the deck. Two other longboats were rapidly pulling away from the burning ship. The fighting was over.

Are they all dead? she thought in horror. *Where is Elise? Is she a prisoner, like me?*

The longboat pulled farther and farther from the burning

ship which tilted further. With a numbing suddenness, it slid under the waves, and a great smoke went up, gray in the night.

Juliette put her face into her hands and wept, filled with grief for the captain, the sailors. For a few moments, she was numb to everything around her, but the merciful oblivion didn't last.

She looked up. The shadow of the xebec loomed above them, and as she watched, a ladder snaked down. The full meaning of her plight hit her clearly.

God help her, she'd been captured by Barbary pirates!

Chapter Three

Juliette stood on the deck of the pirate ship, watching the pirates swarming over the rails onto the deck. She glanced out at the moonlit sea, but no trace of the *Alexandria* could be seen. It was gone, and as the last of the pirates climbed over the rail, she realized she was the only prisoner from the ship. Elise—Elise must be dead, sunk with the ship.

She was alone.

A man detached himself from the group of pirates and strolled down the deck to her. Her heart began to beat too fast with fear as he approached, and her mouth was dry at the thought of what these men would now do. She could almost feel the rose-and-silver cloth being ripped from her body. But bravely, she lifted her chin and tried to show none of the fear she felt as the man stopped in front of her.

For a few silent moments, they looked each other over carefully. He was squat and, to Juliette's eyes, very strangely dressed. A bright yellow turban, clasped with a glittering jewel, framed a dark face with deepset eyes and a curving mustache. His vest, though now stained and dirty, was richly embroidered; his baggy silk trousers were clasped by a magnificent gilded belt. A long curved knife hung at his side.

He grinned, showing yellowed teeth. "You are a prize indeed," he said.

"You speak English!"

"As well as you do," said the man, looking her up and down in a leisurely sort of way. "Ah! You are very pretty. My men were wise to take you." He rubbed his hands and gave a satisfied grin.

"I am an English citizen. How dare you take me prisoner?" Juliette said, hating the cruelty she saw in that smile. "What do you intend to do with me?"

Her captor seemed amused. "If my men did not take you prisoner, you would be dead with everyone else aboard that ship." He waved an arm in the direction the ship had sunk. "My men have given you the gift of life. What you make of the fate that awaits you may be easier, English woman, if you remember that every day you now live is a gift from Allah."

"I would rather be dead than submit to you or your men!" she stated, trying hard to control the trembling fear she felt at what might befall her next. "I will fight you, even if you kill me for it."

He laughed at her defiance. "Set your mind at rest, English woman. Being used by me or my men for pleasure is not your fate. Lucky for you, you have fallen into the hands of a businessman. You are worth a great deal of money to me. Among other things, I am a slave trader. Though I was not after slaves this trip, the quick thinking of Jamauil—the man who almost killed you—saved you when he saw your beauty. Such beauty—"

He paused and lifted up one of the tangled curls that had fallen on Juliette's shoulder. Repulsed, she stepped back quickly, drawing the curl through his fingers. "Such beauty is worth a fortune here. Many a sheik would pay a top price to have this hair like flame and skin like snow inside his harems."

Juliette shuddered. She had heard of the harems of Suleiman the Magnificent, or of the Ottoman Empire, once inside them, there would be no escape! She glanced at the rail of the ship, wondering if she could dive over the side and try to swim to shore. To fail and drown would be better than to be sold into harem slavery forever! What madness had sent her running onto the deck tonight? If she had only stayed in the captain's cabin, she would have drowned with the rest of them. Such a death seemed painless now.

He followed her glance. "Do not think of it, English woman. You have already escaped death once today. Do not court it a second time or Death may oblige you." He pulled the long, curved knife out of his belt, and the blade winked wickedly in the moonlight.

"You will not sell me as a slave!" she cried. "You cannot! If it is money you want, then ransom me! My relatives will pay you more than you could ever get for me as a slave."

"At last you have said something that interests me. So you are wealthy? I thought, from that dress, you might be. What is your name, and where are these relatives that will pay to see you freed?"

"Juliette Hawkins. My cousin is in Malta. He is a rich man."

"In Malta? What does he there?"

"He is a diplomat. He works with the British governor."

The pirate's eyes narrowed. "You are suggesting that Mulay el-Rassouli, the most wanted pirate in the Mediterranean, have dealings with the British governor? Juliette Hawkins, I think not. I have no wish to die before my time. Safer by far to sell you as a slave."

"But—please! I tell you, my cousin will pay you whatever you ask! And he will keep it secret from the governor, I promise!" She controlled her voice with an effort. "Mr. Rassouli, it will be well worth your while to ask for ransom." She watched him anxiously, regretting she had mentioned that Lionel worked with the governor. *Of course that would make this pirate wary. The British government pursued these Mediterranean pirates ruthlessly.*

He stroked his mustache, thinking. Then his eyes gleamed at her as he shot her an assessing glance. "You say your cousin is rich?"

"Very rich."

"Then I will think about it. To the world, you died with that ship. I can sell you without risk, and you will never be heard from again. I see by your defiant eyes you are the type of woman to think of trying to escape. You are not weeping, or crying for mercy. You stand there and face me like a man, and I would wager if you had a cutlass you would fight me like one. Courage is good to an extent—it will help you survive. But to me, such a courageous woman is a risk to keep prisoner for long."

He turned to his men waiting on the deck and called something in Arabic. Two of them stepped forward and flanked Juliette.

He turned back to her. "I will consider whether the risk of ransoming you is worth it. If not, I will sell you as a slave. And now, I am afraid you must be locked up. I will tell you my decision when I have made it." He said something else in Arabic, and the two guards took Juliette by the elbows.

She resisted the instinct to struggle as they grasped her, or to argue further with the hateful Mulay el-Rassouli. She merely nodded coldly to him and walked off down the deck between the guards.

Before she climbed down the dark hatch that led to the lower decks, she took a last glance at the moon riding high and radiant in a black sky. It no longer looked magically beautiful to her. Now it looked cold, casting a sinister light into the dark corners of a world she'd never dreamed she would see.

Derna, five days later

Mulay el-Rassouli sat in his cabin, his fingers steepled, a smile on his face as he thought of the strange ways Allah worked. He had just made up his mind it was too risky to ransom the prisoner, when a solution presented itself.

Ransoming her was full of risks. He knew the instant the ransom demand was received, inquiries as to her whereabouts would be made. The British consulate had an efficient spy service—and they would doubtless offer a large reward for information.

His problem was keeping her safely until the ransom was arranged and paid. The trouble was, he couldn't trust his own men. Any one of them would be tempted to claim a large monetary reward for information on her whereabouts—or even to arrange her escape. It was impossible to keep her aboard his ship . . . or under guard in the city. He had no one he could trust to guard her.

No one, that is, until now.

The door swung open, framing two guards flanking a man

whose arms and ankles were chained. Rassouli rose.

"Ah, you have brought the prisoner," he said with an air of satisfaction. "Leave him with me, but wait outside."

The guards gave the chained man a shove forward, and he stumbled on his ankle irons, falling to his knees before Mulay. Mulay chuckled as the man glared upward at him.

"So, Farouk, now you see that insulting me is not something a man does without consequence. You and that desert rover you call your friend think you are a match for anyone—but you will find you are not a match for me, Mulay el-Rassouli." He thumped his chest proudly and, picking up a glass of wine, drank it off with a flourish.

Farouk rose slowly, his chains clanking, and stared with disdain at the pirate. "You are a braggart as always, Rassouli. You would never have taken me prisoner if I had not been drunk last night. It was hardly in a fair fight you took me."

"So! You continue your insults, dog! If I sell you as a galley slave, I think that hot pride will soon enough be humbled under the lash."

Farouk stared angrily at the pirate, trying to ignore his splitting headache. How had he been fool enough to get himself into this situation? He regretted ever having stepped foot into that waterfront tavern in Derna and, most of all, not leaving when he saw Rassouli was there.

There had been bad blood between he and Rassouli ever since he and Dahkir had refused to deal in the pirate's stolen goods. *Fool that I am, too much palm wine always loosens my tongue, and last night was no exception,* thought Farouk ruefully.

He winced as he remembered how he had gone out of his way to start a fight with Rassouli. The story of rescuing the sheik's daughter from the Bedouin raiders had been loudly making the tavern rounds. Catching Rassouli's eye, Farouk had directed at the scowling pirate a scathing remark about the bandit scum who preyed on honest merchants—and then, he blushed to remember, had bragged about how he and Dahkir were more than a match for such cowards.

Instead of the fight Farouk expected, Rassouli had merely shrugged and dropped his lids over eyes cold with rage. In a mood to celebrate that night, still spoiling for a fight, the evening had turned into a dizzying blur for him. The last thing he remembered clearly was the dancing girl draped over his lap, sharing yet another bottle of palm wine with him . . . until he woke with a splitting head, chained, in the hold of Rassouli's ship.

"Don't make me laugh with threats to sell me as a galley slave," Farouk said. "I know well enough you will demand that Dahkir pay an exorbitant price for my freedom."

Mulay smiled again, enjoying having this hated rival in his power. "But I do not intend to ask a ransom, my friend."

Farouk's eyes narrowed. "What do you mean? I know well enough that kidnapping and ransom is one of your most profitable businesses."

"Yes, it is one of the most profitable. And of course, I have set a price for your release." Rassouli smiled again at the thought of the marvelous way Allah had provided. He met Farouk's discomfited eyes with a mocking glint in his own, and continued, "Yes, there will be payment—but the price is not gold."

Juliette sat on the narrow bunk of the small room aboard the ship, her fingers toying ceaselessly with the lace at her cuff. For days now, she had been locked in this tiny cabin. It had no portholes and was dimly lit by a single candle. But by the motion of the ship, she knew they had anchored somewhere.

Where was she? And what was going to happen to her?

She set her jaw, trying to keep away the despair that kept threatening to engulf her. She had to keep her courage up. She had to.

But it was so hard, locked away alone with so much time to think. The hours crawled past more slowly than she could stand. She kept feeling she would lose control at any moment and start pounding on the locked door, screaming to be let out.

Surely he meant to ransom her. After all, he had made her write a letter to Lionel that first night, hadn't he? But since then, he had not come back.

Twice a day, her guards entered to bring food. She didn't

know which was worse—feeling so frightened, or so filthy, or knowing nothing. Her questions to the guards were always unanswered. Probably they didn't understand her halting Arabic, or they had been instructed to say nothing to her.

The sound of steps echoed in the corridor outside, then the bolts on her door slid back. She stood, wishing her legs wouldn't tremble every time the door opened.

It was Mulay el-Rassouli. At last.

"How long do you intend to keep me locked in this filthy hole?" she demanded at once, facing him with a bravado she was far from feeling.

He stepped inside and looked her over. "I regret I have caused you discomfort. It was necessary to be sure you had no chance to escape. But now—I am taking you elsewhere."

"Are you going to ransom me?" Juliette tried to keep the fear out of her voice, but her stomach twisted as she waited for his answer.

"Yes. I have decided to ransom you after all. You will be taken to a place of safety until your ransom is received. In fact, we leave soon. I have brought you clothes to put on."

He bent and picked up a bundle and threw it at her feet. Juliette stared down at it, dizzy with relief. He was going to ransom her!

"Can you ride a horse, Juliette Hawkins?"

"Yes," she said weakly.

"Good. Then please do change into those clothes. We leave as soon as you are ready."

Recovering herself, she said sharply, "Will you have some water brought to me? I must wash. I asked your men again and again, but they didn't understand me."

His teeth flashed in a grin. "Certainly, if you don't mind cold water. And if you don't take too long."

"I don't mind. Where am I being taken?"

"That"—he grinned—"you will know soon enough."

An hour later, she stood braiding her damp hair. It had felt wonderful to wash, to get out of her clothes. She glanced at the dress lying in a heap in the corner.

Savior and betrayer, she thought, glad she would never see it again.

Quickly, she donned the clothes Mulay had provided: a loose cotton caftan of pale yellow, a pair of tan trousers that fit a little too snugly. Then she pulled on a tall pair of soft leather boots. They fit surprisingly well. Over everything, there was a voluminous gray burnoose like the men on the ship wore, and after a few moment's struggle, she figured out how to put it on properly. Lastly, she covered her head with a white headscarf. Now, if her face were concealed, there would be nothing to show she was a woman.

On that thought, she took the end of the headscarf and pulled it across her face so that only her eyes were revealed. She tucked in the end. Now she was ready.

There was a soft knock on the door, and Mulay opened the door and beckoned her to follow him. To her surprise, he was alone. Her guards were nowhere in sight.

When they reached the deck, it was deserted. Shading her eyes against the dawn light she saw a great city surrounding a harbor.

"Where are we?"

"That is the city of Derna, Juliette Hawkins. Come, climb down to the boat. We are late."

She followed Mulay down the rope ladder to the waiting longboat. As she climbed in and sat, she asked, "Where are your men? Why are we alone?"

"Because I do not wish anyone to know where you are being taken. So I tell them to go to the taverns."

"Where am I being taken?" she inquired, but Mulay picked up the oars and wouldn't answer her. Giving up, she turned and studied the city they were making for.

The streets of the city were narrow, zigzagging and crazily tilted. Flat roofs on different levels crowded each other, walls bleached pale by the desert sun. The spires and onion-shaped domes of the mosques and tall fringed palms stuck up above the city roofs.

As they pulled toward the shore, the waters rippled pink with the rising sun. The harbor teemed with craft of every description, from lateen-rigged xebecs to tiny fishing boats.

Gulls circled and dove around the longboat, their shrieks mingling with the wailing chant of the imams from the top of the mosques, calling the faithful to prayer.

As they pulled up on the shore and climbed out of the boat, Juliette stared fascinated around her, her spirits rising just to be out of the dark cabin she'd been locked in, breathing the morning air and stretching her legs.

The waterfront was crowded with figures out of a dream. Everyone she saw was robed from head to foot, swathed to keep out the desert sun. There were beggars whose turbans were little more than filthy rags, richly dressed merchants whose snowy headcloths winked with jeweled clasps, and women covered from head to foot in shapeless black yashmaks, only their dark eyes showing.

She walked next to Mulay through the maze of streets, his hand clasping her elbow firmly. The narrow streets were barely alleyways through eyeless walls. Now and then she had a glimpse of gardens showing through pointed archways, of brilliant flowers, spilling fountains and richly tiled walls. Her senses were at once assaulted and stimulated by the sights and the odors.

Flowers and oranges, fish and garbage, coffee and spices combined in an exotic wave of smells that was unforgettable and overpowering. They passed swaying camels, lean dogs, holy men waving their arms at small crowds of listeners, merchants sitting with their wares spread on a cloth in front of them, crowds of screaming children weaving through the bazaar and women waiting patiently to draw water from a public well.

She was so taken up with all the strange sights that for a few moments she didn't think of escape. Then she glanced sidelong at Mulay, measuring him. . . .

"Here we are," he said, gesturing with his arm.

A single horse stood tethered in the shadow of a wall. Mulay walked up to it. He turned.

"Get on."

Juliette hesitated. The city all around her had given her hope of escape. After all, there was only Mulay—no guards. If she turned and ran—

"Or I will shoot you."

Suddenly he produced a pistol from beneath his robe and levelled it at her.

She glared at him, then walked to the horse. Fitting her foot in the stirrup, she swung herself up.

In a moment, Mulay was up before her.

"Where are you taking me?" she demanded again.

"Just a short way into the desert. I am delivering you to a man named Dahkir, who will keep you safe for me until the ransom is paid." He wheeled the horse and put his heels to its flanks. They cantered off through the narrow streets, Mulay skillfully dodging passersby and other riders, keeping the horse to a breakneck pace.

As they rode, Juliette's mind worked frantically. Taking her to another captor! This Dahkir was chosen, she was sure, to see she did not escape. If she was ever going to escape, it had to be now, on this ride with Mulay.

They galloped under the great arch of the city gates. Before them, the road wound, dusty and flat, into the low desert hills. Juliette looked down. Mulay's pistol was sticking out of his belt, just below where her hand grasped his waist. If she grabbed the pistol—

She could never shoot him. She shuddered at the thought of killing a man—even a pirate like Mulay.

But maybe—maybe she could knock him out. And get the horse.

As they galloped along, her hands began to sweat lightly from tension—and from the heat. The desert sun was merciless above, the sky almost white. There was no one on the road.

Mulay wheeled the horse, turning off onto a dusty, barely discernable track heading into the hills. In a few moments, he had turned again, and Juliette looked back, trying to keep a sense of direction for the way they had come. All around, all she could see were the low brown hills, featureless sand dunes. Now. She had to do it now, or she would lose all sense of direction.

She stared down at the pistol, willing herself to do it.

She grabbed.

With a shout, Mulay's hand closed over hers on top of the pistol, and he stood in the stirrups, twisting in the saddle. Juliette was almost unseated, and her hand slipped off the pistol. She grabbed desperately at his back to keep from falling, and all at once, they both overbalanced and went crashing off the horse into the dust below.

They rolled over and over, Mulay cursing, Juliette fighting him wildly. She had no hope of getting her hands on the pistol now. She felt his weight come down on top of her, pinning her, and she scrabbled on the ground with her hands for purchase, trying to throw him off.

Her fingers closed on a rock.

Without thinking, powered by adrenaline, she brought the rock up hard in a glancing blow that caught his temple. He fell back with a groan.

Terrified, Juliette pushed him off her and stared down at him, then almost sobbed in relief when she saw his chest rise and fall. Thank God! For a horrible moment, she'd thought she'd killed him.

She scrambled to her feet. She had to get away before he woke.

The horse was standing, sides heaving, thirty feet away.

She held out a trembling hand and began to walk toward the horse on weak legs. It watched her with white-rimmed eyes, unmoving until she was just five feet away.

With a snort, it wheeled and pounded off in terror, disappearing over a hill.

She watched it vanish, open-mouthed. What could she do now?

With a nervous glance at Mulay, she decided she would have to start walking.

She would follow the horse. It must be heading back to the city. She started trudging up the dusty hill under a blazing morning sun. . . .

When the sun reached its zenith, Juliette came to the edge of the low hills and faced the broad, barren expanse of the Sahara. The desert appeared to be a vast motionless sea of white water, like waves caught forever at the peak of their swell, never to crash against the shoreline, perfectly still, oppressively silent and empty. She realized at last that she was lost.

She had tried to follow the horse's tracks and for some distance had been successful, but the hardpacked earth and blowing dust didn't leave much in the way of tracks to follow. And always she felt Mulay at her back, watching her and waiting for an opportunity to overcome her and take her with him. Her naturally good sense of direction had tricked her as she made her way among the indistinct and monotonous foothills and had sent her on a wild goose chase here to the edge of the desert.

Her mouth was dry, and she was nearly overcome by the stifling heat as the sun made its tedious and seemingly unending trek across the desert sky, never once giving her a moment's rest from its fiery eye. She had thought of abandoning her burnoose, but knew she would need it if, God forbid, she had to spend the night in the desert. Her caftan was torn from the scuffle with Mulay, dusty and sweat-stained. Although her boots were hot and chafed her feet, she dared not take them off and wander barefoot across the hot sand.

Suddenly she saw something in the distance that caught her eye. Amid the wavering blaze of the noonday sun, she saw what appeared to be a line of moving forms on the horizon. Like little black dots they moved in and out of the shimmering waves of heat that danced along the edges of what seemed like a not-too-distant sand dune.

She squinted hard, and they seemed to vanish from their previous position and reappear farther away. A caravan, she decided, and her heart beat a hopeful rhythm as she began to run in its direction.

She stumbled from time to time, but she moved with a will that surprised her, and the dots began to grow larger and to take on shape. That one was a man in robes, leading a camel; this one, a man on horseback. Her heart pumped furiously, the pulse pounding fiercely in her temples as she gained ground on the elusive caravan. It was just beyond the next rolling hill of sand.

With a superhuman burst of energy, she crested the sand dune that separated her from salvation and stood gaping and panting at the broad and empty expanse before her. Her heart fell as she gazed in all directions, searching for the human life she was certain she had seen, but was nowhere in sight.

She'd been following a mirage! Panicked, she looked about her, but the foothills she'd left that morning were no longer in sight. Juliette could see nothing but the huge mounds of motionless sand in all directions and the unforgiving sun overhead. She was completely lost and utterly alone.

She collapsed in the sand. She wanted to cry, but the arid desert robbed her of even that small luxury, leaving her unable to even make tears. *I will not cry,* she told herself. *I will not die in this godforsaken place, like some animal.*

A desert wind began to stir, sending the sand scurrying in small dust devils around her, and although it was warm and offered no relief from the desert heat, it roused her. But as she tried to stand, she found she hadn't the strength to do so. She raised herself to her hands and knees and crawled a short distance, before trying to rise. She took several faltering steps as she reached the ridge of the next sand dune and gasped with surprise. She'd misjudged. The caravan was there!

Starting to run down the hill, she tripped on a rock and fell tumbling, rolling head over heels like a rag doll, catching great mouthfuls of sand. Her eyes filled with sand, choking on the dust, she was brought up short as she rolled into something with a jolt. Coughing, she groped, expecting to feel the rock that had stopped her fall. Instead, her hands closed on a pair of tall leather boots.

She sat up, spitting sand, her whole world spinning dizzily before her. Her eyes followed the leather boots upward until they were joined by lean, hard-muscled thighs in tight breeches, and a narrow waist, clasped firmly by a leather belt which held a cutlass. Powerfully broad shoulders under a tossed-back burnoose rose in perfect proportion from the narrow waist.

The stranger towered possessively above her, his feet braced slightly apart. His face was nearly covered by a desert headcloth—all but his eyes. She would remember very little about the rest of his face, but his eyes she would never forget. They were the most piercing shade of green she had ever seen in her life.

"Oh, thank God," she gasped, her mouth dry, words barely

audible. "Do you speak English?"

To her great relief, the answer came. "I speak it."

"Help me, please! I am an Englishwoman—I have been kidnapped by a Barbary pirate who was going to hold me for ransom, but I escaped. He was taking me to a man who was going to keep me prisoner for him—" She swallowed, the world spinning, unable to collect her thoughts. She knew she was babbling and struggled to think of what to tell him next. "My name is—"

"Juliette Hawkins. I know. I am Dahkir," came the unbelievable reply.

Dahkir! The name rang in her ears. She felt fear grip her heart as she realized she had met the very man she was trying to escape from. The last thing she saw before her world went black was that pair of cool green eyes regarding her with chilling irony.

Chapter Four

Dahkir stood looking down at the woman crumpled at his feet, his eyes bemused. She had fainted, and he scowled, wondering how he could bring her around.

It was just as he'd feared. She was a damned nuisance already, an Englishwoman who knew nothing about the desert, or how to survive in it. No doubt delicate as a hothouse flower. He steeled himself for the scene he expected when she woke.

He sighed in irritation at the thought. Why were women so fond of making emotional scenes that left a man helpless and drained? The picture of Amelia's large blue eyes filling with tears came back to him. She'd cried so easily, using her tears as a weapon to get what she wanted. It had taken him a long time to find out that beneath that soft, clinging exterior had been a hard and ruthless heart.

His mouth twisted in a bitter line as he put the thought of Amelia from him. She wasn't his problem now—this woman was. And as Amelia had taught him so well, she would use tears and hysterics as ammunition when she woke. The last thing he wanted was to be stuck with nursemaiding a gently bred female with delicate sensibilities on a grueling trip through the desert. He had neither the time nor the patience to endure scenes, and he would have to make her understand that right from the start.

After all, this situation was no more of his choosing than hers. For the time being, they were stuck together whether either of them liked it or not.

He turned and strode to his waiting horse, detaching a water skin from the saddle. Water might bring her around.

As he walked back to the unconscious girl, he felt a moment's aggravation at Farouk. A shame he wasn't here. With his ready smile and laughing tongue, he could soothe this woman and have her calmed down in no time. He was good at dealing with women, the rogue.

But of course, it was thanks to Farouk he was in this situation at all. *Farouk owes me one for this,* he thought grimly.

Farouk and his penchant for getting into fights when he is drunk. Too bad I didn't go into town with him that night, thought Dahkir. *Maybe I could have kept him out of trouble.* That night, Farouk did not come back to camp from the taverns—not by any means an occurrence that worried Dahkir. Not, that is, until the next morning, when Mulay el-Rassouli rode into camp.

Mulay had grinned as he took a seat in front of Dahkir's tent to explain the business that brought him there. "To avenge the grievous insult I endured from your friend, I plan to sell him as a galley slave," Rassouli told an astonished Dahkir.

Dahkir's fingers itched to pull out his cutlass and run Rassouli through his lying throat, but that wouldn't help Farouk. He concealed his rage at the thought of Farouk in chains, and coolly asked Rassouli what the ransom would be.

As he waited for Rassouli's answer, he winced inwardly at the thought of the huge amount of money Rassouli would no doubt be after—money he and Farouk had been slaving for for so many years, running the caravans through the desert. . . .

But to his surprise, Rassouli didn't want money. He wanted a favor. Dahkir was to take this Englishwoman deep into the desert until her ransom was paid, and to keep her from escaping or being found.

"I can trust you to do this, my friend," Rassouli had said, "because otherwise your friend Farouk—" He shrugged expressively. "But it will be an even exchange. The girl, safely hidden until I want her—for Farouk."

There was no choice. As much as he hated it, he had to act as her jailer until her ransom was arranged. And it looked already like it was going to be a hard job.

This morning, he rode out from his caravan to meet Rassouli in the hills outside Derna and be given the prisoner. Instead, he found Rassouli sitting in the dust, groaning and clutching his bleeding head, made a fool of by the woman.

It wasn't hard to follow her trail into the desert. She was obviously lost, heading deeper into the hills away from Derna. Just like a foolish woman, there was no forethought to this bid for escape. Imagine walking into the desert with no water!

He shook his head, looking down at her. At least she'd had the sense to keep her headcloth and barracan on. If she hadn't, with skin that white she'd have been badly sunburned. Kneeling next to her, he gently turned her onto her back. She didn't wake.

He stared at her for a moment, then unbound her white cloth headcovering and pulled it off. Involuntarily, he drew in his breath at the sight of her face.

She was beautiful.

Her copper hair glinted like fire, framing the creamy curves of her high cheekbones. Long dark lashes swept her cheeks, and her soft, wide mouth was slightly parted.

Asleep, she looked innocent and vulnerable, and for a moment, he was strangely shaken with a surge of protective sympathy for her. For that instant, he forgot his irritation at being stuck with her and thought how frightened she must be.

Then he scowled at his own disturbing softness. Thoughts like this he couldn't afford. Spilling the water onto her headcloth, he started bathing her face and hair.

Her lashes fluttered, but still she didn't wake.

He spilled some of the water onto his fingers and wet her lips with it, pushing away the thought of how soft they felt under his fingers.

She moaned softly and opened her eyes.

He pulled his fingers from her lips as if they burnt as he stared into a pair of lovely dark blue eyes—eyes that were startled for a moment, passing wonderingly over his face.

He braced himself for the tears or the screams that would come any moment when she realized who he was.

He saw memory light her face as consciousness returned to her with a rush. Instead of filling with tears, her eyes suddenly darkened with anger, her delicate brows drawing together.

She sat up and glared at him for a moment, then to his shock, her fist shot out and narrowly missed his chin. He sat back on his heels in surprise as she scrambled to her feet and started to run.

Juliette ran without a backward glance, her head spinning dizzily, making for the horse. She knew even as she ran she had little chance of escape—but he wouldn't take her without a fight! Maybe there would be a rifle on the horse.

She heard pounding footsteps behind her and turned to see him too close. She would never make it to the horse! She bent down to pick up a rock and braced herself, watching with sick fear as he raced toward her. She controlled her instincts, which were screaming at her to run, and stood her ground.

But as she raised her arm to strike with the rock, he surprised her by launching himself into the air a few feet from her, in a low flying leap. His arms hit her waist with a sickening jolt as he tackled her, and the rock went spinning out of her grasp as they hit the ground together. Juliette lay stunned, the breath knocked out of her, feeling sharp arrows of pain where she lay on small rocks. For a moment, they both lay there, breathing hard, his arms around her like bands of iron. She couldn't even move her arms an inch; this man was no Mulay to allow her such a chance.

Juliette stared up at him as she struggled to catch her breath. His headcloth had come unbound during their struggle and uncovered his face. For a breathless moment, she studied her captor. It was a hard face, bronzed by the desert sun, with high cheekbones and a square, determined jaw. He had a wide, sensual mouth bracketed by two deep lines, a mouth that was just now set in an angry line. But all that was just an impression. Her gaze was caught and held by his furious ice-green eyes, arresting eyes under straight dark brows. Could he be an Arab, with those green eyes and that clean-shaven face? His first words answered her question.

"Don't try running away again," he grated. "I have no intention of letting you escape."

Listening to his accent, Juliette's eyes widened in amazement. "You're—you're *English!*" she gasped accusingly.

His eyes narrowed. "So?"

Rage flowed through Juliette. "You—you *bastard!*" she gasped, dredging up the worst word she could think of and hurling it at him like a knife. "You mean to tell me an *Englishman* is helping a pirate hold me for ransom? Unless you let me go, you're a traitor to your country!"

"What I am, madam, is your jailer," he said angrily. "That's all that need concern you. You will do as I say exactly or—"

"Or what?" she dared recklessly, still furious that her captor was an Englishman. He should have been rushing to help her, not tackling her and threatening her!

"Or things will be very unpleasant for you," came the soft reply as his gaze dropped to her lips. Juliette stiffened, suddenly aware that he was still lying on top of her, aware of his great strength as he held her in a steel grip. Dear Lord, this man could rape her if he wanted to, and there was no way she could stop him. She was no match for his strength.

Because he was English she was forgetting he could be as dangerous as any renegade in this part of the world. He dressed as an Arab. Maybe he had adopted Arab ways as well. Fearfully, she looked into his eyes. The anger was gone. She saw desire there, a look she had learned to recognize through her suitors back home like Avery Ashburn. But Avery, despicable as he was, had the conventions to stop him from ravishing her. There was nothing to stop this man.

"I—I won't fight you any more," she faltered.

For a long moment, he measured her. "Good. It is useless."

He rolled off her and, seizing her waist, jerked her to her feet. She felt him grab both of her wrists behind her back. He marched her in front of him to where his horse, a rangy gray, stood quietly. He held her wrists easily with one hand while he rummaged in the saddlebag with his other. He pulled out a piece of rope.

"You're going to bind me?" She was unable to keep still. "I said I won't try to escape."

His answer was a short laugh. "And you think I trust your word?"

She resisted the urge to struggle as she felt her wrists being bound behind her. She gasped as his strong hands seized her waist and lifted her effortlessly through the air, placing her on the horse's back. She looked down at him as he fitted his own foot in the stirrup, but he didn't meet her eyes.

He jumped lightly up behind her. An iron arm came around her waist, causing Juliette to draw in her breath. She felt herself being pulled close to him, her back against his chest, his strong thighs molding hers. He gathered up the reins with the other hand and kicked the horse. They rode off in the direction Juliette had seen the caravan. She could see no sign of it now as the horse labored up another dune.

They crested the hill and beneath, straggling in a long line, Juliette saw the caravan. The camels were strange silhouettes against the pale sky; there were horses hobbled to one side and several tents flapping in the breeze. She could barely make out the form of some men sitting cross-legged in front of one of the tents, and the smoke of a cooking fire.

He reined in the horse. "My camp," came his voice behind her.

"What are you? What is this—camp of yours?"

"It is a caravan. *My* caravan. I am a trader, madam. I run caravans through the desert—Derna, Jalo, Tripoli."

"A *trader*," she said frigidly. "I see. An interesting name for a brigand who holds fellow countrymen for ransom and is in league with a pirate."

She felt his legs stiffen for a moment, then relax. To her surprise, he swung off the horse and landed in the dust. She looked down at him with a glare.

"What are we stopping for?"

"It's time we got a few things straight before we join my caravan," he said, favoring her with a cool determined look that warned her he'd had enough of her defiance.

"A few things straight! Let me get one thing straight, Mr. Dahkir—or *whoever* you are—I despise you for what you are doing. And I will obey you, because otherwise, you'll threaten me with violence, I don't doubt. But if you touch me or—or hurt me, I swear I'll get my revenge on you, even if I have to follow you to the ends of the earth!"

Dahkir's eyebrows lifted in amazement at this speech, wondering how he could ever have feared Juliette Hawkins would scream and faint. Instead, she was a sharp-tongued vixen, looking at him with a fearlessness that suddenly made his lips quirk in the ghost of an amused smile. Her glorious copper hair was tumbling in wild tangles around her shoulders, framing her heart-shaped face which was smudged with dirt. Her burnoose was torn from their scuffle on the ground and liberally streaked with dirt. If she could see herself in a mirror right now, he thought, she might not feel quite so haughty.

"I don't doubt you would. But set your mind at rest. I don't intend to . . . touch you or hurt you, as long as you cooperate."

Was that amusement she heard in his voice? Rage flowed through her at the smug way he was watching her, as if—as if he found her proud words *funny!* Juliette saw red, and spat, "Oh! If you were a man at all, you'd untie me this minute! Are you afraid I'll get the better of you in a fight, like I did Mulay. Is that it? You—"

He crossed over to her, swift as a cat, and grasped her waist and swung her off the horse. Her boots hit the ground with a jolt, and she found herself held close against him in a hard grip. She struggled against him, pushing herself backward. His arms released her so suddenly that she stumbled, then sat down hard on the ground. Sudden tears from the impact filled her eyes as she stared up at him standing above her with his legs planted in a wide stance, hands on his hips.

Damn it! he thought, as he watched sparkling tears fill her wide blue eyes and spill down her cheeks. *Tears—just as I expected.*

But instead of feeling disgusted, he felt a stab of remorse. *Why am I treating this poor girl so roughly?* he thought as he watched her. *What's wrong with me?*

"Don't cry, Juliette," she heard his low voice say, suddenly gentle. He squatted in front of her. "I won't hurt you—I promise." She watched in amazement as his arms came around her and felt for the bonds at her wrists. His face was inches from hers, and there was a soft expression in his eyes as he watched her that was somehow harder to bear than everything else that had happened to her. To her humiliation, she felt real tears rising at the sympathy she saw on his face, and she closed her eyes and burst into sobs as he untied her wrists.

She felt his arms go around her, strong arms that seemed for a moment to promise safety. Her head was against his shoulder, and she smelled the clean scent of him, leather and horses. For a moment, she gave herself up to the luxury of sobbing her frayed nerves out, not even pausing to wonder how she could be comforted by the man who had caused all her misery.

"I'm sorry I was so rough with you."

The low-spoken words brought her back to reality, and she sat up and away from him, rubbing her wrists.

"Let go of me," she demanded angrily.

He sat back on his heels, his hands dropping from her shoulders, and looked coolly at her. "If you've finished ranting and raving at me, maybe I'll tell you what's going to happen to you now. But since you're a woman, I expect you'd rather have a few more hysterical scenes before we can talk in a civilized way."

Color flooded Juliette's cheeks, and she stared at him, enraged. She bit back a scathing remark that he was a kidnapper—how could *he* talk of civilized behavior? Instead, all she said—in freezing accents—was, "Tell me."

"I told you I am a trader, Juliette Hawkins, and I told you the truth. I don't normally hold prisoners who are being ransomed. But I have my reasons for holding you, and I won't tolerate you trying to escape. The caravan is going into the deep desert, all the way to Tripoli, perhaps. You and I will be stuck together for some weeks—maybe even months."

He paused and watched to see how she was taking this, but she only tightened her lips and nodded slightly to show she understood. She was too incensed still to trust herself to speak.

"So, as I am your jailer," he went on, "life will be easier if you understand me. I have six Janissary outriders on the caravan. None speak English. I intend to tell them you are a new—slave I have purchased. When we are in their presence, you will act deferential and hold that sharp tongue of yours."

She glared at him. "Slave! Then—"

He held up his hand, cutting off her indignant remark.

"Once we are in the desert, you will be given your own horse to ride. Try and ride off alone if you wish. Not only will we find you easily, but death waits for those foolish enough to venture into the desert alone. Until then, you ride with me. I will not tie you if you promise me you'll not try to escape."

"I won't promise that," she said proudly.

His mouth curved down in a frown. "Then—you will be tied. Now, we have wasted enough time. The afternoon wanes. We'll go down to my caravan now."

He took her hands and stood, pulling her to her feet with him. For a moment, he held her wrists. "You will obey me, Juliette?" he said softly.

She stared into his beautiful eyes, suddenly feeling a strange shock at his touch that left her knees weak.

When she didn't answer, he released one of her hands. A finger came up and traced the curve of her cheek, stopping just beneath her chin and tilting it up to his face. She couldn't look away from his eyes now if she tried.

"You are a beautiful woman—and one who is in my power. I can treat you as a slave in truth if I so desire. Is that the way you want it?"

Suddenly his voice was rough, his fingers tighter on her wrist. Fear darkened her eyes.

"No—I'll do as you say." The words were unwillingly wrenched from her. But what else could she do? She saw in his face that he was capable of anything if she did not obey him.

"Good." He dropped her wrist and held out one arm in gesture to the horse. "Get on, then."

She avoided his eyes as she climbed on the horse, trying not to feel him as he settled his weight behind her and his arm came around her waist. In a moment, they were galloping down the hill in a flurry of dust, the heads of the outriders turning as they swept into the camp.

Chapter Five

Stretched out against the sky was a long string of camels and horses. The outriders stood in a group as they rode up and her captor reined in his horse. The men were frankly curious, and she tried to will herself not to blush as six dark pairs of eyes devoured her.

Dahkir called a greeting to the men in Arabic and dismounted. He reached up and caught her by the waist, swinging her to the ground in front of the men. For a moment, he held her to make sure she had her balance, then released her. Juliette felt a wave of humiliation as he turned to the men and started speaking rapidly in Arabic. It was too fast for her to catch more than a few words. What must they think! It felt shameful to be standing in front of them while they talked about her. She reddened again as all the men burst into laughter at something Dahkir said. From the appreciative leers on their faces as they looked at her and the tone of the comments they made, she didn't need to understand what was being said to catch the drift of their thoughts—entirely lascivious!

Worse was to follow. Dahkir turned back to her, the grin vanishing from his face, and said coolly, "I have just told the men that you are my new slave, that your name is Juli, and that you don't speak Arabic. Oh—and that I may have to keep you tied because you have not been broken to the yoke of slavery yet. So they are all prepared to help me guard you and see that you do not escape."

Juliette's cheeks burned. She could well imagine the ribald comments the men had made when he said she was not "broken to slavery yet"! She was sure the grinning men had been full of helpful suggestions as to how that could be accomplished! She suddenly hated them all, their dark grinning faces, and controlled an urge to spit in the dust at their feet. Such theatrics would no doubt only amuse them more and gain her nothing. She contented herself with an icy glare at Dahkir. But he only smirked hatefully at her before turning and walking away down the caravan.

With as much dignity as she could muster, she stalked stiffly to a rock some paces off and sat down, trying to ignore the men, not to hear their laughing voices as the group broke up and went back to work. She had no intention of letting Dahkir know she spoke a little Arabic. Maybe she would hear something to her advantage if they spoke freely in front of her.

She watched as Dahkir's tall figure went down the line of the caravan. He was inspecting everything closely, checking that the horses and camels were tethered for the night. He was followed by the men, who kept up a volley of Arabic as he went on his tour. His men seemed to respect him, she noticed, but they were certainly not in awe of him.

They were outriders, he had said. She saw that their horses, which they were unburdening for the night, were swift compact animals, sleek and well-cared for. Their saddlebags, laden with water skins and bedrolls, were also hung about with cutlasses and rifles. The scabbards were worked leather, rather plain, but with scars that told of hard use and with a sheen that told of good care. They were obviously ready to protect whatever goods were in the bulky burdens carried by the camels.

The sun began to set in a startling blaze of beauty that seemed to fill the sky. Juliette sat watching the efficient activity of Dahkir and the outriders as they started to set up camp for the night. They moved with the precision of a well-known routine, without need for commands. Each man silently went about his tasks, setting up tents and starting cooking fires.

Setting up the tents.

She bit her lips. Several tents were going up, their sides billowing in the evening breeze. Was one of them for her? Would they give her any privacy?

Dahkir turned away from the fire and walked toward her. He stopped and looked down at her for a moment.

"You will sleep in that tent. You may go there now. I'll bring you your meal—and join you for it."

She felt relieved. Privacy would make the whole ordeal more bearable. She turned her gaze to where the men were gathering around the fire, squatting or sitting, passing water skins and taking steaming plates of food.

"I don't join your men around the fire? I see that's where they are going to eat."

"In Arab culture, a woman does not join the men for meals. Especially a slave. They would expect you to wait on me . . . and I had an idea you wouldn't agree to act the part without a fight." His voice was dry.

"You were right!" She stood up. "I remind you I am *not* your slave—or anyone else's!" She turned and walked away toward the tent.

It was the one pitched some distance from the others, a fair-sized tent made of striped cloth. She opened the flap and, once inside, was surprised to find the tent more spacious than she'd thought. She could stand without stooping. *Why, it's comfortable!* she thought.

The floor of the tent was covered with rich rugs, and a bedroll with warm covers and piled with pillows lay in one corner along the tent wall. There was a small, X-shaped leather stool that could be folded up, and a low table stood near it. Several cushions were scattered on the floor, and water skins hung on the tent poles. All the materials were richly woven in beautiful soft colors, even luxurious. And it had an established, permanent look surprising for a tent.

She had no further time for thought. The grate of a boot on the sand outside made her turn. The tent flap lifted, and for a moment, he was framed in the opening, a broad-shouldered silhouette, tall, long-legged and slender of hip. He stepped in and let the tent flap fall.

For a few seconds, he said nothing, only let his disturbing

green gaze rest on her face. Then he came in, walking to the low table without greeting her, and setting down a tray he carried. Savory smells rose from the covered dishes on it, and Juliette felt her stomach give a sudden stab. All at once she remembered she was ravenous.

Still he didn't speak. She watched him warily as he bent to light a lamp which filled the tent with a warm glow of light. He pulled off his headcloth with an impatient gesture. It was the first time she had seen him without it, and all at once he looked less like an Arab and more like the Englishman he was. He had longish, tumbled hair that was dark brown, streaked gold in places by the desert sun. He carelessly unwrapped his barracan, revealing a loose white shirt that made his skin look startlingly brown. She watched as he walked restlessly to another oil lamp and bent to light it. He had a hard and reckless look that unnerved her. Why didn't he speak? What manner of man was it that held her prisoner?

He unclasped the belt that held his cutlass and laid it aside. Then he sat on a cushion near the low table and began uncovering dishes.

Without looking up, he said casually, "You aren't eating?"

She reddened slightly at his rudeness, then, following his example, pulled off her headcloth and her burnoose. She sat down on a cushion across from him at the low table.

Silently, he filled a plate for her, with spicy-smelling stew of some kind and flat breads, strong-smelling cheese and some dates. He filled a pewter goblet with wine and set it across from her, then fell to eating his own meal.

As famished as she was, she hesitated. Where were the knives and forks? To her disgust, she saw he was tearing off pieces of the flat bread and using it to scoop up his stew.

He looked up at her then, and she felt disconcerted at the sudden amusement she saw flicker in his eyes.

"There are no knives or forks. I apologize for the offense to your dainty manners, but I'm afraid you'll have to eat the way the Arabs do—or starve."

Tightening her lips, she resolutely picked up a piece of bread and began to scoop up stew with it. As barbaric as it might be to have to eat with her fingers, she wouldn't give him the satisfaction of thinking she wasn't equal to it—or anything.

The stew was so hotly spiced that she gasped at the first swallow and grabbed for her wineglass. As she gulped the liquid with burning cheeks, she saw his lips twitch in amusement.

"*Couscous* can be rather fiery the first few times. Don't worry, it's not so bad after a few bites. Your mouth gets numb."

They ate in silence after that, Juliette deciding there was no choice but to eat the fiery stew. And she found he was right; her mouth seemed to adjust after a time. She even found it tasted good.

As she concentrated on eating, Dahkir found his eyes drawn to her, studying this woman who he now held prisoner. In the lamplight, her hair glowed like copper, a few shining tendrils curling against the curve of her creamy cheekbones. His eyes lingered on the wide curve of her soft mouth, the sweep of her sooty lashes, the slight slant of her dark-blue eyes. Then his gaze dropped before he could stop himself to the line of her neck, the delicate hollow of her collarbones, and the thrust of her breasts under the loose caftan. The pale yellow of the caftan complemented her warm coloring, giving her a soft glow that disturbed him strangely.

He shifted slightly on his cushion, his brows drawing together as he realized his pulses were quickening in a damnably uncomfortable way.

The last thing he wanted was to find her desirable—not when he would have to be sharing a tent with her for some weeks! He took a deep swallow of wine and wrenched his eyes away, determined to keep them away.

As Juliette finished, she sat thinking. Why was she being so defiant to this man? So far—he hadn't harmed her, even if he had been rude. She should make an effort to gain his sympathy. Maybe then, he would let her go, or listen to an offer of money from her. With an effort, she forgot her anger and arranged her face in more agreeable lines.

"Will you tell me your name? I find it hard to call you Dahkir—now that you aren't dressed as a desert bandit."

Her soft question made him break his resolve, and he looked up. For once those lovely eyes weren't sparkling with anger, but instead were searching his seriously.

"Raleigh. Deric Raleigh."

He spoke reluctantly—but more civilly than he'd ever addressed her yet. She felt her spirits rise. Her friends back in England had always been fond of admonishing her that "honey caught more flies than vinegar," but she had scorned their syrupy feminine wiles, always priding herself on her forthright speech. But now—a few words in a sweet tone of voice had already thawed the forbidding scowl of her dark-browed captor. Without the scowl, he looked less like a dangerous bandit and more like the Englishman he was. She found herself wondering what he looked like when he smiled. Perhaps almost human.

"Mr.—Mr. Raleigh," she began, trying to decide whether she should tell him her story first and try to gain his sympathy, or just come right out and offer him money to free her. Deciding on a more subtle approach, she pitched her voice in the most honeyed tones she could manage. "I wondered—what brings a man like you from England to this part of the world?"

"I despise formality. Call me Deric. Manners are one of the English conventions a man has the luxury of leaving behind in this part of the world, as you put it." He paused. "So—I see you've decided to stop defying me. Why?"

He might not be scowling any more, but Juliette recognized suspicion when she saw it. Perhaps she had been *too* sweet. She decided to go back to being forthright. After all, it was more her style, and she'd never been much good at acting sweet. Evidently he could see right through her.

"Because you said today you didn't like this any better than I did. It made me realize that perhaps we could come to some kind of . . . arrangement. I could offer you—"

"There's nothing you could offer me that would persuade me to let you go." The words were curt, shattering the mood that had so briefly existed between them.

Juliette took in a sharp breath of disappointment. For a moment she'd been fool enough to hope he might help her—or at least allow himself to be bought for a higher offer. But of course, he was a despicable mercenary!

"Why are you doing this? Don't you care that I'm English? That you're English, too? What kind of—of bastard are you?" she burst out, dropping all thought of being sweet.

His face changed, becoming cold and set. "What kind of man I am is none of your concern. But I suggest we make the best of this, since we are going to be very much in each other's company for the next few weeks."

There was a footstep and a soft call outside the tent. He glanced at her warningly.

"Cover your face," he said.

"Why?" Juliette felt in the mood to be contrary.

She couldn't mistake the annoyance on his face as he answered her. "Because one of my men wants to enter, and in Arab society, a woman must not show her uncovered face before men."

"I'm not an Arab woman."

"Will you do it—or shall I come over there and do it for you?" he said in a dangerously silky voice.

Hastily, Juliette picked up her headcloth and pulled it on, arranging it so it covered her face below her eyes.

Satisfied, he turned and called something in Arabic. One of his men opened the tent flap and stepped just inside the door. Without even a glance at Juliette, the Arab unloaded several saddlebags, a rifle and a pair of boots in the corner, then left.

She whirled on Deric accusingly the moment they were alone. "This is your tent!"

"Yes." He raised one dark eyebrow quizzically at her. "What did you expect—that you'd have your own tent?"

"I won't stay in here with you!" she gasped.

He looked amused. "I'm afraid you have no choice in the matter. How else can I keep an eye on you? Besides, my men believe you to be my slave. They'd think it very odd if I gave you your own tent—even if I had an extra one, which I don't."

"Do you think I care what your men think?" she said through clenched teeth.

He crossed his arms across his chest and regarded her impassively. "You don't seem to understand that this is no pleasure trip, Juliette. I'm your jailer—whether you approve of it or not. Defying me isn't going to do any good . . . and will only make the situation more unpleasant. Don't worry," he added, and she felt a surge of anger at the contemptuous indifference in his voice. "If you're afraid I'm going to . . . take advantage of you, you can set your mind at ease. I have no interest in taking a woman to my bed unless she wants to be there."

"Oh!" Not pausing to analyze why she found those cool words so insulting, she stared at him through slitted eyes. Infuriatingly, her glare produced an amused smile.

"Of course . . . you will have to share my bed. I'm a light sleeper. I'll wake if you have any ideas about getting up and slipping away in the night, I warn you."

"I won't share your bed!" she gasped.

He shrugged. "Suit yourself. But if you prefer being tied up and sleeping without any blankets on the floor . . . it gets cold in the desert at night."

He turned away indifferently as though what she did mattered nothing to him, and she stared at him as he bent to light another lamp, torn between outrage and curiosity as she watched him. So far, in all of his dealings with her, he had been curt, even rude. But then . . . she had gone out of her way to provoke his anger with her defiance.

And yet, his brusqueness seemed to be more annoyance than cruelty, as if he found her a burden that got on his nerves.

That thought brought back her indignation. He was holding her prisoner! How dare he act as if she were a nuisance to him?

"You would tie me up?"

He glanced briefly at her. "If I have to. It's up to you."

"As you've made clear, I'm your prisoner. Nothing is up to me, it seems, not even where I sleep," she stated coldly.

He shrugged off her indignation. "We leave at dawn tomorrow. I'm tired and want to get some sleep. Will you sleep on the floor—tied? Or next to me in bed?"

A long moment passed. Then she rose, trying to gather as much dignity as possible.

"Tie me," she said in freezing accents.

He stood too, and she saw this time she had managed to push him too far. His green eyes darkened with fury, and his mouth straightened in a grim line.

"Damn it, woman—don't push my patience too far!"

In the face of his fury, she knew it was unwise, but Juliette had never been able to control her tongue. The words were out before she could stop them.

"Or what?" she taunted.

Two strides brought him around the table to her side. Her eyes widening when she saw he was serious, she started to dodge to one side, but he was far too swift for her. He swept her up into his arms, and though she struggled, his strength made it seem an effortless gesture. He strode to the bed and paused.

His face was close to hers, and those furious green eyes bored into her frightened ones. He seemed about to drop her angrily on the bed when she saw his eyes change.

For a breathless moment, their eyes locked. The moment seemed to last forever to Juliette as she was aware of his arms holding her in a steel grip, the beating of his heart against her chest—or was it her own?

Then the moment was broken. He seemed to shake himself, then knelt and set her roughly on the bed. His grip held her hands while he took a short length of cord and wrapped it around one of her wrists.

The look of hurt and betrayal was evident in her eyes. "But—"

"Don't make it hard for both of us," he managed at last. "Prove to me that you won't go running off into the desert in some half-crazed attempt at escape, and I'll untie you." The other end of the cord he tied to his own wrist. "Until then, I want to know your every move."

He reached across her and snuffed the oil lamps. The tent was plunged abruptly into darkness. Juliette lay stiffly, her heart beating too fast, listening to him as he kicked off his boots and pulled the covers over both of them.

She lay rigidly in the dark, still shaken by the sudden violence in the way he'd picked her up and carried her to the bed.

But that wasn't all. She was even more shaken by that moment he held her, by what she had seen in his eyes. She felt angry at herself. How could she find the man who was holding her prisoner attractive? What was wrong with her? He was hatefully arrogant and dangerously rude.

And the handsomest man she had ever seen.

She lay tense in the dark, ready to leap up like a startled deer if he touched her again. For what seemed an eternity, there was only the sound of his breathing in the dark.

She jumped when he spoke.

"Are you going to sleep in your boots?"

As she kicked off her boots, sliding them out of the bed with her foot, she felt her cheeks burning with embarrassed indignation. Not just at his words—the last thing she would have expected him to say—but at the rich note of amusement rippling in his voice.

Fuming, she lay back down.

The damned scoundrel! He was laughing at her!

Chapter Six

Juliette drew the end of her scarf across her mouth and nose, adjusting it snugly against the dusty desert wind. The dawn was breaking, chasing the stars from the horizon, a smudge of pearly green and rose lightening the eastern sky.

She stood alone at the edge of some rocks, watching as Deric and the outriders walked up and down the line of camels, getting everything in readiness to start. The tents had been struck, and she'd had a half hour of privacy to wash, snatch a hasty breakfast of bread, dates and water—and to think.

It was no use fighting him. Last night had shown her he was determined and would go to any lengths to ensure she did not escape. Today, she resolved, she would stop this useless pastime of trading insults with him. She would be cool, frigid, barely speak to him—and though she would obey his orders, she would show him with her remote iciness exactly what kind of a blackguard she thought he was.

The men were mounting their horses now, and Deric came riding toward her on a dark gray stallion with a black mane and tail. He led a spare horse, a dun-colored mare, she noticed with relief. Evidently she was to be allowed her own horse and be spared the humiliation of riding pillion behind him like a captive.

It was not until he halted his stallion in front of her that she saw that the rope he was leading the spare horse with was not held in his hand, but tied to the tall front horn of his saddle.

"I see you intend to keep me tied," she said coldly, looking up. He sat above her on his horse, once more the fearsome desert bandit she'd first seen in the desert: face and head covered, flowing barracan over tall boots, rifle belt across his chest, cutlass hanging at his hip. Only his eyes, green as grass in the dawn light, betrayed his origins.

"Don't waste my time arguing about it. I don't have the patience this morning for any scenes. It would exhaust my horse to carry us both, but I still intend to make sure you don't decide to try riding off."

Juliette glanced at the low brown hills, featureless sand, and then at her saddle. "I see there is no water bag hanging on my saddle. Do you think I'd be fool enough to ride off without water? I don't even know where we are."

His voice was cutting. "Yesterday you were exactly foolish enough to do just that when you ran off from Mulay without any water and without even a horse."

Why am I arguing? Juliette thought, realizing her resolve to barely speak was already broken. But there was something about the man that rubbed her the wrong way—made her long to take him down a peg or two. Silently, she stalked to the dun mare and climbed on, gathering up the reins. His stallion started off toward the line of camels, the mare matching the stallion's pace side-by-side.

"Heee-aaaah!" The long wailing cry of the outriders rose, starting the camels, which shambled reluctantly forward, stretching out in a long string of a line. Some struggled awkwardly to rise, but once walking were creatures of slow grace hypnotizing to watch. The outriders spurred their small, swift horses up and down the line, shouting and chivvying to get the lazy camels started.

Deric steered their horses to a spot at the front of the caravan, and Juliette stole a glance at his face. Little could be seen of his expression, and she looked away. As the light grew, she forced her thoughts away from him, away from her captivity. She would empty her mind, stop fretting. She looked around at the desert and was surprised by the beauty she saw as dawn tinted the world, as the last stars faded overhead. It was a harsh land, stark and spare, but a fascinating one.

She found that when she stopped thinking of her predicament, she could actually enjoy herself. If she forgot the rope that tied her to the stallion, it gave her a sense of freedom to be dressed like a man, riding astride at the head of a caravan that was going deep into the desert. Her spirits rose. So far she was safe, and this was an adventure she would never forget—something to tell her grandchildren about, being captured by Tripolitan pirates and held prisoner by desert bandits. . . .

They rode with barely a halt as the day grew. As the sun painted the sky white and the dust became choking, fine particles of sand gritted in Juliette's mouth, finding their way in beneath her face scarf somehow. They rode at a walking pace along with the slow camels, but relentlessly so the miles were eaten up.

It was midmorning before either of them spoke. He turned in his saddle and studied her for a few moments, then passed across a water skin to her. "You must drink often," he said, "or the heat and sun will make you weak. How are you holding up?"

Juliette could see that the question, put in brusque, clipped tones, was not asked because of concern for her welfare. *He's probably afraid I'll faint and he'll have to stop the caravan!* she thought. Well, she'd never give him the satisfaction of fainting!

"Fine." She drank deeply and passed the water bag back to him with a challenging stare.

"Not starting to feel the heat—or the riding? I'm sure you aren't used to riding for hours—"

She cut him off. "I've spent days in the saddle before. Riding at a walking pace like this is hardly tiring."

He stared at her for a moment as if trying to judge her words. "We can't afford to have you faint or become ill, so you will tell me if you are feeling the heat or becoming tired." The words were a command.

"I never faint and am rarely ill," she said coldly.

He narrowed his eyes, disbelief evident in them. Then he shrugged and turned away, relapsing into silence.

So he thought she was some kind of weak woman who was going to collapse and complain, she thought, irritated. It would be greatly satisfying to prove to him how wrong he was to judge her so. She resolved then and there not to let a word of complaint pass her lips—and at all costs, to keep up with the men. If they kept to this pace, she knew she could ride all day, though she would be stiff when she woke. Well, she'd been stiff before. And as for the heat, the desert robes were surprisingly cool, sheltering her from the fierce dazzling sun. Yes—she'd show him she was as tough as any man.

Juliette didn't bother to analyze why it seemed so important what her captor thought of her, or why she wanted to prove anything to the man who was holding her prisoner. All she knew was his contemptuous attitude irked her; that she was damned if she'd let him think her weak.

They rode until the sun climbed toward its zenith and the day's heat became too great. They stopped under a wall of red, sand-etched rocks that provided shade. Here, Deric told her, they would halt until the worst of the heat had passed. Then they would start again and ride until nightfall.

She climbed gratefully down from her mare, feeling a slight stiffness already in her legs and lower back. By tonight she would be longing for a hot bath to soak her tired muscles. But she knew that by the end of two or three days, the soreness would vanish.

She sat with her back against the rock wall, watching as the men watered the horses. Deric, walking by, tossed her a water skin and a bag of food: more dried dates, flat breads and some cured meat. It felt like dust in her mouth as she chewed, but she determinedly ate everything. She had to keep her strength up.

They all dozed in the shade until the sun started sinking to the west and the shadows lengthened. Then they mounted and rode on again, the caravan a long string in the featureless desert, crawling slowly over its face. All were grateful when the sun went down in a blaze of glory, orange and red and gold.

They halted, and she sat watching the sun sink beneath the rim of the world while the men swiftly set up camp. Darkness fell swiftly like a curtain, and in a few moments, the air turned chill. She'd heard of this desert phenomenon of swift nightfall and dropping temperatures, but there was something awesome in actually experiencing it firsthand. Overhead, a million stars filled the perfectly clear black sky. She sat watching the stars, almost forgetting for the moment the painful throbbing in her legs.

When Deric came striding up to her to tell her the evening meal was ready in the tent, she got up painfully. His brows rose as he saw the stiff way she walked toward the tent, but she threw him a glance that dared him to make a comment.

Inside the tent, she sat and pulled off her boots with a long sigh of relief. As before, he'd set their food on the small table, and for a few moments, neither spoke as they unwrapped their headcloths and robes. She grimaced in pain as she sat down across from him and picked up her wineglass, taking a long drink. Maybe it would dull her soreness.

"I see you are feeling the ride," he said. "I imagine you'll barely be able to hobble tomorrow. Why didn't you say anything? We could have stopped again, or rested longer at noon."

She looked up and saw from his set jaw he was annoyed. She lifted her brows in mock astonishment. "Such concern for me! And here I thought you were merely my jailer. I'm surprised to see you're worrying about my welfare, or about the way I feel. You must have a soft side I never suspected."

He scowled at her, and she gave him a falsely sweet smile and a pair of widely innocent eyes.

"Soft side! Don't count on it," he growled. "I can't afford to have this caravan held up because you're too stubborn and foolish to get the rest you need. I don't intend to let you be more of a burden than you already are."

This was too much for Juliette. "A burden!" she flashed. "You talk as if I'd begged you to let me come along on this caravan! May I remind you, Deric Raleigh, that it is *you* who is holding me prisoner here! So if I am a burden, you only have yourself to thank. Give me a horse and some water, and point me to the nearest town, and I'll gladly be off your hands!"

"You are a burden and one I don't carry by choice. And just because you are a woman and know nothing of the desert, I won't have you exhausting yourself until you collapse. I'm not being unreasonable. I'm only trying to make this whole . . . incident as painless as possible for us both!"

Not being unreasonable! He still acted as if she were to blame for this whole situation! He was utterly infuriating. For a moment, she watched him go back to his eating, turning over a number of crushing replies in her mind. But when she couldn't think of anything insulting enough to say, she went back to eating, too. What was the use? She was just too tired for this tonight.

When she'd finished eating in silence, she rose and went over to the bedroll. She climbed in and lay down, turning her back to the wall and pulling the covers over her up to her chin. She shut her eyes.

For a few more minutes, she heard him moving around the tent. She heard him snuffing the lamps, then felt him climb into the bedroll next to her. For a moment, she lay holding her breath, hoping he would just leave her alone.

But he wouldn't, it seemed. "Juli—give me your arm," came his low voice.

She opened her eyes and stared at the darkness. "I'm too tired to try to escape tonight, Deric," she said wearily. "You don't have to tie me. All I want to do is sleep."

She heard an exasperated soft curse. "And I want to sleep, too, and will sleep better with you tied to me. Damn it, woman—will you never stop arguing with me over every little thing?"

She rolled over and held out an arm. "I am sorry you find me such a nuisance," she said frigidly.

As his hands grasped her arm and she felt the hated rope being tied around her wrist, his voice cut across the space between them like a lash.

"It's no more than I expected. After all, you are a woman—and all women are nuisances."

He dropped her tied wrist on the bedroll between them and lay down. She lay in the dark, breathing hard with suppressed fury. And as tired as she was, it was a long time before she fell asleep.

Chapter Seven

A yank on her wrist woke Juliette. Dazed, she opened her eyes, for a moment not knowing where she was. A billowing cloth ceiling met her gaze, and it all came back in a rush. She turned her head and saw Deric kneeling next to her on the bedroll, untying the knot around her wrist.

"Ohhh!" She let a soft moan escape her lips as she realized that her whole body was sore. Quizzically, he looked at her for a moment.

"That bad?"

She sat up, pushing her tousled hair out of her eyes, feeling stabs of pain when she drew up her knees. "Not too bad," she replied faintly.

He raised a skeptical brow, but got up without comment and left her sitting there. Still half asleep, she watched him, wondering how on earth she was going to move. She hoped he would leave the tent before she had to get up, because she had a feeling she was going to be hobbling.

In a few moments, he'd gathered up some clothes and ducked out of the tent flap. Juliette got up, moving like an old woman, trying to shake out her cramped muscles by walking around the tent. She gave herself a few minutes. Yesterday, he'd gone off, leaving her with a period of much-needed privacy. She hoped he'd be gone again this morning when she came out; she didn't want him to see how she was limping, and it would take some time to walk off this stiffness.

She emerged from the tent and stood for a moment, taking

deep breaths of the cool, fresh air. The sky was showing faint streaks of gray, but dawn was still some time off. It was the still hour before sunrise, without a breath of wind. The world was hushed, and the sounds of the men getting up came clear across the sand.

Another sound, nearer at hand, made her turn her head. She drew in her breath in surprise at the sight that met her eyes.

Deric was standing a few paces off, his back to her—and he was washing. On a rock lay a pile of garments. He'd stripped off his shirt and wore only his pants and boots. Juliette felt heat in her cheeks, but embarrassing as the sight was, she found she couldn't look away.

He was splashing water on his bare skin, and it ran down the valley between his shoulder blades, down his long back to where his pants hugged his hips. She remembered Avery Ashburn when he'd stripped to catch her in the river, remembered thinking contemptuously how narrow his shoulders were, how thin his chest. The same couldn't be said of this man. His shoulders were wide, with muscles that moved smoothly under his skin as he washed. His hair clung wetly to his shoulders.

Against her will, her gaze dropped to the line of his waist, and she found herself admiring the hard lines of his legs and buttocks before she realized what she was doing and blushed. It was at that moment he turned and saw her standing at the door of the tent. She could only hope that the dim light hid her flaming cheeks.

"So—I see you can stand."

She felt her embarrassment grow more acute. Good Lord, was he going to stand there half-naked and make conversation? Why was it that Deric without a shirt seemed so much more . . . *indecent* somehow than Avery Ashburn had? Maybe it was the width of his brown chest, or the hard flat stomach muscles—or the narrowness of his waist. Whatever it was, it was a moment before she could master her confusion and answer him.

"I—I'm a little stiff, but an hour of riding will take care of it, I'm sure."

"Good." He picked up a clean shirt from the rock and put it

on, buttoning it. Running his fingers through his damp hair, he quickly finished dressing in barracan and headcloth. "There's water here for you to wash with—and some food in the tent. I'll be back in half an hour to strike the tent."

She felt herself blushing again, knowing that he gave her privacy so she could take care of nature's needs. It flustered her that he was so matter-of-fact—and so considerate. Somehow it made her feel undressed.

When he walked away, she limped to the rocks where the water skins were. As she washed, she kept picturing the way Deric had looked without his shirt on, imagining the firm planes of his face, the set of his mouth. Angry with herself for these thoughts she couldn't seem to control, she yanked on her boots. So he was far too good-looking for a woman's peace of mind! What did that matter when he was a mercenary rogue holding her captive for money?

Still, as they rode that day, she found herself stealing glances at him from time to time. Last night, he'd said that "all women were nuisances." It had stung her at the time—but had there been a note of bitterness to his words?

What would make a man like him give up everything civilized life in England had to offer and come to this remote corner of the world? She glanced at the rifle hanging across his back, at the cutlass at his side. Evidently, it was a dangerous life out here for a trader.

Trader! She shook herself. *Of course he isn't a trader, Juliette, you fool!* she thought. *He's some kind of mercenary—maybe an outlaw—and I'm sure whatever he does isn't legal. Why else would this caravan need such a heavy guard, all these men, so many weapons?*

Still, because it helped pass the time and take her mind from her aching legs, she found her thoughts often turning back to curiosity about him. He'd been silent to her much of the time and hadn't volunteered much about himself. In fact, she really knew nothing about him except his name.

Deric stood outside the tent, bracing himself to enter. Behind him, he could hear the laughter of the men around the fire and thought for a moment with longing of the gathering he'd just left. They were passing a wineskin and throwing dice, and just at the moment their company seemed much more appealing than the girl in the tent.

She was every bit as much of a nuisance as he'd feared she would be. Oh, it was true, she didn't cry or whimper or need nursemaiding. In fact, he reluctantly had to admit she never complained at all. But it might have been better if she was a little more timid and ready to cry.

As it was, she was always challenging him with those fearless blue eyes—eyes that could flash with scorn or brim with icy anger. Eyes that could make him feel guilty.

As if he didn't already feel badly enough that he was holding her for ransom. That was the problem. He was finding that he liked Juliette Hawkins, and he didn't want to like her.

But that wasn't the worst of his problems. It was bad enough to feel a dangerous sympathy for her, because that made him feel guilty for the part he was playing—no matter that he had no choice—but it didn't just stop with liking her. She was starting to haunt his dreams.

He was far too aware of her when she slept next to him at night, and he had to lie there battling the desire he felt for her. It was damned hard to hear her soft breathing, feel the warmth of her just a few inches away, and ignore it. Damn it, he wasn't made of stone, and it had been a long time since he'd had a woman. Of course that was all it was; but she was a very beautiful woman, and any man would find the situation trying. The comments he heard nightly around the fire didn't help, either. The men assumed she was his slave and that every night they were—

He took a deep breath and forced his thoughts away from this direction. The only hope was to keep avoiding her as much as possible, like he'd been doing. Not talking much, not looking in her eyes— Her eyes. He felt it right through him every time those soft dark blue eyes met his. No, it was best to keep being as brusque as he could. If she hated him for it, so much the better. Soon this would all be over, she could go back to her people, and he'd never see her again.

With a last glance at the night sky, he opened the tent flap and went inside. She was sitting on the bedroll, her caftan pulled up over her knee, her hands working at her calf muscle. With a startled gasp, she quickly pulled the material down to her ankles.

"Oh—I didn't hear you."

For some reason, her obvious embarrassment irked him. "Sorry—there's no door to knock on."

"Still—you might call before you come bursting in here. You give me little enough privacy as it is," she said stiffly.

"Don't worry—I've seen women's legs before. What is it—a cramp?"

She glared at him. "I don't know what you're talking about. I—oh!" Her words were cut off in a wince of pain as the vicious cramp that had seized her leg came back. She doubled over and gingerly tried to massage the muscles, but her touch was rewarded with another giant bolt of agony.

"Let me see." She looked up and found him kneeling in front of her, a look of concern on his face.

"It's nothing. It will pass in a moment. I—"

"Don't be a fool. Let me take a look at your leg. I know how to deal with cramps." Startled, she looked up at him. Though he'd called her a fool, there was a gentle note in his voice she'd not heard there before. He smiled slightly. "I'll try not to hurt you."

Gentle but inexorable hands were pulling up her caftan to her knee, exposing her bare leg. She was about to protest when another wrench of stabbing pain made her gasp, and she forgot all about how improper it was that he see her bare legs. His warm hands ran over her calf, feeling the knotted muscles, then skillfully, he started massaging the cramp. To her amazement, his fingers didn't bring another bolt of pain. Instead, as he worked, she felt the muscle loosening, the pain receding.

She stared at his bent head as he worked away the last shreds of pain. "It's better!" she exclaimed, amazed.

He looked up briefly, amused. "I told you I knew how to deal with cramps. It's something you have to learn if you're going to spend half your life on horseback."

Now his fingers were producing deep waves of pleasure as

they rubbed her exhausted leg. She wanted him to stop—but she hoped he wouldn't; it felt so good.

"It seems like you must know many things, to be able to cross the desert the way you do," she ventured.

"That's true. It's far from doctors or towns. You have to know something about treating wounds, or sunstroke, even broken legs or snakebite. Not to mention where to find water in case you lose your supply, or even food. The desert is no place for those who don't know what they're doing."

His fingers were working their way down her ankle and now were starting to rub her foot. She had to suppress a gasp of pleasure at how it felt to have her foot massaged. "How—how did you learn so much about the desert, about surviving in it?" she asked softly.

"The army—at first. I came out here six years ago as a captain in the cavalry. But I learned as much after I left from a man named Farouk. He—" He broke off, and she saw his brows draw together.

"Who's Farouk?" she asked, wondering at his mood this evening. He'd been kind about her leg, not yelling at her as if her cramp was her own fault. And his touch, though firm, was gentle. Now he was talking to her almost as if he was a human being. Why, a smile had even flickered on his face for a moment.

But she might have known his mood was too good to last long. When he looked up at her, she saw his eyes had darkened and that the stormy look she knew so well already was back in them.

"There. That should take care of your cramp. But for God's sake, woman, take a walk at night before you come into the tent! You can't ride all day and then sit or this happens!" He got up and strode away to the wineskin, pouring himself a glass of wine, then drank off a large swallow.

Stung, she stared at him. "I didn't know I was allowed to 'take walks'!" she snapped. "I thought you wanted me in your sight at all times!"

"I do. But you can walk around the caravan, can't you? Of course I didn't mean go walking off into the hills alone. I'd think even you would have the sense to know there are scorpions and snakes and other dangers out there!"

He saw the hurt anger in her eyes at his furious tone and stared helplessly at her for a moment. God damn it, she had no idea why he was angry. Look at her sitting there, her copper hair falling in a great tumbling river down her back, hair he longed to plunge his hands into! Those gorgeous eyes, with their seductive slant! She obviously had no idea what they did to him.

And it hadn't helped one bit to feel the silky curves of her leg under his hands, see her delicate ankles, feel how damnably soft her skin was . . . and to sit there, wondering what it would feel like to run his hands up over her knees, slowly molding her thighs with his palms—

"I don't see how you can demand I obey you and then rage at me for not doing something you haven't told me I can do!" Her words broke him out of his thoughts. He saw that for all her defiance, unshed tears were glistening in her eyes. Unbidden, a memory of holding her against his chest as she'd cried that first day came back to him—along with how it had produced that strange protective feeling in him.

And right now, he had the same urge he'd given in to before, to fold her in his arms and comfort her. He was definitely going to have to do a better job of avoiding her. If she had another cramp, he'd be damned if he'd touch her again.

He didn't know if he could trust himself to.

He took a long pull from his wine. "Stop railing at me, woman, and go to sleep! You obviously need your rest if you're going to keep up."

She glared at him. "I'm waiting for you to tie me. Otherwise, I'll just have to be woken up again when you decide it's time to go to sleep yourself."

"I may not sleep at all tonight," he said roughly, and to Juliette's amazement, he strode out of the tent and left her alone.

Chapter Eight

"Deric?" she called softly. He rode at her side, straight in the saddle, his attention riveted before him. She rarely spoke to him while they rode, so it had taken some courage to speak up at all—especially after this morning.

His manner had been brusque to say the least. Not a word passed between them as they prepared for the ride. She had even helped him strike the tent, hoping to elicit some comment from him, but he had merely grunted in her direction. And what aggravated her most was his way of making her feel she was responsible for his foul mood.

He hadn't come back to the tent last night at all. She'd tried to fall asleep, but found herself unconsciously listening and waiting for the familiar tread of his feet on the carpets, the weight of his body in bed next to hers. Why she stayed awake half the night for him, she was sure she didn't know. The man was entirely exasperating! One minute he could be kind and caring and the next, as rude and abrupt as anyone she'd ever met in her entire life.

She hazarded a glance in his direction. From his bloodshot eyes and the haggard look on his face, he'd no doubt spent the night hugging a bottle of palm wine, asleep under the open sky. And after the treatment she'd received this morning, she hoped his head was splitting from all that wine.

She'd really wanted to find him in a good mood this morning because she was in desperate need of a change of clothing. Three days had passed since falling prisoner to this man, and in those three days, she'd worn the same yellow caftan and white trousers. And both were in dire need of a washing. If he would just let her wash them, or if he even had a change of clothing for her—

Juliette didn't think it was too much to ask, so she steeled herself against his foul mood and spoke up a little louder. "Deric, I was wondering—"

Her cheerful voice grated against the hangover he was suffering from. "What is it now, woman?"

"It's been three days since I've been able to change my clothes." She spoke haltingly. There was nothing she wanted to avoid more than yet another scene with this man. She would try to be as accommodating as she could—steer clear of any confrontation.

"This is not a fashion parade, madam," he replied dryly.

She laughed softly in an attempt to show him she, too, had a sense of humor, but he remained unmoved. This would be a bit more difficult than she had first anticipated.

"No, indeed it is not. But—"

"Come out with it. If there's one thing I despise, it's a woman who won't say what's on her mind."

Oh, he was really tempting her now! There was nothing more she'd rather do than tell him what was on her mind, but instead she said, "I was only wondering if there might be a change of clothes in one of those bags." She pointed behind her to the camels that swayed beneath their burdens. "I would really—"

"No."

She was stunned at his quick and simple reply. "Well, then, perhaps you have a clean shirt or a pair of—"

He flicked a look of disregard at her. "Nothing that would fit you."

"Would it be possible to wash these?"

"We're days from the next oasis, and we can't spare the water."

Juliette felt the anger rising to her already flushed cheeks. He was being so damned unreasonable! It wasn't as if she'd asked him for the moon. She simply wanted clean clothes.

Through gritted teeth she asked, "Do you have any suggestions?"

"No."

That was it. She could take no more. "Well, I do," she stated, her voice rising.

"And what might that be, madam?" Now his attention was fully on her, and his voice rose to match hers.

"Stop blaming me for the pounding in your head. I didn't make you drink an entire bottle of wine. You did that damage to yourself."

"Do you mean to say I'm drunk?"

"I mean exactly that. Your eyes are bloodshot, you look as if you haven't slept for days and you can barely keep your seat. You're absolutely weaving about on top of your horse. Not to mention your foul manner. I didn't ask you to set me free; I simply asked for a change of clothing. I don't think that's an unreasonable request. After all, I've spent the last three days under this vicious sun, in the same caftan and trousers, while you've had a change of clothes every day. It's no wonder you spent the night out on the desert. The smell of me probably drove you away. I've been a sport about this whole business. I've not complained for a minute. And you've shown me nothing but abuse when I've least deserved it."

If she'd stopped there, she might have succeeded in shaming him into giving her the shirt from his back; but Juliette knew she had a penchant for pushing too far, and she couldn't resist the temptation to go on.

"I refuse to take another step until I have fresh clothing." She swung her leg over the rump of her horse and dismounted, planting her booted feet firmly in the sand. She stood there defiantly, staring up into his hardening face.

"You will get back on that horse," he said evenly.

"Don't count on it. You'll find I can be as stubborn as you, Mr. Raleigh. I am not moving until clean trousers and shirt are given to me."

"You do not want me to get off my horse, I assure you. If you know what's good for you, you will set your dainty little bottom back in that saddle and keep your mouth shut until we pitch camp tonight."

He waited, but she stood firm beside her horse. The caravan came to a halt behind them, the outriders craning their necks to watch this confrontation between their leader and the copper-haired beauty. Their spats had not gone unnoticed by the men, and in fact many had wagers placed on who would bow to the other one's will. Juliette would have been piqued to know the odds were in his favor at this particular moment.

He was off his horse and facing her. "You have stopped my caravan, madam. And have made me get off my horse."

"I noticed, Mr. Raleigh."

Although she felt herself trembling at the power behind his angry gaze, she wouldn't back down now. The fresh clothing was no longer the issue. He was wrong to treat her so badly.

"If by the count of five you are not back in that saddle, I will—"

"You will what, Mr. Raleigh? Turn me over your knee and spank me like a child? Won't your men be amused by that? They seem to be terribly amused already."

He whirled in their direction, just as they politely averted their eyes, but not before he saw the smiles on their faces. He couldn't let this woman undermine his authority with his men, especially since it had taken years to gain their respect and loyalty. But she was making a fool of him, and no matter how wrong he'd been in his behavior, it would not do to have his men thinking him soft and unable to control her. He turned back to her, unsure what it was that he was going to do, and saw the impish spark in her deep, blue eyes. His irritation turned into anger. The wench was enjoying this little display!

He smiled wickedly at her. "You want fresh clothing, Miss Hawkins?"

She felt her resolve turn to hesitation at his sudden about-face, but it wouldn't do to let him know she wavered. "Yes, Mr. Raleigh, I want fresh clothing and I want it now."

"Very well, madam."

Abruptly, he strode through the sand to the first camel. Drawing his sword, he cut the bonds that held a huge bag on the beast's back. It fell with a thud to the sand and sprang open, spilling its contents of silks and satins onto the desert floor.

Then he stepped to the next camel, and then the one behind it and on down the length of the caravan, cutting the cords that held the large burdens of goods, until the desert was strewn with spices and pottery, cloth and rugs.

His voice rose above the braying of the frightened camels and the grumblings of his outriders. "There, Miss Hawkins, choose anything you wish!" He spread his arms to indicate the entire mess. "What is mine is yours!"

He watched her glare at him from the distance. He had succeeded. As he strolled casually toward her, he savored her embarrassment. She had meant to cause a scene, he knew, but hadn't anticipated one of this size. He bent and picked up a peach-colored caftan and skirt from one spilled pile.

He stood above her, looking coolly into her flushed face. "You have wasted my time with this outrageous display. Take this and never"—his eyes pinpointed hers—"ever waste my time again."

He flung the gauzy material at her and stalked from her side, signalling his men to make camp for the night. Six grumbling outriders dismounted and began to gather the spilled contents of the bags. They threw Juliette nettled looks at having to clean up the mess.

As soon as Deric's tent was up, she raced inside to change and to sulk. She tore off her grimy caftan and trousers and flung them in a corner. Indulging herself, she poured some water onto a cloth to wash her face and sponge down the rest of her body as best she could. The cool water felt wonderful but did nothing for her temper.

She wrapped the peach skirt around her waist and tied it at one side. It was full and fell to mid-calf, showing more leg than she was accustomed to. She slipped the cool, gauzy material of the caftan over her head and pulled it down around her hips. It was loose and billowing, and the neckline a bit too low for one without a chemise or proper undergarments, but there was no possible way she would put the old one back on. She found a length of cloth and tied it around her waist to contain the loose billowing folds of the caftan. It was light and felt deliciously clean against her skin. It was worth the battle she'd fought with Deric.

She thought the whole thing over, trying to decide who had been right. On the one hand, her asking for clean clothing was not out of line. His rude behavior, on the other hand, had been completely uncalled for. Granted, she had pushed him too far, and it wasn't in innocence she had done so. She knew how angry he could get, and stopping the caravan had provoked him unnecessarily. But it wasn't her fault she'd been kidnapped and had no other clothes with her! Why did he blame her for everything that happened? Why was he always so rough with her, shouting at her, glaring at her?

She sighed, exasperated by her own thoughts. *And why the hell do I care so much!* She plopped down on the bedroll and lay staring at the ceiling.

"Damn it, woman!" came the furious words.

She sat upright on the bedroll to find Deric standing in the entry to the tent. She expected to see the anger in his voice reflected in his eyes, but it wasn't anger she found.

His hot gaze ran the length of her outstretched body, and she felt the thin gauze of her caftan burning away from her skin like parchment under his stare. She was barely clothed to begin with, but the way he was looking at her made her feel she was absolutely naked. Unconsciously, she moved one arm across her chest to shield herself from his piercing gaze, and as she did, the material slid from one silken shoulder, baring it to his eyes.

It was all he could bear. "Damn it!" he cursed again.

She sat up, pulling the skirt over her bare legs. "Oh, please. Let's not have at it again."

She waited for him to say something and became embarrassed when he didn't. "Why are you staring at me like that? Is something wrong with me?"

Still he said nothing, but she could see his anger rising like a thundercloud. And then it came to her. The caftan was unsuitable for the caravan ride. He thought she meant to wear it on the ride tomorrow. "It's the clothes, isn't it?" she asked. "You have no one to blame but yourself, you know. You're the one who picked them out. I know they're completely unsuitable, and I meant to say something to you."

"Unsuitable!" he boomed. "I will not have you running about half-naked before my men."

"I hadn't intended to wear this outside. I do have enough sense to know what is and isn't appropriate. I only thought that here in the privacy of the tent, it would be fine to wear it. And I didn't know you'd come barging in."

"I don't give a damn where you thought you might wear it or when. Take that flimsy thing off before I strip it from you."

"I beg your pardon, but I will not put those filthy rags back on. I absolutely refuse."

She stonily watched him cross the tent to one of his bags. He pulled a shirt and a pair of pants from it in a heated fury before flinging them at her.

"Take these and get out of that—that thing. And do it now!"

She held the clothing to her chest. She waited a moment, and when he made no effort to move, she glared at him and said, "If you don't mind, I'd prefer to change in privacy, unless you feel it necessary to watch."

He turned in a huff to leave, but her voice brought him up short.

"What grave sin have I committed against you, Mr. Raleigh? What have I done to once again incur your hideous wrath? If you'd only tell me what it is, I swear, I'd stop doing it."

There was a pleading quality in her words that softened his heart momentarily, and he turned. Her blue eyes and their probing made him feel edgy. Could she be as innocent as she sounded? Could she really not be aware of how tantalizing he found her in that outfit?

Before he could help himself, his gaze was drawn to the revealing caftan, her soft curves visible through the see-through material. Of course she knew. She was no innocent. This was some kind of cruel game she was playing, seeing how far she could tease him until he lost all sense and took her right then and there.

"Why are you so damn mean to me?" she asked.

"Because the devil himself couldn't torture me as you have."

And with that he left the tent abruptly.

Juliette was furious. "And what is that supposed to mean?" she shouted after him, but he was gone.

She groaned in complete annoyance and flung herself on the bedroll. *Oh, that man will drive me completely insane!*

Chapter Nine

It was late morning, and the sun was already blazing hot. Scanning the horizon, Juliette saw a line of hills ahead. This evening, they would stop at the oasis of Jofra, which Deric had told her was just behind those hills. She could hardly wait to reach it. In the oasis, there would be water enough to wash—maybe she could even have a real bath. This endless slow riding over the desert was beginning to tell on her nerves, and her eyes ached for the sight of buildings and trees.

She and Deric were riding a small distance ahead of the caravan when it happened. He was slightly in the lead when there was a flash of movement at his stallion's front hooves, something that coiled and writhed. A snake!

The stallion snorted with fear and reared without warning, and Deric gave a shout, clutching for the stallion's mane. The snake was coiled in the dust under the stallion's flailing hooves, but Juliette saw no more. Her own startled scream was cut off as her horse began to plunge violently, backing and rearing. Before she'd barely had time to comprehend what was happening, she was fighting to keep her seat. Vaguely, out of the corner of her eye, she saw Deric being pitched off the rearing stallion and landing with a thud in the dust.

With a squeal, the stallion bolted. Her own terrified mare was tethered to the riderless animal, and needed no further encouragement but galloped off alongside the fleeing stallion. Juliette rose in her stirrups and balanced herself, gathering the reins as best she could, but her tugging had no effect on the mare.

She'd been on a bolting horse before on the hunting field at home and, since she'd not lost her balance in the first moments, knew that she should be able to stay aboard. But this was no normal situation. Her heart was racing with the danger. This was different—the two terrified horses tethered together, racing over rocks and stones. At any moment, a hoof put wrong might bring one of the horses down in a tumbling crash, with both rolling on her.

She had no hope of stopping the mare as she could have if the mare was alone. The stallion was in the lead with no hand on his reins. She whipped her head to the left and studied the situation. She had to get on the back of the stallion somehow! But how—at a full gallop?

For a moment, with the wind whistling in her ears, she had a vision of the wild games she and her friends—all boys—had played on horseback when they were children: pretending they were wild Indians, or Cossacks; doing riding stunts that might have earned them a beating if their parents had caught them. But never at a headlong gallop like this had she tried jumping from the back of one horse to another.

Her mouth paper dry, she steered the mare forward until her own leg was in danger of being crushed against the stallion's flanks. She kicked her feet out of the stirrups and let go of the reins. Before she could think, she threw herself sideways onto her stomach over the stallion's saddle and grasped the side of the saddle with all her strength, holding on for dear life.

The stallion bucked at this strange sudden weight, and for a moment, she almost lost her grip and fell under his flashing hooves. The mare had moved away behind her so her legs were free, and with all her might, she pulled herself forward and got one of her legs over the saddle. It seemed like hours, but it was only seconds before she had managed to right herself and pull herself up in the saddle to a sitting position. Her legs tightened on the saddle, her feet found the wildly bouncing stirrups, and she grabbed for the reins.

Now she could use her experience at stopping a bolting horse. She leaned forward in a jockey's crouch, standing in the stirrups, and shortened the reins until they were a tight pressure on the stallion's mouth. She slowly started to sit down, pulling steadily on his head, bringing it up so he was forced to shorten his stride. As she felt him slow slightly, she began to turn him off to the left away from the mare, forcing him into a curving circle that she gradually tightened.

She knew it was impossible for a leaning horse to gallop headlong in a circle, so she forced him into tighter and tighter curves and felt his steps slowing. His sides were wet with sweat, and she could feel his breath heaving. He was beginning to tire. In a few moments, she would be able to stop him.

Abruptly, deciding he'd had enough and feeling the confident rider's will on his back, the stallion came to a stumbling halt. He stood there trembling, tossing his head and sweating, and Juliette slid down from his back and went at once to his head. She patted him and spoke in a continuous soothing voice as gradually his eyes stopped showing white and his trembling lessened.

It was a few moments later that she heard pounding hooves and looked up to see Deric riding hell-for-leather toward her. He brought his horse to a jolting halt some distance away, so he wouldn't frighten the stallion into bolting again, and slid off his back. He came running toward her, face white with concern.

"Are you all right?" He sounded frantic.

She took a deep, ragged breath. Now that it was over, suddenly her knees felt weak, like they might give way. "Yes—I'm fine—I think," she gasped.

She looked up at him. His face was streaked with dirt. "Are *you* all right? That was a horrible fall you took. Are you hurt?"

"No—I'm fine. Juli—I saw what you did. That was the finest piece of horsemanship I've seen in a long time. I don't know that my men could match it. I thought—I was afraid you'd be thrown or—"

Startled, she searched his face. Why, he sounded like he'd actually been terrified that she might be hurt! And there was a kind of wondering admiration in his eyes she hadn't seen there before.

"It was probably a mad risk to try leaping on the stallion's back; but I couldn't see any other way to stop him, and I was afraid at any moment he'd put a foot in a hole and go down. I guess I didn't give myself time to think. I've been on a bolting horse before, but never on one being dragged by a tether." She smiled weakly. "I—I think I need to sit down now. Look at that—my hands are shaking! And I feel like my knees might give out."

"No wonder." He took the stallion's reins from her hand and stared down at her as she walked a few steps and sat down in the dust, still with that bemused expression on his face. "I don't think it was mad or foolish, but one of the bravest things I've ever seen."

She smiled up at him. "No more nuisance?" she teased.

To her wonder, he smiled back. "I deserve that."

His smile made him look like a different person to her. It was a flashing smile with an edge of recklessness to it, but it took away his hard, dangerous look. And took her breath. Deric smiling at her made her heart glow, and for a few moments, they just sat there, looking into each other's eyes and smiling.

Then they both started to laugh, and once they started, they couldn't stop. They laughed until they were both breathless, until Juliette felt tears start in her eyes. Nothing had ever seemed so richly funny to her, now that it was over.

"You should have seen your face when the horse reared. I swear your mouth dropped open a foot—" she gasped.

"You should have seen the picture you made, flopping around like a rag doll on the back of that galloping stallion—like a bad circus rider!"

They both laughed again and then slowly stopped laughing and stared at each other. Something leapt between them, something new. It was a warm feeling of being comrades—even friends. A feeling of sudden closeness that contained just a ripple of something more, a powerful spark of attraction.

Deric's smile faded as his gaze held hers. After a moment, he said in a low voice, "Why didn't you run away? This was your perfect chance, once you'd slowed the stallion, to point him over the hills. You know where Jofra is. None of us could have caught you with the head start you'd have had."

She stared at him. "I—I don't know," she said at last. "I guess it just didn't occur to me."

He looked at her for another long moment, then suddenly pulled his cutlass out of his scabbard. With a swift motion, he cut the rope that bound the two horses.

She stood on legs that felt normal, though she could feel that she'd been bruised in several places during her wild ride. "Does this mean you trust me now?" she asked.

She couldn't read the expression on his face. "You've earned it." He paused. "And besides, this showed me it's too dangerous to keep two horses tied together."

And will I still be tied at night? The question rose to her lips, but she didn't say it aloud. The sudden friendship between them seemed too nice to spoil.

"Can you ride now?" When he smiled, she liked the way slight crinkles appeared around his eyes.

"I think so. Though I hope it's not much farther to Jofra. I could use a rest. I'm afraid I'll be bruised."

Concern was back in his eyes. "Are you sure you haven't injured yourself—cracked a rib or—"

"I'm fine," she assured hastily. She was afraid he might insist on examining her on the spot. She well remembered how domineering he'd been about rubbing her legs when she had a cramp.

"Let me help you mount."

She walked to the horse and was about to protest when his strong hands grasped her waist and swung her up onto the horse's back with no more effort than if she was a child.

He mounted the horse he'd ridden out, gathering the reins of the stallion to lead him. "Let's take it at a walk," he said. "And hope there are no more snakes. One in a day is enough." He smiled again at her before he started off.

Juliette put her heels to her horse and followed, reflecting that for once he'd said something she completely agreed with!

It was noon when at last they halted to rest, and the hills on the horizon were already much nearer. Stiffly, Juliette climbed down from her mare. As she lifted her arms to loosen the girth, she ruefully reflected that she was already feeling this morning's wild ride.

"I'll do that. You go sit and rest. You probably need it."

She turned to find Deric looking over at her from where he was tending his stallion. Briefly, he smiled at her, then turned back to what he was doing. She stared at him for a moment, then walked away, trying not to hobble too obviously. It was unbelievable. Deric Raleigh was being nice to her.

Three of the outriders were gathered around a small fire, and she caught the aroma of coffee. They looked up curiously as she walked in their direction. Up until now, she'd avoided them, feeling they were enemies—her jailers. But now that Deric was treating her like she was a human being, avoiding them and pretending not to understand Arabic seemed pointless to her. What little she'd overheard of their talk had been too rapid for her limited command of Arabic, so she'd learned nothing useful from them. It would make more sense to practice her Arabic and try to learn more while she had a chance.

Feeling rather shy, she walked up to the fire and halted. Three pairs of dark eyes were fixed on her with avid curiosity, and she felt herself starting to blush.

"Good morning," she managed, wondering how badly she was mispronouncing the words. Badly, she guessed, seeing their eyes widen in astonishment. Wishing she'd just stayed away, she cast about desperately in her mind and managed to add a polite request for a cup of coffee.

The men leapt to their feet, smiles wide and white under dark moustaches, and started a torrent of Arabic so fast she could catch only a few words. She held up her hands with a laugh.

"Please—speak more slowly," she begged them.

"Here, *effendi,* sit here by the fire while we fetch you coffee," said one, a short but compact man with a striped headcloth.

She obeyed and accepted the coffee gratefully, listening to their talk and trying to answer them when she could. They made a great game of it, delighted that she spoke a little of their language, and soon these fearsome soldiers were running around like little boys, pointing at different things and shouting their Arabic names. In short order, she'd learned how to say rifle and water bag, saddle and boot; learned that the smaller swift camels with the lovely dark liquid eyes were called *meharis*.

A laugh made her look up, and she found Deric standing by the edge of the fire. "I see you are getting along with my men. So you speak some Arabic. You're full of surprises."

She smiled. "Barely any, I'm afraid. I tried to learn some before I left England when I learned I was coming to this part of the world, but I didn't have much time and no one to tell me how the words are pronounced."

"It's a good thing to know the languages of the country you're in—though most women don't bother."

"Most *men* don't bother, either," she said tartly.

His eyes danced. "How right you are. If you'd like to learn more Arabic, I can teach you as we ride. Much as I hate to break up this little party, it's time we were going."

The rest of the day, as they drew closer to Jofra, Juliette rode—untied—at Deric's side and got a lesson in Arabic. He interspersed teaching her new words with telling her about the desert they rode through. A whole new world of life she'd never suspected opened before her eyes. He pointed out hawks and vultures hovering high in the sky, mere wheeling dots, and showed her where holes in the sand or rocks meant some small creature slept away the heat of the day. He showed her plants she hadn't noticed before, telling her which ones could be broken and their juices drunk when water was scarce, and which ones could be used to bind wounds.

All afternoon they rode side by side, often laughing. She found Deric had a quick wit and an ability to say things that made her laugh. And he seemed to be enjoying their new-found friendship as much as she was.

As he talked, she heard a note in his voice that told her that he loved the desert—and more, told her that he loved this life he led, roving free and without fetters.

"You're fascinated by the desert, aren't you?" she ventured.

"The desert? Yes, maybe." He rode along, staring ahead into the vast expanse before them, and for a moment she thought his straight brows looked grim. "Or maybe I'm fascinated by the challenge of a raw land like this—a land where cities haven't choked every available space of earth and blotted out the sky. I suppose it was something I didn't suspect about myself until I'd been out here a few years." He threw her a wry look. "Many say the desert gets into your soul and is impossible to forget. Maybe it's the vastness, or the silence—or the stars at night."

She wanted to ask him what had brought him out here in the first place, but was afraid so personal a question might make him clam up. It was rarely enough that he told her anything of his feelings. So instead she contented herself with saying, "Yes—the stars. I'd never imagined stars could look like they do out here. So many of them—so brilliant. It's beautiful—but somehow it makes one feel very tiny. I can see how the desert could get into one's soul."

"I'd think you'd be missing the city by now. Balls and parties—and wearing silk dresses."

"I was never much of a one for parties," she said lightly, surprised that he'd made a comment about her feelings. Usually he avoided any reference to how she felt, as if he'd rather not know. "And as for dresses, they aren't as comfortable as what I'm wearing when all is said and done. Besides, my last dress—" She broke off.

"Your last dress what?"

"I was going to say my last dress didn't bring me very good luck—but then I realized that really, it saved my life."

"How could a dress save your life?"

She shook her head and smiled. "It's a long story," she said.

"I have nothing else pressing to do at the moment," he said in a dry tone that made her laugh.

But then she glanced at him uncertainly, wondering if it was wise to bring up that night she'd been kidnapped by Mulay el-Rassouli. After all, he was holding her captive for Mulay until her ransom was arranged.

The thought was like a slap of cold water on her face. As well as she was getting along with him for the moment, the true fact was, he was her captor, and all she was worth to him was money. Some of the bright glow that had lit her heart since the wild ride's ending evaporated, and she stiffened slightly in the saddle.

"It was the dress I was wearing when Mulay el-Rassouli attacked our ship. It was of rose-and-silver brocade—and only the light on the silver threads saved me from being spitted by a pirate's sword. He saw I was a woman and decided not to kill me. Instead, he brought me to Mulay so I could be sold as a slave. It was only because I managed to reason with him that he decided to ransom me instead," she finished coldly.

She glanced at him and was glad to see he was looking distinctly uncomfortable. He opened his mouth to speak, but she spoke first.

"When *will* I be ransomed, by the way? You haven't seen fit to tell me how long you plan on holding me—how long it will be before I can gain my freedom?"

He was staring at the horizon again, mouth drawn in a grim line. "I haven't told you because I don't know myself. I've told you I don't like this any better than you do, but it seems I should explain to you why I am holding you for Mulay—"

"Explain! As if anything you say could excuse what you're doing!" she said indignantly. "I don't want to hear your self-serving explanations—trying to justify yourself when the truth is you're a criminal who holds women for ransom!"

She glared at him and reined in her horse, stopping it. "In fact, I don't know what is wrong with me, riding along talking to you as if—as if I *liked* you! I don't! And I am heartily sick of your company! So if you don't mind, I'll ride behind you from now on!"

He stared at her for a long moment. Then he shrugged. "If that's what you want—"

"That's what I want."

He turned in the saddle and rode off, and she sat fuming until he was some distance ahead of her, then started her horse. She didn't glance back or she would have been more angry to see the knowing looks the outriders were exchanging. She just rode, giving in to the luxury of being righteously incensed.

The trouble was, it didn't last long. Before a mile had passed, she began to feel rather miserable. She even regretted her outburst of temper, knowing that she'd just put a stop to whatever it was that had been growing between them. From now on, he would avoid her and go back to his old unspeaking, unsmiling self.

And that's best, she told herself firmly. It *was* best. Because the truth was, she was developing dangerous feelings for him—feelings that could only end in disaster and humiliation for her.

Juliette's innate honesty made her admit before she'd ridden much farther that the whole trouble was—she was attracted to Deric Raleigh. More than just attracted, in fact. She'd had crushes on gentlemen before, had felt her heart beat faster when a handsome man bent over her hand at a ball, but this—what she felt for Deric—was different. Like comparing a puddle to a raging river. It was the way her heart beat faster when he just came into her sight, the way she couldn't stop thinking about him—or stop stealing glances at him when he wasn't looking. . . .

She hadn't been able to fall asleep for hours the last few nights, too restlessly aware of his long frame stretched beside her. When his breathing told her he was asleep, she found herself turning to study his profile, the lean hard jaw, the lock of sunstreaked hair that fell over his forehead, wishing she could reach out and smooth it away.

But it wasn't just at night she found herself stealing glances at him. During the day, she would discover with a start that her gaze was resting on the straight broadness of his shoulders, taking in the arrogant way he sat a horse, his bronzed hawk's face dark against his snowy headcloth. He had a competent coolness, a silent sure way of doing things she found herself admiring. He was a man of few words—but what he said meant something.

He was a man who one moment she found unreadable, infuriatingly closed in on himself. Then the next moment, that determined mouth could dissolve into a flashing smile that had the trick of disarming her. His men admired him . . . and these were men who were fierce and free and hard, but they acknowledged him as their leader.

You want him, Juliette, admit it.

She let her eyes rest on his distant straight back, his blowing robes. It was true. She did want him. He made her feel a desire for him she'd never experienced with any other man. But that was all it was—desire.

And if she was fool enough to let it show, Deric Raleigh would take advantage of her feelings, use her and then forget her. After all, he was a mercenary rogue who was holding her for ransom. No better than a pirate. No, it was definitely for the best that she'd driven him off with her sharp tongue.

But all the logic she could use couldn't drive away the bleak cloud that seemed to have settled on her heart. With a sigh, she realized he hadn't given her any idea of how long she was going to be on this caravan.

For her own sanity, she hoped it wouldn't be much longer.

Chapter Ten

A line of palms threw blessed shade from the late afternoon sun as the caravan rode into Jofra. Juliette sighed with relief as they passed through the outer walls and into the shade of the date palms. It was a shock to see the green of an oasis in the middle of the desert. Looking at the miles of barren sand and rocks they had crossed, she hadn't been able to imagine anything growing on them. But all that the desert needed to be fertile, it seemed, was water. Water here was more precious than rubies, a treasure taken for granted in other parts of the world.

The town was lovely with the sun painting violent contrasts of white walls and deep blue shade. The green of the palms and gardens soothed Juliette's eyes, which were used to the monochromatic grays and browns of the desert.

That night, she stood at the front of their tent, looking out at the moon rising huge and white behind the black fringed leaves of a palm. All around, the breeze rustled the dry palm fronds with a continuous flutter, and she could hear music from the tavern down the street, the faint wailing of a zither. A dog started barking and a voice shouted at it. After the awesome silence of desert nights, the tiny oasis almost seemed like a city to her.

For the moment, she was alone. Deric had gone off to the tavern with his men after they'd set up the tents and eaten, and watered the horses and camels. She'd helped to draw water from the well near their camp, delighting in being able to plunge her wrists into the cool water. Now was her chance before Deric came back to take the bath she'd longed for.

She went inside the tent and quickly gathered up her old, dirty clothes, the ones she'd worn in the first days and fought with Deric to change. She could wash them—and wash the shirt she wore, too. Then she'd have a change of clothes in the days to come between here and the next oasis. Kneeling, she rummaged in Deric's bag until she found one of his clean shirts. She'd borrow it for an hour and then replace it before he got back. He'd never know it was missing. She grabbed a few cotton cloths used for headscarves to dry herself with, and she was ready.

Once outside the tent, she paused for a moment to make sure the village near their camp was deserted. They were camped just inside the outer walls, and the first houses of Jofra were some distance away. She saw no one and started off toward the well, walking quietly.

It stood behind their camp near the wall, so she'd be screened from the view of anyone walking through the village by their tents. She walked up to it, a wide, round low wall filled almost to the top with dark, motionless water. The moon's reflection rippled in one end of the water.

She knelt on the edge of the well and plunged her dirty clothes into the water. How wonderful the cool water felt on her arms! She knelt, enjoying the night, the shimmering moonlight, the rustling palms, and the fact that she was washing her clothes and would soon wash herself.

When she was finished, she pulled out the yellow caftan and wrung it out, then spread the pants on the side of the well. Now for the most risky part. She glanced around carefully, but saw no movement in the dark tents beyond. She held her breath listening, but heard no footsteps. It seemed she was alone.

Quickly, she stripped off her white shirt and pants, the ones Deric had so grudgingly given her. For a moment, she was a silver vision of loveliness in the moonlight, like some naked nymph come to play in the well's water. But as lovely as it would be to plunge into the cool water as she was, it was unthinkable to risk getting caught. She pulled the soaking yellow caftan over her head. It stuck and clung, but it fell to her knees and would serve as a covering in case anyone surprised her here.

In a flash, she was over the side, up to her neck in the silky cool water. It felt like heaven. The well was quite deep, she could feel no bottom with her toes. She took a deep breath and dived under the surface like an otter, then came up, shaking the wet hair out of her eyes.

For a few moments, she swam and splashed softly, luxuriating in the feel of the water slipping over her skin. She hadn't realized until now how dry the desert air was, how her skin cried out for water. She turned on her back and floated, staring up at the great misty moon, now rising above the fringed palms. It seemed an enchanted night, and she felt all her weariness and uncertainty slip away as the spell of the moonlit water took her.

How wonderful it was to be free! Back in England, she'd never been allowed to swim because it wasn't ladylike. She'd only swum when she'd been able to slip away in secret. With a shock, Juliette realized that she was happy—maybe happier than she'd ever been. How strange that when she was being held prisoner, she should feel free for the first time in her life! Though she'd always flouted the conventions, she saw that still so many restrictions had hemmed her in.

But not now. Now she rode like a boy and ate with her fingers. Now she didn't have to worry about her reputation or watch her wayward tongue. Why, she could say anything to Deric—anything at all—no matter if it was something that would be thought too bold or opinionated back home. Even her arguments with him were stimulating, she realized with a kind of wonder. She'd never felt quite so alive.

Yes, she was enjoying so many things that would be considered shocking back home—

Like sleeping in the same bed with Deric? The thought came unbidden into her mind, and she smiled as she stared at the moon, thinking of what Lionel's expression would be if he knew she was sharing a tent with a man.

The water caressed her skin like satin, deliciously flowing over her arms, and the floating caftan felt like the lightest of touches on her skin. *I'm enjoying so many things about this—but is sleeping in the same tent with Deric one of them?* she wondered, struck by this wicked thought.

Maybe it was the enchanted silver moonlight that got into her, but she felt a tingling in her veins at the thought. There was something very comforting—no, even nice—about hearing his breathing beside her at night, feeling the warmth of his body close to hers. She felt a sensual kind of thrill she'd never felt before as she dreamily stared at the moon and abandoned herself to thinking about this interesting subject.

Yes, she did enjoy sleeping in the same tent with him. Why, she'd even missed him the one night he had stayed away. Then an even more wicked thought popped into her mind. Suddenly she was picturing him lying next to her in bed one night, with the tent walls closing them in, in their own private world, as he turned toward her. She imagined how his hand would slowly reach out and trace the line of her face, and then, he would draw her to him ever so slowly until his beautiful green eyes were staring into hers. . . .

And then he would kiss her. Juliette felt a warm glow of a new kind of pleasure she'd never felt start in her stomach at this thought, and she stared at the moon as she pictured what it would be like if Deric Raleigh ever kissed her. He would kiss her softly, so softly, and tenderly, like she was a precious, fragile flower he feared to bruise—

An angry voice broke into her reverie. "Damn it—what the *hell* do you think you're doing!?"

She gave a gasp and twisted in the water, grabbing the side of the well, and found herself staring up at Deric's furious face. He was little more than a threatening black outline above her, but there was enough moonlight to see the dangerous set to his jaw.

"Get out of that water right now!" came the furious command, and before she could open her mouth to protest, he'd stooped and seized her under the arms and was hauling her like a wet and spitting cat out of the water.

He set her with a jolt on her feet in front of him, but his iron grip didn't release her. She shoved angrily at him, then raised a hand to push the dripping hair out of her eyes. "What does it look like I'm doing! Let go of me!" she cried.

Deric stared down at the woman he held in his arms, feeling

unreasonably angry. A few minutes ago, he'd come out of the tavern into the night, telling himself he wanted a breath of fresh air, to get away from the smoke. That was all it was, he'd thought firmly as he made his way back toward the tent, a little unsteady on his feet from the strong wine he'd been drinking. It wasn't that he wanted to see Juli—just that for some strange reason, tonight the men's company was making him restless.

Reaching the tent, he'd called and gotten no answer. To his disbelief, the tent was empty. Without stopping to think, he'd rushed out of the tent, feeling a black anger at her and at himself for trusting her. So she was trying to escape, damn it all! He'd been running along toward the horses, wondering how he was going to track her with only the moonlight to guide him, when the soft sound of splashing halted him in his tracks.

He'd run up to the well, only to see to his utter amazement, Juliette floating on her back without a care in the world. The anger that rushed through his veins then was because she'd given him such a scare; he hadn't stopped to think before he'd hauled her out of the water.

And that had been a grave mistake. His eyes swept down over her. Her hair hung in wet waves, plastered to her shoulders and back. In the moonlight, the glistening curves of her cheekbones and collarbones were bewitchingly alluring, as was the way she was staring at him with a parted, inviting mouth. She looked like a moonlit water nymph who was bent on ravishing the man who had caught her. . . .

And the thin caftan she wore was completely transparent! It clung wetly to her body, outlining every tantalizing curve, more arousing than if he'd found her completely naked. He felt his anger turning to blind desire for her and knew that he couldn't stop what was going to happen next any more than he could stop the moon from rising. His hands of their own will circled the indrawn curve of her waist and moved around to her back.

Juliette stared up at Deric, her heart starting to hammer as she saw the anger leave his eyes and felt his hands sliding over her wet caftan, pulling her closer. She felt a wild thrill go through her as she saw his mouth tighten with passion.

His hands plunged into her wet hair, and he pulled her

roughly to him, molding her tightly against his strong frame. She gasped under the first touch of his lips, at the shock of feeling him draw her so close that the whole length of his hard body pressed against hers. His mouth seared hers, taking her lips with a savage passion she found frightening and sweet all at once. It was a kiss like none she had imagined, bruising, demanding, masterful.

Never had she been kissed like this! His hard kiss softened as she twined her arms around his neck and let her mouth open slightly under his lips. She felt her knees grow weak as his lips explored hers, as his broad chest and strong arms molded her body with electricity. For a timeless moment, she clung to him in a dizzied, whirling world where everything vanished except the new tide of feeling that was rushing through her.

With a ragged gasp, he pushed her away and stood looking down at her for a moment with a look of desire in his eyes she found shattering.

"Juli—" he said thickly, as if he were fighting for control. Then he scowled. "Damn it—you'd better put some clothes on, or in a moment I'll rip what little you're wearing off!"

She widened her eyes at the sudden harsh note in his voice, then looked down at herself. She gasped when she saw her body gleaming through the wet cloth, her peaked breasts showing clearly as if she wore nothing. "Oh!"

She wrenched herself out of his arms and turned away, bending over to pick up his shirt. A tortured groan came from behind her.

"Damn it, woman, are you trying to tempt me beyond endurance?"

She whirled around, straightening, and held the shirt in front of her. Her cheeks were flaming.

"Don't you know any better than to flaunt yourself in front of me when every night we have to—oh, hell!"

He turned and strode away from her, anger making his strides longer, and called over his shoulder, "I'll wait out of sight while you dress—and make it fast!"

Trembling, Juliette stared after him as he vanished between the dark row of tents. She was mortified! He'd seen her almost—*naked!*

But as her heart slowed its frantic beating and she pulled on her clothes, a dart of anger entered her. He'd accused her of—of *flaunting* herself in front of him, when he'd been the one who'd hauled her out of the water!

And to think that just a few moments before, she'd been dreaming of what it might be like to kiss him—imagining a tender kiss! Color burned in her cheeks anew as she pulled on her pants. She might have known he'd kiss a woman like that, like a savage! So different from the soft kiss she'd imagined, it wasn't thrilling at all!

Wasn't it? A mocking voice seemed to speak of itself in her head. Hastily, she gathered up the clothes and walked rapidly away from the well.

Chapter Eleven

"Are you ever going to get up?"

The words penetrated Juliette's consciousness, and she rolled over groggily. She was tangled in the bedcovers as if she'd spent a restless night, and it took her a moment to get them untwined from around her legs. A faint gray light filled the dim tent, and she realized it was Deric's voice, calling her from outside.

From outside. She winced. Outside where he'd spent the night. Last night, when she'd returned to the tent, she'd found him rolling up his bedroll. Somehow she hadn't been able to meet his eyes when he'd straightened and said brusquely, "I'm—sorry about what happened. It was just the wine—and seeing you dressed like that—"

"Please," she'd cut in, in an agony of embarrassment. "You don't need to apologize."

Now her face flamed again as she thought of *that* stupid remark! It made it sound as if she'd *liked* it when he'd kissed her! Oh, why did *she* feel so foolish about the whole thing?

But he hadn't seemed to notice the comment. "I'm leaving you some blankets. It's best I sleep outside tonight."

She'd dared to glance up as he brushed past with a set face. She saw he wasn't looking at her, either. "You don't have to sleep outside—I mean, you'll be cold," she'd burst out, then wanted to clap her hand over her mouth in mortification at the way it sounded. Good Lord—like she didn't want him to leave! Like she *wanted* to sleep with him!

That remark had at last caused him to look at her. Juliette writhed as she remembered the look of angry disbelief in his eyes. It seemed like the moment was the most humiliating moment of her life—but worse was to follow.

"For God's sake, Juli, do you think I'm made of stone?" he'd exploded, staring at her with something like hatred. "Or are you deliberately enjoying torturing me?"

She'd not been able to move under the force of that scathing green gaze. To her humiliation, she felt her eyes widen and tears start. Why? She couldn't have said. Maybe it was the anger in his eyes. Or maybe she was just tired of fighting with Deric Raleigh.

But her soft tearful eyes and slightly trembling lips only seemed to anger him more.

"Damn it, Juliette, don't give me those wide eyes and hurt looks! I kissed you—and that's all there is to it! A mistake I've apologized for—and one I regret already! Don't you think I know better than to kiss nicely-bred English girls like you? Don't you think I know what it means to you?"

Her temper was coming back, and her eyes started to snap; but maddeningly, it was too late to stop the tears, and a few slipped sparkling over her lashes to streak down her cheeks. "And what do you think it means to me? Do you actually think I *liked* it?"

"Liked it? I know damn well you liked it. Don't you think I've kissed enough women to tell?" Juliette gasped at this outrageously conceited statement, but before she could say a word he was going on. "And already, one kiss and you're looking at me with tears! I know what kisses mean to women like you. They mean love and romance—a man to marry!"

His strong fingers closed around her wrist in an irresistible grasp. He turned on his heel, and Juliette found herself stumbling, being dragged along out of the tent flap and into the moonlight. She yanked at her wrist, but was answered with an angry yank back that almost sent her sprawling. Deric stalked into the night, boots grating on sand. He was taking her somewhere and damned determined she come along.

"Let go of me," she hissed, trying to dig in her heels.

"In a moment. It's time you and I got something straight,"

was the answer.

He halted, fingers still tight around her wrist, a tall robed shadow in the desert night.

"Do you see those?" His arm described an arc. Black against the gray of the walls were etched the outlines of the caravan's camels, strange humped silhouettes with long curving necks, lying down for the night.

She could only nod, mouth dry, blood raging with a mixture of fear and fury and indignation.

"My camels—my caravan. That's what I am—what I do. A trader. I sleep under the stars, and I call no walls my home. If there are women in my life, they are women I can leave with a smile, who understand that the desert is my wife."

His fingers left her wrist; but before she could move, they were on her shoulders, and he was drawing her close, almost holding her against him, looking down at her.

"I won't give this life up for a pair of lips, no matter how tempting your kisses are. The price of living inside four walls in one place would be too high to pay—even for you."

She stared up at him, felt his fingers tighten slightly on her shoulders, and knew that for all he was denying it, it was going to happen again. He was going to kiss her; she could see it by the way his mouth was drawn with passion, his eyes suddenly devouring her face. Damn him! After that speech he'd just given her—how dare he think of kissing her again?

"What makes you think I'm interested in ever, ever having you touch me again, Deric Raleigh?" she cried angrily, then put her hands on his chest and shoved him away. His hands dropped from her shoulders, and she felt a surge of relief, because as his head had bent toward hers, his gaze dropping to her mouth, she'd felt her bones being to melt, her blood tingling.

God help her, she wanted him to kiss her again, and the anger she felt at herself lent venom to her voice. She wanted to strike out—to hurt him. "Though I'm sure—as you said—you're more than familiar with kissing women—you aren't familiar with *me!* I find you and your kisses disgusting!" she lied, and almost believed it as she worked herself up into a pitch of righteous indignation. "Oh! I can't believe you are so conceited to think I'd want a filthy, low-life pirate like you to kiss me even *once,* much less again. You forced that kiss on me, and now you're blaming me for it!"

"Forced it?" He laughed. "If that was force—well, maybe I was wrong to kiss you in the first place. But don't pretend injured innocence with me! Not when you've been deliberately tempting me beyond all endurance every night—going out of your way to let me see just what a desirable body you have, looking at me through those damned seductive eyelashes until all I can think of is— Damn it, it's not entirely *my* fault that we kissed!"

"Deliberately tempting you! Is it my fault that you've kept me *tied* to you so I have no privacy? Not even when at last I get to take a bath? I'm hardly flaunting myself when I can't get a moment alone from you. And then you force me to kiss you, then blame me for it! And that you have the *gall* to think that a kiss from you is so wonderful it would make me want to *marry* a despicable vagrant like you—"

She stopped, heaving for breath, unable to think of anything bad enough to say. "You must thing I'm *mad* if you think someone from my background would even dream of *speaking* to someone like you if we weren't on this damned caravan together! You seem to forget that you kidnapped me, and I'm here against my will!"

"I haven't forgotten." His low voice cut into her tirade and stopped her, all anger gone from it. "And I'm glad to hear you have some sense. That's all I've been trying to tell you—a woman like you wouldn't normally even speak to a man like me. So let's keep it that way until this damned trip is over."

There was a pause, and she tried hard to see his face in the night; but it was unreadable. All he was, was a dark shape looming over her, a shadowed face. "Then you can go back to your lords and dukes—and to the marriage and the life that awaits you," he finished, sounding angry again.

"And you can go back to your—your Arab *houris!*" she heard herself spit, to her horror.

His voice was even, his control back. "And I can go back to my Arab *houris.*" He paused. "It won't happen again—I'll see to it." The words held grim promise.

Then he turned and strode away, leaving her standing there. She stared after his tall figure, robes cracking from shoulder to heel, as he disappeared into the night.

And then the sobs had started. She'd stood, gulping helplessly, feeling a searing pain in her tight throat, a burning hole of loss pressing her heart. He was gone. She hated him! She wanted to call him back. He was a damned, conceited womanizer, an arrogant devil who had the temerity to tell her he'd have none of her kisses! Rage struggled with a tearing feeling of loss, and at last, she'd crammed her fist into her mouth to stifle the sobs and stumbled back to the tent. It had been many wakeful hours she'd lain there, reliving the scenes between them, torn between hatred and that awful, contrary feeling of loss she couldn't shake.

How was it possible, she'd tortured herself, that she could sink so low as to still want a man who'd told her he wanted nothing more from a woman than—than to make love to her and then leave her, never being tied down to one woman or one place? Was she the biggest fool ever born? What was wrong with her?

But still, still she hadn't been able to stop the bitter tears that had come, tears that were cried out of loss for what they'd had growing between them—tears because she wished he would come back, even if it was only to fight.

In impotent rage, she had turned over and punched at the pillow, furious with herself for missing him, for wanting him, for *caring* when he was no more than a bastard.

The whole awful scene came back now with a rush as Juliette sat up and her hands went to her swollen eyes. At last, exhausted, she'd cried herself to sleep, but only a couple of hours ago. Oh, God—it was morning. How would she face him?

As she dressed, she chewed her lip and fretted at what she would say when she saw him. Should she be freezingly cold, cutting? Should she tell him in no uncertain terms that his behavior last night was *despicable* and she would have no more of it?

And how would he act toward her? Would he be ashamed? Apologetic? Or just hatefully sarcastic, still angry? Her face felt hot, her hands cold, as she mentally lived a hundred different encounters with him while she slowly dressed.

At last she was finished dressing and could put off her emergence from the tent no longer. She held up a hand mirror and winced. Her eyes were red-rimmed, puffy. It was all too obvious she'd spent the night crying—and it was humiliating that he'd think she was crying over *him*. Even if she had been, he was the last person on earth she wanted to know it. Swallowing, she opened the tent flap, trying to ignore the way her heart was beating far too fast.

He was sitting cross-legged a short distance away from the tent, mending a bridle. He glanced up, and his eyes rested briefly on her face; then he looked away. His face was unreadable, his voice even when he spoke.

"Good morning." There was the slightest of pauses, and then he went on, "I imagine both of us regret the scene between us last night. I meant it when I said I'll see it doesn't happen again. I'm sure you'll be relieved to hear I think it's best to avoid your company. I've asked Ahmal to ride with you from now on."

"I see." She too paused, taken aback at his expressionless tone, but he didn't look up at her. She had been prepared for anger, sarcasm, cruelty even, but not this chill indifference. "Ahmal will ride with me so I don't escape, I suppose?" she said cuttingly. Then, as he opened his mouth to say something, she cut in, "Don't answer. You're right. After what happened last night, Ahmal's company is far preferable to yours. I'm glad you're good enough to spare me your presence."

There was a keen flash from his eyes—just one. Then he stood. "I'm glad you agree. Since that's all I wanted to say, I'll take my—uh, *despicable* presence out of your gentle one. I wouldn't want to offend your delicate sensibilities any more than I already have."

She cringed as she heard her words of last night tossed back at her, then drew her brows together as she saw the small taunting grin that fleetingly touched his lips. He turned and walked away before she could say anything, but before he left, she caught a moment's glimpse of his eyes. They didn't match the grin. They were bleak.

The anger suddenly going out of her, she watched him go. Why fight with him any more? He was right. It was much better that they stayed away from each other.

With eyes as bleak as his had been, Juliette started to strike the tent.

Chapter Twelve

An uneasiness seemed to ride with them after they left Jofra. Although the skies were clear day in and day out, it felt as if a storm were brewing, and Juliette often scanned the horizon for clouds. But she found only the endless miles of sand and the clear blue skies above. Still she couldn't seem to shake the feeling that something was lurking just beyond the next hill.

Deric's reticent mood hadn't helped in calming her anxiety, either. He'd barely said a word to her since their last meeting, choosing to limit their conversation to the orders he barked at her or the others. There was no more talk of the desert, no more lessons in Arabic, and she found that hurt.

He had never been boring, nor had he ever tried to impress her with his knowledge of the desert. He had shared these secrets with her because they truly fascinated him, and the tone of his voice had told her that he thought she, too, would find them interesting. And she had. But now—oh, why couldn't she hate him as she should? Why must she miss his friendship? And why must these long rides with him so silent grip her heart and leave her aching for his nearness?

She had decided Deric was very much like his desert. On the surface he showed her a bare landscape—all rock and grit—but beneath his austere and harsh surface was another Deric, teeming with life, dangerous, humorous and appealing all at the same time.

She could picture him nowhere else in the world, and that's what left her feeling so empty. Even if she could stop time and rearrange the lives of the people she had known—change the circumstances of her meeting with Deric—she could never, ever take him out of his desert.

It's best this way, she told herself. She stole a glance at him as he rode at the head of the caravan. The cut of his figure in the saddle, riding proud and tall, his robes unfurling in the warm breeze, filled her with an admiration she'd tried not to admit these past days. He was no London dandy or foppish Avery Ashburn. This was a man she could fall in love with. This was a man she could stand beside and call her equal. But fate, the wicked imp, had placed a desert and so much more between them. Once again they were strangers, and soon they would part.

She rode alongside Ahmal in thoughtful silence until the voice of one of the outriders pierced her reverie.

"*Sirocco!*" he cried and waved a frantic arm toward the southern horizon.

She followed the direction of his signal and saw in the distance the rolling cloud of dust that was heading in their direction. Like a wall of brown fog, it obscured the view of the desert beyond, and above, dark clouds churned ominously. For the first time, they felt the hot and humid wind that carried the thick clouds of dust swiftly toward them.

Deric dismounted and began shouting orders to set up camp. The caravan suddenly came alive, the swift movement of the impending sandstorm giving urgency to their actions.

"What is it?" Juliette cried as Deric ran to her and Ahmal. All she could see were his eyes. He and the others had already pulled their headcloths around their noses and mouths. Juliette did likewise.

"Sandstorm. We've got to get the tents set up, or we'll be buried alive. Help Ahmal with the horses," he ordered before sprinting away.

She and Ahmal quickly led the horses behind a low hill. There they tethered them together, securing them as best they could against the encroaching storm. Ahmal showed her how to cover the horses' heads with cloth, securing the fabric in the bridle so that the sand wouldn't get underneath. She felt the wind pick up in a sudden gust, and her curls came flying out from beneath her headdress. The sand whirled around her, cutting what bare skin was left exposed to the air. It got in her eyes and mouth and flew up her nose, nearly choking her, but the welfare of the animals came first. Ahmal looked to her when he finished tying the animals together. There were three horses left that needed head coverings. She gave Ahmal a nod indicating that she would take care of them, and he left her, disappearing into the billowing sand.

It was five minutes later when Deric found Ahmal pounding in a tent stake.

"Where's the woman?" Deric shouted over the wind, and when Ahmal pointed to the low hill where he and Juliette had secured the animals, anger seized Deric. "You fool! Why did you leave her alone? She could get lost in the storm. I ought to—" He left his sentence unfinished and raced for the hill to find her. Panic rose with each step he took.

He rounded its side and searched frantically for her among the animals. The sand was so thick now that the sun was nearly blotted out, and the raging wind was deafening. He raised a futile arm against the stinging particles of sand that ripped at his face, then called her name.

"Juli," he shouted against the howling wind and strained to hear her reply. But there was no answer. He called again louder, but only the wind answered him.

The high-pitched scream of a horse caught his attention as his head whipped in its direction. Through the swirling sand, not more than fifty yards from him, he caught a glimpse of Juliette, trying to calm a rearing stallion—his stallion. The animal raised itself up on its hind legs and clawed the dust-filled air around it. She reached for the reins, but they slipped from her hands.

He pushed forward into the resistant wind, his mouth set in a grim line. She was still alive, but in danger. He had to get her back to the safety of the tents.

"Juli!" he shouted. "Juli, for God's sake leave the horse!"

Just as he came within feet of her, the full fury of the storm lashed out at him, A huge wave of sand, dark and thick, rose up from the desert floor and swept between them, blotting her out. It was moments before he could even see dimly again. Deric looked around in disbelief through the eddying sand. She was gone. It was as if the desert had swallowed her up.

"JULI!" he cried in despair. He stood, panting, the sand stinging his face raw. His eyes watered, yet still he searched everywhere for her, his heart pounding a dull rhythm. Frantically, he spun around, looking through the whirling storm for any sight of her, but she was nowhere. She'd vanished.

Then he heard the rifle shots coming from his camp. The shouts of his men rose above the raging storm. His disbelief doubled. What in the devil was all the shouting about, and who had fired the shots?

From nowhere, he got his answer. A Bedouin raider appeared through the gusting veil of dust and swept down on him, scimitar raised.

Without thinking, Deric drew his own blade and unhorsed the raider. The man rolled in the dust and sprang quickly to his feet, facing Deric in the ungodly storm.

He gave the raider no time to think. He lunged forward, slashing the air with his sword until it made contact with the Bedouin's blade. Their swords were held high above their heads as each man grappled for the advantage, straining against the other's power. Deric gathered reserve strength and sent the raider sprawling against the rocky slope of a low hill. Before his opponent could recover, Deric was at him again with his sword raised. He dealt him a glancing blow to the shoulder.

The Bedouin groaned and slumped to the ground, holding his wound. Deric left him there and stumbled back through the storm toward camp. He would get his men. They had no doubt taken care of the raiders by now. They could help him find Juli. God help him, he had to find her.

Juliette finally managed to control the startled animal when she heard the shots coming from beyond the hills. Quickly, she secured Deric's horse and grabbed the rifle he had left slung over the animal's back. Choosing her way carefully, she moved toward the hill that stood between her and camp. The storm was blowing with less fury, but the air was still full of dust.

She lay on her stomach at the hill's crest and peered over the edge. The sight that met her eyes was unbelievable. Two Bedouin raiders stood over Deric's men, who were tied belly down in the blowing dust; two others were ransacking the caravan goods. The raiders must have been trailing the caravan and had seized the opportunity to attack under the cover of the sandstorm.

But where was Deric? She scanned the camp below, desperately searching for his familiar figure; he wasn't there. And then a fifth raider pushed him forward from one of the tents and held him at knife-point on the ground.

Juliette drew in her breath as the raider lowered the knife to Deric's chest, catching the front of his shirt and cutting the material. She couldn't watch!—nor could she tear her eyes away. She felt so helpless. It was clear the raider meant to kill Deric. She wanted to race down the hill and throw herself at the Bedouin, tear his eyes out, beat him with her fists.

Her mind raced. She couldn't lie here and let Deric die. She had to do something. The loneliness she'd felt these past few days would seem like nothing compared to losing him forever. In a flash, she felt what it would mean to never look into his eyes again, even if they were angry eyes, or feel his touch, even if it was a furious grasp. She would gladly have his anger, his fury, if he would only live. But what could she do? There were five of them.

But she had a rifle.

She heard the raider shout something in Arabic at Deric and saw him thrust the knife closer to Deric's throat. She gasped and, without thinking, lowered her rifle and fired, aiming for the hand that held the knife.

The Bedouin yelped, and the knife leapt from his hand as the report echoed across the desert. The raiders' heads jerked in the direction of the hills, searching for the source of the shot.

There was only one way. It was a gamble, but she couldn't stay there and watch them kill Deric. She raised herself and ran along the hills. She threw herself down again, took aim and sent a volley of shots into the air above their heads and into the dust at their feet. Then she was up again, running to fire from a new direction.

The raiders hit the dust as a new round of fire rained down

on them. The shots seemed to be coming from all around them. They rose crouching and ran for their horses, thinking themselves surrounded.

Deric quickly sprang into action, cutting the bonds of his men, who immediately leapt to their feet, grabbed their weapons and were off after the bandits, soon disappearing from sight.

The camp was all at once very quiet.

Deric squinted into the slowly settling sand. From the hills he saw a figure rise and approach him, its silhouette proud and sure, yet slender and delicate, not the figure of a man, but of a woman. It was Juli! She was safe—and she'd been the one firing those shots with unbelievable accuracy.

The air was as still now as it had been before the sudden storm. Low thunder rumbled across the desert, and streaks of lightning lit up the sky. Large drops of rain splattered to the ground, leaving big pock marks in the sand.

For a long moment they stared at each other in relief, then the distance between them became too great.

Juliette ran down the hill toward the center of camp. Deric met her halfway and threw his arms around her in a protective embrace.

He whispered her name over and over again as if to reassure himself that she was really in his arms. He pressed her to his chest possessively and held her firmly to him, afraid she would slip from his grasp. He had almost lost her.

"My God," he whispered into her hair, "you're safe."

The pressure of his arms around her filled her with calm, and she felt grateful tears spilling down her cheeks. He had almost been killed. But now he was safe.

"I didn't know you were such a crack shot," he said softly. He wanted to tell her how relieved he was that she was safe, but he avoided it. She thought him a brigand. His words would only sound false. "Where were you? I tried finding you in the storm," he said instead.

"I tried to make sure the horses were settled. I think I may have lost one," Juliette replied against his shoulder. She didn't know why she mentioned the horse. It seemed absurd in light of the danger they'd both just faced. But she couldn't tell him how she feared for his life. He might laugh at her. "I know a good outrider would have—"

"Stop," he said, stroking her hair, still holding her to him. "I don't give a damn about the horse." She felt him swallow hard before adding, "It was you I was worried about."

They parted and looked at each other as the rain began pouring down. For a long moment, the relief in his eyes held steady. Then he raised his hand to stroke her cheek—and the relief changed to something else entirely.

The moment his fingers touched her skin, a blaze of heat as sudden as the rain leapt between them, too strong to deny any longer. And as the rain pounded down around them, everything was forgotten except what they saw in each other's eyes.

Chapter Thirteen

Juliette felt her heart begin a wild beat as Deric suddenly pulled her close. She saw his eyes darken with passion as he bent his head to kiss her.

His mouth closed over hers as his arms encircled her, one hand sliding up under the waterfall of her hair to caress her neck. She almost struggled—but was it against this male who held her so tightly pinioned in his arms, who was kissing her as if he would never let her go, or was it against the treacherous tide of feeling that was suddenly flooding her? She was dizzy as she felt his mouth plundering hers, and she felt his passion mount as her hands, almost against her will, rose to caress his chest and twine in his hair. His tongue parted her lips, and he pressed her so close to the heat of his body that she felt they might melt together!

The rain lashed them unheeded, forgotten as they stood lost in the wonder of kissing each other, in the delicious relief of giving up the futile fight they'd fought to try to stay apart. Deric's hands were stroking her hair, her face, and he broke their kiss and moved his mouth close to her ear. He held her tightly as he murmured, "Juli—Juli, I cannot fight you any more. I've tried to resist touching you, but you are like a fire in my heart I cannot put out."

His words sent a wild thrill through her, for she heard a tender note in his voice, the kind of note she'd dreamed of hearing. With the rain beating around them, she wondered for a moment why it didn't seem wrong to be in Deric's arms, why it seemed like the only place in the world she'd ever been meant to be. It was magic. And if it was madness too, Juliette found it didn't matter. He was her lover, the lover she'd always yearned for and never known it, and every kiss twined them closer in a destiny they couldn't deny.

As his mouth met hers again, she kissed him with an ardor that matched his, her body alight with desire for him, tingling with the pleasure of the new sensations he was arousing in her. His lips left hers and softly wandered over her wet face and throat, leaving a trail of fire. She trembled and arched toward him as his questing hands came slowly up her waist to cup her breasts. His burning lips travelled down to meet his hands as they traced the thrusting shapes of her firm breasts. With a low moan, he pulled open the soaking cloth of her shirt and let his tongue touch, then gently circle the nipples that tautened under his lips.

"So sweet," she heard him murmur. "You're more beautiful than I dreamed, and I couldn't stop dreaming of you." His head came up, and he stared into her eyes. She drew in her breath at how dangerously beautiful he looked. "I had to try to stay away from you, from the spell you've cast on me. It was torture trying to sleep in the same tent with you and not touch you—"

"Then if this is a spell, you—you have cast it on me too," she whispered shyly.

He stroked her cheek and her lips. "I want you, Juli—my Juli. And you are driving me to madness by showing me you want me too. If I kiss you again, I won't be able to stop."

For a long moment, she looked up at him, feeling her resistance melt, feeling the wild magic that leapt between them. When the words escaped her lips, they were so low he barely heard them.

"Kiss me again," she breathed.

With a ragged indrawn breath and a low groan, he suddenly picked her up. His lips closed on her tilted-back mouth as he strode through the wild rain, carrying her in his arms to the tent.

He ducked inside the tent and carried her to the bed, then knelt. He deposited her in a glorious tumble of copper curls, clinging wet garments and taunting breasts. He thought he had never seen a more desirable picture. Her half-closed eyes burned up at him, and he drew in his breath as her hands found his open shirt and pulled it over his shoulders, baring his chest.

With slow, caressing fingers he unbuttoned her shirt. Holding his breath, he slowly slipped it off, then trailed his fingers down the silken skin of her stomach and grasped the edge of her pants.

Juliette shivered convulsively at his touch and gave a low moan of pleasure. She lay back watching him, hypnotized. She was hardly conscious of who she was or where she was. There was only the night, this lean man above her, the muscles of his wide shoulders and arms rippling in the dim light, shut inside this secret world of a billowing tent and drumming rain. He was silhouetted above her, naked from the waist up, narrow hips circled by his scabbard's belt, his boots somehow—she could not remember how—gone. He had bared her breasts and was staring down at her with those long, wicked green eyes as he slowly pulled her pants down her legs—so slowly, so caressingly that she shuddered!—leaving her naked. She was revelling in his gaze, feasting her eyes on his as he knelt above her, hot and flushed with some strange emotion that had possessed her and shut out the world.

His eyes drank in her naked splendor with a burning gaze. She was a vision of lustrous beauty, all curves and long legs, slender waist and luscious breasts and tumbling hair. "You're perfect," he breathed at last. "My Juli . . ."

He lowered himself to her, his mouth hungry on hers, her arms circling his neck. It suddenly seemed that neither of them could get enough of the other, their lips seeking, their hands exploring, their passion mounting to a wild desire neither could contain. He felt her long, silken legs twine around his legs, her back arch as she fitted her body to his, her hands helping his as he pulled his last clothes away.

As his fingers touched places that made her gasp, teased her, played with her, stroked her, as his lips travelled over her twisting body, she felt silver thrills like a thousand shooting stars racing through her veins, and she ached for—she knew not what.

At last Deric could keep his passion in check not a moment

longer, and he was on top of her, his mouth thirstily covering hers. With a spearing thrust, he entered her, and she arched against him, crying out. For a moment, he was still, holding her as if she was the most precious wonder in the universe, conscious of her untried newness at love. Then he began to move slowly inside her until he felt her relax against him and felt her hands on his neck, pulling him closer.

With his ragged breath in her ear and his lips kissing her mouth, her cheek, her eyelids, she felt the pain of receiving him quickly vanish and a wondrous new feeling filling her. She found herself meeting him thrust for thrust as passion caused him to quicken. The tingling sensation that flowed over her body carried her up and up, into an unknown world of dark nights and flowers opening like stars in the darkness. Upward she travelled, free of the earth, yet chained to it by his mouth at the deep valley of her breasts; chained to it by shivering sensations that were at once hot and cold as his strong hands caught her waist and then moved slowly lower to hold her hips as he pushed deep inside her; chained by his passionate thrusts that made her wonder how two people could become as one, united by the melting heat of their bodies.

Then white-hot passion rose until it exploded like a thousand pulsing sprays of liquid flame, scattering like stars. Juliette clung to him weakly as he slowed, gasping, their bodies unable to stop that sweet rhythm that had brought them to the heights, then tossed them down again.

At last, he rolled to her side, pulling her possessively close to him, her head on his shoulder, his hands twining in her soft curls. Their bare chests, warm like silk against each other, slowed in breath and beating heart. She felt wonder fill her, a contentment and pleasure that was as deep as velvet and as relaxed as sleep. She was back on the earth once again, lying in a desert tent, imprisoned in the arms of this magnificent male, whose satiny skin covered heavy muscles like steel, lean muscles like iron. She felt his mouth press softly, so gently, on her forehead—a lover's caress.

She lay naked in his arms and didn't care, because it was right that she was there. Tonight there was only the magic between them; tonight there was only the incredible feeling of oneness with her lover. Tonight there was only the memory of that pulsing, shattering feeling that had run through her as he lay, one with her. Tonight . . .

She turned slightly in his arms, and they looked long into each other's eyes. And their eyes told each other everything that for now, their lips could not say.

Chapter Fourteen

The next days brought Juliette a happiness she had never dreamed of owning. From the moment she had awakened in Deric's arms to find him staring down at her with a kind of tender wonder, the world became an entrancing place in which everything but their delight in each other ceased to matter.

That afternoon, the battered caravan rode into the oasis of Bu Ngem, the next stop on the great caravan route that stretched from Egypt to Tripoli. Here they would take a much-needed halt to repair the damage the storm had inflicted.

While the men were busy setting up the tents, Deric came riding up to her and looked down at her with a glinting smile. He'd disappeared when they reached the oasis and left her with the outriders, and she'd helped with the tents, wondering where he had gone.

He leapt down. "Come with me and leave setting up that tent. In fact, leave it folded. We won't be needing it."

"Leave it folded?" she asked, amazed. Usually Deric was adamant about camp being set up, the animals seen to, before anything else was done. "Where are we going? And why won't we be needing the tent?"

"Because I have a mind to sleep with you in a bed for a change. And let you have a real bath so you won't be driven to running off to swim in wells at night." He grinned. "I find I don't like the thought of you running off anywhere at night."

Juliette blushed, but it was a blush of pleasure. Then she squealed as he scooped her up in his arms and carried her to his horse, leaping up behind her. His arms came firmly around her waist, and for a moment, she felt his lips in her hair. Then he kicked the stallion, and they were off with a flourish, riding toward the buildings of the oasis.

Behind them, the men laughed and looked after the pair. "So, the fiery beauty has tamed the hawk," one said. "It looks as if I win our wager."

The other outrider laughed. "But it seems to me he is the one who has won the battle. *Bism'Allah!* But if I knew where I could find a slave so beautiful, I would kill the horse under me riding there!"

Juliette leaned against Deric's broad chest, delighting in the feel of his hard thighs against hers, in the security of being clasped in his strong arms. She looked around as they rode at the low, flat-roofed buildings, white walls and archways, chattering women in a group drawing water from a well, palms lining the dusty streets. The oasis seemed the most beautiful place on earth to her at that moment.

Deric reined in the horse in the courtyard of a low rambling building. A fountain splashed and flowers grew.

"It is a *caravanseri*—an inn," he explained. "And I have taken a room—and a bath."

They climbed the stairs to find themselves in a sun-splashed room. It had white walls, a clean floor of red tiles and a deep window that overlooked the courtyard garden. Though the furniture was plain, there was everything for comfort: a big bed cleanly made with white linens, a table and chairs—and a bath.

Juliette gave a cry of delight when she saw the big copper tub and the curls of steam rising from the water. She turned to Deric with shining eyes. "A *hot* bath! I can't believe it!"

"It's amazing what gold can do." He paused. "Well, are you going to stand and stare at it until the water grows cold?"

"I'm waiting for you to leave," she said primly.

"But I have no intention of leaving. In fact, I have every intention of sharing that bath with you."

"Deric!" she began, but her protest was stilled as he crossed the room and quieted her with a dizzying kiss. He was in no mood to be gainsaid, it seemed, for his hands were opening her shirt, divesting her of her clothes so quickly it made her head spin. It seemed but a few moments before he had stripped her of her garments, picked her up and deposited her, blushing and protesting at this bold treatment, into the bath.

"My water nymph," he murmured. "It seems my best memories of you are when you are soaking wet. I couldn't forget dragging a bewitching temptress out of the well, or kissing her in the rain. Now I will see if we can make this water hotter than it already is."

With wondering eyes, Juliette watched while he stripped off his clothes so he could join her in the tub. It was the first time she had seen him naked in the light, and she couldn't suppress an admiring gasp at his tall strong frame, so beautifully proportioned.

As he sank into the water and pulled her shyly struggling onto his lap, she made another feeble attempt at protest. "You have no shame, Deric." She laughed, trying to cover her breasts with her damp hair and shield them from his burning gaze.

"If it is shameful to think your loveliness is like none I have ever seen—to want to look at you—to kiss you like this—to touch you so—and to have you touch me like you long to do—" His hand was guiding hers over his body in bold ways she'd never dreamed of touching him, and he was kissing her until she was senseless. "Then I have no shame where you are concerned, my love."

When at last their passion was spent, to Juliette's amazement, Deric insisted on bathing her. He soaped her tenderly, making her laugh, and plunged her head under the water, then washed her hair like she was a helpless child. When she insisted on washing him in turn, it was not long before his passion quickened again under her hands. But this time he hauled her out of the bathtub and carried her to the bed, vowing that otherwise they'd flood the floor with the water they were splashing on it.

At last they fell into a sweet exhausted sleep, holding each other closely while blue night deepened in the windows.

Juliette woke to find Deric smiling down at her, his fingers playing with her now-dry hair. For a moment, they said nothing, just smiled into each other's eyes. Then Juliette stirred, stretching deliciously.

"I wonder what the time can be? I'm ravenous!"

"I find you drive all thought of food—and time—out of my mind." He laughed. "But since I would have you happy, I'll go see if I can find us something to eat."

But it was a few moments before he could tear himself from the bed. First there were a few delicious kisses to claim, a few murmured whispers to exchange, in the manner of lovers since time immemorial.

Juliette watched him with a misty glow in her eyes as he dressed and left the room. Then she rose and, pulling the sheet around her, went to the window. She leaned her elbows on it and took a deep breath of the scented night air. She could smell flowers, jasmine and frangipani, and beneath the window a nightingale began its heartachingly sweet song. Above her the hollow dome of the heavens was black and sparkling with stars. Briefly, her soul seemed to expand outward in the most perfect happiness she had ever felt.

It was not long before Deric returned.

"I see I will have to get you some clothes."

She turned from the window and sashayed demurely in her sheet. "Why? Don't you think this is becoming?"

"Too becoming. With your bare shoulders uncovered, I've a mind to put that sheet back where it belongs—on the bed."

He made a grab for the trailing end of the sheet, and she eluded him, laughing. There was a knock on the door, and she clapped her hand over her mouth to stifle her giggles.

"Stay there," he said warningly. He was in no mind to let any other man catch a glimpse of her wrapped in a sheet, with her pearly shoulders gleaming and her hair falling in rich copper waves down her back.

He opened the door a crack and said a few words in Arabic. In a moment, he was shutting the door again, holding a tray filled with dishes and a tall wine bottle.

They sat down and both suddenly realized how hungry they were after their hours of love. When they had finished, it was long they lingered, sipping their wine and talking, laughing softly together, before at last they slept again, clasped in each other's arms.

The days followed one another like pearls on a string, each more lustrous than the last. They rode out together side by side into the desert, and Juliette learned more and more about its ways from Deric. They slept late and sought their bed early; they spent lazy hours talking and laughing, each learning more every day about the other.

But the one thing they never spoke of was the future.

For now, it was enough to forget that she was his prisoner—that the day was coming when they would have to part. For now, it was enough just to be lovers who were snatching a few precious hours together in the face of their enemy, time.

Chapter Fifteen

The days drew out, and to Juliette's surprise, no mention was made of leaving. It was nearly a week now that they had lingered at the oasis. It seemed that Deric was as content as she was to take each day as it came with no thought—or mention—of the future.

On the morning of their sixth day there, she was awakened by a resounding slap on her bare bottom.

"Oh!" Pushing her hair out of her eyes, she rolled over to find a smiling Deric standing dressed near the bed. Hastily, she grabbed for the sheets, only to have him snatch their tangled remnants off the bed with a wicked grin. She blushed, still finding it hard to get used to being completely naked in front of him in the daylight. "Stop that! To what do I owe such a rude awakening?" she cried, making a futile grab for the sheet.

"You sleep late this morning; I thought you'd never wake up. You didn't even stir when I got out of bed and dressed. So I had to wake you—for I have plans for us today."

She threw him a mischievous look. "It's no wonder, when you scarcely allow me any rest!"

His eyes swept over her face and then lingered on the softly rounded curve of her breasts. "And is that to be wondered at, when the sight of you makes me forget everything else? Maybe I dressed too soon this morning."

Juliette's eyes sparkled playfully at him as he made a sudden lunge at her, and she rolled over and got up just as he landed on the bed. She laughed down at him.

"Juli—don't test me too sorely or—"

"Or what? I'm curious to learn what this plan is you have, and I won't have it driven out of your mind!" She grabbed a caftan and pulled it over her head.

A groan from the bed greeted his move. "You are hard-hearted. But—maybe it's best. I have a mind that our play will be sweeter if we wait a bit. But if you don't stop tempting me, I promise you, you will make me forget all about it."

"Tempting you? How so, when I have put on these clothes?"

"Clothes? What you wear makes you more alluring than before, if that is possible—at least when you are standing in front of the window!"

Juliette looked down and realized that the strong sunlight was rendering the outline of her body clearly visible through the thin caftan. With a laugh, she moved away from the window.

"Tell me this mysterious plan!" she said, starting to dress for the outdoors. But there was no reply, and when she glanced up, it seemed Deric was more interested in watching her pull on her pants and change into a shirt than in telling her what he had in mind.

"You'll see soon enough," was all she could get out of him, and she had to be content with that. But it delighted her that Deric was planning something to please her. She was excited as they mounted their horses and rode out of the oasis into the desert. Not far away was a line of hills they seemed to be making for, and she wondered where he was taking her.

They rode up into the low hills, following a faint track. Suddenly they rounded a rocky spur, and Juliette gasped with pleasure.

In front of them was a small sheltered grotto, surrounded on every side by towering rock walls. Down the face of one of the walls wound a silver ribbon of falling water, and it was gathered into a shining pool. All around the pool, unexpected in the dry desert, grew lush growth fed by the water. Soft green grasses and moss framed the pool, and several tall palms shaded it from the blazing sun. It was a wild garden spot, a hidden green jewel set in the dry hills.

"Oh—how beautiful!" she cried. "I never dreamed such a place could exist in the desert! How did you find it?"

"My friend Farouk showed it to me. All places that have

water are marked by those who travel the desert. There are many springs that come up from far underground, like this one. Without them, the desert would indeed be impossible to travel."

They slid off their horses and tethered them where they could crop the soft grass. "Farouk? Once I asked who he was—he is a friend of yours?"

Strolling to the pool's edge, they sat on the grass. He was silent a moment before answering. "Farouk? A friend of mine, an Arab I met when I was in the army."

"The army? You said that's how you came to this part of the world?"

He smiled, but it was a smile that held an edge of bitterness, she thought. "Yes—I came out here first as an officer in the cavalry, stationed in Derna. It was the expected thing for me to do. You see, I am a younger son. My father was a lord, and I grew up near the edge of the Pennines on a huge estate. But my eldest brother is now Lord Davencourt and runs the estate—and I, as is the way with younger sons, was left almost penniless." He glanced at her, and his expression lightened. "Which is just as well, for I would not have made much of a squire. I find I am of too restless a disposition to settle down in one place for long—at least a place as tame as England."

Juliette listened to him curiously. It was rare he would speak of himself this way. Not wanting him to stop, she ventured softly, "So—you chose the army as your profession?"

He shrugged. "The army seemed the best choice at the time. Younger sons in our family have a tradition of choosing the church or the army, and as I could see that I hardly fit the church—!"

"But—why did you leave the army?"

Again the bitter set was back to his mouth. "I came out here six years ago on captain's wages—starvation pay. I found it didn't sit well with me to spend my life guarding those who were grabbing fortunes and getting nothing for it in the end but a pension. So I took my skills with a horse and rifle and put them to good use. Running caravans—trading in ivory, spices, silks—is profitable. In another year or two, with luck, I will have earned that fortune I saw others grabbing."

So money is that important to you? It was on the tip of her tongue to ask, but suddenly he turned to her with a smile.

"But enough of such serious talk! I brought you out here so that we might have a swim. As I recall, you seem to enjoy swimming!" He grinned at her, and both of them laughed as they remembered the night at the well.

"It sounds wonderful!" She sighed, looking at the inviting water. The sun was hot, and she pulled off her boots and stuck a toe in the water. It was refreshingly cool and clear, and the pond looked deep. "What shall we swim in?"

He smiled wickedly. "In the water, of course."

She picked a flower and threw it at him. "I mean what should we wear?"

"I vote for nothing at all."

"But what if someone comes?" she asked, pretending to be scandalized.

"Then they will hopefully have the sense to turn right around and leave. If not, I'll chase them off with my cutlass!"

She giggled at the entertaining picture of a naked Deric, cutlass in hand, chasing some poor intruder down the path.

In a few moments, they had their clothes stripped off. Juliette looked up to see Deric's eyes fastened on her with unmistakable intent, but as he reached for her, she dodged away.

"You promised me a swim," she reproved him. For a moment, she stood poised in the sunlight, her hair a shining cloak of fire, her smile arch and winsome. Then she turned and slipped into the pool with a splash. She surfaced, shaking the water out of her eyes and laughing, in time to see Deric's lean form diving into the pool after her.

With a smile, she swam away, eluding him. She heard his spluttered, laughing curse as he struck out after her, the light of purpose in his eyes. In a few swift strokes, he was close enough to grasp her ankle, but with a kick and a twist, she shook him off again.

But he was the faster swimmer, and this playful pursuit did not last long. Coming up gasping, she felt his long body sliding up along hers from under water, felt his arms coming around her in an unbreakable grip. Then his head broke the surface, and he was looking down at her, holding her imprisoned against him. She could feel how unmistakably this chase had aroused him as his lips came down on hers.

They floated, twined in a kiss, until he broke it off and looked down at her. In the sunlight, his eyes were green and clear, and she felt her heart catch.

"My water nymph—my Juli. Are you part mermaid or siren? Your eyes are sparkling like the sunlight on the pool."

He didn't wait for an answer, but let his lips touch hers again in a soft slow kiss that took her breath away. Lingeringly, sensually, he kissed her, his tongue gently tracing her lips until she was dizzy. His hands felt like silk as under the water he explored the curves of her body. She let her own hands roam over the sinewy muscles of his back, of his thighs.

His hands clasped her waist and turned her until she was floating on her back, as his mouth went down her throat and found her breasts. She twined her legs around his waist and let her fingers stroke his wet hair as his mouth teased her nipples until she was moaning with pleasure.

Then his strong arms were carrying her, lifting her dripping and dazed out of the pool to lay her on the soft grass next to the pool. She moved to pull him close, but she felt his hands grasp her wrists and spread her arms wide over her head, holding her pinioned. She opened her eyes to find him staring down at her, bemused.

"You are so lovely," he breathed. "I will never get enough of drinking in the sight of you, I think."

Releasing her arms, he lay on his side, propped on one elbow, and let his fingers lightly run down her wet skin, from her collarbone to the base of her stomach. She shivered with pleasure and reached for him to clasp him close to her, but he pressed her down again, and again spread her arms wide.

"Let me pleasure you, my Juli. Don't you know what it does to me to see you gasping with desire?"

She stared at him, feeling a flush rising to her cheeks at the thought of him watching her while he touched her. But at the same time that it was embarrassing, it was also unbearably exciting. She shuddered as his hand continued to stroke her wet skin, with a featherlight touch that left no inch of her alone. He stroked the arch of her foot, running his fingers slowly up the inside of her legs, brushing them over her stomach, lightly touching her nipples until they sprang up under his touch and she twisted beneath his fingers, not able to hold back a low gasp. Waves of heat seemed to be rushing through her body as his fingers continued their sweet torture.

Just when she thought she could bear not another moment of his delicious shivering touch, he parted her legs slightly, and his fingers found her most sensitive spot. She cried out and clutched his shoulders, but he was bombarding her with sensations and would have no mercy on her. He rolled half on her, and his mouth found her breasts as his fingers drove her to new heights of pleasure that were shatteringly sharp. She threw her head back, neck arched, as his tongue slid over her jawline, her neck, her collarbones. She cried out with an ecstasy she couldn't hold back.

Just when she knew she could bear no more, with a groan of his own, Deric rolled on top of her and entered her with a powerful thrust. She held on to his shoulders as they wildly rode together, their breath tearing their throats, fused into one being by the miracle of their passion. At last they both cried out at the fulfillment of their desire, and clung together, gasping, as their hearts slowed their furious beating.

It was a long time before Juliette could even open her eyes. She just lay, her arms around Deric's neck, her fingers twined in his damp hair, feeling his weight on her, his chest rising and falling in rhythm with her own. At last he raised himself on his elbow and looked tenderly into her eyes.

They didn't speak, but she reached up a wondering hand to stroke his cheek, to trace the firm line of his mouth. He bent and kissed her softly, and with a hand smoothed her hair back from her brow. Then he rolled over onto his back, pulling her with him so that her head was resting on his chest and she was held closely in his arms. For an endless time, they just lay together, listening to the rustling palms overhead and the musical murmur of the falling water.

At last he stirred.

"I didn't let you swim very long. Would you like to take that swim now?"

She gave him a squeeze. "That sounds like a wonderful idea.

Maybe the water will cool me off."

"Did something make you hot?" he inquired innocently.

She made a fist and punched his ribs, feeling a quick blush at the memory of how he had watched her in the throes of desire while he touched her. But evidently it had pleased him too. Never before had he loved her so strongly and yet so tenderly.

She got up and, casting him a misty smile, dived into the pool once more. This time he sat on the bank and watched her as she swam and splashed like a child in the water. She felt as free as she ever had, swimming without clothing while her lover sat and smiled down at her from the bank.

Deric watched her, delighting in the sparkling happiness he saw in her face. She had blossomed during this week under his very eyes. His Juli. She had been beautiful before, God knows, but now, with the flush of love in her cheeks, she had a radiance that caught at his heart. She had awakened to passion under his touch and seemed to glow with happiness as she discovered the delights that love could bring.

A shadow seemed to pass over him then as he watched her. His Juli—so happy. She had cast her spell on him so that he had taken her love because he hadn't been able to stop. As he watched her laughing in the water, his heart gave a sudden twist at the thought that he might be the one to bring unhappiness to those sparkling dark blue eyes.

The next evening, Juliette stood before the small mirror on the wall, twisting this way and that, standing on tiptoes to try to get a better view of herself. She stroked the gossamer-thin silk of the caftan she wore. It was a fragile lavender, so fine that it was like a whisper on her skin. It fell to her knees, and beneath was a narrow skirt of the same material, split to the thigh, that stopped just above her ankles.

On the bed was a riot of finery, and she'd spent the last half hour amusing herself by deciding which was the most becoming. Deric had plundered the caravan's wealth for her and come in the second day with an armload of garments to lay at her feet. All of them were alluring, seductive, destined for sale to the wives and favored slaves of wealthy Arab potentates.

And, he had warned her, they were for her to wear only inside this room. She gave a little impish smile as she remembered the thrill his possessive words had given her—that he'd be damned if he let any other man see her so dressed!

Now she twisted a belt of silver cloth around her waist, letting the knotted ends dangle, and tied another silver scarf around her head, so her hair fell unbound down her back. Then she smiled at the trouble she was taking, for like as not, he'd barely see her in her finery before he had it off her.

Taking a piece of fruit from the table, she sat in a chair by the window and stared dreamily out, hardly able to wait for the moment when the door would open and he would come back into the room.

She was falling in love with him. She had never suspected that her whole being could seem to light like a flame just with one glance at him. And it had all happened so fast—so unexpectedly—with the force of a thunderbolt from a clear sky. That night of the bandit raid, it had seemed so natural to fall into his arms—and once there, she had lost the power to think. He had given her no time that night to wonder if what she was doing was right or wrong. And once he had become her lover, she had wanted nothing except to be held in his arms.

She heard a footstep in the hall and tried not to hope too much it was his. He'd gone to speak to the men, to make arrangements for their departure on the morrow. If only they never had to leave this place, she thought with a faint stab of sadness. The happiest hours of her life had been spent here.

The footsteps receded down the hall. *Once they left.*

Juliette put down the piece of fruit, suddenly feeling a cold chill strike her heart. All this time, all this blissful time, she'd been content to take each golden moment as it came, never thinking where it was all leading. But now, tomorrow they were leaving, and then—

And then—what?

She was going to have to leave him—at least for a time! She had to go back to Lionel. Poor Lionel—he must be frantic with worry for her, and she'd hardly spared him a thought in days. He had to see her, to know she was safe. And then—

She tried to picture Deric at the governor's mansion in Malta, dressed in fine black broadcloth and a ruffled shirt, among a glittering gathering of British society, herself at his side in a ball dress. . . .

She couldn't.

She could only picture Deric as he was, roving free over the desert, or maybe in some equally wild land. Such untamed panoramas seemed to be the only backdrop she could see him against.

Then, she would be his desert bride. She would follow him from well to well, and they would make their home a camp under the stars. She had never been happy in society anyway. Weren't her happiest days these last ones?

For a moment, she quailed at the thought of Lionel's incredulous face were she to announce she was riding off into the blue as a roving adventurer's bride.

Then she shook her head fiercely. What did she care what Lionel thought? It was her life, and life without Deric would seem as dry as the dust that blew from the dune tops.

Bride? a mocking voice spoke in her head. *You are making castles in the air. He has never spoken a word of love to you, or asked you to be his!*

But, she argued firmly, putting aside this doubt, *what about the love I have seen in his eyes?* No lover could have been more tender than he'd been these last days, she knew it.

And how do you know that, since you have no experience at love?

The mocking voice wouldn't seem to go away, and the sound of the door opening made her turn with relief. She saw Deric standing in the door, swathed in his barracan. To her surprise, his rifle belt crossed his chest. He looked at her for a moment, then came in and closed the door. She thought the old wary expression was back in his eyes, and some of the bright joy she'd felt when he'd entered the room vanished.

"Is something wrong?" she asked, watching him as he went to the table and poured a glass of wine. He drank some, then answered her without turning around.

"No. Nothing." He paused. "There is just much to do before we leave tomorrow."

His curt tone wounded her, but his next words filled her with dismay.

"The men have been chiding me for not doing my fair share

of guard duty these last nights. So tonight I must go and watch the horses and camels. Even in an oasis, bandits have been known to make a raid."

She fought not to let her disappointment show. Their last night together here, and he had to go guard the caravan! But it was only reasonable. "Perhaps you could use some help then, if there are bandits to drive off," she said lightly.

He didn't smile with her. Many times in the last week, he had jested with her about her shooting ability, vowing that if she was at his side, he could shepherd a caravan through the desert without bothering to hire guards.

When he was silent, she added teasingly, "I wouldn't mind spending the night under the stars."

He threw her an unreadable glance, and his voice was abrupt. "I'm afraid I can have no distractions while I am on guard duty. It's serious business, not a game. And you would be a definite distraction."

Stung by the short way he spoke, she stared at him, hurt. Then she became annoyed. If something was wrong—and obviously something was—why didn't he tell her?

"I didn't mean to imply that I thought it a game," she said stiffly. She gestured at the table. "Dinner is here. Are you going to eat it wearing your rifle? It might make me nervous and I'll lose my appetite."

"I'm sorry—but I have no time to eat. I just came to tell you where I'd be. I'll eat something while I'm on guard."

She strove to keep the irritation out of her voice. "Fine. Then please—waste no more time. I don't mind eating alone." She winced a little. How shrewish she sounded! "I hope you have an uneventful night," she added more softly.

"No doubt I will. Get some rest. We have a long ride tomorrow, and we leave at dawn."

"I will."

He stood for a moment, and she could have sworn she saw hesitation in his eyes. "Well, then—goodnight," he said abruptly, and swung on his heel and left the room.

She sat staring at the door when it closed with a bang.

What on earth had put him in such a foul mood?

Chapter Sixteen

With a wrenching effort of will, Deric pulled his hand away from the door and walked down the hall. He'd already done enough harm to her, he told himself, harm he'd never meant to do, and all because he'd acted without thinking. And he hadn't been thinking clearly these past few days. He couldn't have been or else he would never have allowed his feelings to get so out of hand. But Juli had a way of making him forget everything else. When he was with her, there was only her. His caravan, his men, Mulay el-Rassouli, everything seemed to disappear.

Even now as he stood in the doorway of the inn, she filled every corner of his being with her smell, her voice and her touch. No other woman had dominated his heart and his thoughts like she had, no other woman, not even Amelia. His Juli was truly extraordinary.

He owed it to her to take some time to think it all out before he let his emotions rule his actions again. That was why he'd taken guard duty tonight, their last night. He couldn't let her cloud his reason, and how easily she could do just that and without knowing she was doing it.

Swearing softly under his breath, Deric stepped out of the building and into the street. In a few moments, he was climbing the hill where he would stand watch for the night. He would have plenty of time to be alone and think. The whole night, in fact. The thought did little to comfort him.

At the top of the hill, overlooking the animals, he could see the familiar shapes of Ahmal and Rindu silhouetted against the setting sun. They waved in acknowledgement, and he returned their greeting, indicating he would relieve them for the night.

As he approached he could see the wide smile on Rindu's face as he spoke. "I have just been telling Ahmal how we have been performing the most serious duties of the outrider this past week."

Deric raised an eyebrow, anticipating Rindu's teasing. "And what might those duties be, Rindu?"

"Some would think it is to fight off the desert bandits, to bring the caravan goods to market safely. But this week has proved this false." He paused. "Dahkir pays *us* to clean our saddles, mend our tents . . ."

"Trim our beards and drink the tavern dry," Ahmal added.

Deric laughed ruefully.

Rindu turned to Ahmal, mock disbelief on his dark face. "Yes—strange, is it not, that the man who was always in such a hurry to get somewhere, always complaining about delays and extra money he must pay us if we halted for but an hour, now dawdles here for many days?"

Ahmal carried the joke further. "Strange? You may call it strange, my friend, but I call it the work of the arrow of desire. A man who holds such beauty in his grasp is mad if he does not first admire it before he lets it go."

"And who is to blame him if the beauty desires his grasp in return," Rindu quipped.

Ahmal laughed at his friend's most accurate observation. Throwing Deric a knowing look, he put his arm around Rindu's shoulder, guiding him down the hill. "Come, my friend, there is a bottle of palm wine in the tavern that longs to feel *your* grasp."

Deric listened as their hearty laughter faded into the night. They would be heading for the tavern where drink, women and fellowship awaited them. And he—he sighed and lowered himself to the ground.

The last rays of the dying sun washed the horizon in a rosy glow, and the moon rose, pale and white against the night-blue sky. Deric settled down with his rifle over his knees. He shifted uncomfortably. The ground he sat on seemed hard and unyielding, the night air chill, after the warmth and velvet softness of his last nights. His Juli was making him soft. He had no business getting used to such nights—though he had to admit they could be damned easy to get used to. He tried to force his thoughts away from that direction, but Ahmal's words echoed in his ears.

Such beauty in his grasp.

And he must let her go.

All she'd told him of herself during their week together—her cultured background, her stuffy cousin—had reminded him like a sharp slap to the face that he had no real claim on her. The future she had every right to expect was unspoken, but crystal clear to him in her words. She would return to London and marry a man with a title, an estate and wealth, a man who would give her the stability women wanted. All too well, he knew that her beauty and her shining spirit could easily snare a man's heart—the right man's heart, the one who would give her the settled, secure marriage she deserved, the beautiful home and children he was sure she wanted.

He was so wrong to have taken her innocence simply because he was too weak to resist, too selfish to think how wrong it might be for her. He had fought the hardest battle of his life trying to resist her. Just the slightest touch of her skin seemed to burn his fingers. He had no control where she was concerned. But in the end, she would be the one who hurt the most and deserved it the least.

He looked out over the bare landscape shadowed by the night. A warm wind stirred the grass on the hill, while a jackal cackled in the distance, a lonely, hollow and empty sound.

And then there was Mulay el-Rassouli. That was the thing he dreaded most—telling her that he had to turn her over to the pirate. But he would have to tell her soon. In less than a week, the caravan would reach Homs Misurata, where Mulay's contact would be waiting for them with instructions for the trade.

As for Rassouli, if he so much as laid a hand on Juli, he would slit the pirate scum's throat. She needn't know that once the trade was made, he had every intention of making sure Rassouli ransomed her without harm. He would follow them until he saw with his own eyes that she was safely aboard ship at her cousin's side.

But how to tell her she would still be traded to Rassouli? He didn't know. There was no easy way. The choice of words didn't matter. She would feel betrayed and hate him, pure and simple. But then maybe her hurt would be less—because she'd forget him sooner.

Until she was gone, it would be hell to resist holding her in his arms to comfort her, knowing that the hurt in her blue, blue eyes was caused by him; hell to forget the intoxicating touch of her silken skin against his, to forget the way she'd made him feel—the way no other woman had made him feel.

If the desert was an empty and lonely place now, what would it be without her?

Ignoring this dim prospect and the emptiness it left in him, he stared up at the stars, his mouth a bleak line.

He breathed a curse. In time, he would be able to forget her, he convinced himself. After all, he'd forgotten Amelia, hadn't he? His feelings for her had evaporated once he'd discovered what she truly was, and hadn't he been mad with love for her?

Yes, he would forget his Juli in time.

He would force himself to.

And maybe someday she would forgive him for the terrible way he'd taken her innocence.

As he stared unseeing at the stars, he knew that even if she forgave him, he would never be able to forgive himself.

Juliette rode behind a grim and silent Deric. Something had changed. For three days they'd been riding the caravan route between Bu Ngem and Homs Misurata, and Deric had spoken barely a word to her.

Those wonderful days together in Bu Ngem seemed like a dream to Juliette now that Deric had taken up his old abrupt self again. He spend his days riding ahead of her, his unyielding back to her; his nights he no longer shared with her in the tent, but outside. He was busy or the horses needed tending; his men needed instruction—merely excuses not to be near her or to talk to her.

Something had indeed changed. The old familiar wall that their days in Bu Ngem had nearly torn down was once again raised. And it was Deric who had raised it and without warning. How many times in the past three days had she gone over everything they'd said to each other, searching for the one word that would explain his stony silence, the one gesture that would tell her why he was pushing her away. At times she would catch his eye and was certain she'd seen a flash of pain shoot through it, but as quickly as she'd caught his gaze, he'd give her his back again. If something was bothering him, why hadn't he come to her?

In the last three days, she noticed, too, that the pace of the caravan had increased, as though Deric were racing toward what she didn't know.

To the end of their journey? Where this adventure would end was the one question she desired and feared most to have answered. Would he ask her to stay with him, or would he let her go?

If there are women in my life, they are women I can leave with a smile, who understand that the desert is my wife.

His words came back to her. Oh, God—was that it? Was it over to him now?

She spurred her horse to quicken its pace. The uncertainty she felt in her heart wouldn't rest until she'd spoken to him.

She brought her mare alongside his stallion and waited for him to turn in her direction. His stony silence stabbed at her heart like a blade until she was sure she would cry. *Why won't he look at me?*

"Deric, please, speak to me. Tell me why you're so angry. What have I done?" She willed her voice to remain steady.

It's just like her to blame herself, he thought. "Nothing," he said.

"But in Bu Ngem—"

"Bu Ngem is behind us," he replied as evenly as he could; but the pain in her voice had been obvious, and it cut him to the core.

"You say that as if it never existed—as if it were all some fanciful dream. Damn it, was I the only one who dreamed it?"

He felt her eyes searching his for an answer, and when he

thought her gaze would pierce him, he turned his head away from her. "Perhaps it's best you forget those days," he heard himself saying. "I have." Quickly, before she could read the lie in his face, he goaded his horse into a trot and pulled away from her.

In disbelief, she watched him ride ahead of her. A sickening feeling—an empty feeling—tugged at her chest. She was losing him. He was going to leave her, and she would never see him again. He would take her to Tripoli, put her on a ship and send her back to Lionel. And she would never see him again!

And then a new doubt began to gnaw at her. There was still Mulay el-Rassouli. Her stomach began to churn as the doubt began to take shape in her head. Surely, after all that had happened between them, he wasn't going to hand her over to Mulay el-Rassouli? He could never bring himself to do that, not after all they'd shared, she tried to tell herself. She'd never be able to forgive him if he returned her to that beast. She studied his rigid back and felt a sudden panic riding over her. Or could he?

She spurred her horse after him and drew up alongside him. "Look at me, Deric Raleigh," she ordered him. "Look at me and tell me where you're taking me."

He didn't answer.

"Look at me and say it to my face. You're taking me to Mulay el-Rassouli, aren't you?"

He stared straight ahead, then swung his leg over the back of his horse to dismount. He walked a short distance from her. She dismounted and followed. He'd avoided her too long. If he was going to betray her, he'd have to tell her straight out.

She faced his rigid back and demanded again, "Look at me, you coward, and tell me that you are taking me to Mulay el-Rassouli."

Deric knew he couldn't run from her now. He had to face what he'd been dreading since his night alone under the stars. No matter how much it hurt her, it was best. He would make it as easy as possible.

He turned and took her arm, drawing her to his side. He felt her hesitation, her reluctance at his touch, and cursed himself for it. He had no one to blame for her hatred but himself.

Below, an oasis stretched before them, a long line of multicolored tents, scattered palm trees and low buildings. He pointed in its direction.

"That is Homs Misurata. And beyond that in the distance—Tripoli, where you will be ransomed."

Although she had guessed it, his words still cut her. "You would still ransom me after all that has happened between us?"

"I mean to return you to Mulay el-Rassouli—as I promised to. What has happened between us has nothing to do with it. I never meant for it to happen." He paused. How could he make it easier? Would she understand about Farouk? For a quick moment, he thought he would tell her. "I have no choice, Juli. You've got to understand."

"Don't say another word," she warned. "Don't say anything. Nothing . . . nothing you could ever say would make me understand why you've done this."

The hurt and confusion in her eyes was evident. He could tell her about Farouk, but that would only prolong his dreadful task. No. It was best she thought his only concern was the ransom she imagined he would receive for her. The sooner she learned to despise him, the sooner she would forget him.

Juliette felt that at any moment she would not be able to hold back her tears, and more than anything else, she didn't want him to see her cry. She turned her back on him and missed the anquish that was mirrored in his face.

"Just leave me. Leave me alone. Go."

The caravan had moved ahead of them, marking a path down the dune toward the oasis. Deric glanced first in its direction, then back at her. She stood alone at the edge of the dune, staring down into the valley of sand. He longed to take her in his arms and kiss her tears away.

With gritted teeth, he mounted his horse instead and waited for her.

When she didn't move he said, "Come, Juli, we must make the oasis before dark."

She moved mechanically to her horse, grabbed the reins and swung herself into the saddle. Taking her place behind him, she urged her horse on toward Homs Misurata.

Chapter Seventeen

Sheik Abd ul-Yazza himself rushed out into the courtyard of his house when the caravan arrived, to welcome them. Juliette stood for the moment forgotten, as the sheik embraced Deric with glad cries of greeting. Abd ul-Yazza was a stout man in his fifties, with a full black beard streaked with gray and shrewd eyes that missed little. He was opulently dressed in a long striped robe corded at the waist with gilded braid. As befitted an Arab man, he took no notice of Juliette as he stood back to look at Deric, stroking his beard.

"*Bism'Allah!*" he exclaimed. "I welcome you, Dahkir, and bless the good fortune that has brought you to my house. As always, I am delighted to offer you my home, for do I not owe you the life of my daughter?" He laughed expansively. "Raneiri will be lifted to the skies when she knows her brave rescuer is once more in our tents."

He spoke figuratively, of course, for behind him stood no tent but what could pass for a small palace. Though he lived in utmost luxury in Homs Misurata, still he was a desert sheik and spent part of each year travelling the desert among his nomad people. Juliette stood listening, able to catch the gist of what he said, and wondering who "Raneiri" was.

"But Dahkir—this time your friend Farouk, whom I am also eternally grateful to, is not with you? It saddens my heart not to see his face!"

"No, this time Farouk does not journey with me. He is—on business elsewhere. My good friend Abd ul-Yazza, I need to stay in Homs Misurata until I receive a certain message. It could be some time. I cannot so impose on your hospitality—"

"Impose! On me! When you saved my daughter from death—from worse! It would not be an imposition were you to spend your life here, my friend. In fact, such a fate would please me—and my daughter—to no end. Never a day passes that she does not speak of you. You are already like the son I do not have; so speak no more of leaving!"

There was a roguish gleam in the sheik's eyes when he spoke of his daughter, and Juliette felt a dart of jealousy. It seemed as if the sheik was hinting that he would be pleased to have Deric as a son-in-law!

"And my . . . slave?" Deric turned and glanced at Juliette.

"Of course, of course, my friend. Now, come—"

His slave! So that was what she was to be while in this house! She glared at him, but he turned back to the sheik. She wanted to shout out that she was no slave—but a prisoner! But the sheik was already walking off with Deric at his side, and at the wave of an arm, two servants were hurrying to her side to lead her into the house.

Once inside, Juliette barely had time to glance at the lovely interiors scattered with beautiful rugs, low divans and tables, the doorways hung with sheer curtains. Almost at once a silent slave came forward, her eyes lowered, and led Juliette off to the women's quarters at the back of the house. They were separate from the rest of the house, as in all well-to-do Arab homes.

Abd ul-Yazza, she soon learned, had three wives, ranging from a thin, wrinkled woman, to a fat, middle-aged dark-eyed wife, to a young wife obviously chosen for her beauty. Her name was Bazia, a lovely, slender woman with skin the color of coffee, a long, graceful neck and gazelle-like dark eyes. She welcomed Juliette with soft words, exclaiming wonderingly over her strange clothing. She told Juliette she was from one of the tribes along the Nile, and settled her with a glass of lemon water.

Also present in the women's quarters were several slaves and the sheik's daughter, Raneiri. She stood looking Juliette over with sparkling black eyes in which there was a trace of resentment. Juliette faced her gaze without flinching, letting her own eyes examine Raneiri as boldly as she herself was being examined. So—this was the girl who would be so *pleased* at Deric's return!

She was beautiful, with a ripe, alluring attraction Juliette knew she herself did not possess. Her long hair was a shining midnight river, her dark eyes almond-shaped, her full lips very red. And she moved with a catlike grace that made the most of the generous curves of her body.

"So—you are slave to Dahkir," she said after a moment, narrowing her eyes. "Dahkir never kept a slave before."

"And he does not keep one now!" Juliette replied tartly, in what was probably garbled Arabic.

But Raneiri understood. "Then, what are you, if not a slave?"

"I am—a hostage," she said after a moment, her temper high enough at the way Deric had been treating her not to care how she blackened his reputation to his friends. "I am being held for ransom, and as soon as the money arrives, I will be freed. I am an Englishwoman."

All the wives clucked at this interesting information, and Bazia fluttered her hands in sympathetic dismay. But the relief in Raneiri's eyes was evident.

"So—he is keeping you for ransom, not as a slave. Good." She started to turn away, as if dismissing Juliette as of no further interest.

"You think it's good that he's holding me for ransom?"

Raneiri turned back. There was a little spark in her black eyes. "Why not—such things are done all the time! Why, Dahkir saved me from the same fate as I was about to be carried off by Bedouin raiders." She shrugged. "A man must make his fortune somehow—usually by the sword."

Juliette persisted. "But why are you glad I am not his slave?"

Raneiri smiled. "Because, a man can sometimes get very attached to a slave he has purchased to share his bed. Sometimes, he may even marry such a slave. And"—she threw Juliette a smug, self-satisfied look—"Dahkir is going to marry me."

"Marry you?" Juliette could not contain her startled words.

"He—he asked you to *marry* him?"

Before Raneiri could answer, Bazia put in with an arch smile, "He has not asked her yet—but we hope it is not long before he does. Her father, the emir, wishes it. He thinks Dahkir would make a fine son, and he is pleased his daughter has chosen such a man!"

"And last time he was here, he as much as told me. Why, he could not keep his eyes off me then—or his hands." Her eyes challenged Juliette. "And he makes any excuse to come and visit us, like this."

A slave entered the women's quarters through a beaded curtain and bowed before them. "The guest Dahkir has asked that the English woman be sent to his rooms. I will show her the way if she will follow me," she said meekly.

Juliette rose, trembling with a number of emotions. So he'd sent for her! It was on the tip of her tongue to refuse to go, when she caught sight of the frown the words had produced on Raneiri's face. She changed her mind. "I will follow you," she said to the slave, and walked after her to the door.

When she reached the swinging curtain, she paused and looked back over her shoulder at Raneiri. She couldn't resist adding, "Just because I am not his slave—doesn't mean I don't share his bed!"

And she had the dubious satisfaction of seeing Raneiri's scowl before she left the room.

That night, she paced up and down in the room she'd been given, like a caged animal. A whole world of conflicting emotions was raging in her breast. He was selling her! After all that had happened between them, he was selling her!

The first numbed disbelief had given way to a dull rage at him—and most of all, at herself for being such a fool. What an utter, utter fool she'd been to believe he actually *loved* her! It was all too clear now that he'd only desired her and now was ready to discard her without a backward look.

Oh, how *could* she have been so naive as to believe he cared about her! From the beginning, she'd known that he was an adventurer, a mercenary, known that he was holding her prisoner for money! She'd known all these things and she had—

She stopped her furious pacing and sank to the floor, fists pressed to her burning cheeks. She had no one—no one to blame but herself for what had happened! Not even Deric. Scoundrel though he was, he'd never lied to her; never spoken false words of love; never made any promises he was now breaking. He'd never spoken any words of love at all. Now that she thought of it, all his words had been of his desire for her.

But like a fool, she, knowing all that, had ignored it all! She'd been caught up in the lovely dream-world of falling in love for the first time, while all he'd ever wanted was what she'd so freely given. Her body. No doubt, to a man like Deric, the time they'd spent together was nothing special. Why, this very moment, he might be bending his head to kiss Raneiri as he'd kissed her, might be—

Stop it, stop it! her anguished mind cried, but as hard as she tried, she couldn't stop torturing herself. She pictured him doing with other women what they'd done together, and felt the grinding torture that only jealousy can bring to the heart.

Tears ran down her cheeks as she thought of their confrontation this afternoon. He hadn't called her to him to explain, not to apologize. Instead, he'd stood like he was carved out of ice and told her in a wooden voice that he'd sent a message to Mulay and that within the week, she could hope to be ransomed. She had heard him out in stony silence and returned to the women's quarters, where Raneiri's triumphant look of how short a time she'd been gone was only salt to her wounds.

Now, alone at last, she gave herself over to misery. Bitterly she thought of how blithely she'd wondered how she would tell Lionel she meant to be Deric's desert bride. Furiously, she leapt up and paced again, filled with rage against Deric, at what a *bastard* he was to use her so when he knew—*knew* he would leave her! Sorrowfully, her heart ached as she thought of those precious moments between them—all of them lies! Her emotions changed wildly, so that sometimes tears flowed down her cheeks, and other times she struck her fist into her palm and cursed aloud.

But most often, they swung back to self-blame.

In the end, it was she who had known no better than to see a noble character under a handsome rogue's face!

She sank on the bed and stared at the night sky through the latticed window in utter misery. So why, if he was such a damned bastard, who'd used her heart and then thrown it away—why was there such a cloud of grief weighing down her heart at the thought that soon, she would never see him again?

Chapter Eighteen

Raneiri stood under the arch of the courtyard doorway, looking meditatively at the stables. She tapped her cheek with a long nail, then, seeming to make up her mind, headed purposefully for the stables.

In the stables, she knew, she would find the caravan outriders, and she wanted to talk to one of them—about Dahkir.

Though he had not sent for the English prisoner again in these last two days, something had definitely changed him. On his last visit, while he was always reserved, she'd been able to flirt with him and see an answering spark of interest in his eyes. Now he treated her with a cool, remote politeness, and his eyes looked right through her.

She had to find out if it was because of the damned English prisoner! She'd made up her mind that Dahkir was going to marry her. Why, it was her father's wish, was it not? He was a powerful sheik with wealth and regiments at his command, and Raneiri could not imagine him not getting what he wanted. He always did—and in that way, she took after her father.

She walked into the stables and saw one of the outriders just about to enter one of the long rows of stalls. He looked up and saw her, and she halted him with an imperious gesture, then waved him to her side.

"Yes, *effendi?*" he asked respectfully, walking up to her.

"What is your name?" she asked haughtily, as befitted a sheik's daughter addressing a common soldier.

"Ahmal, *effendi.*" He waited, obviously wondering what it was she wanted. But she hesitated for a moment, casting about for a way to begin.

"You have been in Dahkir's employ long?"

"For four years, *effendi.*"

"Then you—know him well. His habits."

He nodded. "At least when he is on caravan—and with Dahkir, that is most of the time."

"Does he ever have women travelling with him? Or—does he keep a slave or a mistress in one of the towns?"

Ah, here we have it! thought Ahmal, trying to keep his face straight and his eyes from dancing. *This little beauty has set her sights on Dahkir. He is lucky in love just now, to have so many women sighing after him!*

Soberly, he answered, "*Effendi,* if Dahkir keeps a woman somewhere, I know of it not. And never before does a woman travel with us on caravan. This is new for him, keeping a—slave."

So the men do not know she is a prisoner, but think she is a slave! Raneiri thought. "And tell me—how do Dahkir and this slave get along?"

Ahmal smiled. "My lady, like the sea crashing against the shore. They fight like demons. Never have I seen a woman like this before, with such a temper and who dares to speak out like a man. Very angry she can make him. But like the waves crash against the shore and draw away, always they are drawn back again." He spread his hands, shrugging.

Raneiri scowled. This was worse than she'd thought! But at least they fought. Maybe that was encouraging. "So they fight all the time?" she pursued.

"No, not all the time. When the fighting stops, he carry this slave to his tent with a passion I do not see in him before. And sometimes, they laugh together and exchange soft words. Why, we stayed a whole week in Bu Ngem, which is very strange for Dahkir. Usually he is in a hurry. They were happy all that week. But now"—he shrugged again—"they barely speak or look at each other."

"I see." She tossed a handful of coins at his feet with a ringing sound and turned to go. "You will not tell Dahkir I was asking these things," came the command over her shoulder.

Ahmal stood looking after her, the coins in the dust at his feet. *You cannot pay me enough to be disloyal to Dahkir, foolish woman,* he thought, a smile of contempt on his lips.

As he turned to go back into the stable, leaving the coins in the dust, he reflected that of the two women who wanted Dahkir, he much hoped that the slave, Juli, would win. For all her fiery temper, she had earned the men's respect and liking. Look how she never complained, rode all day like a man and shot like an outrider. The other one was beautiful, but her eyes were cold like a snake's.

Juli's eyes were soft when they looked at Dahkir.

But he didn't think he needed to worry much about it. If he was any judge, it would be the slave, Juli, Dahkir chose. He had known Dahkir a long time, and never had he seen him look at a woman the way he looked at her. Well, whatever happened, it was the will of Allah, he thought, and went back to his work.

Abd ul-Yazza lolled back on the cushions, cheeks flushed, a pleased grin on his face. Before him on a long, low table was spread the remains of a lavish banquet. The table groaned with delicacies, and attentive slave girls hastened to fill the wine goblets and offer plates of grapes and figs. He turned and surveyed his guest Dahkir, lounging next to him, with an expansive smile.

"Now that we have eaten and drunk, my friend, we will have music and dancing!" He sat up straighter and clapped his hands, sending the slaves scurrying.

"Dancing!" Raneiri turned to Abd's wives, a pleased smile on her face, and then threw Juliette a malicious look. They were all seated behind a latticed wall that shielded them from view, but through which they could watch the banquet. The women were allowed to see and hear, but not to be seen unless summoned by the emir. "Good! I shall be able to dance for the guest."

Juliette looked at Raneiri with distaste. For the whole afternoon, she and Bazia, along with some of the young, comely slaves, had been perfuming and dressing themselves in anticipation of being called to dance at the banquet tonight.

"Your father allows you to dance—in front of men?" Juliette inquired. "I would think he wouldn't want you to make such a display of yourself to strangers."

"Ah—but Dahkir is hardly a stranger to us!" Raneiri said smugly. "And what do you know of our customs, Englishwoman? It is one thing to dance before strangers—another to dance before the man your father intends you should marry. All Arab girls are taught the art of the dance, and it is much admired in our culture."

She smoothed her hands down her torso and turned this way and that before the mirror, checking her appearance, as Juliette watched sourly. Raneiri was clad in a long caftan of dull gold cloth, modest enough except for the slits at the side that showed her bare brown legs, and the plunging neckline. A sheer veil covered her long hair and her face, and her bare arms and ankles were ringed with jingling gold bracelets. She held two shimmering gold veils in her hands. Her eyes were painted with kohl, her lips and cheeks reddened. She looked almost indecently alluring, Juliette had to admit and bit her lip at the thought of her dancing in front of Deric.

She didn't have long to imagine this. In a few moments, the lamps in the banquet room had been dimmed to a soft glow, and several slaves had taken their place in a corner with their instruments. The soft clashing of cymbals and the rhythmic wailing of the zither filled the room with an insistent, exotic melody. One of the slaves started a pulsing beat on a drum. Raneiri, with a last mocking smile at Juliette, swept out of the room.

Juliette watched as she swirled into the banquet room through parted curtains. She began a slow, erotic dance to the rhythm of the music. Her hips swiveled slowly back and forth, her body posturings graceful and taunting.

Gradually, the music increased its tempo, and the dance became wilder, more abandoned. She bent to the floor, her hair swinging in a wide circle, and raised herself gracefully, her hands swirling the veils she held in a hypnotic display.

Her dance was sensual, tantalizing, and Juliette tore her eyes away from Raneiri to look at how Deric was taking this.

He was leaning slightly forward, his eyes fixed intently on the sensual creature who arched like a cat in front of them. Juliette's lips tightened as she saw that Deric was frankly enjoying this taunting dance.

Now Raneiri's black eyes were fixed on Deric's as she danced slowly forward, her reddened lips pouting invitingly under her transparent face veil. She arched her back so her breasts were thrust out as she danced daringly close in front of Deric, performing obviously for him alone. Juliette felt a spurt of anger as she saw a smile of appreciation form on his lips.

She fumed as she watched the girl tempt Deric—and Deric responding so blatantly! She felt her breast tighten as if a flame burned inside her heart, and she breathed faster in anger. So he was everything she'd accused him of in her heart! Now that he'd discarded her, he was ready to go to the bed of another with no thought; it was obvious!

And then, to her disbelief, she saw Raneiri take Deric's hands and pull him to his feet. She stood just in front of him, looking up. Suddenly, her arms twined around his neck, her hands in his hair, bending his head to hers. Juliette sat frozen, feeling as if someone had just delivered a tremendous blow to her stomach as she watched Raneiri's mouth meet his, watched her arch her body and press her breasts against his chest.

She turned away, suddenly feeling ill, not able to watch any more. So she didn't see Deric break the kiss and put Raneiri from him with a smile, nor did she think that maybe he'd only allowed it so as not to offend his host.

She saw Bazia looking at her sympathetically as she fled, her feet stumbling, heading for her room. All she wanted was to get away from the sight of the man who had cared nothing for her.

Get away, she thought as she opened the door of her room, her heart beating in funny jerks, her hands hot and cold. If only there was some way she could get away from here—get away from him! She knew that after tonight, every day here would be torture—every day close to him, hating him.

She never, never wanted to see him again!

Chapter Nineteen

Raneiri sat before her mirror, combing her long, dark hair. The other women of her father's house sat across the room, eating a mid-morning snack of figs and melon slices. They giggled and chattered among themselves. At a distance from them, Juliette sat in a low-slung chair, gazing out of the window into the garden below. Raneiri's eyes narrowed with hatred at the sight of the English prisoner. She would be more of a problem than first thought. This had become obvious the night before when Dahkir pushed her from his lips. His polite smile had only been for the benefit of her father; Dahkir felt nothing for her.

Her face turned down in a pout. She had so little time. In a few days, Dahkir's caravan would be leaving for Tripoli, and she might never have her chance again. His heart would never be free of the copper-haired witch—not as long as she was here as a constant reminder.

True, he did not call the prisoner to his bed at night; she had slept here since arriving. It would not take much to capture his attentions, especially if the witch were no longer around. *If I had him to myself . . .* she thought, and for the first time a smile twisted her lips.

Juliette stared into the garden below, her unseeing eyes looking beyond its exotic beauty into the desert beyond. Tripoli was just a few hours ride from here. Her resolve to get away from Deric had grown stronger. It was too painful to see him day in and day out, especially with that—that she-viper, Raneiri, constantly hanging on him.

The way Raneiri danced before Deric had been an absolute disgrace. That trollop had no shame to writhe and wiggle like a bowl of plum pudding in front of his leering face. Their kiss of last night flashed before her eyes, and the anger she had felt doubled and resurfaced. He had enjoyed it! The look on his face was as obvious as the meat hooks Raneiri was trying to plant in him. *Fine,* she thought. *They deserve one another!*

Her thoughts were interrupted by Raneiri standing at her side. She threw the Arab girl an acid look and turned her eyes toward Tripoli again. Raneiri followed her gaze.

"I have been there." Raneiri's syrup-sweet voice came to her.

Juliette looked up for a moment. Raneiri smiled at her and pointed out the window. "I have been to Tripoli."

Juliette ignored her attempt at conversation.

"It is a beautiful city," Raneiri continued. "The markets are known the world over for their quality of goods. Traders from China, India, even the Americas trade there. You will like it."

"I doubt it very much," was Juliette's cold reply.

"Ah, the pirate Mulay el-Rassouli troubles you?" offered Raneiri. "As well he should. He is not a very honorable man. Not at all like my Dahkir."

Juliette's voice dripped with sarcasm. "Your Dahkir is the most honorable man I've ever met, Raneiri. He's so honorable, he's—" She sighed. "Oh, forget it."

Raneiri moved around Juliette like a panther. "Still, I would be much troubled if I were to be delivered into the hands of that jackal, Rassouli. His reputation as a kidnapper is nothing compared to his renown as a cheat and a liar."

Juliette wished Raneiri would go away. This talk about Rassouli was making her nervous.

"I think it was last year about this time that he kidnapped the wife of a wealthy merchant and held her for ransom. When it came time to trade her, he took her husband's ransom money and sold the wife into slavery. The merchant lost his money and his wife."

Juliette looked the Arab woman in the eyes. "Why are you

telling me this? Is it to scare me?"

"I only tell you these things because I see in your eyes a wish to escape. We may not be friends, but that does not mean we cannot help each other."

Juliette's eyes narrowed suspiciously. "Why would you help me? From the moment I arrived you've shown nothing but dislike for me."

"And you have shown me the same." Raneiri's gaze lowered to her lap as she leaned nearer to Juliette. "I will be honest. I wish to marry Dahkir and find it difficult to do so with you here."

"He doesn't care about me," was Juliette's short reply.

"But there was something between you?"

She didn't answer.

Raneiri leaned away, smiling smugly at her foe's lowered head. "He has hurt you, yes?"

Juliette nodded her head reluctantly.

"You wish to leave this place, yes?"

Again she nodded her head, the aching in her heart threatening to squeeze the life out of her.

"Then there is no need for you to be delivered to Rassouli. He is a scoundrel who will only cheat your relatives out of their money and increase his profits by selling you. And if you were no longer here to remind Dahkir of your time together, he would be free to marry me." Here she paused, waiting for this to sink in. Then lowering her voice to a whisper, she said, "If I told you my servant, Binzari, could get you to the British embassy in Tripoli safely and by tomorrow, would you be willing to leave here?"

Juliette looked at her suspiciously. "Your servant could get me to the embassy tomorrow? But—what if Deric sees me leaving?"

"He will never know you are gone. We can pretend you are here in the women's quarters for a few days. After all, he never sends for you anymore, does he?"

No, he never did.

The tears ran hot and stinging down Juliette's cheeks, but she nodded her head. It was what she wanted, wasn't it? To be gone from here, as far away as she could get from Deric. She nodded her head again. "I'll go," she whispered. "I'll go."

Chapter Twenty

The world was still dark as Juliette followed the shadowy form of Binzari out of the courtyard gate and into the street. He led her through the twisting narrow streets confidently, and in a few minutes, she lost all sense of direction.

Soon she could hear the rushing roar of the sea ahead, and they emerged from the shadow of the alleyways. Ahead were a long sea wall and several quays that held many moored boats. Already, fishermen were loading their nets in the growing gray light of dawn. None of them took the slightest notice of the two as they walked along one of the quays to a longboat.

"This boat. It is not far to Tripoli, and safest to make the trip by rowing along the coast. Then no horse will be missed," said Binzari. He watched as she climbed into the boat and settled in one of the seats. Unmooring it, he jumped in and pushed off, then took up the oars.

Juliette tried not to look at Binzari as they rowed away from the harbor, away from Homs Misurata. There was something in his eyes, in the way they glinted when they passed over her, that made her uneasy. But she ignored this small disquiet and tried to feel happy that she was escaping. In perhaps an hour, they would reach Tripoli, and she would make her way at once to the British embassy—and send a message to Lionel.

But her heart just wouldn't obey her by feeling happy at the prospect. It was a traitor, with a will of its own that wouldn't listen to what her head firmly knew was how it should feel. She should be overjoyed that she was gaining her freedom, that she would never see that bastard Deric Raleigh again.

She stared desolately at Homs Misurata as it began to recede behind them. The sun was coming up, a red ball of fire on the horizon. It was going to be a beautiful day, a day that would end this disastrous episode in her life and bring a new start.

Fiercely, she told herself that she would get over it all in time. The day would come when her heart would stop aching every time she thought of Deric, when her sense of humiliated betrayal would not be so keen. She would learn from what happened, she thought, and learn to guard her heart more carefully—not to be an innocent girl. No, when love came again—*if it came again,* said that traitorous voice she could not still—she would go into it with her feet firmly on the ground, a woman grown. And she would, she vowed, learn much more about the man before she gave her heart away again!

After they had rowed for perhaps an hour, the boat came around a headland, and before her, Juliette saw the great city of Tripoli. Its low buildings, white and tan, lay around a long, narrow harbor. The city was on a flat sweep of land, and behind the buildings rose two hills. On the left was a huge white palace, sprawling imposingly behind frowning walls. She saw the shapely spikes of the minarets, the domes of the mosques, the huge covered roof of the bazaar. Now that the sun was up, the place was alive with activity, and lateen-rigged boats crowded the harbor. Somewhere in the maze of those connecting, flat-roofed buildings, under those fringed palm trees, stood the British embassy—and safety.

As they rowed into the harbor, she noticed that Binzari was pointing the boat toward the long quay that jutted out from the foot of the palace walls. She pointed. "We are going to the palace?"

"Yes—there is where the embassy is near," he said, his eyes glinting at her.

She nodded, satisfied, and waited as the boat drew up to the quay. On the quay stood a number of strange figures, staring at them as if they were waiting for them. In the front stood a huge man in baggy white pantaloons and a red jacket, wearing a white turban; behind him were drawn up ranks of what seemed to be soldiers or guards, in brilliant livery of baggy yellow trousers, scarlet jackets and black turbans. But she could see that for all their finery, curved scimitars hung at their belts, and each pair of hands held a rifle at attention.

"Who are they?" she asked nervously, glancing at Binzari. But he didn't answer her, just concentrated on maneuvering the boat until it touched the quay.

Four pairs of soldiers' hands reached down and grabbed the gunwales, arresting the boat. Juliette looked nervously up at the man in the white turban who stared impassively at her.

"What—what do they want?" she asked turning to Binzari, her fear mounting.

"Get out," he said.

She stared at him, at the coldness she suddenly saw in his eyes, and swallowed. What—what did this mean? She glanced again at the men, and then back at Binzari, realizing she had no choice but to obey.

She climbed out of the boat and stood on the quay. Binzari followed. She opened her mouth to say something to the man in the white turban, but he spoke first to Binzari.

"This is the English woman?"

"This is she."

The man in the white turban turned and studied her for a long moment, his eyes devouring her face, then dropping down over her body. "So—you take her from Mulay el-Rassouli, the pirate swine. It is good that you have done so."

Juliette felt a rush of relief at these words. Obviously, the man was some kind of official—authority. He would know where the embassy was. "It's true—I escaped from being held by Rassouli for ransom. Now I want to go to the British embassy. Who—who are you?" she asked in Arabic.

"I serve the sultan of Tripoli. I am Giza. You have landed at his palace and must be brought before him."

"But—why can I not go straight to the embassy? I am sure the sultan would have no wish to detain me any longer. I have been held against my will for some weeks now and am anxious to contact my cousin."

"You do not understand." His eyes were like stones, his mouth down-curving in a cruel line. "You are not going to the embassy at all."

"What do you mean?" cried Juliette, feeling her heart begin

to beat in uneven jerks.

He looked at Binzari. "Her face is all you say, but I would see more of her before I decide if I want her. Take off her headcloth and barracan for me."

"If you want me?" she gasped, as Binzari stepped forward and reached for her. She backed away, her fist striking out at him vainly. "What do you mean—don't touch me!" she cried wildly.

Giza folded his arms impassively on his chest at this display. "She is not biddable, my friend," he said with a tone of regret. "This is not good."

"She will do *my* bidding!" growled Binzari, and he lunged at Juliette. Her arm was caught in a cruel grip and shoved up behind her until it felt as if it would break. Crying out with pain, she was forced to her knees and felt her headcloth being torn off. As her hair spilled out, Binzari's rough hands unwrapped her barracan and pulled it off her, so she was left wearing a shirt, trousers and boots. Tears started to her eyes as she was yanked to her feet.

All around her, the soldiers had stepped forward and ringed her. A dozen rifles were pointed at her heart.

"I would fight no longer, woman," came the soft voice of Giza. "Let me look at her. Turn her around."

Giza's eyes narrowed as Binzari slowly turned Juliette around. In the sun, her hair shone like fire, rippling in shining waves over her shoulders, falling in a torrent almost to her waist. He noted the proud thrust of her breasts against the thin cloth of her shirt, the narrowness of her waist and the long legs outlined by the clinging trousers. Most of all, he noted the white skin like velvet with a flush of rose on her cheeks, the alluring wide pink mouth and those intriguing eyes, blue as the deep evening sky on a midsummer's night. Wonderful, unusual eyes. He had not seen such eyes before.

What did her temper matter? That could be tamed. A woman like this was worth every penny he had to pay for her—but he would not let the stupid avaricious Binzari know that.

"Perhaps—I am interested. But"—he shrugged—"the sultan has already the most beautiful women trained in the arts of pleasure in his harem. I have heard English women are cold.

And she is not meek, but looks to be much trouble."

Binzari said anxiously, "No, no—she is not cold! She is no virgin, this one, but spent many weeks in the tent of the man who held her prisoner. I understand she was most passionate, wild in her lovemaking, driving this man almost to distraction! Every night his men heard their cries of pleasure. She is a woman whose fire matches her hair. And look—see her white skin! The sultan has no such woman in his harems!"

Juliette listened with disbelief to this exchange. The sultan—his harems! Her cheeks flamed as she heard Binzari's description of her passion, and she began to struggle wildly in his grip, kicking and twisting to free herself. She'd forgotten all about the rifles pointed at her. All she cared about was getting away!

"You see, my friend. She is a tigress!" exclaimed Giza.

"And a tigress in bed!" panted Binzari, struggling to hold her.

"Guards!" snapped Giza.

In a moment, the fight was over, for she was held strongly pinioned by two brawny guards. She stopped resisting, suddenly going limp. Fighting was no use here; she had to use her brain.

"How dare you abduct me like this," she cried, her eyes on the one called Giza. "Have you considered what it will mean, abducting a British citizen? My guardian is aide to the governor in Malta, and when they hear of this, it may mean war. Can your sultan afford war with England?"

Giza smiled. "I do not abduct you; I merely steal you from Mulay el-Rassouli. If it comforts you, woman, he would have doubtless sold you on the auction block after he'd collected your ransom. He would not have released you. But now—I buy you instead; for I am the slave master of the sultan's harems, and you are unusual enough that you may please him. Besides—I do not risk war for the sultan by buying you." His eyes gleamed with malice. "For who will know you are here? Binzari tells me you left telling no one where you had gone—escaped in the night."

Juliette swayed as his words sank in, a low moan on her lips. It was true. No one would ever know where she had been taken, for Binzari would never tell! And Raneiri—had this been her doing? Oh, God—she was completely at this man's mercy!

"I will buy this woman. Here—this is all I will offer you, because of her temper." Giza handed a leather bag to Binzari, and he poured a stream of gold coins into his palm. Binzari looked up, eyes shining in an eager face.

"It is good," he crowed. Evidently whatever he had been paid for her was more than he had dreamed of getting.

Giza turned away and started down the quay toward the palace. The guards tightened their grip under Juliette's elbows and marched her along behind him.

It was a short walk to the palace, but it seemed like a long ordeal to Juliette. With every step, the great white palace, the high walls, drew nightmarishly closer. She stared at it dumbfounded, unable to believe that she'd been sold as a slave—that in a few moments, she was going to disappear behind those massive walls, maybe never to come out.

And it was all her own fault! Why, why had she been such a fool to leave with Binzari, to think she could arrange her own escape? To trust the treacherous Raneiri? If only—if only Deric knew where she was!

But he would never know where she'd been taken. He'd think she'd made her escape and had reached the safety of her cousin's protection. He was probably cursing the loss of the money she'd have brought him at this very moment and turning his caravan toward the desert again. Even if he came into Tripoli to trade, he would never know she was here.

They reached a great outer gate in the palace wall and stood as door guards unbarred its massive portal. Giza turned to her.

"We will take you to the sultan—just as you are."

Chapter Twenty-One

The iron gates of the palace clanged shut behind Juliette and the guards. They led her through an inner courtyard and another barred gate, then marched her through a dazzling splendor of palace hallways straight to the Royal Chambers. There Oman Kazamali, Sultan of Tripoli, awaited them.

Inside, the palace itself was a vision of Eastern splendor. The wide hallways were lined with pillars; the floors, made of patterned tiles. Pointed arches opened on courtyards where fountains played and flowers grew. Everything was decorated in patterns almost too complex and ornate for the eyes to follow, in gold and blue, scarlet and emerald, purple and white.

Slaves with crossed swords stared impassively through her as she passed, in livery that was straight out of the *Arabian Nights*. At the entrance to the Royal Chambers, two door guards lifted their scimitars to let them pass.

It looked like an endless expanse to Juliette, a long, echoing room with a grandly worked floor in gold, white and blue designs, lined by marble pillars marching down the sides. At the far end, an assemblage of nobles and courtiers were being fanned by slaves, and they all turned at once and eyed Juliette avidly.

The sultan himself sat above all of them on a raised throne, watching her approach over the echoing floor. Her guards stopped her a few feet from the throne.

Juliette looked up at him, and he saw that the dark blue eyes looking into his showed no trace of fear. He frowned slightly, then smiled cruelly. *This woman would have to be taught to fear him—and he would enjoy that.*

The sultan stared down at her coldly for a moment, then turned and spoke to the slave master. She stood, tensely studying the man to whom she'd been sold.

Oman Kazamali had a cruel face marked by power and desire. His skin was dark, his nose hooked, his eyes dark under heavy brows. They were cold eyes, and there was too much flesh in his cheeks and lips. He had an air of evil sensuality, of complete command.

He was the most magnificently dressed man Juliette had ever seen. His white turban was clasped by an enormous crescent of emeralds and gold. He wore white silk trousers and shirt, but over them a purple vest encrusted with gold embroidery, and a turquoise sash fringed with gold.

She stood trying to swallow her fear as he talked to the slave master. She felt her knees shake and her mouth go dry, but she struggled to show no outward sign of fear in front of her captors.

At last he turned his cold regard back to her. He nodded at her, and Juliette's two guards shoved her forward, jerking her wrists downward until she was forced into a low bow.

She straightened and met his gaze, lifting her chin proudly. He took a pull from his goblet, and his eyes travelled over her at leisure. Juliette felt herself blushing and cursed herself for it.

"Your name, slave?" he asked.

"I am Juliette Hawkins."

"You will call me Your Supreme Highness!" he barked sharply.

She swallowed. "Your Supreme Highness, I was on my way to join my cousin in Malta when—"

"Silence, miserable woman!" he roared, his face turning red with fury. Juliette took an involuntary step backward, her hand flying to her throat. "You are a slave and speak only when spoken to. Your beauty is great. But you will learn the bearing of a slave or you will suffer for it. You should never have come here, English woman." He sat back and smiled at her—a malevolent smile.

Juliette faced him as bravely as she could and dared to speak oncc more. "You Supreme Highness, though I have been sold to you as a slave, my value to you would be greater if you let me be ransomed. If word is sent to the governor in Malta, I am sure he would pay what you ask in exchange for my freedom. My cousin is a British diplomat—"

"I have no need of money . . . but your beauty will amuse me." He turned to his waiting slaves. "You will take her to the harem."

"Your Supreme Highness!" she cried, flinging herself out of the guards' grasp and kneeling at his feet. "Please—be merciful! Send word to the governor and allow me to be ransomed! Consider what abducting a British citizen will mean! Oh, I beg you—"

"Silence!" he roared, and the rage on his face was truly terrifying. "I do not abduct you! You are my slave.

"Be silent and grateful, foolish woman," he went on, looking at her with enjoyment as he saw her lips whiten. At last she showed fear, as a woman should! He continued, "Be grateful that I do not have you sold on the auction block! Or that I do not have you whipped for defiance and thrown into the foulest prison where, after murderers and thieves have taken you again and again, you die like an insect of disease! My harems are places of greatest comfort. Be grateful that I send you there. Or do you argue with me, woman?"

Juliette stared up at him for a long, despairing moment. She clearly saw the enjoyment dancing in his eyes, behind the façade of rage.

She bowed her head. "No, Your Supreme Highness, I do not argue with you," she said. "I am grateful for your mercy."

He regarded her for a moment with satisfaction, and two slaves stepped forward to lead her away.

She stared at him for a last, despairing moment, before the slaves grasped her arms in an unbreakable grip.

Word of the new arrival spread through the harem like wildfire. The harem was in a separate wing of the palace and had just two entrances, both heavily guarded. One entrance was off the central palace courtyard, and the other, the sultan's private entrance was a winding stair and tunnel that led from the Royal Bedchamber. It was a world shut in on itself, and the arrival of a new inmate—slave, concubine, or more rarely, wife—set the rooms and corridors alight with whispering and rushing feet as the gossip spread.

The harem was a square surrounding a central courtyard and gardens. The gardens were carefully tended, with trees and paths, and even a small lake in the center that boasted an island on which stood a pleasure pavilion. All around the garden was a shaded walkway behind rows of graceful pillars. Many pointed windows shuttered with delicate latticework overlooked the central courtyard.

The outer rooms not overlooking the courtyard were windowless, so that no escape or entrance could be made—except for the rooms on one side. These rooms faced the sea and had windows that looked out on the outside world. They were barred with iron latticework that was strong for all its dainty appearance. But they could not be entered even if the bars were broken; beneath the windows, the ground fell in tumbled cliffs of rock to the sea below; an impossible climb.

It was impregnable.

But Juliette didn't discover all this until later. She was taken at once to a chamber, and two old women immediately came in to wait on her. They brought water for a bath and stripped her of her clothes, deaf to her protests. They exclaimed over her hair as they helped her into the water. One of the crones began to untangle her hair, while the other one bowed her way out the door and rushed away down the hall.

The old woman was headed to the grand central chambers of Farah, the sultan's favorite concubine and, for the present, at least, the virtual ruler of the harem.

The old woman bowed her way into the chambers. Farah had been waiting impatiently, striding up and down, eaten up by curiosity and malice. She *must* hear about this—this foreign newcomer! Already she knew the woman was beautiful enough for Giza to pay an outrageous price for her. That in itself was unusual enough to put Farah in a rage of jealous worry.

She had the sultan well in thrall now and feared no real competition from the other members of the harem, not even his two official wives. They were diversions, mere diversions to amuse him. But it was she, Farah, he was dependent on.

She paced wrathfully, thinking of how secure she was in his favor. Did she not live in the most opulent chambers in the harem? Did he not prefer her two sons to his legitimate ones by his highborn wives? He was *her* slave—not she, his!

As she strode up and down the dark red and orange tiles of her chambers, she looked like an angry cat. She had clawed her way to the top, to her position of power, and she would do anything to keep it. She'd had rivals poisoned before now—yes, even their sons!

Her gaze flicked over the gold and red hangings of the bed, the finest gossamers and silks brought from the East by caravan. The floor was scattered with rich rugs and soft cushions; her divan was scarlet damask. She had jewels, costly cosmetics, rare perfumes, attentive servants, slaves and loyal spies. All this had his favor brought her!

And that exotic, flame-haired slave might snatch his favor from her if she was beautiful enough, clever enough! Especially now that Farah was once again pregnant. It wasn't obvious yet, but there would come a time when she could no longer entertain the sultan. And all that she had gained could be taken from her easily.

Farah remembered well that she had snatched all she possessed from another. She had been young then, just fourteen, but already well-skilled in the arts of love and seduction. Her body had been ripe, enticing as she danced before him—and he had noticed her.

Once she caught his eye, it had taken all of her cleverness to keep him amused, all of her innate sensuality to keep him fascinated—and all of her ruthlessness to eliminate her rivals.

Now she must make sure the English bitch did not become a rival!

She arranged herself on her couch as she heard her servants admit the old woman to her chamber. She looked perfectly composed as she lay on her side on the divan, no longer a spitting cat, but a languid panther at rest. Her full, supple body was barely veiled by tangerine gauze, her dark hair unbound and rippling to her waist.

She watched the old woman cross the floor through long

narrowed eyes, eyes that could burn, throw off sparks, or freeze like ice. Just now they were cold black pools, beautiful but considering.

"So," she demanded.

"Your ladyship, your ladyship," the old woman said, bowing nervously. She was afraid her news would send Farah into one of her rages. She was a tigress when she was angry! The old woman's eyes were fearful as she rose from her bow. "She is a pretty creature, your ladyship. But her skin is like paste, and she is thin—too thin! And her hair—it is the hair of the devil—!"

"Silence!" Farah sat up, black eyes snapping. "I do not pay you to tell me lies! I *know* she is beautiful! My spies have already told me so! I must know *how* beautiful she is. So tell me the truth, or by Allah, I will have you roasted over a slow fire!" She leaned back, panting with fury.

"Ladyship." The old woman was trembling with fear. "It is true. She is very beautiful. Her hair shines like fire. I have never seen hair of this color. Her skin is very white, and soft and smooth. We looked at her everywhere, but we could find no blemish."

Farah frowned. "Go on," she commanded.

"Her eyes are as blue as the night sky, ladyship. But she glared at us like she would like to stab us. She looks fearless, like a man."

Farah smiled briefly. That was the first good thing she had learned. The sultan would not find a defiant woman attractive.

"That is all. You may go now." She tossed two coins carelessly in the air and turned away as the old woman scrambled for them then bowed her way out.

In a few moments, a plan occurred to her, and she clapped her hands for her slave. It was bad that the foreign devil was a novelty—white and red like flame. There was no doubt the sultan would enjoy her—unless her rebelliousness could be encouraged. . . .

"See that Halide is brought to the English woman's room. She speaks the language of the woman," she commanded.

The slave bowed and left the room, ready to obey her order without question. But it was an unusual order. Farah never cared about anyone . . . much less a new inmate! It was uncharacteristic of her to care if the Englishwoman had someone to talk to.

Juliette sat in her room, alone at last. The slaves had bathed her and helped her into a loose caftan. She sank onto the bed, exhausted.

She felt numb. Why had she been such a fool—a fool to believe Raneiri? To leave Deric?

Deric! Her heart twisted. At least he had always protected her from harm. She'd been safe with him. And even if she'd been his prisoner, he was taking her back to Lionel. Bitterly and clearly, she saw where her anger with him, her jealousy, her hurt love had led her. She'd let her emotions think for her—and now she had no one to blame but herself for the horrible situation she found herself in.

She was alone. There was no Deric to rescue her. If she was going to get out of this place, it was up to her.

She considered the room. The door led only to the guarded hallways of the harem. Two arched windows in the wall were securely barred with iron latticework. She was in one of the outer rooms overlooking the cliffs. Scented air poured in, warm and heavy with the aroma of jasmine, juniper and tuberoses. The room was opulent, with green and white tiles on the floor, thick rugs in muted patterns of green and apricot. The bed was draped with pale green hangings. Everything was rich, in soft shades accented by dull gleams of gold. But as beautiful as it was, it was still a prison.

She started at the soft sound of her door opening. She stared at the woman who stood in the open door.

Two gentle dark eyes regarded her. The woman held a tray of covered dishes and fresh fruits. She inclined her head slightly, a soft expression on her lovely oval face. Juliette thought she read compassion in the woman's eyes and the slight, benevolent curve of her mouth.

"I am Halide," she said, her voice as soft as her dark eyes. "May I enter your chamber? I have brought you food."

Juliette stood, surprised. "You—you speak English!" she exclaimed.

Halide nodded and came in, setting the tray on the low table in front of the divan, then shutting the door. "Yes. I am afraid I do not speak very well. What are you called?"

"Juliette Hawkins. I—I'm from England."

Halide threw her a look of sympathy. "This I have been told," she said gently. "It is hard to be here against your will, I know. Not being born to be a slave, such a fate is difficult to accept."

Juliette stared. "You—you are a slave, too?"

Halide shook her head and sat gracefully on the divan, arranging her flowing coral caftan around her slim legs. "No. I am not a slave, but a prisoner. I am—what do you say?—a hostage. My husband is Oman Kazamali's brother."

Juliette sat across from Halide, fascinated. "His *brother?* He holds his own brother's wife prisoner? But why?"

Halide smiled. "You have much to learn about this man who holds your fate in his hand, I see. He holds me here—and my son—because otherwise my husband Aznan would fight him for the throne. You see, he has the better claim."

"Then why isn't he the sultan?"

A trace of steel came into Halide's eyes. "Because Oman gained the throne by murder. There were three brothers, and Oman was the youngest. So he killed his oldest brother the sultan, and then took us hostage. Then he claimed the throne for himself. Aznan cannot fight him openly or we will be killed."

Juliette listened wide-eyed. So the man who held her really *was* ruthless. She felt moved by Halide's plight, separated from her husband. "So you and your son—how long have you been prisoner here?"

"Almost a year now. Now, it is best you eat some of the food I brought. You will need your strength if you are to survive here."

Juliette looked uncertainly at Halide, wondering what she meant, then nodded and reached for a piece of fruit. She felt her hope rising. Halide could tell her so many things she needed to know about this place!

As she ate, Halide told her how the harem was structured, under the command of eunuch slaves and an older woman, Lilla, was the *valide-sultan,* who ruled every detail of its strict hierarchy. But the real power in the harem, Halide whispered, was the concubine Farah.

"You must beware of angering her." Halide's eyes held warning.

"Is it possible to escape?" Juliette ventured, feeling she could trust this woman. If anyone would know, a fellow prisoner should.

"Not without help from the outside. The harem was built and is guarded night and day to prevent escape. You must hope the sultan will change his mind and ransom you. In the meantime, you must learn patience." Halide searched Juliette's face anxiously. She liked the Englishwoman already, but her eyes sparkled with a defiance that made Halide uneasy. The sooner she learned to accept her lot, the easier her time here would be. But this one didn't look like she would easily bend to the yoke of slavery without fighting.

"Will . . . will the sultan—visit me?" Juliette held her breath, dreading what Halide's answer might be.

"He may," she replied quietly. "Each night slaves will come and prepare you for his visit. But you must wait on his whim. Many of the women here he never visits since he has become so enthralled with Farah." She didn't voice the thought that she doubted the sultan would leave Juliette alone. She was too beautiful for that hope. "If he does come, do not fight him, but submit. If you defy him, he will have you whipped . . . or worse."

Before Juliette could answer, Halide rose. "I must go now. In a few moments, slaves will come to make you ready. But I will see you tomorrow. I hope we will be friends. Keep your courage, for it is all you now own." She smiled her soft smile and slipped out the door quickly. Juliette stared at the door, thinking over everything Halide had said. A friend! With a friend, maybe things would not be so bad. . . .

But she couldn't—*wouldn't*—believe it was true there was no way to escape from this place. *I'll find a way to get out of here,* she vowed, *if I have to dig a way out with my bare hands!*

The slaves were gone, and Juliette was alone again. She walked to the mirror slowly, afraid to see what they had done.

They had dressed her to please the sultan—in case he visited her tonight!

She gasped at her reflection. Looking back at her was a stranger she didn't recognize. Her hair was unbound and rippled down her back in long, loose waves. A transparent veil of metallic bronze was bound at her forehead by a thin gold cord and fell over her hair to the middle of her back. Dangling pagan earrings like gold scimitars hung almost to her shoulders. And they had painted her face! Her eyes were rimmed with black kohl, making them look enormous and slanted, her lips reddened to a beckoning pout.

But worst of all, she was almost naked! She was clad in diaphanous bronze silks: a brief bodice that left her stomach bare and a long skirt slit at the sides so her legs showed when she moved. They had clasped gold bracelets on her arms and ankles, but most insulting was a fine gold chain of delicate braided links circling her bare waist, fastened in front. It was a blatant reminder that she was nothing more than a slave!

The door opened, and she jumped, turning from the mirror. The sultan stood framed in the doorway.

He came in with an air of arrogant ownership. These were his harems, and everyone inside belonged utterly to him. He closed the door behind him. His eyes raked her.

"So," he said after a moment. "You are now mine. Mine to do as I please with. I can use you, beat you, or have you beaten for my enjoyment. Outside the door wait my guards. They are skilled with a whip if you choose to fight me. Of course, if you fight me, I might enjoy proving to you how much greater my strength is than yours."

Juliette said nothing as he prowled across the floor toward her. He stopped close to her and lifted one of her curls from her shoulder, drawing it slowly through his fingers.

"Do you understand you are my slave, woman?" he asked in a voice soft with malice.

"Yes, Your Supreme Highness," she replied, sick with the revulsion she felt for this man. Her hands curled into fists at her sides, and she longed to rake her nails across his cruel, smiling face. She swallowed. "If I do not obey you, you will have me whipped. I have no wish to face that. So I will not . . . resist you."

Her words were meek enough, but her eyes told a different story. He saw clearly enough that she was far from afraid of him . . . far from meek. That would soon change. He smiled again, enjoying this game.

"I shall enjoy your beauty . . . your skin like moonlight. You will be wise to please me, my beauty, because you are my possession to use as I wish."

Suddenly, he reached out and seized her shoulders in an iron grasp, drawing her against him. His mouth covered hers, and she gasped and stiffened in his arms. His hand found her bodice, and with a violent motion, he ripped it open. Then he let her go and stood back.

His eyes were malevolent as he looked at her. She stood, trembling slightly, but meeting his eyes with cool contempt. Her coral-tipped breasts were proudly thrust forward, tempting him to take her. But there was hatred in her eyes, not fear . . . not yet.

He reached out and slowly pushed aside her torn bodice, his fingers brushing her breasts lingeringly. He saw the fear at last come into her eyes, and he smiled, a slow, wicked smile. She had been cold when he took her in his arms, cold and resisting. For now, it was enough to frighten her, subdue her. Soon she would welcome his embrace with a show of warmth. That, or he would have the pleasure of watching that white skin beaten until it bled.

"Yes, I shall enjoy your beauty in time," he said, his hand falling from her breast. "But now I have those waiting for me who know how to satisfy me. Your coldness displeases me. When I next visit you, you will be warmer . . . or you will no longer be kept in these harems." He strode to the door and turned, saying before he left, "And I will visit you again."

The door closed with a bang. Juliette stood staring after him, trembling with fear and hatred. Fighting inside her was relief that he'd left her alone, and despair at his parting threat. He would be back, and then he would have her—if not tonight, then another night!

She sank onto the couch. *What am I going to do?* she thought.

Chapter Twenty-Two

The sultan sat pensive and moody on the great gilded throne in his audience chamber. A restive silence in the room hung like heavy velvet curtains between the large man seated on the throne and those courtiers surrounding him. A dissatisfied frown crossed his face, and an angry sigh heaved his great chest beneath his robes. The courtiers exchanged apprehensive glances. He was in a foul mood this morning, it was plain, and each hoped to stay clear of his legendary wrath. They watched for some sign of the calming of the storm that raged within him, but none was immediately in sight.

The silence was broken by the drumming of his heavily jeweled fingers against the gold of the throne. He grunted. The Englishwoman was a nuisance. With his visit to her bedchambers had come the onslaught of Farah's jealous rampage, and last night it had reached its pinnacle. The fiery odalisque had nearly destroyed his chambers with her rantings and raving and then had lain like a dead woman with him, denying him his pleasure until he promised to get rid of the girl.

His anger rose when he thought of how Farah could twist him around her finger. But she was his favorite, to be sure, and his household would not rest until Farah was satisfied.

And of the new slave? He could not deny she was beautiful. The sight of her bronze curls and milky skin had often recurred in his mind since the night he had visited her. He saw again those rebellious blue eyes filled with hatred and loathing. It would take time before she was willing to have him in her bed, and he had no taste or time for rebellious women. He was certain that beneath those lovely white breasts beat the heart of a passionate women—but those eyes, those eyes told him everything. Such a one would never be tamed to the yoke of slavery, he reflected.

"Giza," he growled.

The slave master stepped forward, inclining his head and murmuring, "Your Surpreme Highness?"

"Giza, come closer."

The advisor obeyed, reading the sultan's wish to confer privately with him.

"Perhaps I wish to sell the English slave."

Giza cleared his throat before answering. "Forgive me, Your Highness, but it would not be advisable." He averted his eyes, fearful of what he was to say next. Giza played with the great ruby ring that circled his finger and continued, "The war is in a delicate balance. It is rumored your brother, Aznan, negotiates with the Americans and is seeking the aid of the English. To sell the English slave might unnecessarily bring the English troops to Aznan's aid. For then they would know you held her."

"Let the impudent jackals come. I fear them not," the sultan bellowed. News of Aznan irritated him. His scowl deepened at the thought that Giza was probably right. Ransoming the prisoner might put the English squarely on Aznan's side. And he would do nothing that might help Aznan gain his throne!

"His Supreme Highness's courage is well-known, and his troops are inspired by his fearless valor. They wait for the day when they may follow Your Eminence into battle and reach the gates of Paradise by dying gloriously for your cause."

The sultan scowled at the man's flattery. Giza often rendered him invaluable information, but his obsequious manner was vexing.

"Curse the woman!" the sultan roared. The English bitch was becoming more of a nuisance every moment. "You were an utter fool to buy her." He waved Giza from his side. "Leave me now. Your presence nettles me."

Giza's pointed teeth showed between thin lips in a snarl as he turned to leave the chambers. Poison and a quick removal of the girl's dead body from the palace was the only answer, he thought, as he passed the great portal of the audience chamber.

The sultan remained scowling on his throne, brooding further about his dilemma. His thoughts were interrupted by a slave who bowed low and announced the arrival of a newcomer.

"The trader Dahkir has come, Your Supreme Highness. He begs for an audience."

The sultan smiled broadly for the first time and nodded for the slave to grant the trader entrance. Dahkir! The trader would take his mind from his problem. He was always amusing. And he would have gifts, valuable gifts to offer for the privilege of bringing his caravans to Tripoli. He straightened on his throne, watching the trader cross the tiled floor to stand before him.

Beneath his robes, the trader carried himself with the straightness of a military bearing. And though his bow was graceful and properly deferential, when he brought himself to his full height, there was an air of easy confidence in his posture as he faced the sultan. This man belonged to no one, and that was one reason the sultan enjoyed his company after tolerating crawling snakes like Giza.

"Dahkir! I did not expect you back so soon," the sultan said. "You must have found a way to avoid the Bedouin robbers that plague the routes."

He was answered with a smile and an indifferent shrug. "They are beginning to avoid me, Your Highness."

The sultan laughed loudly, and a ripple of relief went through the waiting courtiers at this sign of his earlier black mood vanishing. "Well said, Dahkir! News of your exploits reaches me even here. The Bedouin have come to respect your aim with a rifle. I could use such a rifle myself in these perilous times."

The statement hung in the air for a moment as Dahkir's eyes measured his. Then he laughed and gave a slight bow. "The sultan knows I am not political," he said, his words edged with challenge. "There is more money to be made in trading than in soldiering—and less risk, even considering the bandits that hide in the desert like wolves. But I am complimented you think so highly of my skills."

The listening courtiers held their breath as they waited to see how the sultan would take this. No one contradicted him and lived! But somehow, he seemed to enjoy this trader's insolent ways, because he laughed again, seeming much amused by this blunt refusal to work for him.

"You are a wise man to see that the profit in life is in trade, rather than the arts of war. Unless you are a ruler like me, eh? I profit well from war, but I fear my soldiers do not. As a trader, you can find many ways to profit if you are sly. For example, I understand Sheik Abd ul-Yazza is most grateful to you. You rescued his daughter from bandits, did you not?"

Dahkir shrugged with an air of depreciation. "Allah favored me then. I thought she was just a tribesman's daughter, snatched from the village well perhaps. I have just come from the emir's tents. He sends his greetings to you."

The sultan smiled cynically. "Allah favored you indeed, Dahkir, to see that you have the sheik in your debt. Powerful friends are most convenient. It is wise to do favors that leave others owing you something."

"Unfortunately, he had an idea I should marry his daughter. Since marriage is not to my taste, he perhaps looks on me with less favor now. But I say, why should a man take on the trouble of a wife when he can purchase a slave who will fill all his needs just as well? Better, even, for a slave does not nag the way a wife does."

As the sultan laughed, Deric laughed with him, but it was the hardest thing he'd ever done in his life. He was in a blind rage at the thought of what the man sitting before him might have done to Juliette—*his Juli!* He could barely restrain himself from leaping on the sultan; his fingers twitched, itching for his dagger, longing to drive it into the sultan's heart.

But he had to stay calm for her sake, if he had any hope of trying to buy her back from the sultan. How long he could contain himself he didn't know, when a red rage at the thought of the grinning Oman's hands on her was so blinding him. He took a deep, calming breath and stared at the sultan.

If Oman had seen the deadly light in the green eyes so

ferociously regarding him, he would have shouted for his guards. But as the sultan, who'd thrown back his head in laughter, again fixed his eyes on the trader, he found him half turned away, clapping his hands for a slave.

At this signal, a waiting slave came forward from the entrance of the hall, carrying three rolled bolts of cloth. When he reached the throne, the slave bowed low, then knelt and unrolled the first bolt at the sultan's feet.

The material unwound in rich folds, its threads of gold glimmering and glinting against the brilliant mosaic floor. A sigh of approval escaped the sultan's lips as the second bolt flowed beneath the slave's hands in wispy transparent waves of purple silk shot through with fine silver threads. The third bolt brought a greedy gleam to his eyes—the finest French brocade of palest cream and lavender. Goods such as these were costly to come by. What shrieking of joy there would be in the harems over the extravagant bolts of cloth. Dahkir had, as always, done well.

"I was fortunate in my cloth trading," Dahkir said, watching as the sultan tested the weave of the brocade. "If you are pleased to accept them, these 'gifts' are for you." The emphasis on the word did not go unnoticed by the sultan. Both men knew the "gifts" were bribes paid in return for the favor of trading within the city gates. The sultan laughed softly. This Dahkir would flatter no one. That was why it was such a pleasure to fence verbally with him—a game both men enjoyed.

"I am pleased," he purred, turning his attention back to the brocade. He would give it to Farah. Perhaps she would forget her jealousies over the English slave once she saw the cloth. Then he sighed. It would take more than this cloth to appease her rage.

Suddenly his eyes narrowed, and he considered the trader who waited before him. "So—you say you prefer to keep a slave instead of a wife. Very wise. You have one now who warms your tent?"

Deric drew in his breath at this piece of luck—the sultan bringing up the subject first. "Alas, no—but I thought to visit the slave-blocks while I am in Tripoli. Perhaps there I will find a slave to my liking. But I find I tire of dark hair and eyes." He paused. "Perhaps your slave master knows where I could find a slave who is fair-skinned like my countrywomen. I would pay a great price for such a woman."

The sultan sat back, smiling. "You will dine with me tonight," he said, and it was a command, not a request. Then he grinned broadly, white teeth showing beneath his dark moustache. "Perhaps I know where you can find such a slave—though I warn you, the price *is* very high."

Deric bowed. "It will be a pleasure," he said, a smile on his lips and murder in his heart, "to dine with you tonight."

Chapter Twenty-Three

Juliette watched with narrowed eyes as Farah made an almost royal progress through the baths. She stood behind a screen of potted palms, hidden from casual view. She wanted to see what Farah was up to.

She well knew that Farah was her enemy. Farah seldom lost an opportunity to make life uncomfortable for Juliette. And Halide had warned her that Farah hated her with an exceptional viciousness.

How dangerous this place was! She was a helpless prisoner, and information was her only hope. Yet it was so hard to get! She had a better grasp of spoken Arabic now, but still the other harem women shunned her and were suspicious of her, as befitted a foreigner.

Yet there were things she had to know. So far, the sultan had not made good his threat to visit her. She'd been left alone, to adjust as best she might to life as a prisoner . . . to dreams and plans for escape. Escape seemed impossible, so well were the harems guarded. And every day she lived in dread that the sultan would decide it was time he visited her. It had been a week now, and he still had not come to her chamber, thank God!

She knew from Halide that one of the reasons he had not yet come to her was Farah's jealousy. So she had to know what Farah was up to now.

In her explorations of the harem in the past days, trying to find a way to escape, she had found ways to spy on Farah. She knew the odalisque's favorite places to sit, and had found hidden ways to conceal herself near Farah and learn what she said to her servants. It was a dangerous game, but one she felt she had to play if she hoped to survive here.

She watched as Farah sat gracefully on a scattering of cushions in an alcove. Around her waited anxious slaves. Juliette's eyes swept over the alcove. It was screened on one side by open latticework. Once before, she had listened to Farah as she sat in that alcove; she had found a route to get behind the screen if she was careful.

Cautiously she slipped out from behind the screen of palms and worked her way slowly along the wall. Using the plants that stood along the wall to hide her from view, she slipped from the shadows of one to the other. At last she stood just a few feet from an open space in front of the screen she had to get behind. She held her breath and waited for an opportunity to glide unremarked to the next hiding place—the one that would bring her within earshot.

In a few moments, it came. A slave stepped forward with a peacock feather fan to fan her mistress, and her back blocked Farah's view. Juliette rapidly crossed the floor and stood behind the screen, her heart beating fast. To be caught would mean whipping. Maybe even death. But as her breathing stilled, she heard the voices on the other side continue unabated. She had not been seen!

"What is taking Giza so long?" Farah was asking impatiently.

"He should be here at any moment, *effendi,*" came the soft deferential voice of a slave.

Giza! The eunuch slave master who had bought her! His hateful face rose before her eyes.

She waited, looking through the shadowy screen at the shapes beyond it. She heard the slap of sandals on the tiles and knew Giza approached.

"*Effendi,*" he said, and she saw a stout, robed shadow bow low at the entrance to the alcove. "I have done as you wished and cast the foreign slave's horoscope."

Juliette softly drew in her breath. So Farah had had her horoscope cast! She must indeed believe Juliette to be a dangerous threat.

"And what did you find?" demanded Farah impatiently. "How long will she remain here?"

His voice was smooth. "Not long, most gracious lady. I see in her stars that it is not her destiny to live her life as a slave."

She heard Farah's long indrawn breath of satisfaction. "That is good news. How is it she will leave here? Will she be sold? Or perhaps . . . she will die?"

Juliette stiffened at the soft threat in Farah's words. Die! Then Halide's warnings were right. Often Halide had cautioned her that Farah was known to have her rivals poisoned.

"The stars do not tell me the manner of her departure, most gracious one. Only that she will not be here long."

"Then there is no danger of her catching the sultan's favor?" Farah asked sharply.

"I do not believe so," was the cautious reply. "Yet I must tell you that this woman has great power over men's hearts. It is written in her stars that she will inspire a great passion. But I do not believe this love will be with the sultan, for the stars tell me she will return this love. It is her fate. And it is common knowledge this slave despises the sultan."

"Yet hate can turn to love, as we all know!" snapped Farah. "The emotions are two sides of the same coin! I will not take the risk of them being together. Your words make it clear that I cannot, if she is destined to inspire great passions in the men she loves! Perhaps her stars can use a helping hand to speed her departure from these walls."

"Perhaps they can, *effendi,*" said Giza smoothly. "Many are not strong enough to survive slavery. This is well known."

A cold sweat broke out on Juliette's brow, and the palms of her hands felt clammy. Slowly, cautiously, she backed away from the screen. She must not be found here! If Farah knew what she had overheard, it would be her death warrant!

She slipped from behind the screen rapidly while Giza still held Farah's attention. Cold chills were running down her spine as she made her cautious way along the wall, back toward the baths. She felt like a hunted animal. She must get back to her quarters—to Halide!

The last rays of afternoon sunlight poured through the window of Halide's apartment, giving it a warm, safe look—a refuge. Halide looked up as Juliette entered, startled. Taking one look at Juliette's face, she kissed her son Ismail and rapidly whispered for him to return to his chambers.

Ismail threw Juliette an anxious look, then obeyed. He was fond of Juliette, enjoyed the hours she spent every day teaching him English. But he could see by her face that his teacher, whom he thought brave as a lion, was badly frightened.

"What is wrong?" asked Halide at once, when Ismail was gone.

Juliette turned to Halide, her eyes enormous in a white, strained face. She threw a quick glance at the hangings of the room. It was not safe to talk freely here—but talk to Halide she must! Too many rooms of the harem were spied on continually, especially rooms of prisoners such as Halide. She couldn't be sure the walls didn't conceal a hidden listener or watcher. So she crossed to where Halide sat on the couch and sat next to her. She would have to whisper her news. It might bring the guards in, in a few minutes, but she would chance it.

"I overheard Farah with Giza. She had him cast my horoscope. I believe Farah may mean to kill me, because he said I would not remain here long and Farah asked if it was because I would die soon. I am in danger. Halide, I must find a way to escape!"

Halide's soft eyes widened at this rapid whisper. "But you know there is no way to escape," she whispered back.

"Halide, if the sultan sends for me, I am dead. Farah will have me killed. What can I do?"

Halide's face was filled with fear as she looked at Juliette. But Juliette saw clearly there was nothing Halide could offer her. And whispering between them any more was dangerous and would surely bring the guards. Halide's worried eyes followed Juliette as she rose and paced the room like a caged animal, the yellow silks she wore rippling against her long legs.

"I can see you are anxious," Halide said aloud, mindful of the role she must play to deceive the listening ears. "You are unhappy because the sultan has not favored you with a visit yet? But you must learn patience. He will not be attracted by the unwomanly qualities you display—your impatience, your anger."

Juliette's gaze went to the window that held the dying glow of the sun, and followed the dimming light as it crawled across the thick carpets scattered on the floor. How she hated to see night fall, knowing that every night he might send for her. But she and Halide had played this game many times, pretending she did not dread such a summons but longed for it. Only when they were alone in the gardens could they speak freely without fear of hidden listeners.

"But it is the uncertainty that maddens me, Halide! Am I to stay here—or be ransomed? Or even sold on the slave block? If I am to be happy here, I must know what is in store for me!" Juliette played for the listeners as she said this. Too docile an acceptance of her fate would only cause them to suspect her more deeply.

"You must learn to accept what Allah sends you," said Halide serenely. Inside, her heart was wrenched with worry. Juliette was in terrible danger that worsened every day she stayed here.

Juliette crossed to the window and leaned her forehead against the iron bars, breathing in the salt air. A ship could be seen tilting carelessly on the horizon, its sails tinted a rosy pink with the setting sun. Juliette was reminded of the *Alexandria*.

"I just want to be free," she breathed between the iron bars.

Halide was silent in the face of her friend's despair. Too well she knew how hard it was to live as a prisoner, your every moment an uncertainty. At least she had her son. Juliette had no one.

"To exist without freedom is hard, but to exist without love is hardest of all," said Halide.

Juliette turned to her friend. "You miss your husband very much, don't you?"

Halide's eyes held a wistful yearning. "I miss him every moment. And I think, from what you have told me of this Deric, you have the same pain?"

Juliette's lips tightened. So Halide saw through to the sorrow in her heart. "It's a pain I must learn to forget," she said, wondering how it would ever be possible.

There was a soft knock on the door, and Juliette jumped. Halide's eyes held a flicker of fear in their soft brown depths, quickly extinguished. Both were thinking that their earlier whispering had brought the guards. Now they might be whipped mercilessly until they divulged what secrets they kept.

But Halide's voice sounded steady and unconcerned. "Come in," she called softly.

A slave girl entered and bowed low to the two women. Juliette suppressed a sigh of relief that it was not one of the harem guards.

The slave girl finished her bow to Halide, and her eyes shifted to Juliette. She spoke.

"The sultan has ordered that you make yourself ready, *effendi.* You are to be taken to chambers where you will receive him. I am here to help you with your bath."

Halide's gaze flew to Juliette's and locked. Juliette had paled, her lips whitening.

"Dear God," whispered Juliette. The dreaded summons had come at last.

In a short while, she lay numbly in the tepid waters while the chattering slaves oiled and perfumed her body. A dazed Juliette moved without purpose while she was dried and dressed in her apricot silks. They painted her unresisting face and combed her hair until it gleamed like rubies down her back.

Two hours later, she followed a phalanx of guards through the sultan's private tunnel to the harem. The slaves carried torches to light their way, and as they unbarred the door at the end of the tunnel, she swallowed, trying to banish the knot rising in her throat.

They entered a hallway and passed several doors. At last the guards opened a door and motioned her inside.

She had no sooner entered the room on tentative bare feet than the door slammed behind her and she was alone. She heard the latch fall in place on the other side of the door.

The elaborate bedchamber was dominated by an enormous bed surrounded by transparent, shimmering hangings of pale pink gossamer shot through with thin golden threads. Low tables and chairs and rich hangings on the walls made the room a lavish dream. But Juliette didn't spare them a glance. Her attention was riveted to the window.

It was unbarred.

She rushed to it and looked out, hope rising in her heart. But when she gained the window, she gasped in disappointment. The window overlooked a courtyard surrounded by palace walls.

Six guards stood motionless at intervals around the courtyard, their scimitars catching the torchlight and throwing it in challenge at her.

She choked back a sob as she crossed to the bed and sat. Turning her eyes to the door, the door he would be entering all too soon, she grasped a pillow and flung it in impotent anger.

The moon rose over the palace walls and shone in the narrow window, filling the room with beautifully frail shafts of silver moonlight. One glimmering tendril touched Juliette's cheek as she sat, a motionless statue on the bed, staring at the door.

Footsteps in the corridor and the soft voices of the guards warned her that he came at last. She rose, her heart hammering. The door was unbarred, and it swung open.

The sultan stepped inside the room and stood looking at her. As he walked in, she kept her eyes fixed in fear on his hated face. It was some moments before she could wash the hatred from her eyes, before she could make herself bow.

She bent at the waist, blood rushing to her head, wondering if there was any way she could kill him. She straightened and looked at him again.

And then she realized he was not alone.

To her disbelief, she found herself looking over the sultan's shoulder into a pair of familiar green eyes. The room rocked under her feet.

It was Deric!

Before she could even open her mouth, he raised a warning hand behind the sultan's shoulder, stilling the cry that leapt to her lips. Just in time she stopped herself from reacting to the sight of him, but she couldn't take her eyes off his face. Her vision swam and the room tilted dizzily, and from the lightness of her head, she thought she was about to faint.

"This is the slave I told you of at dinner," she dimly heard the sultan say. "She is fair of skin—and look at that hair. Is she not beautiful?"

"She is truly magnificent," said Deric, his eyes locked with hers, steadying her, giving her hope.

"Magnificent indeed," agreed the sultan, with a knowing leer at Deric. "You, slave! Turn around for this man, slowly, so he may look at you!"

Feeling unsteady on her feet, Juliette walked forward and turned slowly. How had Deric found her here? How—how had he learned where she'd been taken? And what was he doing here?

"It is with great reluctance I offer to sell the girl to you. Her beauty is only surpassed by her passion. She is a tigress, this one," the sultan boasted, a crafty gleam in his eyes. "She has pleased me to distraction," he furthered the lie, not seeing the leap of fury in Deric's eyes at his words.

"You! Listen to me, slave," came the harsh voice of the sultan, his eyes on her. "By my rights as your owner, I may decide to sell you to this man. He will try you tonight, and if he is pleased with you, he may buy you."

The sultan spoke to Deric, watching Juliette with narrowed eyes. "You will tell me in the morning if she does not satisfy you. For if she fails to delight you, I will find you a more suitable slave. I would have you go on your journey well pleased tomorrow."

"I will try this slave with pleasure, Excellency. Her beauty is more than I ever hoped for."

"Good," said the sultan. "I have already ordered wine to be sent to this room, so you can refresh yourselves." He grinned, a satisfied leer. By Allah, after what he'd said, the Englishwoman would do anything to please her new master. And once he sent her on her way with Dahkir, she was no longer his concern. Dahkir could keep her or let her go; it mattered not.

"Enjoy her," he said as he strode from the chamber, pulling the door shut behind him.

For a moment they stared at each other. Then both rushed forward, and Juliette was safe in his arms.

Chapter Twenty-Four

She stood, clasped tightly in his arms, her head pillowed against his chest, and never had arms offered such safety. His hands stroked her hair, and he said her name over and over again.

Then he took her by the shoulders and held her back from him, looking down into her face. His eyes glazed with a green fire it took her a moment to realize was fury.

"Juli—are you all right? Did he hurt you?"

She shook her head, feeling tears trembling on her lashes. "Oh, Deric—thank God you're here!"

His lips were set and white, and he said through clenched teeth, "Did he—touch you?"

"No—no, not really," she faltered, remembering the sultan's hands on her bodice, his brutal kiss. He swore, and she felt his fingers tighten convulsively on her shoulders.

"What do you mean—not really? If he touched you—if he harmed you in any way—then I swear he's going to die for it tonight!"

She stared at him, barely able to comprehend that she was really hearing these unbelievable words. He was speaking as if he cared about her! And he looked ready to rush out of the room after the sultan, never mind that the palace was swarming with guards!

"No—no, Deric, he never visited me! I've been left alone since I came here. I swear, he didn't hurt me."

His face changed with a wave of relief, and he let out a long, pent breath. "I've been nearly driven mad since I found out you were sold, thinking of what he might be doing to you—"

He broke off. It was no more than the truth. He'd been like a madman from the moment he'd found out she was gone. Never again did he want to experience anything like his wild ride here, panic, anguish and killing rage all mingled in his heart.

"But Deric—how did you find out I was here?" she began, filled with a thousand questions. But there was a soft knock at the door, and he hastily put a finger to his lips, then put her from him. "Say nothing," he warned in a whisper, then walked away from her and called, "Enter!"

The door opened, and two servants bowed their way in, bearing trays of food and wine. They swiftly arranged the supper on the table, and Juliette and Deric stood silently until they were finished. A swift glance from the slaves' eyes, another bow, and they were gone, closing the door behind them.

Deric poured two glasses of wine and turned to her, holding one out. "A glass of wine? I think we both need it."

"Yes—my nerves are still in pieces. I can't believe you're really here. Just a few minutes ago, I was sitting there staring at the door, thinking the sultan was going to—visit me at last, thinking I would never escape from this place, and now—" She stopped. "Deric, how did you know I was here?"

"From Raneiri." His voice was terse. "I didn't find out until today that you were gone. She kept up the pretense you were still in the women's quarters, and since you didn't seem to want to see me, I thought it best not to send for you. Then I had the message from Mulay that all was in readiness, so I sent for you. It was then that she told me you'd 'escaped.'"

"But—how did you learn I hadn't really escaped? That I'd been sold to the sultan?"

His voice was dry. "I—ah, persuaded Raneiri to tell me the truth." He didn't add that his rage at discovering she was gone was so great that he had taken Raneiri by the shoulders and shaken her; that he had seen the lie in her eyes, the sudden malice there, and known she was hiding something. He had shaken her mercilessly and shouted at her until at last she had screamed the truth at him—that it was too late for him to find his *houri* ever again, for she'd been sold into the sultan's harems and would never come out again!

He'd thrown her from him onto the floor and had stared

down at her with disbelieving revulsion in his eyes. For a horrible moment he'd wanted to hit her as she panted up at him, her face a mask of malice, but then the terrible import of her words had sunk in. He had turned and strode from her, shouting for his men, not even hearing her wailing cry that followed him.

By God, he never wanted to live through anything like that moment again as long as he lived.

His brows drew together in a thunderous scowl. "What the hell did you mean by going off with Raneiri's man? You little fool! What on earth possessed you to do something that stupid?"

She stared at him, stung by the sudden tone of contemptuous anger in his voice. "I know now it was a mistake—but Raneiri told me her man would take me to the embassy in Tripoli. I believed her because—" *Because I wanted to get away from the sight of you two together*—"because she said she was planning to marry you and wanted me out of the picture. So she would help me escape. I never even imagined that she would betray me like that."

"But why did you suddenly decide to escape? For God's sake, Juli, you knew you were going to be ransomed in a few days!" he exploded.

"Because Raneiri told me that Mulay el-Rassouli might not let me go—might collect the ransom and then sell me as a slave anyway! I couldn't take that risk!"

"Do you think I'd let anything like that happen to you?" He was almost shouting. "I would never have turned you over to Mulay without making sure he was going to let you go! You little fool, I was planning to watch the whole thing until I saw you safely on a ship with your cousin!"

"How was I supposed to know that?" Juliette flashed, losing her temper. "You've been holding me for Mulay for the money he would pay you! You're his *partner!* Why would I think you gave a damn about what happened to me? For all I knew, you were planning to sell me yourself after the ransom was collected!"

Deric groaned inwardly. So that was what she thought—and he deserved it. "I'm not Mulay's partner and never have been," he said quietly. "And I didn't hold you prisoner for him for money. I should have told you before, but—" He made a gesture of futility with his hand. It was impossible to explain why he hadn't told her.

He went on, his voice level. "You've heard me speak of my friend Farouk? Mulay holds him as a prisoner—a galley slave. He blackmailed me into keeping you for him—as the price of Farouk's freedom. So you see, I must return you to Mulay, because Farouk's freedom—his life—depends on the exchange tomorrow."

Juliette felt her heart growing lighter as she listened to him, a great bubble of joy growing inside her. "Then you—you—" She couldn't find the words to say. It had never been for money. Her heart had been right when it had stubbornly refused to believe he was a black-hearted mercenary! "Oh, my God—why didn't you tell me?" she whispered at last.

His eyes locked with hers, and for a long time, he didn't look away. They seemed to be telling her something, but when at last he spoke, all he said was, "At first I didn't think there was any reason you should know. And what does it matter? Now you know the truth. All that matters is that you're safe."

"Then—you said the exchange is tomorrow?"

He nodded and took a deep drink of his wine, still watching her.

"But Deric—you haven't told me how you got inside the harem—how you convinced the sultan to sell me to you! I still can't believe it! I can't believe we're going to get out of here safely tomorrow!"

"And you haven't told me what has happened to you in this week here. It seems, if nothing else, you've learned a new way of dressing." His eyes swept her from head to toe, lingering for a moment on her face, then slowly travelling all the way down to her slender, gold-braceleted ankles. She felt herself blushing as she suddenly remembered how little she was wearing, but also felt a familiar flicker of heat at his gaze on her body.

"Come and sit down," he said softly. "There is food and wine here—and I would hear your story, Scheherazade."

She followed him to the low table, and they sat on tasselled cushions across from each other, both picking at the food as they talked, telling each other what had happened since she'd made her bid for escape.

The lamps burned low, casting a rosy circle and mingling with the silver bars of moonlight that streamed in the window. The rest of the room was shadowed with a velvety blueness. The hated room now seemed an enchanted place to Juliette, a dream from the *Arabian Nights.*

At last, they finished speaking. There was a silence in which the tension grew as the moments slipped past. Juliette was all too aware of the big bed behind them, shrouded in gauzy curtains, of the perfumed night air that blew into the windows from the gardens below and slipped like a caress over her bare arms.

Evidently, Deric's thoughts were turned in the same direction.

"We should get some rest. We leave at dawn tomorrow. We will need our wits about us for the exchange," he said, and he wasn't meeting her eyes anymore. Before, he'd stared at her as if he couldn't tear his eyes away from her, as if he was committing to memory every line of her face.

She looked at him, seeing him as if for the first time again: his square-jawed, high-cheekboned face, bronzed by the sun; his sun-streaked hair, the two lines that bracketed his mouth, lines she loved; but most of all, his emerald eyes, brilliant beneath dark, straight brows. She didn't have to commit his face to memory, for how could she ever forget it?

As if he felt her steady gaze, he looked up, then stood quickly as if her eyes made him restless. "I'll—I'll sleep on the divan here. You can have the bed."

She stood, too, unsure of what she felt, unsure of what she thought. Then, suddenly shy, she nodded and walked to the bed, opening the curtains. For a moment, she stood framed there, looking over her shoulder at him.

His heart twisted at the picture she made, a vision that glittered with gold, a vision indeed that threatened to vanish like a mirage. It was all he could do not to cross to her side.

Thank God, she'd soon be out of the range of his touch, enclosed inside those bed curtains where the sight of her could no longer haunt him. Then he could lie down on the divan, not to sleep but to toss with desire for her and wrestle with this battle to resist her.

"Goodnight, Juli," he said quietly.

"Goodnight," she whispered, and climbed inside the bed.

He turned with a sigh and put out the lamps, leaving just one burning dimly. Then he stretched out on the divan, and clasping his hands behind his head, he lay staring up at the ceiling.

Juliette lay in the bed, also staring into the night, and thinking. *Tomorrow, tomorrow.* Tomorrow, she was going back to Lionel. After tomorrow—she might never see Deric again.

But tonight? Tonight she'd learned he wasn't the mercenary pirate she'd thought him, but a man doing his best to save his friend. He wasn't selling her for money. And he might not care about her the way she cared about him, but tonight she'd learned he cared at least a little.

Yet he'd let her go alone to this bed. It was clear enough from his actions that whatever had once existed between them was finished as far as he was concerned. Tomorrow, he would make the exchange. Tomorrow, he would be gone from her life.

What would it be like without him?

The thought made her shiver with absolute fear, a fear greater than any she'd experienced on this adventure—a fear that after tomorrow she would never again feel what she had felt with him. There were no more lies she could tell herself. There was no one like Deric. No one.

But he didn't love her. He'd never said the words. He may have desired her, but that was not the same. She had to forget him. She had to. She would leave him, plod through each day, immerse herself in society, until this unbearable pain in her heart grew less and less and was nothing more than a dull ache. It would happen, she told herself. She would make it happen.

It's not fair, she thought. It was so unfair that her time with him would eventually become the dream, and the dull days ahead, the reality. Her days with him had been the most exciting, passionate and vital time she had ever known. He'd taught her to live, to feel, to love. He was her life's breath. Nothing had existed before him, and now nothing would exist after he was gone.

Tomorrow.

Slowly, she sat up, her hand going to the shimmering curtains to part them.

There was only tonight.

Chapter Twenty-Five

The oil lamp flickered low, casting wayward shadows on the walls, and the scented night breeze rippled the curtains so they sparkled where the gold threads caught the light. A turtle dove cooed once beneath the window, then fell silent.

Juliette stood beside the bed, a quiver going through her body, her heart racing. Across the room, Deric lay bare-chested on the divan, a sheet to his waist. His clothes were slung carelessly over a chair beside him. She could hear his breathing, slow and even, could see the gentle rise and fall of his chest. Was he asleep?

Suddenly she felt ridiculous. What if he was angry with her for waking him and sent her back to bed? Wasn't she being fool enough by going to him now? She would die if he turned her away like some child.

Her confidence wavered, and she started to climb back in bed. Then Deric turned on his side to face her. He was awake, his movement slow, deliberate, as if he had sensed her standing there and had felt her hesitation. Raising himself up on one elbow, he gave her a half-puzzled look.

His gaze swept her from head to foot, then he lifted his eyes to hers. She couldn't turn back now if she tried. All at once, she was light-headed, trembling, her mouth cotton-dry. Everything in the room seemed to spin and fade around her, time spiralled endlessly. The only two objects she could focus on were his eyes, and they pierced her to the soul. The all-too-familiar heat flared between them and ran crackling through the air.

Juliette hesitated again, searching his eyes for the love she wanted to see there. What she found, she wasn't sure: a mixture of desire, longing, need, sorrow? But love? Damn his eyes! They said so much, but told her nothing. She groped for the resolve she'd had only moments before and found it. Being with him tonight was all that mattered.

She took a sure step forward. "This is our last night together. We may never—"

"Juliette, no," came his ragged warning as he sat up, his weak resolve nearly melted by the sight of her.

She took another step. "I want to."

He stood, and the sheet slipped from his lap. In two hurried strides, he was standing naked before her, holding her away from him as if the touch of her would burn him.

"You must go back to bed."

Her reply was firm. "Not without you."

He relaxed his hold on her as she reached behind her back to unhook her bodice.

"Juli, no," he repeated, but the conviction in his voice had all but faded.

The hooks came free; the bodice hung loose. His fingers clutched the material at her shoulders and desperately held it in place. He was only a movement away from turning her around and sending her back to her bed. He could still do it. He only had to turn her away from him. . . .

With a groan, he slid the diaphanous material from her shoulders, down her arms and let it fall to the floor, leaving her naked to the waist. Her bare breasts, frosted by the moonlight, rippled temptingly as the material slid away; their pink tips grew hard under the cool night air.

In a second he had her pressed to him, her warmth and softness against his bare skin infusing him with desire. How many times had he fought this very battle, only to lose? She wanted and needed him tonight. And for all his denials he needed her, too. Damn tomorrow and all it would bring.

His hands moved to her waist and untied the cord that held her skirts in place. They slid to the floor, and he stepped away from her to view her completely.

She was like an apparition, ethereal, innocent and lovely. An aura of moonlight surrounded her. Her hair hung loose in tousled curls around her shoulders, her skin silvery and luminous. He wanted to take her now, but warned himself not to rush tonight. He wanted to hold her, to explore every glorious inch of her physical being, every expression of her soul, because after tomorrow he would only hold the memory of her.

Juliette didn't blush, or turn from him, but felt breathless under his gaze. Oh, how he could suffocate her with a look—the very look he gave her now, his eyes so heated and impassioned like summer lightning.

And then she was in his arms again.

His lips moved closer to hers, hovering near them, brushing them lightly, hesitating, then pressing against them, hard and harder still, a bruising and hungry crush. She could feel desperation in his caress, and it frightened her. He was always so strong, so confident. Instinctively she tightened her arms around him as if to drain his desperation into herself.

At last, his grip eased, and she was allowed the intense pleasure of his kiss, the demand of his lips on hers, the feel of his lean, muscled physique against her pliable one. She was ever amazed at how weak his embrace could leave her, helpless and trembling, the most splendid feeling in the world. It would be one of her last, and she would revel in every bittersweet second of it.

He pulled her away from him and looked down at her, trying to memorize every curve, every plane of her face, trying to etch into his mind's eye the portrait he would carry with him when she was gone. Though he denied it, he knew how she would haunt his nights in the desert, how his skin would thirst for the feel of her, and how his soul would rage for wanting her.

He kissed her again as he swept her in his arms and carried her to the bed.

She sighed and opened her eyes to find him watching her.

"You should have gone back to your bed when I told you to, woman. Now I'll keep you up half the night," he said, his lips curving in a roguish smile.

"Do you promise?"

His soft laughter mixed with hers in the quiet room.

Then he fell silent. Why was he so aware of the way her eyes sparkled just then, the impish lift of her eyebrow when she spoke, her full lips so near his, slightly parted? Her every expression tugged at his heart. There was so much he wanted to know of her, and tonight he would barely scratch the surface.

He smiled at her wistfully and pulled a stray curl from her face, running his finger along the creamy curve of her cheek. Like a kitten she closed her eyes and leaned into his caress.

Then tenderly, his lips touched her forehead, her cheek, her neck.

"Juli, if the sun were mine to rule, I would command it never to rise again," he murmured against her flushed skin as his mouth moved down over one nipple and suckled it until it became firm. Fiery thrills sang through her, radiating from her center to the very tips of her fingers and toes. She arched her back as he played with the other, teasing it into a hard peak, flicking it with his tongue. Then he began trailing feverish kisses along her collarbone to her neck.

He lay stretched at her side like a sleek panther, and she allowed her eyes to roam his body, smooth, lean and unashamed.

He assaulted her senses with his every touch. Her pulse quickened, her breathing came in gasps, and her heart thrummed madly in her chest. A wake of goosebumps rose, beginning at her shoulders and rippling downward as a hand cupped one breast, then followed the curve of her waist to her sleek hips, across the smooth skin of her stomach to the curly tendrils of hair at its base. One finger dipped to touch the honey-sweet recesses of her, sending shivers all through her.

She twisted the fingers of one hand in his hair, pulling his head closer to her, her hips rocking, straining for the feel of him against her. The other, she slid between them, along the taut muscles of his abdomen. She heard him draw in his breath as he loosened his embrace, allowing her to explore further. Her hand stole between them to take his hardness in her grasp.

A long shuddering moan came from deep within his throat as she moved her hand along him. He was a wonder—firm, hot and responsive. The feel of him made her deliciously warm as she thought of what was to come, of what he would do to her, of how he would soon make her feel.

"Say my name," she purred in his ear. "I need to hear you say it." And he did over and over again, until they were both drunk with the sound of it.

She stroked him, caressingly, delighting at the reaction she could elicit from him with such a simple movement. And then both her hands were slipping along his skin, testing his responses to her palms on his chest, her fingers trailing along his back, her hands grasping his buttocks to urge him gently on top of her.

Her touch was driving him mad; her movement beneath him, quickening his own responses. He was unable to hold back any longer, and he masterfully penetrated her. He heard her breath catch in her throat, then even, as he began his silken rhythm.

Her eyes fluttered open.

His movements were slow and willful as he held her gaze firmly with his own. He thrust against her and watched the pleasure light up her blue eyes, the faintest smile crease her lips, heard the moan that escaped between them, a whisper, a sigh. All his being was focused on discovering what brought her pleasure. He wanted nothing more than to make her happy tonight—tonight was all he had. After tonight another would take his place, would hold her and make love to her as he wanted to. The thought made him feel empty, despairing, and he crushed her against him.

The spell that rode between them couldn't have been broken if she'd wanted it. His eyes so intent on her had fanned the flames deep inside her and sent her logic packing. And then there had been the sparks that had flown from his eyes only a moment ago, increasing his ardor and leaving her gasping for breath.

His thrusts became quicker, stronger.

She cried out in delight as he moved inside her, commanding the tide of sensations that ran deep in her to ride hot and pulsing to the surface. When she thought he'd given her all the joy he could, he drove deeper, and yet another surge swelled and threatened to burst. A pressure built up inside her, and she strained against him to release it, as only he could. He felt her need and plunged deeper. The tension doubled, and she arched against him, tightening her embrace. He thrust once more, and she cried out. Wave after wave of delicious tremors quivered through her, spreading outward, spiraling upward, and finally exploding inside her like a thousand points of fire and ice.

Her cries of fulfillment sent him over the edge, releasing his own tensions as well. Panting he lay on top of her, unable to move for the moment, entirely spent. When at last his breathing evened, he rolled to one side and pulled her close to him. Her head rested on his chest, and he could feel her breath warm on his skin.

Her legs entwined with his, her hair brushing his arm. Her fingers tracing lazy circles on his chest filled him with such longing. No other woman could satisfy him and at the same time leave him hungering for more. The feel of her, the smell of her, the taste of her had become a part of him. And at the moment, he knew what he wanted. He wanted her to stay. *If I thought you would,* he thought bitterly, *I would ask you.*

She felt his fingers at the nape of her neck, toying with the curls there as his heart beat strongly in her ear. Why did his arms around her make her feel so safe and secure? Even tomorrow seemed less dreadful when seen from the fortress of his embrace. She could spend the rest of her life with him, if he'd only ask. *Oh, Deric, why won't you ask me to stay?*

As if they could read each other's thoughts, they pulled away and looked into each other's eyes, searching, as a silent dialogue passed between them.

His eyes seemed to say, *I want to ask you something.*

Hers to answer, *Then ask.*

I'm afraid to say it.

And I'm afraid you won't.

Am I a coward?

No. Am I a fool?

Never.

Then ask.

But between them there was silence.

Juliette closed her eyes briefly, feeling the tears beginning to well, then opened them again. Bravely she held his gaze. *I understand,* she seemed to tell him, then she hopelessly lowered her head to rest on his chest for the last time.

Chapter Twenty-Six

Juliette walked down the long corridor, one of the hundreds that twisted mazelike through the palace, thinking of her tearful farewell with Halide and Ismail this morning. It had been a wrench to leave her friend behind, to be gaining her own freedom while for Halide there was no hope.

She followed the guards' naked backs down the hall to a massive double door that was flung open, letting in light.

The late afternoon sun was just lighting a small, enclosed courtyard. Two great dark archways faced each other, one leading to the stables, the other a side-gate to the outside world. Here it was that the smaller troops of the sultan's cavalry could dash in and out, easily reaching the stables, far from the crowds and confusion of the main palace entrance.

Two horses waited in the center of the courtyard. Deric stood holding their reins, watching Juliette as the guards led her across the cobblestones.

He was dressed for the desert, swathed from head to heel in a coarse gray and tan burnoose and white headcloth. He held the reins of his tall gray stallion and Juliette's smaller mare. She tried to see his face, but his expression was shadowed by his headcloth.

He chose his words carefully in front of the guards. "You are dressed for the desert. Good. We're late. The caravan waits for us."

She nodded at him, remembering their plans of last night. They would ride directly from the palace to the harbor, where

Mulay el-Rassouli and Lionel would be waiting for the exchange. Deric had insisted that all parties be present to prevent that vagabond Rassouli's pulling some trick.

She fitted her foot in the stirrup and swung herself up to ride astride, grateful once again to Halide for the desert leggings, boots and burnoose she had given her that morning. She nodded to Deric that she was ready.

Without a backward glance, he squeezed his stallion into a canter and headed for the gate. The clattering hooves of his horse echoed through the courtyard, raising a burst of startled doves from the roof tiles.

She gathered her reins and turned the mare's head, which broke into a following canter at the barest urging.

She felt the sun's hot rays dazzle her eyes as they galloped through the yawning gate with a clatter of hooves. She was free of the despicable sultan and out of the harem!

As she rode into the city, she was filled with an odd feeling she couldn't put her finger on.

Through the congested streets of the city, through the mass of traders and farmers streaming into the morning markets, the throngs of carts and donkeys and people carrying precarious loads of goods, Deric picked a skillful path. As she drank everything in, the simultaneous filth and opulence of the mysterious crowds of people in turbans, women veiled in black, dark eyes showing through slits in the cloth, the feeling grew stronger—a restless feeling of having left something behind, of having lost something.

Deric interrupted her thoughts. "Are you frightened?"

She saw his sturdy face and shook her head. "No," she said evenly.

He pointed ahead. Through the crowd, she could see the sparkling waters of the bay, the sails of the ships seesawing on the waves. As they drew nearer, shouting arose from the sailors who hoisted massive crates onto the bobbing decks of the ships, among the whirring of sails being run up the masts. A whirl of color and a rush of smells bombarded Juliette. She was reminded of her ride through Derna with Mulay el-Rassouli. These things had seemed so foreign and threatening to her then. But now—

She saw the looming shape of Mulay el-Rassouli on the dock. Moored in the harbor was the familiar ship of the pirate, his men lining the decks. A slumped figure was held between two of Mulay's men on the dock. *That must be Farouk,* she thought, following Deric's lead and dismounting at the dock's foot.

Rassouli moved forward. "I see you have taken good care of the woman, Dahkir."

"Better than your care of Farouk, I see," came Deric's terse reply at the disheveled form of his friend. How he wished to slit this ship rat's throat. "Let's get this thing over with."

Juliette watched horrified as Mulay's men pushed Farouk forward. He was painfully thin, lank dark hair falling into his shadowed eyes, a dark beard hiding some of his gauntness. It was obvious Rassouli's treatment of him had not been kind. How lucky she was that Rassouli had given her to Deric. What happened to her could have been much worse.

Farouk stumbled and fell into Deric's arms. He righted himself and weakly said, "I'm sorry, my friend," in a voice that cracked.

Deric helped him to sit on a crate, for the moment, all else forgotten. He turned back in time to see Mulay's men taking Juliette to stand beside the pirate. He felt anger rising uncontrolled at the sight of her in their grasp.

"I'll have no tricks, Mulay," he shouted. Six armed men dislodged themselves from the crowd and came to stand behind Deric.

The outriders from the caravan! she thought, amazed. The whole time they rode through the city, his men must have been following, and Deric—she gave him a bemused look—hadn't said a word. She looked them over, remembering each one from their days on the caravan. She never knew they could be so menacing.

Rassouli's men on the ship came to attention, drawing their own rifles. Tension sang through the air like a high-pitched whistle, and Juliette felt her skin ripple with goosebumps.

Rassouli grinned slyly. "There is no need for fireworks, Dahkir. The girl's cousin is quite generous with his money. I have thoughts of retiring after this." He laughed, and his men laughed with him.

The mention of Lionel's money grated on Deric's pride. "I will personally slit your throat if anything happens to the girl."

"So—I see you have become attached to the girl! Such violence." He grinned mockingly at a glowering Deric.

Juliette searched the activity on the docks. "Where's Lionel? I don't see him," she called to Deric.

Deric heard the note of anxiety in her voice. "He knows where to meet us. He'll be here shortly."

No sooner had the words escaped his lips, than a gleaming white coach-and-four rattled to the edge of the dock, and the staid and stately figure of Lionel got out. Juliette waved to him in acknowledgement.

Deric turned to Rassouli, a look as hard as flint. "I'm warning you," was all he said.

The pirate grinned. "No tricks, my friend."

Lionel walked forward, his eyes locked anxiously on Juliette. Then he looked to Mulay, annoyance for the pirate crossing his face. "Well, now, let's get this nasty business over with. Mr. Rassouli, I presume? Good. Well"—here he signalled to his groomsman, who brought forward a leather satchel—"I will be quite happy to put this entire hideous episode into the past. Mr. Rassouli, your ransom."

He tossed the bag at Rassouli's feet. From the bulge in its side, Deric surmised that indeed Lionel had been generous in his ransom. His eyes went over Lionel, seeing the perfect cut of his dark suit, the fine lace of his cravat and the diamond stickpin that held it. A perfect—and wealthy—English gentleman. His lips tightened as he took in this evidence of the world Juli came from—and was going back to.

The pirate knelt to check the contents of the bag. When he was satisfied, he tossed it to one of his men on his ship.

"And now, my cousin," Lionel finished. Mulay pushed Juliette forward. She ran into Lionel's arms.

His arms went around her, pulling her to him. "Thank goodness you're safe, Juliette! Are you all right? Unharmed?" He pulled back and searched her face, and she saw how worried he'd been. He looked careworn.

Tears pricked her eyes, all her differences with Lionel

mistily forgotten. "I'm fine, Lionel. They didn't harm me. I was treated very well."

"Thank God! I've been quite worried."

"You must have been. I hate to think what you must have felt—"

He took her under the arm and started gently pulling her down the dock. "My God—what *I* must have felt—! When I think of what you've gone through—! But come along, Juliette. We can't talk here. Let's get in the carriage. There's a ship on the next pier bound for Malta, and I've booked us cabins. Let's get out of this devilish, heathen city! I have a doctor standing by on board in case you—in case—"

Lionel's face reddened, and Juliette felt her own cheeks pinken in turn. God knows what Lionel imagined had been happening to her since she'd been kidnapped.

She stopped. "No, Lionel, really—I'm fine," she said firmly. "Really I was not harmed. In fact I owe thanks to the man who—who held me for Rassouli. He saw to it that nothing happened to me, and he even—" She was about to say he'd even rescued her from the sultan's harems, but the way Lionel's eyebrows shot up when she mentioned thanking Deric stopped her. Obviously he believed she was mad to think she had anything to thank one of her captors for.

Maybe she was mad.

She turned away from Lionel as his mouth opened to protest, merely saying over her shoulder, "In fact, I really must thank him before I leave," as she started across the dock to where Deric stood.

He was alone, watching her. She felt his gaze on her as she walked toward him. But she couldn't meet his eyes yet. If she looked at him, she knew the tears that were threatening would fall, and she didn't want him to remember her that way. She swallowed hard against an aching throat, dimly conscious of the crowd on the deck watching them. A disapproving Lionel behind her, a jeering Mulay off to one side, the slumped figure of Deric's comrade . . . all eyes were on her.

Including Deric's

She stopped in front of him and at last looked up and met his eyes. Her heart hurt as she took him in, so tall and proud, desert robes tossed carelessly back around his shoulders, long booted legs braced. His unforgettable face was framed by long hair glinting in the sun, ruffled by the wind. Was any other face so strong? Was there another mouth so determined—and fascinating? Or eyes as clear as the green water of the sea?

She attempted a smile and offered her hand. "Deric" was all she could say.

He took it. "Juli." He too was studying her, knowing this was a moment he would carry with him. Her burnoose had fallen away from her head. Her curls were loose and lifted softly in the gentle sea breeze as the sun stroked her cheeks with its morning light, and he saw the Mediterranean mirrored in her eyes.

"I don't know quite what to say." Her heart felt like it was weighted, too large for her chest. "Except that I'm grateful for—all you've done." Why was she saying such meaningless things when what she really wanted to say was, *Will I ever see you again?*

He didn't seem to know what to say either. "So—it's all over. And you're off to a safe life in Malta."

"It's over," she agreed, trying to smile. *Oh, Deric, after last night, is it so easy for you to say good-bye?*

The silence stretched between them until she knew she must break it. "What are your plans?" she asked, wanting to know where in the wide world he would be, and if there was any chance she might ever see him again.

His gaze pulled away from hers to the open seas. "Maybe I'll sail to the Americas. Who knows?"

The Americas! She felt her heart drop to her feet. No, she would never, never see him again. This was her last moment with him. It was time to say something she meant.

She looked at him directly and knew her eyes were swimming with tears. "I'll never forget you," she whispered.

Both her hands were captured in a grip that squeezed her bones. "I won't forget you either," he said, and she heard the catch in his voice. No, she could never forget his face, or the pain of this moment.

Lionel appeared at her side, but she didn't spare him a glance. Neither did Deric—and he didn't release her hands.

"Juliette—we must hurry," Lionel urged, and she could hear the displeasure in his voice. "Really—the ship is leaving, and—"

She nodded, still not looking at Lionel. She took in the green depths of Deric's eyes one last time.

"Good-bye, Deric," she whispered.

"Good-bye, Juli."

Their hands dropped apart, the contact between them broken. She turned quickly as Lionel took her elbow. She walked away as rapidly as she could, not looking back, her head bent, uncaring that Lionel would see her tears falling.

Deric watched her go, then felt Farouk at his elbow.

"Dahkir, who was the woman?" Farouk asked curiously.

For a moment, Deric didn't answer as they stood together watching her walk down the dock.

She was at the steps of the waiting coach, climbing them. She turned and for a moment stood poised in the coach door, the sun turning her hair to copper flames. Then Lionel hustled her inside, and the coach door closed. She was gone.

"She was nothing more than a mirage," Deric answered. There was a pause, then he added, "Let's go."

"Really, Juliette, I cannot imagine what possessed you to make a spectacle of yourself on the docks with that—*pirate!* Why, you were *holding his hands!* And I cannot condone your insistence that you should be grateful to him. The man is nothing more than a common brigand! Your captivity—all that riding you said you were doing under the desert sun—must have affected your brain. I insist you come below and let the doctor look at you. . . ."

Lionel's voice droned on and on, until his words were a meaningless jumble of sounds. Juliette stood on the deck of the ship, doing her best to ignore him for the moment. In the coach, she'd tried to answer his questions, but he'd been absolutely scandalized already by the little she'd told him about being on caravan with Deric. She couldn't even imagine what he'd think if she told him she'd spent time inside a *seraglio.* Right now, she didn't have the energy to reassure him.

Right now, she was saying good-bye.

Malta, her new home, lay in the other direction, but it was the shores of North Africa she now faced.

As the ship pulled away from the pier and the rocking motion of the sea carried them farther and farther from the city of Tripoli, the odd feeling she'd had before rushed in at her.

She realized she was leaving behind the kind of life she was meant for.

The frightful adventure that had started that fateful night on another ship was over. And her heart was desolate.

She watched the roofs of Tripoli dwindling on the horizon as the sun went down in a blaze of rose light and turned the waves to silver, dazzling her eyes through her tears.

Part Two

A book of Verses underneath the Bough,
A jug of Wine, a Loaf of Bread—and Thou
Beside me singing in the Wilderness—
Oh, Wilderness were Paradise enow!

Omar Khayyám, *Rubáiyát of Omar Khayyám*

Chapter Twenty-Seven

On a morning four months later, Juliette descended the sweeping staircase at the governor's mansion in Malta to the breakfast room. She was up earlier than usual, but she wanted a few moments to drink a cup of tea in peace—and to prepare herself so she could appear more animated than she felt. Lionel and his wife were coming to breakfast this morning.

She found the governor, Sir John Wright, and his wife, Lady Margaret, already at the table in the sunny, gracious room. Sir John was deep in his morning newspaper, and she threw an affectionate glance at his kindly face and silver hair. She'd become very fond of him in the months she lived here, and equally fond of his wife. They'd been kindness itself.

"Good morning, my dear," beamed Sir John, setting his paper aside. "You're up early this morning. I suppose because you had an early night last night. No parties or balls for a change. I think Margaret sets you to harder duty than I ever have. You must be worn out with all the gadding about you've been doing after putting in a day's work with me."

Juliette was about to protest that the work she did for the governor was hardly taxing—helping him with his daily correspondence and paper work—but his wife spoke first.

"Nonsense, John," said Margaret crisply. She looked the picture of an English lady at home in her lavender morning dress with a mauve sash and soft lace collar. Juliette thought that no matter what climate or part of the world Sir John took her to, Margaret would always be a living reminder of a more gracious life in England. Her brown hair, faintly streaked with silver, was elegantly piled on her head. She had a patrician beauty and blue eyes that for all their soft loveliness, had an autocratic way of falling on people. "Juliette needs to have some fun, too, after all the drudgery *you* subject her to! At her age, a girl needs to go to parties and balls! How else will she ever find a husband? She can't be your underpaid factotum for life—most unsuitable for a girl of her beauty, training and station! Besides the fact that it must get very boring for her, shut up all hours in a dreary room, bent over and trying to decipher that chicken-scratch Arabic writing! Why, I get angry every time I think about it!"

Sir John sent Juliette a searching look. "*Do* you find it boring, my dear? If I thought—"

"No, Sir John—and dear Margaret—I most emphatically do *not* find it boring! It's far from being the drudgery you make it out to be, Margaret. It's fascinating to learn about the politics of this part of the world, and I much prefer it to afternoon calls and dressmaker's fittings!"

"There, you see, Margaret? I've often told you Juliette is a young woman of rare good sense."

"But John, with all respect, this work she does for you doesn't help further her position in society, or go far toward finding her a husband! Which is what my balls and parties, which you scorn so much, do! Why, look at the way Lord Ormsby is positively *pursuing* her, and—"

"Yes, yes, Margaret, I concede! I agree she needs to go to all the parties she can. Why, haven't I allowed you to nag me into holding a damned ball next week?" he said, his eyes twinkling.

"John Wright, you know very well you are looking forward to that ball as much—more!—than I am, and—"

He held up his hands. "Let's not get into a row. Not that I wouldn't enjoy it; but I hear the butler coming, and I imagine our guests are here. How shocked Lionel and his wife would be to find us quarreling over the breakfast teacups!"

Juliette laughed, then turned in her chair to await Lionel's entrance, trying to put a pleasant expression on her face. But it wasn't easy. Lionel had been so trying since she'd come back!

She sighed. He hadn't changed a bit in all the time she was

gone. He still watched her every move and never stopped commenting on her behavior. And he worried incessantly about what a scandal there would be if people found out she hadn't arrived in Malta straight from London, but had been kidnapped.

She hadn't told him much about what had really happened to her . . . the expression on his face when she'd told him she'd actually spent part of the time in a harem! And if he knew the truth about Deric—

She cut that thought off before it could finish forming. There were some things she firmly did not let herself think about these days. That was the one good thing that had come out of the whole terrible experience. Now she'd grown into a woman, determined that it would be her own hand that shaped her destiny from now on, that she'd control her own life. And that included putting certain thoughts forever behind her.

Thank God the governor and his wife had been kindness itself in those first dark days after her arrival in Malta. If it hadn't been for their support, she could never have faced it all. Lionel's air of half-condemnation, as if the whole thing had been her fault, and the sadness that she couldn't seem to shake back whenever she thought of—

Again, she turned her thoughts firmly away. Taking a sip of her tea, she cast another fond glance at the governor and his wife. How glad she was Lionel was married now and she didn't have to live with him anymore! He had been so disapproving when, on his marriage two months ago, she'd not gone to live in the new house he'd built for his bride. Instead, she'd stayed on here, gratefully accepting the governor's offer to help him with his correspondence. But the "position" was no more than his kindness, so she could live here without feeling she was taking their charity. She knew that Sir John and Lady Margaret realized how out of place she'd have felt, moving in with Lionel and his new bride, and so they'd generously rescued her from an awkward situation.

Yes, she was much happier here, she thought, as Lionel and his wife entered the room. Sir John and Lady Margaret were her friends, and she could talk to them with a freedom she never could with Lionel. Or his bride. Lady Anne Jermyn was a sweet, quiet girl, a trifle on the heavy side, with a placid manner. Juliette was sure Lady Anne never caused Lionel a moment's disquiet over "improper" behavior. They were perfect for each other.

"Ah—good morning, Cousin Juliette," Lionel was saying now, a twinge of reserve on his mouth as always when he looked at her. "I'm glad to find you in health."

"But what a lovely dress, Cousin Juliette," remarked Lady Anne, unconsciously touching her own sand-colored hair as she sat. "That pattern of dusty pink mixed with yellow is quite striking with your hair. I declare, I never thought redheads could wear pink! Is it voile?"

Juliette turned to Anne with a smile but an inward sigh, prepared to spend some time discussing dressmakers, materials and the latest trim for bonnets. That and gossip were Lady Anne's chief subjects of conversation.

Margaret gamely joined in, saying, "Yes—and voile is *such* a good material in this climate! I declare, I love silk but positively *wilt* in it in the heat. They just got such a lovely shipment of voiles at Madame Renard's, you can't imagine!"

"And a whole new supply of picture hats—the kind with sweeping feathers and a thousand yards of gauze veiling," Juliette added, trying to sound animated.

Lady Anne giggled. "A thousand yards! How you do exaggerate, Cousin Juliette! Lady Margaret, do you really shop at Madame Renard's? I thought she wasn't *chic* enough to be patronized by fashionable society!"

"Yes, but her prices, my dear . . ."

Juliette lost the thread of the women's conversation. With half an ear, she heard Lionel holding forth about the American navy in the Mediterranean to Sir John. He was so ponderous! But he was a good diplomat, for he would never say anything offensive or without careful thought.

She realized that Lady Anne was asking her something. "I'm sorry?" she said, and caught Margaret throwing her a reproving twinkle.

"I asked you, what are you wearing to the governor's ball. I'm sure everyone will be dressed most spectacularly. I myself can hardly wait for the night to come. No one is talking of anything else. I've heard that simply *everyone* who is anyone is planning to come! It is so very exciting!" cooed Lady Anne.

"Yes, quite everyone will be there," said Margaret complacently. "I'll wear black and silver lace myself, and of course, the Wright diamonds. Juliette is planning to dazzle in ivory, and I'm hoping that there will be plenty of eligible young men in attendance to be dazzled by her." Margaret threw Juliette an arch glance.

Juliette smiled brightly, wondering if the smile fooled Margaret's sharp eyes, and tried to feel excited at the prospect of all those eligible young men. Her mind wandered as Margaret went on, "And we are having chilled champagne and an orchestra, and the most divine lobster patties. . . ."

With an effort of will, she forced herself to pay attention again. She was happy now, she told herself firmly, happy with her life. If she found some of it boring now that she was back . . . if she had a hard time adjusting to the quiet routine of life, that was all that was wrong with her.

Nothing more.

Chapter Twenty-Eight

Juliette stared impatiently at her reflection in the mirror as she coaxed her curls into place, weaving a yellow ribbon edged with gold lace through them. Her stays felt so tight she could scarcely breathe, and as for dancing—!

She knew how hot it would get at the ball tonight, even though the governor would throw open all the doors to the verandah and push wide all the windows to let the night breeze in. It was not that the night was over-warm; it would be the heat of tightly packed bodies and the dancing. She could almost already feel herself stifling.

But it's not the crush tonight, or the air you find stifling, is it, Juliette? she asked herself as she shook out her full sleeves and stood to check her toilette.

Her silk ball gown of ivory and cream stripes was trimmed with buttercup-yellow ribbons edged with gold lace like the one she'd woven through her hair. She pulled on her long ivory gloves with disgust, cursing the fashion that made them *de rigueur* even in the tropics. At least the sleeves were short, the neck low and her shoulders almost bare. As a concession to the heat, she'd piled her hair on top of her head, leaving only a few curls to drop on her shoulders.

She picked up her fan (necessary), her reticule (a bother), and her heavy skirts (a torture in this heat). She sighed with a sudden memory of how light and airy, cool somehow, had been the voluminous burnoose she'd worn in the desert. Well, no wonder, there was no corset under it, nor pantaloons and petticoats and chemise! She tried to set her mouth in more pliable, sweet lines than the rebellious ones she saw in the mirror, to remind herself that she was Juliette now, not Juli.

As she crossed the echoing polished ballroom toward the governor and his wife, she could hear the musicians tuning up behind the great screen of flowers and potted plants. The scent of flowers filled the room, from the gardens below and the floral decorations in the ballroom. She found the scent cloying and felt her stomach knot. She had a momentary remembrance of the keen freshness of the desert air under a sky full of stars.

"Good evening, my dear, you look lovely," greeted Sir John, bowing to her. "James, champagne for Miss Hawkins. I'm glad you're early. You can help us receive. We've just time for a bracer before the hordes storm the gates."

She accepted her glass with a sympathetic smile at Sir John. He felt the same way she did about parties.

"Juliette, that dress looks marvelous on you! Not but what you could wear rags and dazzle in them, my dear," said Lady Margaret. "I'm glad you chose the pearls. So suitable. You shall have a declaration out of Ormsby tonight or I miss my guess."

"I hope not!" Juliette laughed, sipping her icy champagne. It soothed her to hold the cold glass, and she knew the effect would indeed brace her for the boredom of the receiving line.

"Honestly, I don't know what to do with you, Juliette," said Lady Margaret, fixing Juliette with a fond but vexed stare. "He's quite suitable and so good-looking."

"His suitability is overwhelming," rejoined Juliette dryly.

"Stop making light of it! I don't understand how I have simply *pitchforked* eligible men in your path these past weeks and you do not develop a *tendre* for any of them! It is too provoking. I suppose you're waiting for a duke to offer. Though, perhaps, with your looks, anything is possible; still, I would not have you sniff at a lord!" She shrugged.

Juliette and Sir John both burst into laughter, and after a moment, Margaret joined in.

"You two! John, you encourage her! And I suppose you're not looking forward to tonight, Juliette! At your age, I would have sparkled like that champagne at the thought of it!"

"Well, Margaret dearest, you *know* how I am coming to feel about parties, but you are right. I am an ungrateful beast! I'll do my best to have a wonderful time tonight, and I promise I'll even sparkle like champagne!"

Margaret's eyes warmed, and she smiled. "Oh, good—I hope you do! I just would *so* like to see you find—"

"A suitable young man," finished Sir John and Juliette, and they all laughed.

"And then I should lose her quite invaluable services, and that would never do," said Sir John gallantly, taking their arms and leading them toward their positions near the entrance for receiving guests.

An hour later, Juliette, her face sore from smiling, was excused from the line and allowed to go "enjoy the ball." Guests thronged on every side, and she was quickly claimed to join a group of chattering acquaintances, then whirled off to dance. As she had feared, the ballroom was growing warmer, and she was already so bored with the small talk she felt she would scream. But she concealed her boredom with almost professional graciousness, accepting dances and allowing refreshments to be fetched for her, but resisting any walks on the terrace to see the moonlight.

A waltz ended, and her partner escorted her to the sidelines. Marie-Claire Corraine waved gaily at her, and she curtsied to her late partner in relief, glad of the excuse to escape him offered by Marie-Claire.

"Juliette! You look marvelous tonight," enthused Marie-Claire, taking her arm warmly. She was an outrageous flirt, forever tossing her dark curls and sparkling her green eyes at all the gentlemen, but she was fun, always filled with high spirits, the latest gossip and a seemingly inexhaustible supply of chatter.

"That yellow-and-cream is an indecently pretty color on you. None of the gentlemen will *look* at me next to you—but then, I could use a break!" Marie-Claire laughed. "Tell me, how have you avoided Ormsby all evening? You haven't danced with him once!"

"There's an art to it." Juliette smiled. "I contrive never to leave one dancing partner until I'm certain another—*not* Lord

Ormsby—is nearby and will get to me first. But I can't avoid him forever. Margaret thinks he means to make me an offer tonight, so I suppose he'll corner me sometime!"

"How dreadful for you!" sympathized Marie-Claire, making a *moue* of distaste. "He'd be quite a good match, I know, but what does that matter if you don't love him? And it's so tiresome having to listen to proposals you intend to turn down! But everyone will say you're mad not to accept him, you know."

Juliette nodded, struck. Especially Lionel. He was bursting his waistcoat with pride that his unconventional cousin had actually managed to attract a suitor like Ormsby, and he'd be incredulous when she refused him.

"*I* intend to marry for love if I can," declared Marie-Claire. "But parents can be so difficult about these things! If I can't, then I at least hope to land someone wicked and lusty, like Viscount Enfield. For all that he's a dreadful rake and would never be a faithful husband, at least he would be fun!"

"You're so right! I—I also would rather marry some desperate adventurer than a man I didn't love, no matter how secure he would make me—oh, Lord, Ormsby's seen me! What shall we do?"

Marie-Claire was never at a loss in these situations. She adroitly took Juliette's arm and steered her toward the gambling rooms.

"We're safe enough for the moment." She laughed, positioning them behind a silver loo table. "Ormsby loathes gambling. We can wait here a few moments, then go back into the ballroom by another door—and find you a new dancing partner before Ormsby sees you again!"

Juliette smiled gratefully at the younger girl, feeling a momentary pang of envy at her uncomplicated high spirits. This was the apogee of Marie-Claire's world: balls, parties, dancing and flirting. She would never pine for a desert moon at midnight, for the freedom of being treated like a man. She would never be bored with the small round of society—afternoon calls, dances and the opera—where one saw the same endless round of faces and heard the same endless stream of gossip. If Marie-Claire pined, it would be for London, or some handsome guards captain, or a titled rake. Life was so simple for her.

As it was for me once, thought Juliette, *before that fateful night when my life was changed forever. Before being a prisoner, before being a harem slave, before riding like a Janissary soldier through the desert, before Deric. . . .* She glanced at Marie-Claire's guileless face next to her and thought, *How shocked she would be if she knew. . . .*

"Don't you . . . don't you ever get bored, Marie-Claire?" asked Juliette wistfully.

"Bored?" Marie-Claire looked at her quizzically, then laughed. "Lord, all the time! I ache with it! Afternoon calls to Mama's friends, church, beastly sewing—"

"No, I mean with this whole life, not just the church and the sewing. With—with parties, and people, and having to put on frilly dresses and—" She stopped. Marie-Claire was looking at her as if she'd gone mad.

"With *parties?* Never! Parties are *too* divine!" She cocked her head to one side, considering Juliette. "I know what your trouble is! You need a bit of romance—a cavalier—a handsome buck to make your head spin and make you forget all about being bored! I don't wonder you're down. Come on. We'll go back to the ball and see if we can't find one. And if we do, I promise I won't even look *twice* at him," she said generously, taking Juliette by the elbow and dragging her to the door

Juliette laughed and let herself be led. It was so like Marie-Claire to simplify the problem to men. "I hope you *do* find me someone. Someone who can make me forget—someone else!" exclaimed Juliette recklessly.

"Oh, so *that's* it! I knew it! You're pining for a lost love! Oh, how romantic! Did you meet him back in England? You shall have to tell me *all* later. But right now, we're going to find you someone to help you forget him. Here—this is perfect! See, Ormsby's over there and won't see us through the palm trees, but we can see most of the room."

Marie-Claire had found a spot for them near the stairway where a few potted palms indeed screened them from a casual glance from Lord Ormsby's direction across the room. Juliette could see his fair head and aristocratic profile through the screen of leaves. There was nothing wrong with him as a suitor. He was very handsome, and decidedly intelligent. But like many of the men she'd met since she'd arrived here, he seemed almost too refined—a trifle *too* civilized. She didn't want to admit to herself that the trouble was, other men seemed almost boyish compared to Deric. She lent half an ear to Marie-Claire's chatter, staring dreamily out at the dancing couples, the twinkling chandeliers, the banks of flowers.

". . . there's Lieutenant Bolling—hmmm. Handsome, but not quite handsome enough, I think. And James Taverner—well, he *is* a bit stout, but he's said to be a hand with the ladies, though I don't see the attraction. . . ."

Suddenly Juliette was roused from her daydream by Marie-Claire gripping her arm, quite hard. "Oh, my goodness—will you look at *that!* I don't know if I shall let you have him after all—he's too divine. What gorgeous eyes!"

"Where? Who are you talking about?" Juliette scanned the dance floor but saw no one she thought was that handsome.

"He's just come in—near the door. They're going to announce him. Oh—you can't see him now—he's behind that crowd of people."

"Where?" Juliette craned her neck.

"There! Why, Juliette, he's seen us! He's staring at us! There, just to the left of Lady Davenish. The tall man with golden-brown hair!"

Juliette found herself staring across the ballroom into Deric Raleigh's green eyes.

Chapter Twenty-Nine

"Juliette—Juliette! What *is* the matter? You've gone quite white!"

Marie-Claire shook Juliette's arm, but Juliette didn't answer. She was staring at the man across the ballroom, obviously not hearing a word Marie-Claire was saying.

"I—I—it's someone I know," stammered Juliette at last.

"It's *him?*" Marie-Claire squeaked, enthralled by the drama of the situation. "Is it? Oh, I can see from your face that it must be your old flame! Juliette—he's coming toward us!"

Juliette's face told her this man—whoever he was—was indeed someone special. All these months, Marie-Claire knew perfectly well no man had caused Juliette's heart to flutter. But now—! She was staring at this man like an infatuated schoolgirl! What kind of man could make the cool and collected Juliette look like she was about to faint?

Delightedly, Marie-Claire turned to study the man as he started toward them. He came straight through the colorful throng, dressed in black, accented only by a white neckcloth and a white satin waistcoat. For all his finery, he looked dangerously out of place in this crowd, like a pirate who had come to rob them all. He walked with a long, loose stride, his tanned skin making his eyes look vividly green, and there were streaks of gold burned in his brown hair. Obviously, this was no dandy who spent his time indoors, but a man used to life in the open air.

He stopped in front of them, looking down into Juliette's

face. Marie-Claire had to stifle a giggle at this intriguing development. Why, his eyes were positively devouring Juliette! And what divine eyes they were, too. *If such a man was looking at me like that, I would burst my stays! He is indecently good-looking!* she thought.

Fascinated, she wondered how long they could stare at each other without speaking. The electricity between them was making the air tingle. And it wouldn't be long before behavior like this would cause a delicious stir!

"Hello, Juli," he said at last.

"Deric" was Juliette's answer, just a whispered breath, and Marie-Claire had to resist the urge to elbow her. Why didn't she say more, Marie-Claire wondered in frustration—something witty, flirtatious, romantic, dramatic?

But for the life of her, Juliette couldn't speak. Those dark green eyes she'd never thought to see again were locked with hers. She'd forgotten how his mere physical presence was an impact she could feel all the way across a room, how she could drown in that gaze once she met it, everything else vanishing. Around her, the room seemed to have dimmed, the music muted.

At last she remembered Marie-Claire at her side.

"Oh, Miss Corraine, may I present Deric Raleigh? Mr. Raleigh, it is my pleasure to make you known to Miss Corraine," she heard herself saying.

Marie-Claire giggled and extended her hand to be kissed as Deric bowed to her.

"Such a dramatic meeting, sir! I take it you two are—old friends?" she quizzed.

A hand grasped her elbow, and a still-stunned Juliette turned to find herself staring blankly into the blue eyes of Lord Ormsby.

"Ahem, Miss Hawkins," he said, bowing. "May I have the honor of this waltz?"

Deric's voice cut in smoothly. "Very sorry, old chap. 'Fraid Miss Hawkins has just promised it to me," he drawled.

Juliette's eyes flicked nervously from Deric to Lord Ormsby. They stood facing each other, the polite smiles they maintained in contrast to the challenging looks in their eyes as they measured each other.

Ormsby drew his attention from Deric and laid accusing eyes on Juliette, "But you will save a waltz for me, will you not?"

"But of course," she murmured in embarrassment.

Lord Ormsby released Juliette's elbow and bowed politely. "'Til then."

Juliette found herself being whirled out onto the dance floor in Deric's arms, followed by the curious stares of Marie-Claire and Lord Ormsby.

Her head was spinning, her heart beating like a hammer in her chest, her mouth dry as paper. She was flustered to the depths of her soul. She couldn't for the life of her think of a word to say. She knew she was staring at him like he was an apparition, alternating with avoiding his eyes, and she detested herself for it! If only she could have run off for a few moments to the ladies' boudoir, plunged her wrists in cold water, taken a few deep breaths and gathered her wits about her! Then she could have faced him with cool aplomb, not with this shaking nervousness that made her cheeks flame, then pale!

How could he simply walk back into her life and be so damnably cool about it? When she dared to look at him, she saw he was studying her face with an intensity that sent a thrill all the way down her spine.

"Juli," he said at last, "it seems like more than just four months since I held you in my arms."

"You're holding me too closely," she managed, feeling as if every eye in the room was on them, fighting the thrill his words gave her. "And please, I must ask you not to call me Juli. No one here knows about the—when you and I—about how we—about that time." She was trying to maintain her composure, but she was failing miserably. "It will be difficult enough to explain how I know you. Everyone thinks I arrived here straight from England. And Marie-Claire—why, she is such a gossip that I'm sure she's telling everyone who will listen that you're an *old* friend of mine!"

His smile made her weak. "I've been on the desert too long and have completely forgotten my manners. Forgive me, Miss Hawkins," he said and pulled her just slightly closer to him.

There was that intimate tone of his she remembered too well. And he'd purposely ignored her request not to be held so tightly.

She averted her face, feeling her cheeks heat up.

"The desert has nothing to do with your lack of manners," she began as primly as she could manage. "You have been and always will be the rudest man I've ever met." And with that she pushed him to a safer distance.

"Then we're even, because you will always be the most stubborn woman I've ever met," he teased.

She was pressed against him again, her embarrassment rising. "I am not stubborn. I may be opinionated and strong-willed, but I find the term, stubborn, utterly incorrect." Her gloved hand properly pushed him away again.

"'Opinionated and strong-willed'? I've been all over the world, and in most countries that's called stubborn."

She felt herself at his mercy once more as he pulled her to him and held her fast. She could no longer avoid looking in his eyes.

Juliette felt Marie-Claire at her shoulder and heard her whisper delightedly in her ear—"What an amusing dance, my dear. You'll have to teach me that step"—and danced away.

Embarrassment flooded her cheeks hotly. Then she caught the devilish glint in his eye and his rakish smile, the smile that would always melt her heart. Her laughter came first, followed by the mellow tones of Deric's low laugh.

Chiding herself for being so flustered, she relaxed in his commanding embrace and let herself be led across the floor. Surprisingly, he carried her with an effortless grace through the steps of the waltz, and she found him a wonderful change from the stiffly proper dancing partners she had danced with before.

The moments flew by, and she forgot everything except the pleasure of floating across the floor, actually dancing with Deric Raleigh. She couldn't believe he was really here, that she was truly seeing him again. It was like a dream. Above, the chandeliers sparkled; the scent of flowers came in through the open doors.

As she stared up at his face, the sight of him made her feel breathless. She couldn't sustain his gaze, so her gaze dropped to his mouth and was caught there, fascinated.

She was going to faint; she knew it.

He'd come back for her.

They whirled together down the length of the ballroom, their steps matched perfectly. The ivory silks of her skirts flared out as he turned her, and she caught a glimpse of the two of them in the long mirrors as they danced past. He was a tall strong figure, the black he wore a perfect contrast to the frail softness of her ivory gown.

Oh, yes, she would faint.

At last he spoke. "You seem to have done quite well for yourself. Tell me, what's happened to you?"

"The governor and his wife offered to let me stay here. I live with them now," she replied.

"And Lionel? You don't live with him? Is he still here?"

"Yes, but he's married now. I'm doing some work for the governor. I just didn't want to move in with Lionel when he has a new bride."

There was a brief pause, and it seemed his eyes searched hers keenly for a moment.

"And you? Are you engaged?" he asked.

She laughed nervously. "Engaged? No. Why?"

"I thought—" He indicated Lord Ormsby who watched from the other side of the ballroom, then shrugged. "It seems you have no lack of suitors."

She looked at him wondering, but his face was bland. "Deric, what are you doing here?" she asked, still feeling like she must be dreaming.

"Some urgent business brought me."

Something inside her seemed to burst—a great, rosy bubble that had swelled when she'd seen his face at the door. For a few precious moments, she'd thought—known—that he'd come to find her. But business . . .

"Business. I—I should have guessed," she stammered, blushing at the fool she was making of herself, hoping her feelings didn't show too obviously in her face.

He was here on business! He hadn't come to find her, he didn't care. He had never cared!

"Juli, I need to talk to you," she realized he was saying. "I'll explain everything, but it's delicate and a rather long story. I need to see you alone—quite alone. I need your help."

"Why would you need *my* help?" she managed.

The last strains of the waltz sounded, and he bowed over her hand. "Here comes that fair-haired chap, and he looks determined. Meet me on the terrace in twenty minutes. And, Juli, if you don't, I swear I'll cause a scandal by climbing in your bedroom window tonight!"

She was left standing there, stunned, as he kissed her hand and walked away. Then Lord Ormsby joined her, to lead her onto the floor. She smiled at him mechanically and let herself be led, feeling like a marionette.

Deric's smile vanished as he crossed the room to stand at the row of French doors that lined the terrace. He adjusted his cravat, feeling terribly uncomfortable in the binding suit. Through the crowd he caught a glimpse of Juliette in the arms of Lord Ormsby and experienced a quick stab of jealousy when she smiled at the young lord.

Gruffly, he pushed open the French doors and stepped out onto the terrace. There he lit a cigar and puffed angry clouds of smoke into the cool night air.

Chapter Thirty

Juliette walked out onto the moonlit terrace, at least fifteen minutes late for her rendezvous with Deric. It had been very difficult to escape from Lord Ormsby, who was indeed determined to get her alone. Only by pleading the need to retire for a few moments had she shaken him at last, without hearing his proposal. Then she'd had to wait until his back was to her before sneaking across the ballroom and making it out a terrace door unobserved.

And now where was Deric?

He was watching her from the shadows near the railing, and for a moment, he didn't move, taking in the elegant vision she made in her elaborate ball dress, hair piled high, pearls glowing against her graceful neck. He took a deep breath and tossed his cigar away, glad he'd had these few moments to regain some control. He'd been half on fire from holding her during their dance, half burning with unreasonable anger at the sight of her dancing with another man. It had taken more than a few deep breaths to regain a measure of control, but an ember of jealousy was still smoldering.

He stepped out of the shadows.

She turned and saw him, and felt his eyes sweeping over her like a hot wind.

He crossed his arms on his chest. "How was your dance with your lord?" The words were a lazy, insolent drawl.

Stung, she stared angrily back at him. "He's not *my* lord," she replied. He wanted her help—but that didn't stop him from being insulting! She felt her temper rising at the thought that not only had this man walked out of her life without a backward glance . . . now he came back and mocked her about a man who at least treated her with *respect!* She strode to the balcony rail and snapped open her fan, then fanned herself rapidly as she stared out over the gardens.

"So this Lord Ormsby . . . I suppose he's courting you?"

"Yes, and everyone thinks he means to propose to me tonight, so you can see it would not do to have him discover me on the terrace with another man," she said, nettled.

"And you mean to accept him?"

She turned searching eyes on Deric. There had been an unmistakable note of suppressed anger in his voice. Could he be jealous . . . could it matter to him? But his face was as unreadable as ever.

She avoided answering him. "I cannot be absent much longer. No doubt, Lord Ormsby will come looking for me. If you have something—"

"Will you accept his offer?" he interrupted.

"It doesn't concern you," she said frigidly.

"I know, but it concerns the business proposal I have to talk to you about. If you are to marry shortly, perhaps leave Malta, it could change my proposal to you."

"I see." Juliette indeed saw. Jealous? When would she learn to stop being a fool where Deric was concerned? He couldn't care less if she was going to marry, except as it affected his business proposals!

Incensed, she said, "I imagine I *should* accept him, if he asks me. Everyone tells me I'd be mad not to. Besides being very handsome, he's wealthy. And of course—he *is* a lord." She said the words to hurt him and was glad when she saw his mouth tighten.

"So you mean to marry him—just because he's a good catch?"

The words were heavy with sarcasm, sounding like they were gritted out through clenched teeth. She stared at him through her lashes for a long moment before turning and presenting a cold profile to him.

"If I marry, it will be because of how the man makes me feel—not for his money," she said icily, refusing to look at him. How dare he question her motives? Imply that she would marry Lord Ormsby for his position—not that she *was* going to marry him, but at least—

Warm hands fell on her bare shoulders.

She felt herself being turned irresistibly around. Startled, she was pulled against the length of his hard body.

"Does he make you feel like this?" he demanded.

For a moment, he stared down at her, eyes dark as a stormy sea, mouth a slash, jaw set. Then his head came down and his lips closed over hers in a harsh kiss that was punishing in its possessiveness. His arms locked around her like steel and pressed her so tightly against him she could hardly breathe. He was almost violent, like a primitive savage staking his claim to her, taking her kiss whether she wanted to give it or not, not caring if she struggled, if he hurt her.

She did struggle—after a moment. But first a wild thrill went all through her as his arms encircled her and his lips met hers, crushing her almost bared breasts against his chest. For just a moment, she surrendered to his mastery, letting herself mold softly against his hardness, as a passion leapt between them which seemed to make every cell of her body crackle into flames.

Then she twisted wildly in his arms, fighting against his grasp. She shoved herself backward, freeing her lips from his kiss, and her hand came up as she slapped him across the cheek with a resounding blow.

"How dare you, Deric Raleigh?" she gasped. "How dare you treat me like that? Do you think all these months I've just been—*waiting* for you to come back so I can fall into your arms again?" The words were all too close to the humiliating truth. He'd done exactly that—walked out of her life, then casually back into it. And instead of being cold to him, in moments he had her aching for his kisses! Furious at him and at herself, she finished, "I may have fallen into your arms once—but I won't be such a fool twice!"

He stared at her, the fury in her eyes answered in his. His hands dropped to his sides and were jammed in his pockets.

"You still haven't answered my question. Does he do that to you? Are you as passionate with him as you were once with me?"

The words were like a slap. Her cheeks burned, but at the same time she felt a perverse thrill at his words. So he *was* jealous of her! It was obvious he hated the thought of her kissing another man. She took a deep breath and tried to steady herself, wrenching her eyes from his compelling—and heat-making—gaze.

"That doesn't deserve an answer," she said. "You—I believe you brought me out here for a reason. You wanted my help? If you expect me to stay and listen, stop insulting me—and keep your hands off me. I've done my best to forget all that."

He didn't need to know she'd been unable to forget. Maybe her cold words would stop him from kissing her again, because if he did, God help her, she might not be able to resist him.

There was a long silence, during which she almost held her breath. She stared into the garden, unable to meet his eyes, afraid of what she might see in them.

After what seemed an eternity, he spoke. "Very well. I'll keep my hands off you." His voice sounded tight, as if he spoke with an effort. "But you still haven't answered my question. Are you going to marry this lord or not?"

That made her turn and look at him in astonishment. "Why do you keep asking me? What does it have to do with this mysterious business proposal?"

"Everything. If you're going to be married, then I can't ask you to leave."

"Leave?" Her heart began to beat faster. "With—with you?"

"With me." His gaze searched her face, then dropped to her dress and swept over her. "Though you look damned—pretty in that dress, I was hoping that under it some of the old Juli still exists. The one who rides like a soldier and shoots straight."

"Why?" Her words were a whisper.

"Because I want you to ride off with me on an adventure—this time of your own free will."

"An adventure? What—what are you going to do?"

That reckless green gaze held hers captive. "I'm going to rescue Halide," he said. "And I need your help."

Chapter Thirty-One

That evening, Juliette paced up and down in her bedroom, her thoughts in turmoil. She pulled the sash of her dark red wrapper tighter and bit her lip, looking around at the room as if searching for some clue that would help her come to her decision. She felt at the mercy of conflicting emotions: fear, elation, caution, recklessness.

A warm breeze came in the opened latticed windows from the governor's gardens below. She felt safe in these rooms; in her time here, the mansion had become her home. There was the beautiful old rosewood furniture she had come to love so well. There stood the writing table near the window, littered with papers and books. She loved the room, the muted sea-green walls set off by white trim and soft landscape paintings. Here she had found peace and a sense of worth that came from doing a man's job for the governor—and doing it well.

And yet she had not been content. Oh, happy enough, it was true, when she compared her present situation to her other alternatives: live with Lionel and Anne, or marry.

But there had been the restlessness. It was as if her time in the harem and her time on the caravan had changed her forever, changed her beyond the point of going back to who she was before. As terrifying as the harem had been, it had brought out a side of her that she never knew existed. She remembered the desperate fascination of those days of plotting to escape: learning to school her face so that no one could read what she was thinking or feeling; learning to judge the secret happenings in the harem by reading the lift of an eyebrow, the way someone held their shoulders, by who was being insolent to whom, by who talked to whom in the baths. It had been a secret world, a dangerous world, a world of intrigue.

And there was a part of Juliette that had liked that.

Then there was the caravan through the desert: the daily challenge of keeping up with the men, of proving her worth and her battles of will with Deric; the free feeling of mounting her horse and turning her face to the morning breeze, hearing her comrades praising Allah; feeling her rifle secure against her thigh, riding into the wind with a wild exhilaration as her burnoose cracked like rifle shots.

There was something fierce and rebellious in Juliette's heart, something that refused to accept that a life of dull boredom was the lot of a woman, all she could ever hope for. It was the part of Juliette that had sent her to the Mediterranean in the first place. It was the part that had helped her survive her times of captivity with her will and her sanity intact, her spirit unbowed. And it was that part that these last months, had been bored to death.

Now Deric was back, and she was no longer bored.

Her reckless streak was taking over now—had been ever since Deric had said the words, "I have spoken to Aznan . . ."

Aznan, Halide's husband, was offering a fortune to anyone who could effect his wife and son's escape. And word had reached him from his spies in the palace that the trader, Dahkir, had bought a slave from Oman's harem.

So he'd sent for Deric and had been disappointed to find he no longer had the "slave." He was desperate for news of his wife and son . . . and even more desperate to get them out, because he loved them, and because then he could fight his brother for the throne.

He'd offered Deric a fortune to find Juliette, and more if together they could think of a plan to release Halide and Ismail. With her inside knowledge of the harem and Deric's prowess, Aznan felt they might succeed where others had failed.

She thought of the way Deric's eyes had blazed as he'd spoken of the adventure—and of the fortune they'd all earn when they succeeded. He was sure they could find a way.

The trouble was, it could never work. There was no way into or out of the harem, and she knew it.

She sat down at the writing desk and briskly took out a piece of paper and pen. She would do as Deric asked and write down everything she remembered about life inside the harem. Then she'd draw the maps he wanted.

Maybe then an idea would present itself. She knew from the light she'd seen in Deric's eyes that nothing would stop him from trying this adventure. But no escape attempt, she knew, could succeed without help from the inside.

"From the inside," she wrote swiftly. "Who?"

A chill ran down her spine as the germ of an idea came to her.

Halide and her son had to be warned of the escape attempt in advance. Otherwise it was too risky. But how could they contact Halide? If they tried to bribe a guard, chances were the guard would reveal the plan to the sultan. And Halide would never trust a guard or anyone they could contact. There were too many plots in the harem. She might risk herself, but she would never risk her son.

But she would trust me.

With a shiver, Juliette put the thought from her mind and went back to drawing maps. A few moments later, she stopped.

She had it!

The window! There was a window in the harem that opened—just one. It was in one of the high upstairs rooms reached by a small staircase that Juliette had found when playing hide-and-seek with Ismail. She well remembered her delight at being able to lean out the small window and look down on the dizzying view below, while breathing deeply of the air. It had been a momentary illusion of freedom, to find a window that was not barred.

It was clear why it was unbarred. Below the window, the wall dropped for a hundred feet, and below the sheer wall, the face of the cliff the palace was built on dropped several hundred more. There was no way to reach the small window from below.

But it could be reached from the roof above.

If a rope could be lowered . . . and if someone inside could get Halide and Ismail to the window at the right time.

Would the sultan buy her back?

It was a chilling thought, and she swallowed. If he would—then there was a way to get Halide out of the harem. Suddenly she could see it as clearly as if it had already happened.

The sultan's dark face rose briefly before her, and she swallowed, feeling a *frisson* of revulsion. What if he wouldn't buy her back?

What if Deric wouldn't agree to what she thought would work?

She frowned. If she decided it was the only way that would work—she'd *make* him agree. Or she wouldn't give him the harem plans he needed. A less sure plan would result in death—not just for Deric, but for his friend Farouk, who he said would help with the escape. And maybe for Halide and Ismail, too.

But if she could get back in . . . it could be done.

But then, so many things could go wrong, she thought.

When she had left the harem, Halide and Ismail had been free inside the harem confines. With Aznan now actively raising an army to try to get his throne back, they could be confined to their quarters, guarded more closely. If that was the case, she would have to escape the harem without Halide. But it would be hard to leave her behind.

What if . . .

"The sultan could send for me," Juliette wrote, again underlining the words. She shuddered at the thought. If anything prevented their escape on the first night she was back in the harem, then she would have to submit to him if he wanted to make love to her. It was a fact she had to face. Could she risk that, even to save her friend Halide?

But there was another, more serious danger she had to consider. What if something happened and Deric and Farouk were caught while she was inside the harem? They would be executed, and she would probably be slain with them. If she wasn't executed, they might sell her on the slave block, throw her in a rat-infested dungeon, or simply keep her forever in the harem. She could become the sultan's plaything, at the mercy of sadistic slaves like Giza.

Forever.

"It is clear that no escape attempt has a chance to succeed

without inside help." she wrote, and stared at the words. If she did not help, Deric would try anyway. She knew he would never give up easily on a chance at an adventure—and a fortune. Without her help, the risks were so great it dried her mouth to even think about them—not just for Deric, but for Halide and Ismail. She thought of Halide helping her when, if not for her help and friendship, she might have gone mad. Perhaps killed herself. *I may owe my life to Halide,* she thought.

But the picture that haunted her the most was one of Deric in a filthy dungeon cell, Deric kneeling, the executioner's blade poised above his head. . . .

If it was courting disaster for her to go back into the harem, how much more perilous it seemed for her to allow him to try it without her!

Juliette stared at the stars out the window and thought how it would feel to see those stars once more from behind bars. *But this time, it will be different. This time, Deric will be on the outside. And as long as Deric is not caught, I stand a good chance of saving my friend Halide.*

"I will go to Tripoli," Juliette resolved. "And let the rest depend on what we find when we get there." She'd faced dangers before and could stand facing them again. The hardest part, no doubt, would be to convince Deric to accept this plan.

But what of the danger she faced from Deric himself?

Seeing him again had made her realize the truth. No matter how hard she'd tried to forget him, she'd only been fooling herself. During the day, she'd only managed to put him out of her thoughts by forcing them away from him at least twenty times a day.

But at night . . .

She'd tossed and turned, haunted by a green-eyed ghost. When at last sleep came, too often she'd wake from heated dreams in which Deric was entwined with her in bed, his hands sliding over her naked skin. . . .

Her dreams were telling her what her mind refused to admit during the day.

A rogue he might be, who could love her and then leave her—but a rogue she couldn't forget. A fool she might be, not to see she meant nothing to him, but her heart was stubborn and refused not to thrill at his very glance. And her body was a traitor, refusing not to melt at his merest touch.

Whether she denied it or not, Deric had captured her heart and held it. Whether she wanted to admit it or not, she'd fallen in love with him the moment she'd first fallen down that damned dune and found herself confronted by a pair of angry green eyes.

But he hadn't come back here for her.

Juliette knew then that all along a part of her had been waiting for him to do just that—come back for her. A part of her hadn't been able to believe he could forget what had once existed between them when she couldn't.

And he'd come. But he'd come because he needed her help in making a fortune.

Was the reason she was deciding to go just so she could be with him once more? Because if that was the reason, she was the greatest fool ever born.

She shook her head. If she went, it was to help Halide, she told herself—wasn't it?—not because for a few more precious weeks, she'd be with the man she loved. Not at all.

She smiled bitterly as she picked up her silver-backed brush and sat down at her dressing table to give her hair a hundred strokes. Well, whatever her motives, she was going to do it. So what was the use of wondering why?

Chapter Thirty-Two

A week later, Juliette sat next to Margaret as their open carriage bowled through the streets. They were on a shopping expedition that was part of the deception she was using to explain her imminent departure.

She glanced at Margaret's profile, shaded under a wide picture hat, and thought of how hard it was to deceive her—and Sir John. But it had been hard enough to convince them she should be allowed to go to Tripoli at all. Margaret had been quite faint at the thought of traveling without a proper chaperone, and Sir John had actually cursed for the first time in her memory.

If they knew she was thinking of going back into the harem—!

They would probably turn her over to Lionel, and she wouldn't put it past him to have her locked in her room.

Really, it wasn't fair. She was over twenty-one and had spent months surviving dangers during her kidnapping much worse than this one. And she was hardly an innocent any more either, thanks to Deric Raleigh.

But they all acted as if she were a weak flower which had to be sheltered, just because she was a woman. Really, what choice did she have but to lie?

She sighed, half exasperated, half sad she couldn't take the Wrights into her confidence about going back into the harem.

If she did go back in. Deric was being impossible about it. Oh, he'd wanted her to come to Tripoli all along, to be on the spot while he and Farouk planned the escape. But he'd exploded when she'd told him her plan. It had taken her an hour of arguing and all her stubbornness to get him to even admit her plan *might* work.

Still, he insisted they go to Tripoli and see what they found before anything was decided.

Pulling her thoughts from Deric, she reflected it had been a week of arguments. The silly one over the chaperone had taken up the most time. Good God, why was that so important when the Wrights knew she'd spent months alone with Deric before?

"It's not your judgment I question, Juliette," Margaret had said firmly. "It's your reputation I'm worried about."

"Do you think I care about my reputation when there's a chance to free Halide?" she'd countered.

"Well, if you don't, you should," declared Margaret roundly.

"I agree," had come a voice from the doorway, and they'd all turned to find Deric standing there, looking the sober picture of respectability in a charcoal-gray suit. His eyes had caught hers for a moment with a glint in them, then a mask of seriousness descended over his expression.

His courtly good manners during the subsequent hours of talk had left her almost speechless. This was a Deric Raleigh she hadn't seen before . . . one who could behave like a duke when he put his mind to it!

At last, the Wrights had been swayed, in large part because of Deric's grave, respectable act. He and Sir John had spent hours discussing how important Aznan's interests were to the British army here. That was what had convinced Sir John. Margaret? It had taken promising to lie to everyone to protect Juliette's reputation.

Margaret protested that Juliette couldn't just pick up and leave Malta with no explanation given of where she was going. It would cause too much talk. When Juliette had suggested saying she was going back to England for a visit, Margaret had wondered what would happen if Lord Ormsby decided to follow her there? Throwing a hasty glance at Deric, Juliette had said she thought that was hardly likely.

"I think it very likely," Margaret had declared, "for a more determined suitor I have never seen."

She'd shot another glance at Deric but read nothing in his eyes, except perhaps there was a trace of flint in them? Finally they'd all decided it was best to put it about that Juliette was joining a school friend and her family in Italy, and would travel with them for a time. Her itinerary would be unsettled, so the Wrights would declare they had no idea exactly where she might be. They also agreed to keep up the fiction to Lionel. All of them knew he'd never approve of the truth.

Deric had told her to go shopping and buy clothes for such a trip. He'd take care of getting everything she needed for their real trip. In a week's time, she was to meet him on the docks. They'd cross in a ship and meet Deric's caravan a short distance from Tripoli so their arrival in that city would be unsuspicious.

Now, as their carriage pulled up in front of a row of shops, they heard a hail from the street. Juliette saw Lord Ormsby hurrying across the crowded street to their carriage's side. He reached them and stood in the street, looking up at them, a delighted smile in his eyes when they rested on Juliette.

"Good morning, Lady Margaret—Miss Hawkins! Pleasure to see you! What brings you into town?"

"Shopping, what else? Good morning, Lord Ormsby," said Margaret, smiling at him.

"Yes—I have been raiding the shops in such a hurry," said Juliette, glad they'd run into him. It was the perfect chance to tell him she was leaving. "I've had the most exciting news. I've been invited to join some friends who are traveling on the continent. I'm going to Italy, but I have to be ready to leave by the end of the week!" She smiled at him as if she were tremendously excited by the news.

"You—you are leaving?" Lord Ormsby stared up at her as if he could not believe his ears. Juliette made a pretense of tightening a glove carefully, pretending not to see the distress in his eyes.

"Yes, almost immediately. It is so fortunate to run into you this way. Lady Wright and I were planning to call on you to tell you the news, and beg your forgiveness that I will not be able to attend the ball on Friday. But I must take ship at the end of the week if I am to catch my friends in Italy."

Lord Ormsby stood in the street next to their carriage, his hat in his hand, obviously at a loss of words. "Oh—but, I say! That's—that's too bad! How long do you expect to be gone? I—I'm dashed disappointed you have to leave so quickly," Ormsby stammered.

"I'm not certain yet, Lord Ormsby, about the length of my visit. Some months, I would expect," Juliette said coolly. She almost felt sorry for Ormsby, so taken aback did he look at her answer.

"Some months! I—that is, I had hoped to call on you on Thursday morning—counted on it! A chance for a word with you alone—" Again Ormsby blushed at his boldness and lack of delicacy in alluding to being alone with her. But dash it, this was so sudden, and he was sure she couldn't know he meant to propose to her, otherwise she would never be planning to leave like this!

"I am afraid Juliette will be much too busy to receive any callers before she sails, Lord Ormsby," put in Margaret smoothly, but with kindness in her voice. She sympathized with what he must be feeling, but really—! To allude so indelicately to being alone with Juliette, it was too much! "You have no idea the tizzy we've been thrown into, trying to see that she has everything she needs before she sails! I am quite distracted, I assure you. In fact, it was our good fortune that we found you just now. It will save us some time this morning, which we are sorely in need of. Don't fret, my lord. I feel sure our dear Miss Hawkins will be back in Malta before we know it!"

Juliette threw Margaret a grateful look. She put out her hand for Lord Ormsby to shake, saying with a smile, "It has been a pleasure knowing you these last months, Lord Ormsby. Thank you for all your kindnesses. I am sure I will see you when I return."

As Ormsby shook her hand, frantic thoughts sped through his mind. This couldn't be happening—so quickly! She would never be so calm if she had the least idea she was missing a chance at being Lady Ormsby by leaving on this dashed journey! Ormsby simply couldn't imagine any girl not being bowled over by a marriage proposal from him, and scrambling to accept it. For too many years his looks and his title had ensured that he was energetically pursued by marriage-minded females.

"I *said,* we must make our farewells, Lord Ormsby," came the voice of Lady Margaret for the second time, breaking him out of his thoughts.

"Oh—our farewells—yes, of course. I—I wish you a safe journey, Miss Hawkins, and a speedy return. Malta will miss you very much." His eyes said that it was not only Malta who would miss her. Juliette smiled at him once again, Margaret rapped on the coach with her parasol, and the coach started forward with a jerk, leaving Lord Ormsby staring after them mournfully.

"Well," exclaimed Margaret crisply, with a little smile, as she reached up and adjusted her enormous feathered hat to her satisfaction. "That certainly threw *him* for a loop! He was heartbroken, anyone could see that! But I won't say a word about Lord Ormsby and what might have been. You don't love him and that's that. Now let me see, where must we go next? Ah yes, to the milliner's! They have a shipment of new hats this week, I'm told." She threw Juliette a glance from under the brim of her hat, trying to read the girl's face.

"And I can see why you don't love Ormsby," she went on, seeming to instantly forget she'd just promised not to talk of him. "Though he is very handsome, with his impeccable manners one always knows exactly how he will behave. And we women seem to have a soft spot for more unpredictable men. Now, Deric Raleigh—there's a man one could call handsome and unpredictable, I think."

Juliette forced herself not to look at Margaret but to keep staring out the window. Damn Margaret! Sometimes she was very perceptive under her line of insouciant chatter. She strove for a casual tone as she answered, "Yes, I think one could call him very unpredictable indeed." There! Said with just the right note of indifference, she hoped.

But all illusion that she might have fooled Margaret—Margaret who was like a hound with her nose to the trail whenever an affair of the heart was concerned—vanished as

Margaret answered, "Just the type of man, in fact, that one could easily fall in love with, I would imagine. So handsome, so brave, so daring! Particularly if one were rescued by him in a rather *dramatic* way!"

"Margaret—" began Juliette, turning to look at her friend at last.

"Don't say it! Don't say a word to me! I just would be *very* surprised, that's all, if you haven't developed some tenderer feelings for Mr. Raleigh, my dear. Why, I could scarcely believe my eyes when he walked through the door! So tall and so very, very handsome, my dear! Why, if I were younger myself—! And to think he was the man who rescued you from the harem, and then you spent so much time with him on that caravan journey . . . well, *now* I can say I don't really wonder why you haven't looked at the men I've been throwing at you lately. Even if you are not in love with Mr. Raleigh, they would seem very boring—almost like boys, I would imagine—beside someone like him. Are you in love with him, Juliette?"

"In love with Deric Raleigh!" Juliette protested, then cautioned herself to cool off. After all, she had portrayed Deric to Margaret as her brave and gallant rescuer from the harem. She could never tell her now how Deric had taken advantage of her, used her—and never loved her at all. "Of course I'm not in love with him, Margaret. I admit he is handsome, but . . . I find him too arrogant for my liking. I don't think he respects women!" she finished, hoping her indignation had convinced Margaret.

"Respects women?" Margaret looked at her quizzically, then laughed. "Of course he probably doesn't, my dear. Most men don't until they are taught to . . . by being in love. Before that, women are conquests to them, playthings . . . or nuisances. But from what I saw of Mr. Raleigh, I would say that he respects *you.*"

"Would you? Why?" asked Juliette quickly, then cursed herself for her eagerness. Margaret would see right through her if she continued being this transparent. In fact, she probably already had! But did it really matter? Perhaps she should take Margaret into her confidence, at least part of the way. She could use the older woman's advice, which was always wise on the subject she cared most about—men.

"Because of the way he looked at you, dear, as if you were one of his—comrades! Certainly not as if he thought you were a silly girl. Even *I* could see that there was a mutual trust between the two of you, as if you'd shared some difficult times in the past and learned to rely on one another."

"Really?" said Juliette, pleasure brightening her face and warming her heart, and she didn't even care if it showed. Could it be true that Deric had grown to respect her in those months on the caravan?

"Yes, really," said Margaret decisively.

"I—I am not in love with him, Margaret, really I am not. But I confess that I feel *something* for him. You're right, we did go through a lot together on that journey." She didn't dare to meet Margaret's eyes, afraid of what her own eyes might be showing as she said that sentence. "But he can be so—so *infuriating* sometimes! Cold, and sarcastic, and—mean! There are as many times that I hate him as times that I like him. But none of that matters. I am sure he is not . . . in love with me, and I don't want to fall in love with him! He is too changeable, too wild. He would break my heart like a toy. So I must merely be businesslike with him, and he with me, that's all. Halide's escape is what really matters."

"I see," said Margaret thoughtfully, her eyes bright with sympathy. And she did see more than Juliette thought she had revealed. She saw that Juliette knew she was perilously close to falling in love with this man. But she wasn't sure her heart could be trusted to him. She was afraid he was a wild rover, who would take the gift of her love for a time, then leave it behind without a second thought—leaving Juliette behind, too, broken-hearted. Why did women always fall for the rakes and the rogues, to their heartbreak? Margaret wondered. She sighed. *Perhaps it is our lot,* she thought.

But *was* Deric Raleigh a rake and a rogue? She didn't know enough about him to answer the question. She had warmed to him at once—but then, he was so handsome, and Margaret knew she had always had a soft corner in her heart for a handsome scoundrel. Poor Juliette! Not only was she going to risk her reputation on this journey—but she was going to risk her heart as well!

Then Margaret smiled a small smile. Ever the optimist when it came to romance, she thought of the way she'd seen Mr. Raleigh's eyes rest on Juliette. He might not be a lord, but he was so *very* tall and handsome.

If she came back married from this journey, her reputation wouldn't have been at risk after all. He might be a rogue . . . but didn't they say a reformed rake made the best husband?

Chapter Thirty-Three

Juliette leaned over the rail near the bow of the *Merry Chase* and stared at the sea. A fine mist of spray blew in her face, and there was a good stiff breeze today. The small ship rolled on the waves, not too violently, and they were making good headway. How good it felt to be sailing with the wind once again along the coast of North Africa!

The sea was a deep blue unique to the Mediterranean, with glimpses of green and even purple in the shifting waves. Overhead the sky was a heartbreakingly high, clear blue with trailing wisps of white clouds far above. The coast was a dark smudge on the edge of the horizon. The thought crossed her mind of her first voyage on the Mediterranean, and how that had ended. She shivered. She hoped that this time, her journey would end better.

They would reach the city of Zaafran, down the coast from Tripoli, on the second day. After she'd boarded this morning, she'd been shown to her quarters, a small cabin snuggled below the quarterdeck.

Neatly stowed on her bed and on the floor had been several soft leather bags. Curious, Juliette had unpacked her own small bag and turned to the other bags. This must be what Deric had outfitted her with for the journey.

Indeed, she thought, as she lifted out items, he had forgotten nothing. To her pleasure, there were breeches, a burnoose, some caftans and some shirts. A pair of tall riding boots and pairs of slippers were also included.

Something gleamed dully at the bottom of the clothes bag. She pulled it out. Beneath a black yashmak that would cover her from head to foot and make her indistinguishable from any other Arab woman, there was a soft, diaphanous dress. It was of translucent green material shot through with a leaf pattern in silver threads. There was a silver veil with a green twisted headband to bind it, and a pile of clinking silver jewelry: armbands, necklaces, earrings, ankle bracelets.

She stared solemnly at the outfit. So Deric was willing to admit she might actually have to go back inside.

With something like a shiver, she finished her unpacking and hastily climbed to the deck. It was all at once too confined in her cabin; she wanted the air.

For half an hour, she stood, staring at the sea, before a footstep made her turn. Deric joined her silently, not saying anything for a few moments, and she felt a companionable ease in his company. There had been times like this on the caravan, when they'd been able to ride for hours at each other's side, not saying anything . . . but it seemed they understood each other's thoughts. At moments like this, she thought, she could have wished the ship was leaving to sail around the world. . . .

"Beautiful, isn't it?" he said at last.

"Yes . . . I love being at sea." She paused. "Thank you for the clothes. They all fit well."

"Just part of enlisting in Aznan's cause. There's no need to thank me. As for the fit—I guessed from memory."

Something in his tone made her want to change the subject. This was dangerous ground. "The . . . green dress. Is that what I will wear when I go back into the harem?"

His eyes, as dark green as the waves, pierced hers. "*If* you go back in, you mean. There may be some other way . . . a less dangerous way."

"No other way that will work, and you know it. It's just because I'm a woman that you don't like to see me take a risk. If it was you or Farouk who had to go in, why—"

"You're right. I don't like you taking the risk." The words were a disagreeable growl.

She opened her mouth to argue, but something in the way his dark brows were frowning, his jaw set, made her close her mouth again. "Let's not argue about it again. I want to do my best to enjoy this journey—and not look too far ahead if I can." It was true. The very thought of going back inside the harem chilled her, though she would never admit it to the man at her side.

"That's best." He startled her with his curt readiness to drop the argument, adding, "You haven't really had the chance to meet Farouk yet. I've arranged that we all dine together tonight, so you two will have a chance to get to know each other."

"Good. I'll look forward to that." When she'd boarded the ship, she'd briefly been introduced to Farouk. She'd liked him at once. He had merry dark eyes, a sweeping moustache and black hair. His dark skin gleamed with health, and he was the picture of vitality, very different from that thin ravaged figure she'd seen on the docks in the arms of Mulay's men. He'd regained his health and strength in the last months.

"Then, I will see you tonight at seven," Deric said, bowing slightly. "I will escort you to the dining quarters if you will allow me."

Juliette's eyes twinkled up at him, amused at his sudden almost courtly formality, his gentlemanly manners. He was treating her like a lady, and it made her want to laugh for some reason. "I will be happy to accept your escort, sir," she said, smiling mischievously at him.

He bowed again, and she watched his broad back as he walked away from her, something almost painful tugging at her heart. She would never have believed she'd miss the old Deric—the one who argued with her, infuriated her, but never treated her with respect. And yet—she wasn't sure she liked the new, gentlemanly version of Deric.

That evening, Juliette put on the only decent dress she had brought along. It was nothing so fine as the rose-and-silver brocade worn for her last shipboard dinner, but it was pretty enough for all its simplicity.

It was of apricot-colored silk with full sleeves that were caught up with pale green ribbons. Another pale-green ribbon wove in and out of the lace at the low round neckline that skimmed her shoulders. The apricot darkened her hair to garnet in the lamplight, and she gave a last anxious glance in the mirror as she heard his soft knock. Suddenly she felt ridiculously nervous as she crossed her room to the door.

He leaned in the doorway, outlined against a flaming sunset. His eyes went over her slowly, bringing a flush of heat to her cheeks. "You look . . . wonderful, Juliette," he said.

"Thank you—I suppose." She strove to sound light, like she would to a flirtatious suitor in a ballroom. But the way he was looking at her made her feel flustered. "How is it that you manage to make even compliments sound indecent? I feared your gentlemanly act was too good to be true!"

"Indecent? I didn't *really* mean it to sound that way . . . though, if you prefer it, I will be happy to stop acting gentlemanly any time you wish." His mouth curved in a slow smile.

"I should have known better than to say anything. Of course I prefer you to act like a gentleman—though I know it's just an act." But secretly she smiled, glad he was acting just a trifle less respectful.

"And I know well how important a man's *manners* are to you."

Was that bitterness in his tone—or was it sarcasm? Was he baiting her about Lord Ormsby again? An uncertain glance at his face told her nothing. Ruffled out of her insouciant act, she managed, "I believe you came here to escort me to dinner, and Farouk is expecting us?"

Silently, he offered his arm, and Juliette took it. As they walked along the deck, she forgot all about Deric as she gazed at the sunset. The whole sky was splashed with red and purple, barred by dark clouds along the western horizon, fading up through violet and palest green to the dome overhead where the evening star burned white. Even as they walked, the savage colors were fading from the sky, growing more muted, and darkness was falling fast.

"Red skies . . . according to the old sailor's saying, that foretells good weather for tomorrow. Good. That means we won't be delayed by any storms, though they can blow up fast. Here we are."

He opened the door to a dining cabin and ushered her in.

Farouk rose from the table.

"Good evening, *effendi*," he said, coming and gallantly bowing over Juliette's hand, then kissing it.

Juliette smiled as he straightened and dropped her hand. "But please—not so formal! If I am to call you Farouk, you must call me by my first name, too."

"Very well . . . then I will call you Juli, with pleasure," he said, pulling out a chair for her.

She turned and gave Deric a quizzing look, her eyebrows raised. He had the grace to look embarrassed. So he'd told Farouk something about her. As the cabin boy came in and poured wine for all of them, she wondered how much.

"So, Dahkir tells me that you are a brave woman, able to face hardships without complaining, and to think coolly in the face of danger. This is good because this plan you have made carries many risks," said Farouk, as the cabin boy moved to the sideboard, starting to set the first course on the table.

"Dahkir! I'd almost forgotten he was called that," said Juliette, then added, "but this plan carries less of a risk with one of us inside. To break in by force would surely end in disaster."

Farouk smiled. "Not by force—by stealth. But please—there is no need to argue. I am on your side. I think your plan is the one that could succeed, and that if you are brave enough to try it, then such daring should not be denied."

"At last, a man who judges a plan on its merits," she cried, throwing Deric a sparkling look of challenge.

But he refused to be drawn . . . in fact, didn't really seem to be listening at all. Piqued, she turned back to Farouk.

"But what a woman, eh, Dahkir?" Farouk winked, getting for his pains a quelling look from Deric that didn't repress him one bit. "One who scares off six Bedouin riders in the middle of a sandstorm—and who leaps on the back of a bolting stallion without a thought for safety. And is a very good shot, I'm told."

Deric scowled, but Juliette glowed. So Deric had told Farouk more than a little about her!

Deric opened his mouth to say something, and hastily, Farouk turned back to her, knowing that black look of old.

"But if you do go in, never fear that we will get you out," he promised her, suddenly grave.

"If we have to rip down the harem walls with our bare hands," came Deric's grim voice.

Juliette's eyebrows rose in surprise. What was wrong with him? He was positively glowering. "Comforting words, I'm sure, but I wouldn't—*won't*—do it unless I think it will work, and . . ."

Deric lost the rest of her remark as his gaze rested darkly on the cabin boy.

There was a look of open admiration on the lad's face as Juliette leaned forward to answer Farouk. Deric scowled and picked up his wineglass, draining the contents abruptly, not even aware of what he was doing. He saw the lad's gaze drop inadvertently to the front of her dress, and then rise again quickly to her face, a faint color staining his cheeks. Deric's own eyes followed the path the lad's had taken, and he cursed under his breath. As Juliette leaned forward, her breasts strained and swelled against the low bodice, creating a deep valley between them. It was a tempting sight—a damned sight *too* tempting for on board a ship with a bunch of randy seamen! Dammit, didn't she know any better than to wear a dress like that in front of men who had been at sea for months? But as she settled back in her chair, and the dress rode back up slightly, he had to admit to himself that it wasn't really a particularly low-cut dress. Too well he remembered her in the ball dress she had worn. Now, *that* one had been cut almost indecently low, with a bodice so form-fitting it left little to the imagination. This dress was far more discreet.

Deric sighed, looking away. It wasn't her fault, really. She was just so beautiful she looked like a temptress no matter *what* she wore. His eyes were fastened on Juliette's face as she laughed and talked. He ground his teeth. It galled him for some reason to see men looking at her that way, whether it was her fault or not! He watched the cabin boy broodingly as he left the room.

As they ate, Juliette looked around herself warmly. She was enjoying this dinner on shipboard, Farouk's laughing talk, and if Deric barely spoke, well, that was his loss! she thought. For all Deric's taciturn manners, she felt free, happy. After the dinner, the men lounged back in their chairs with cigars and brandy, but she stayed. In society, women always had to hustle off after dinner and leave the men alone. Here on a ship, such formality seemed a world away. And this dinner had been far from boring—unlike so many dinners in Malta, where she'd had to stifle yawns or hide them behind her lace fan.

As he leaned back in his chair, Farouk looked meditatively at Juliette. So this was Juli. The woman Dahkir had told him so much about—and at the same time so little. He had told him all about Mulay's blackmail, of course. And other things. The way she'd saved them in the bandit attack. That she'd had spirit and at least had not spent the time wailing and fainting as he'd first feared she would. About the way she'd run off to the harem and he'd had to go get her out so he'd have her to exchange for Farouk.

Yes, many things. But he'd never once mentioned that she was beautiful. Or spoken of what their relationship had been.

Strange, when now that he saw her with his own eyes, she was one of the most beautiful women he'd ever seen. It was strange a man wouldn't mention that fact.

And then there was the odd way he'd behaved ever since the trade and ransom. He'd had the disposition of a camel: black moods all the time, snapping at his men, stalking off to be alone, going days sometimes with barely a growl at anyone.

Now, thought Farouk, looking from one to the other, *maybe I begin to see why. Look at the way they both avoid each other's eyes—but then each looks at the other when they think the other is not looking! And never,* he thought speculatively, *have I seen Dahkir look at a woman the way he is looking at her right now.*

Neither had he missed the way Dahkir had been glowering at that poor cabin boy who'd been gaping at Juli all evening. Why, she'd hardly noticed the way the lad had turned scarlet when she'd spoken kindly to him—but Dahkir had. He'd looked like he was ready to leap on the boy.

Farouk picked up his wine and smiled. This was going to be a very interesting trip, it seemed.

At last, Deric rose to escort Juliette back to her cabin. On the deck, he held out his arm without a word. The sky above was studded with stars, the Milky Way thick above them. The softness of the night air was like a caress, and Juliette breathed deeply, glad to be in the fresh night air and out of the smoky cabin.

After a few moments of silence, Deric said in a tight voice, "That lad—I didn't like the way he was looking at you, Juli. And you were encouraging him by flirting with him! You'll have to be more careful with men in these parts of the world. They haven't been around a young lady such as yourself in months—maybe years. It's all too easy for them to misunderstand your behavior. It's necessary your behavior on this journey be most circumspect, most discreet. You can't flirt as if you're in the governor's ballroom."

Juliette listened with growing disbelief to this lecture, delivered in patronizing tones with a hint of roughness that sounded like anger. When he came to the last sentence, she gave a smothered gasp.

"*What* lad? What on earth are you talking about?"

"The cabin boy! He—"

"I was *not* flirting with him!" she interrupted indignantly. This was ridiculous! She'd barely looked at him! "I was merely being polite—something you, perhaps, do not understand! But for you to accuse me of encouraging him is just too much!"

"If you don't keep your voice lowered, I'll be forced to find some way to silence you—like throwing you overboard! I didn't mean—" Deric was about to apologize, but Juliette swung on him, enraged, before he could get the words out. How dare he lecture her on her behavior!

"Just *try* to throw me overboard! I swear I'll take you over with me! Oh! That's your solution to everything, isn't it—brute force? Well, you can't scare me, Deric Raleigh, into behaving like a meek little—" Juliette gasped as Deric, face darkening with anger, stepped forward and grasped her shoulders roughly.

"You've *never* been meek, have you, Juliette?" he snarled angrily. "I told you I'd find a way to silence you, and so help me God, I will!"

He bent his head toward hers and covered her mouth in a

brusque, suffocating kiss.

And Juliette forgot everything as she surrendered to the authority of his touch. She didn't want to, but her body had a will of its own that made her melt against him.

And he wasn't just kissing her.

She felt his hands at her waist as she was being maneuvered back into the shadows of the deck, half-lifted in the air. He never broke the kiss, and she tightened her arms around his neck as he laid her, half-standing, half-reclining on top of an upside-down lifeboat.

He slipped one knee between her legs, parting them easily, then pulled her to him, driving his hips into hers. He looked down at her and felt his loins tighten. Her head was tilted back, her eyes closed, her lips slightly parted, waiting for his kiss.

His kiss deepened, and his hands moved as if they had a will of their own. He reached for her shoulders, impatiently sliding the sleeves of her gown down, until he could see the bare tops of her breasts above the corset she wore underneath. He was so used to seeing her in loose desert robes, that the sight of her in creamy lace and pink ribbons, feminine and enticing, was a new sensation. He could see a hint of her pale skin through the lace that edged the top of the corset and remembered how soft that skin was.

But the damn corset, as thin as it might be, was in the way.

His fingers fumbled with the ribbons to unlace it, pushing the material away. He heard her breath catch, and she pulled him closer. He revelled in this simple movement. There was nothing he loved more than to feel her responding to his touch.

Then his hands slid up, lifting her skirts, her petticoats, rustling silk and filmy lace, cool and soft beneath his touch—as cool and soft as she would be. The anticipation of feeling her bare skin made him groan. These garments were damned annoying . . . and incredibly arousing. He ran his restless hands along her legs to find satin garters holding her stockings securely in place. Loosening them, he rolled the stockings down, then at last slid his hands back up her bare thighs. They were like silk beneath his fingers, and he moved his hands behind her to grip her firmly.

Juliette gasped at the physical impact of him pressed so

tightly to her. She was half-naked beneath him, feeling his need for her, and wrapped her legs around him to satisfy her need for him. For all the thrills that were racing through her body, he might as well have been making love to her.

The faint sound of someone talking floated down the deck.

She opened her eyes.

The sails were fluttering above her, and she could hear the creaking of the masts; and suddenly, she was aware of where they were and what they were doing. She was lying under him, dress half-off her shoulders, skirts pushed up around her waist!

Desperately, she turned her head as his lips came down and felt his mouth graze her cheek.

"Deric—stop it!" she gasped. "Let me go!"

To her astonishment, his hands dropped from her shoulders, and he pulled away from her.

She could feel his nearness like the heat of the sun, but she didn't dare look up at him. It was all happening too fast, and she needed to think—think before feelings swept her away. No, she couldn't look up at him. So instead she did the one thing that would save her. . . .

She sat up, gathering her loose clothing to her breast, and slid on weak legs to her feet. Then she turned on her heel and ran down the deck to her room, slamming the door behind her.

Chapter Thirty-Four

Deric stared after her as she ran away from him, shaken. Then he walked to the rail and, cursing, gripped it like he would break it with his bare hands.

Her words echoed in his mind, and he heard again the angry, wrenched tones they'd been spoken in—*"Let me go!"*

That I must, he thought, gritting his teeth. But that was going to be hard—damned hard. Like tonight. Just now, when she'd stood before him, gorgeously angry, he hadn't been able to stop himself from kissing her. And even as she'd lain beneath him, her face averted, and pleaded with him—*"Let me go"*—he'd wanted nothing so much as to make love to her! It had taken all of his willpower to pull himself away. His fingers even now remembered the soft feel of her skin, and he clenched the rail even harder.

He swore and wrenched his thoughts from that. Why was he trying to rekindle their love affair? It was over, as she'd said tonight. She'd made that clear.

But it was so hard for him to forget. After he had left her in Tripoli, he'd found her image recurring to him time and time again. He had wondered what she was doing . . . and God help him, longed to hold her in his arms again. But as much as his body ached for her, harder to take had been the emptiness of those months. In such a short time, it seemed she'd become a part of his life. He even missed their fights, her temper, and most of all her sudden smile that could wrap itself around his heart. His tent had seemed as empty as the desert since she'd been gone.

He stared into the water. And it had been worse since he had seen her again. He thought of the ball, how eagerly he'd raced to Tripoli after meeting with Aznan, telling himself it was because of the fortune they could earn, but really—if he was honest with himself—on fire to see her again.

Just to see her again, to—

To what? he asked himself bitterly. To tumble her back into bed and taste that unforgettable passion once more?

Or to ask her the question he'd almost asked her that night in the harem?

He scowled. He'd spent too much damned time these last four months wondering what her answer would have been—if he'd asked. Too much time missing her in an empty tent, too much time riding alone and picturing what it would be like to have her always riding at his side. . . .

That was the hell of it. That picture was nothing more than a fool's fantasy. Having a woman always at your side didn't mean roaming the world like a pair of nomads. It meant a house in one place—for a woman of Juliette's aristocratic background, a capital like London, Paris or Malta. He saw cobblestoned streets crowded with carriages and passersby, himself bored and restless at the opera, walking up a paved walk after another day's work to his well-upholstered prison. . . .

He shuddered.

No, Juli, not even for you.

But he'd have to be careful. Damned careful. It would be far too easy to fall in love with Juliette. In fact, he was already acting like a lovesick fool around her, unable to keep his hands off her, unable to stop thinking about her. Look at the way he'd come so close to asking her to stay that night in the harem. It had been a close call. But then, when he held her close, it seemed like he could never let her go—like nothing else mattered at all.

It's no more than desire, he told himself firmly. He knew damned well what the world called love was just desire that would eventually fade. Hadn't that been the case with Amelia?

No—he was damned glad he'd left it all unspoken. It was obvious Juliette was going to make the kind of marriage that was right for her, and obvious what her reaction would have been.

. . . everyone thinks he means to propose to me tonight . . . I imagine I should accept him if he asks me . . . everyone tells me I would be mad not to. . . .

Her words on the balcony echoed in his mind. Did she love that damned Ormsby? Had he proposed to her that night? But no, she'd come on this trip. *What kind of fool would let the woman he intended to marry come on a trip with a man like me—or leave his side?* he thought angrily.

And then paradoxically: *But if he didn't propose to her, what kind of an idiot was he to let a woman like Juliette slip through his fingers? Or—*

Had he asked her, and she turned him down?

And what does it matter to me? Angrily, Deric tried to shove this train of thought out of his mind. It was an all-too-familiar route his thoughts were taking, and he wanted no more of it. He wanted control back.

I'd better never be alone with her if I can help it, he resolved. But it would be difficult to keep away from her when they were under the stars on a caravan once again. Difficult? It would be hell.

"I need a brandy," Deric growled aloud, and stalked away from the rail, taking a fine temper along.

A few moments later, Farouk looked up as Deric walked into the dining cabin. He lifted his brows at the frown he saw on Deric's face. He watched without comment as Deric grabbed a brandy bottle and poured.

So. It was Miss Juliette, no doubt, mused Farouk, his eyes narrowed and thoughtful. He hadn't seen Dahkir in such a black mood since the days just after he'd left her in Tripoli. *She gets under his skin like the sting of a scorpion,* he thought. *And for some reason, he stays away from her room tonight, though he burns to go there. Perhaps he believes she does not want him—though I saw the way she looked at him, and he's a fool if he thinks that! Ah well, I do not understand them. Why do they deny themselves when it is what they both want? If a woman as beautiful as that wanted me, I'd be in her bed this moment. . . .*

Farouk sighed. He hoped that Juli would soon invite Dahkir

into her bed, because otherwise—he shot another glance at the scowling face of his companion, who was staring without speaking at the floor—this journey would be very unpleasant for everyone!

Juliette sat on the tiny bed in her darkened cabin, her heart still beating too fast whenever she thought of the scene between her and Deric on deck, even though nearly an hour had passed since she'd run into her cabin and slammed the door. At first, she had paced up and down, breast heaving, until she was slightly calmer. Then she had undressed and brushed her hair with vicious, jerking strokes and climbed into bed. She had snuffed the candle and lay, twisting and turning, until at last she had sat up in the darkness. Sleep was far off.

How dare he! she thought, angry all over again. First to accuse her of flirting with that poor boy, when she had hardly spoken to him all evening! And then—to try to make love to her as if he expected that she'd fall into his arms again after he'd left her without a backward glance before. Well, Mr. Deric Raleigh was going to have to learn she wasn't going to be such a fool twice!

But it was obvious she was more than weak where he was concerned. One kiss and he'd practically taken her there on the deck! Why did he have the power to blind her to all else but him?

All evening she'd barely been able to take her eyes off of him. At one point, she'd found herself staring at his arm, the shape of it, the way his muscles moved under his shirt, and been aware that forbidden memories of his magnificent naked body were assaulting her mind. . . .

Was she so easily angered at Deric because he'd taken her to his bed, and then been able to forget her?

He doesn't treat me with any respect, she argued to herself. *It's not that I'm easily angered . . . not that I'm holding a grudge because he left me . . .*

Respect women? . . . most men don't until they are taught to by love . . .

Margaret had told her that. And then she had added, *But he respects you, my dear.*

She frowned. Why Margaret had said that she didn't know. Deric Raleigh had treated her with a fine contempt since the beginning. Hadn't he tied her up? Made her his prisoner without telling her why? Let her believe he was a pirate?

And then swept her into his bed when he'd felt a need for a woman—and swept her out again when that need had been fulfilled?

All he'd done was desire her the way he'd desire any woman, she told herself. There was, she thought wryly, no doubt he desired her.

Unbidden, she saw again the tenderness in his eyes during the blissful week they'd spent together in Bu Ngem. The way he'd held her like she was precious, laughed with her, been her friend, paid her the compliment of seeking her opinion, listening to her—that week she had believed she'd seen love in his eyes.

She had been so sure he'd loved her then, she'd been confidently planning how to break the news to Lionel she was marrying a desert trader.

And then he'd changed, become cold. She'd never understood why, but hurt pride had whispered it was because he'd tired of her, had never loved her at all. Well, maybe he hadn't and she'd been wrong. Ever since, she'd alternated between hurt and anger, her feelings warring with her pride.

He desired her, it was true. But could he love her?

At this thought, Juliette sat up straighter in bed, staring across the tiny cabin with unseeing eyes, fingers fidgeting with the bedspread edge.

Once—he had loved her. That magical time they'd spent—or at least, she cautioned herself, trying to dampen the sudden hope she was feeling, he'd cared.

But for some reason, his feelings had cooled.

Or had they?

A small thrill whispered down her spine as she saw again the angry passion in his green eyes tonight, the way his mouth had been drawn with desire. He still wanted her. But could he ever love her?

She was stilled by the thought. She thought of life back in

Malta, of Lionel, of Anne. She thought of what it would be like to marry a man like Lord Ormsby and stand at his side, brilliant in brocade, feathers and diamonds in her hair and long gloves on her arms, endlessly gracious. Could she stand endlessly by his side in glittering ballrooms, at political dinners, politely receiving him for his visits to her grand and formal bedroom . . . enduring the lack of passion because it was her duty, because it might bring her children to fill the lonely places in her heart? . . .

And then she thought of the way Deric's mere glance falling on her made her feel alive.

She thought with a shiver of how dull—unbearable—life had been these last four months without him.

She made her decision. He might never come to love her. He might want no more of her than the pleasure her body gave him, but if there was a chance he could love her—

Because without Deric at her side life would be an empty show. She loved him with her whole heart and soul.

Besides. She smiled in the dark. *Juliette Hawkins, give up without a fight?*

Never.

Chapter Thirty-Five

Juliette shifted the rifle that hung behind her saddle to a more secure position and put her heels lightly to her mare's side. It was morning, and the caravan was on its way.

She glanced down the line to where Farouk was riding and smiled at him, lifting a hand. He smiled back, a wide grin that warmed her heart. How nice Farouk was, with his eyes that looked on life with an almost madcap zest, his ready laughter and his courteous tongue. No wonder he and Deric were such good friends—no wonder Deric had been so determined to do anything to free him from Mulay.

Farouk, spurring his horse along the line, rode up to her and slowed at her side. "So—this must all seem familiar to you. It's good you're already used to the desert. Many English find it hard to bear when first they come out here," he said, waving his hand to take in the endless dunes. "No green, like your land. They say England is very green."

"It is. You should see the grass there, and the trees, Farouk! And it rains almost all the time, sometimes for weeks on end, and the skies are always gray. We almost never see the sun."

"Then I do not know if I would like it there," he said, grinning. "Though I would like to see a place with so much rain. Here, rain is precious, and everyone runs out to stand in a downpour."

She smiled. "There, we hide from the rain and sit inside, staring dismally out the windows and wishing for the sun."

"Do you miss it there—your home?" he asked after a moment, studying her curiously.

She sighed. "Sometimes. I find that sometimes I do miss the green and the rain. But I've also come to love this part of the world. Strange, isn't it, after all that's happened to me here? But if I may miss a cloudy day sometimes, I don't really miss life in England. It was sometimes—very dull."

"And now Dahkir has seen to it that your life is maybe too exciting again? Are you not afraid?" His eyes searched her face, and she saw kindness and concern there for her. "They *say* it is harder to be a spy even than to be a prisoner . . . keeping secrets, waiting, always in fear. It is a brave thing you do, Juli."

They were silent, then he added, "Dahkir was very glad you decided to come." It was a question, but he made it almost like a statement.

"I . . . think he was, because he is anxious to help Halide and earn Aznan's payment." Juliette looked down.

"Yes . . . because he is anxious to earn Aznan's payment." Something in Farouk's tone had made her turn and search his face, but it was bland and innocent.

She studied him for a moment. "You've known him for some time," she said at last.

"Dahkir? Longer than either of us cares to admit. We met in the army under very unusual circumstances." Farouk's mouth twisted in a wry grin as he continued, "When I joined the army, I was given a horse with the disposition of a donkey. When I wanted to go, this animal wanted to stop. When I wanted to stop, this animal wanted to go. We were sent to Derna to fight the Turks, and in one particular skirmish, this stupid horse decides he wants a new master. I pull him one way and he goes the other. I find myself racing into the front lines. This horse has made me look like a fool. I have no choice but to draw my scimitar and wave it like a madman. Then that stubborn animal makes up his mind to stop. I am thrown right over his head and sent rolling into the dust. When I come to a stop, I look up to find a very large Turkish soldier on horseback with a very large rifle pointed at my foolish head. And then from out of nowhere, Dahkir rides within inches of me. He looks me in the eye and asks, 'Do you need some help, my friend?' The next thing I know I am swinging up behind him on his horse, and the Turk is lying dead on the ground." He paused. "Dahkir is a very brave man. I owe him my life. We have been friends ever since."

"And how did you become his business partner?" she asked.

"Dahkir decides to sell his commission and leave the army to start trading. He has a deal to buy six camels, but he needs money. The next thing I know, I am selling my army commission along with him and buying not only camels, but goods to trade. Pretty soon, we have ten camels, and a little later, we have twenty; and even later we have more camels than we can count." Farouk sighed, reminiscing. "But there were days when we had no money and nothing to eat, and then there were the desert raiders who would try to steal everything you owned. We were fearless in those days, challenging anyone who got in our way."

Juliette was thoughtful. "Deric isn't afraid of anything, is he?"

Farouk looked puzzled. "What makes you say that?"

She shrugged, at a loss for how to put it into words. "I don't know. He meets everything head on. Nothing seems to rattle him. Just once, Farouk, I'd like to see him shaking in his boots."

Farouk laughed. "But Dahkir does 'shake in his boots' as you put it. There is only one thing he fears more than any Bedouin raider. If you promise not to say a word, I will tell you what it is."

"I promise," she said, returning his smile.

"Women," was the one-word reply.

Juliette's curiosity was piqued. "Really, that would have been my last guess." She tried to keep her tone nonchalant, but inside she was dying to know more. "He certainly didn't seem to be afraid of Ranieri. He couldn't keep his hands off her."

Farouk shrugged this off. "His interest in her was as fleeting as rain in the desert."

"She did want to marry him, you know. But that didn't scare him off."

"She meant nothing to him." He saw the puzzled look on her face. "Juli, for Dahkir there are two kinds of women. There are the women who are nothing more than a cloudburst. The rain comes and then goes. All is forgotten. But there is the woman who storms his heart and leaves him thirsting for more. That is the woman Dahkir fears most." Farouk chuckled. "Dahkir is so sure he will never let this kind of woman into his heart."

She sighed. How true. Deric wore armor around his heart so thick it seemed nothing would penetrate it, not even her.

Then Farouk smiled mischievously. "But then Dahkir doesn't know everything, least of all his own heart."

Juliette's head came up fast, but Farouk didn't give her a chance for any more questions. He spurred his horse and rode ahead of her, leaving her to her own thoughts.

Farouk smiled to himself. Maybe he was wrong for giving her some hope where his friend was concerned. But if any woman could steal Dahkir's heart, he hoped it would be her.

They rode until the sun began to sink. The last traces of the sunset vanished quickly as they halted and set up camp. Juliette found that the routines of making camp came quickly back to her. As the outriders saw to the camels, she set up her small tent and neatly stowed her belongings inside. Every movement was familiar, swift, comforting. It always amazed her how quickly the caravan could make or break camp. Then she went in search of Farouk to help him prepare the evening meal.

She found him bent over a fire and silently joined him about his tasks. She glanced up as the men, one by one, appeared and sat cross-legged around the fire. Skins of date wine were passed, and pipes were lit as they waited for the evening meal to be ready. Two men threw dice, and the rest chatted in relaxed tones. Deric was the last to join them as always, having first satisfied himself that every detail was done correctly.

Juliette had barely seen him all day, for he had ridden ahead of the caravan. She felt a small jolt as his eyes met hers, and he nodded to her in greeting—but then he looked away. She watched him through her lashes as he bent to fill his plate, pondering the problem that had been nagging at her all day. How was she going to get him alone? Since she'd run from him on the ship's deck, they hadn't had a moment alone.

But what exactly was she going to say to him when she *did* get him alone? Her cheeks colored faintly. Apologize for running away? Ask him to kiss her again? Today as she'd ridden she'd planned a hundred things to say to him, and rejected all of them.

But she had to say something to thaw the coolness she'd caused; that was certain. But when? She felt far too embarrassed to announce at the fire she wanted to speak to him alone. She winced as she imagined the reactions of Farouk and the men. Well, she'd find a way after the meal—even if she had to go to his tent. And somehow, when the time came, she'd find the right thing to say. She had to. Every day was precious—every hour one of the few she had with him.

Though she would have sworn he was absorbed in eating, Deric was watching her profile in the firelight as she ate. She always surprised him. She looked so delicate, so well-bred, with that slim nose and high cheekbones and her slender, graceful hands. But she could be as tough as nails—almost as tough as a man. Look at the way she had adjusted all over again to the caravan. She looked as if a day's ride hadn't bothered her a bit.

He put his plate down and stood, not able to meet her eyes. "I'll take first watch tonight," he said shortly, then strode off into the night.

Juliette watched him, wishing she could get up and follow him. Instead, with a sigh, she helped Farouk gather up the dishes, telling herself her chance to speak to Deric would come later.

But it didn't. He was nowhere to be found when she took a last stroll around the encampment, straining her eyes for a glimpse of him. Disappointed, at last she went to her tent. She hadn't managed to see him tonight—and tomorrow, the outriders and Farouk would be most effective chaperones. And one more precious day together would be gone.

It was near midnight when Deric walked into camp, after patrolling the perimeter for hours—the only cure he could find for the restlessness that beset him. He paused as he came within sight of Juliette's tent, set up a short distance from the others so she could have some privacy. He had deliberately pitched his tent as far as possible from hers.

He stared at the outline of her tent as the memory of Juli tied to his wrist to sleep came back . . . of the curve of her back as she slept, pressed against him, while he himself tried to forget her nearness and fall asleep. What a sweet torture it had been to have her share his tent but not his bed. And then at last when she had come to him— He shook his head and cursed softly.

He was turning to go when a soft light appeared inside her tent as she lit a lantern. He froze, looking at her silhouette outlined against the tent wall in the lantern's light. He knew he should turn and go, but his feet wouldn't obey him. They were rooted to the spot.

He watched as she moved inside her small tent, readying herself for sleep. His mouth went dry as she bent and lifted her burnoose up over her head and folded it. For a few moments, he could clearly see the curves of her form outlined against the tent's luminous wall. She swiftly lifted her arms and dropped a nightgown over her head; and a moment later she snuffed the lantern, and the tent was once again a dark shape against the night sky.

Deric stood staring at the tent. What would she do if he strode across the sand now and lifted the flap of her tent? He pictured her sitting up, eyes wide in the starlight, her hair falling around her shoulders . . . then opening her arms to him; he swiftly crossing her tent and kneeling in front of her, his hands on her shoulders, her nightgown falling away as he untied it and bent to put his lips to hers. . . .

He swore again and turned on his heel, heading for the safety of his own tent. He was a fool. If he parted the flaps of her tent, she would scream. He knew that. She wanted no part of him.

"Deric!"

Her soft voice calling him from behind froze him. It was some moments before he could turn.

She was a dark shape in front of her tent.

"Could I speak to you a moment?"

He took a deep breath. She just wanted to ask him something—that was all. But right at the moment, there was nothing he wanted to do less than exchange polite conversation with her.

Stopping a few feet away from her, he studied her as she stood in the dim gray night. Her hair was a dark cloud that fell over her shoulders and down her back, her face soft, her lips trembling. She was the most desirable sight he'd ever seen, and he clenched his fists at his sides.

"What is it?"

Juliette swallowed at the brusque tone of his voice, shaking inside, unable to think of what to say.

"I wanted to—to tell you I'm sorry," she began, feeling her cheeks flame.

"For what?"

The two words were clipped, and she winced. It took an effort to answer him around a dry tongue. "For the other night. For running away. I shouldn't have—it was rude," she stammered.

"It's I who should apologize. Not you. I had no right to treat you as if—you are right to remind me that what is past, is past. If that's all—?"

She swallowed. He sounded so abrupt, so coldly formal. Her hands felt like they were ice cold, her stomach shaking, her cheeks hot. He was turning to go, to walk away once again, the rift unbridged. Desperation gave her courage.

"Is it past?" she asked in a low voice. *I don't want it to be,* she wanted to add, but didn't have the courage.

She saw him stop, then turn.

There was a long silence while he stared at her through the darkness.

"It is," he said, and strode away into the night.

Despairing, she watched him go, her heart seeming to fill her throat. Then she turned and ducked back inside the tent.

She let the flap fall and sat abruptly, a great space of emptiness in her chest where her heart should have been. She had gambled, and lost. Too stunned even for tears, she just sat and sat, staring into the darkness. She could feel each thudding heartbeat marking out each endless minute that passed. She had never felt so utterly alone.

There was a grate of boot on sand.

She looked up, her heart giving a great leap as the flap to her tent was lifted.

He was a black silhouette against a gray night sky, and she couldn't move.

"It isn't," he said. "It never was."

And then he was inside, clasping her in his arms.

Chapter Thirty-Six

Juliette let out her held breath as his arms came around her, raised her own arms and slid them around his neck. His mouth covered hers, and nothing had ever felt so right as being back in his arms. Her heart, so bleak a moment ago, seemed to sing with love and joy as she gave herself up to his kiss.

Deric! Her fingers stole along the line of his jaw, tangling themselves in his hair; she inhaled his male scent and felt the hardness of his muscular body as he clasped her against him. How she had missed him, how she had longed for just this! What use was there in ever resisting such feelings?

Suddenly he broke their kiss and held her tightly against him. Her cheek was pressed against his chest, and he was running his hands over the long sweep of her hair where it fell down her back. She could feel his arms trembling, and knew the kiss had shaken him every bit as much as it had shaken her. Rough and low, he spoke against her hair.

"If you want me to stop this, I must stop now—and leave you."

But he didn't let her go, instead kept her held hard against him, so that she couldn't have moved if she wanted to. She could hear the thudding of his heart.

"And do you want to stop?" she murmured. A wicked little smile curved her lips, and she let her fingers slide slowly along his neck. She smiled more to herself as she felt his shudder.

"Damn it—you know I don't! But I don't understand you! First, you push me away, and now—"

He pushed her away from his chest and held her away from him. In the dim light, she could see his eyes were blazing, whether with anger or desire she didn't know. "I don't know what you want of me, but I know I can't promise you anything. I know damned well I should stop!" The words sounded desperate, for he was losing his battle to resist as surely as he was being won by her touch.

A stranger seemed to take over her then as she was filled by a sensual abandon she'd never felt before. More than anything else, she wanted him to kiss her again. To touch her, to make her his. Nothing else mattered—not what he thought of her—nothing.

"I ask you for no promises," she murmured. She stared at him full for a moment. "All I want from you is this—now."

Her hands slid up his arms and under his shirt, daring him to hold back his desire even an instant longer, while her eyes were openly seducing him. The last of his resistance melted away in the blaze of heat her shameless words caused.

With a groan, he pulled her close again, his hands cradling her narrow waist, then slowly sliding up her ribcage as his mouth found hers. He kissed her roughly, and she matched him, matched him with a wild, wanton passion she'd never show him before. They kissed as if starved for each other's touch.

Never had Deric been so mad for her. It had been too long, and he'd dreamed of just this too many nights. His lips were teasing the line of her jaw, his mouth tracing the sweet line of her neck, his hands running, fingers spread wide, through her hair. She moaned softly and felt him shudder in response to her uninhibited sound, as her seeking hands found his shirt and struggled to open it. His breathing was ragged, and he suddenly swept her onto his lap, then tumbled her, twined with him, down onto the bedroll.

His hands were all over her, burning through the thin material of her nightgown, setting her aflame. She pressed herself against him with an abandoned delight. It seemed he found the thin material too much of a barrier to his touch, for he was soon untying the ribbons at her bodice, her shoulders, pushing the delicate cloud of material down around her shoulders, her breasts, over her rounded hips, and then she was kicking it away.

"Oh, God—you are more beautiful than I remembered you. No woman has ever done to me what you do."

He stared at her naked body, and she gloried in this groaned admission, only raising her own hands to push open his shirt, to slip it off his shoulders until his chest was as naked as she was. And then, her hands were sliding lower, to open his pants, to help pull them away. She heard his intake of breath as her fingers closed around his erect maleness, slowly sliding down with the most delicate of touches.

Then they were both naked, and she continued to stroke him, delighting in her boldness, marveling in his eager hardness, wondering how she ever managed to accommodate the size of him. She could feel from his response, from the way he was breathing as he lowered his head to her breasts, she was making him wild with passion.

Soon, she too was afire. First the tip of his tongue touched one of her nipples, softly slipping over it as she gasped with pleasure. Then he moved to the other nipple, and his tongue teased it lightly, delicately. He barely flicked her nipples with his featherlight tongue until she was shivering and crying out low in her throat. And then he took her nipple fully into his warm mouth, sending a burst of pleasure all through her. She arched convulsively against him, and her fingers tightened around his swollen manhood. She felt his excited throb, and knew that neither of them would be able to hold back much longer.

But his sweet torture of her was not so soon finished. She felt his fingers sliding down her abdomen, felt his warm touch find her center of pleasure. His other hand raised to her mouth and lightly brushed her lips, outlining them inside and out, until she cried out again, begging incoherently, afraid she would go mad unless he stopped this play and made love to her at last.

To distract herself from the aching want she couldn't stand, she ran her hands over his back, feeling the long smooth muscles, then up to his shoulders. Her fingertips brushed over his arms, delighting in the feel of him, so long remembered, longed for—but now, at last real. Her touch found his long legs, his stomach, hard and flat, his chest. As he was making her flame with desire by what his hands and his lips were doing to her, her uninhibited exploration of his body was driving him to a peak of desire he'd never experienced before.

His fingers traced her lips inside, ran lightly over her tongue, and then were replaced by his kiss. His mouth came down on her begging lips, and she welcomed him as he shifted over her.

Her arms twined around his neck while, with his mouth on hers, he slid into her with a spearing thrust that filled her to her depths, sending a burst of pleasure through her so intense that for a moment the world seemed to disappear.

Then they were moving together, both clinging close, unable to keep their cries of pleasure to themselves, in a sweet rhythm that was as fast as it was wild. Together they climbed to the heights, both shaken by wave after wave of unbelievable, nearly unbearable passion, and by that wonderment that is the fusion of two souls who love and become one. With a final cry, Juliette felt stars burst inside her, felt Deric's shuddering gasp, and both at last—slowly—came down from the heights they had discovered as one.

She lay, feeling his precious weight above her, her lips against the skin of his shoulder. Never had she felt so much that she belonged to anyone. She was his. This man was the man she loved—the man she'd given her heart to. Even if he was never her husband, there was no changing the way she felt. Tonight—in the very wild abandon she'd given herself up to him, the way she'd trusted him to show him her most sensuous side without fear—those had been her vows.

At last, he stirred. Rolling off her, he nevertheless drew her close, into the position she had so often slept with him: her head on his shoulder, his arms encircling her, his hand toying softly in her long curls.

He spoke. "Juli—how am I ever going to let you go again? Let you spend even a night away from me, after tonight?"

She smiled in the dark and pulled him closer.

It might not be a declaration of love. But it was a start.

Chapter Thirty-Seven

"Are you never going to get up?"

Deric opened his eyes and rolled over sleepily to find Juliette gone from the bed. In fact, she was up and dressed, across the tent, briskly folding her clothes and packing them away.

Bemused, he stared at her for a moment. She was dressed for riding, in a trim pair of breeches and a white blouse tucked into them. His eyes raked the long curves of her legs, clearly evident beneath the clinging breeches, and dwelt for a moment on her slim waist. Then his gaze rose a bit higher, and he felt his loins stir as he thought of untying the ribbons of her nightgown last night . . . how irresistibly desirable she'd looked wrapped in a whisper of white lace with her hair down her back like a bride. . . .

And yet, right now he'd be ready to swear there was no more seductive way for her to be dressed than as a boy, hair twisted into a knot that showed the lovely lines of her neck. It was a good thing she wore a shapeless burnoose over her riding dress, for he'd never allow another man to see her looking this tempting.

He stifled a groan as she presented a trim rear end to him, and it was on the tip of his tongue to tell her to come back to bed. But then, with the force of a fist slamming into his stomach, a realization hit him.

It was happening again.

She was making him forget everything else. He was ready to let their need for speed—his vows to stay disentangled from her—go hang while he spent the day in this tent with her.

And before he knew it, she'd have him wrapped around her smallest finger, fatuously happy to do her least bidding. . . .

He frowned. "We've got to talk."

Juliette straightened, startled by the abrupt growl of Deric's voice behind her. She turned to find a stormy pair of green eyes narrowed at her accusingly.

Her stomach sank. She'd woken early this morning with the first light and, for a long time, raised on an elbow, had simply stared at him while he slept. Serene love filled her with a glow rosy as the dawn, and she'd spent a long time just savoring the miracle that at last, they were together again.

Then finally she'd torn herself away, dressing quietly, planning to slip outside and make coffee, come back and waken him with the softest of kisses, so she could see his eyes open and fall on her with that new tenderness she'd seen in them the night before. . . .

The same eyes that were now furious chips of green ice.

"About what?" She could barely get the words out of a mouth dry with apprehension.

He sat up, sheet to his waist, all bare-chested muscles and cold eyes. "About last night. About what happened."

"What—" She swallowed, feeling sick at the look in his eyes. "What do you mean?"

"What I mean is just this—what happened didn't mean what you think. So stop thinking it!"

"Thinking what?" Welcome anger was rising now inside the sick shock, and she grasped at it, drowning. "What do you mean, didn't mean what I think? What do you think I think?"

He got to his feet, tying the sheet emphatically around his flat waist and, dragging a restless hand through his hair, started striding up and down like a panther. He looked angry—worse yet, accusing! And she still didn't know what the hell she'd done!

"You know damn well what I'm talking about, so don't play innocent! I had no intention of spending the night in your tent last night—none at all! But then you call me over to your tent and stand there wearing nothing more than a nightgown—" He rounded on her furiously. "What did you expect to happen? And don't pretend you didn't know exactly what you were doing!" He paused, and she saw his jaw muscles jump. "So, I won't have any of your tears or accusations that I've taken advantage of you. What happened last night was your own damned fault and you know it!"

"Taken advantage of me?" she gasped. Her temper was flaming as red as her hair, and now the blue fire in her eyes was a match for the green ice in his. "And I suppose *you* had nothing to do with it? Are you trying to tell me you were in my tent against your will last night?" She laughed, tossing her head in derision.

"I am trying to tell you I am not a marrying man—so don't expect it!"

He stopped and shouted these words at her, and for a moment, they so stopped her with hurt and rage and insult she couldn't speak. Then she found her tongue and shouted back at him as uninhibitedly as he'd shouted at her.

"I know that damned well, Deric Raleigh. Haven't you been drilling that into my head since I first met you?"

"I know what a woman like you expects when she shares a man's bed, and dammit, I made up my mind to stay away from you just for that reason! But then last night—don't tell me you didn't know what would happen when you called me to your tent—"

Light broke. He was so furious because he was guilty. He was angry with her because he hadn't kept away from her . . . and angry with himself because he couldn't give her what she deserved. So he was lashing out, convincing himself she was to blame.

But this understanding only brought deeper fury. God in heaven, how dare he feel guilty about what they'd shared last night? Or worst of all, presume she was *manipulating* him into marriage—

It was her turn to use anger to deflect a guilt that cut too close.

"Marry you! Damn you, Deric Raleigh, not if you were the last man on earth!" she shouted. "What makes you think I want anything more from you than to share your bed, you conceited—"

She whirled, possessed by anger, ready to stalk out of the tent, but the red rage was too much. She spun back, hand raised to slap him.

But her wrist was caught as she raised her hand above her head. He towered above her, and for a long moment, her arm strained against his strength and her eyes battled against his, telling him if he loosened his grasp she meant to slap him with all her might. Silently, they strove. And stopped. Stopped by each other's eyes.

"Then—share my bed," he rasped.

She was yanked against him, the rage running red-hot in their veins turning all at once to passion. But still she resisted it.

"Get your hands off me!" she hissed, pushing hard against his chest with her free hand, but all the time feeling him against her.

"Is that what you want?"

The words were a taunt, angry and knowing. He was daring her to stop pretending she didn't feel what was happening between them.

For a breathless moment she stared up into eyes that were mocking her for the coward she'd be to deny it.

"No."

She formed the word deliberately, giving him cool blue eyes through lowered lashes, as taunting as his own. Her free hand slid down his chest and found the edge of the sheet taut against his hips—and pulled.

It came away in a slither, and she let it fall from her fingers, her eyes never leaving his. His eyes blazed as she was pressed, fully dressed in boots and breeches, against his nakedness. His fingers grasped her other wrist and spread her arms wide, bending her back, and his mouth came down to claim hers with a fury.

She could feel all the force of his anger at her for his own surrender as he forced her backward, holding her wrists in an iron grip, showing her just how much stronger he was, even though he was naked and she was fully clothed. He was punishing her with his mouth, all angry male, and in his anger he would prove he possessed her.

He let go of her wrists, and she almost fell backward, head tilting, limp in her total surrender; but he caught her in an iron grasp before she fell, placing his mouth under her jaw at her throat. She punished him back by running her own hands wantonly up and down his body from the straining muscles of his back to the iron curves of his thighs.

"Damn you—witch!"

The words were a curse against her mouth, and she laughed.

She felt his hands move to her blouse, then they were grasping it, a hand on each side of the neckline. With a jerk outward, the thin material parted, and the remnants of her shirt floated unheeded to the floor.

He cursed her and kissed her, staking an age-old claim to the woman he possessed.

And she was glad to be claimed as they tumbled to the floor together, their differences vanishing.

For now.

Chapter Thirty-Eight

The noon sun was blazing in a white-hot sky as Juliette emerged from her tent. For a few moments, she just stood, stretching, filled with a delicious contentment.

She heard Deric behind her and felt his arms go around her waist and lock in front of her. Smiling, she leaned back against him, giving herself up to happiness. His lips caressed her hair.

"Mmm—I can't seem to let you go. We're already hours late in starting, and all I can think about is touching you."

She turned in his arms, held against him. She found him looking down at her with a light in his eyes that took her breath. She smiled up at him.

After the storm of their passion was spent, she'd woken to a rain of tenderness. She felt loved, and now as she laughed, she saw the same unmistakable glow she felt in her heart, burning deep in his eyes.

He smiled ruefully at her. "I fear my men will wonder what we're doing, stopping for a day. You make me forget everything else, Juli."

"And you do the same to me," she admitted, shyly.

"Oh, Juli—" He started to bend to kiss her softly, when from behind them there was a shout.

"Dahkir!"

He straightened reluctantly, grimaced at her, turned, but couldn't release her just yet.

"What is it?" he called over his shoulder.

One of his men, some distance away, was pointing.

"Rider!"

They both turned, squinting at the horizon behind them. At first, Juliette could see nothing. Then she saw it—a wavering black cloud of dust. She shaded her eyes against the sun as Deric released her.

"He's alone?" she ventured.

"And riding fast in our direction. . . ." He tried to appear unconcerned as Farouk walked up and joined them, but Juliette wasn't fooled. She saw the crease in his brow deepen each time he looked in the rider's direction. She was sure the rider must be one of Aznan's messengers. Anything inconsequential could have waited until they reached Homs Misurata, but to send a rider, alone into the desert to catch up with the caravan . . .

"News, my friends," Farouk said quietly. Deric nodded grimly.

They stood in front of the tents, waiting silently until the rider galloped into camp and came to a jolting halt, sand spraying from his horse's hooves.

"Dahkir?" the rider gasped.

Deric nodded, stepping forward and grabbing the bridle as the exhausted rider slid from the saddle.

"I am Patak Osir. I come with news . . . and a request from Aznan." He stopped to catch his breath. "We have word from the Americans. They have finally pledged their support to Aznan."

"They've pledged their support before, and nothing's come of it," Farouk said. "Why the rush for such a message?"

"This is more than just a promise. Within the last week, they have set up headquarters at Derna. The American navy has sent ships," Patak answered.

"Then Halide and her son are in danger, if Oman knows of this," Deric said flatly.

"As he must know," said Patak. "There are no secrets of this magnitude that escape his spies. Oman is frightened now that the Americans have given us promises. He trusts no one. He has had some of his most loyal courtiers publicly executed as spies; others he has had thrown in prison on the thinnest of evidence."

"Tell me—" Juliette swallowed. "Halide and Ismail—do you have any news of them?"

"Our last report was that they were alive. That was three weeks ago. But Oman is trying to gather an army. Fortunately, his royal coffers are nearly empty, and he has very little money to pay his soldiers. Oman is finally growing weaker. With the Americans behind us, Aznan feels victory is certain if he strikes now, but—"

"But he won't do it if Halide and Ismail are still held prisoner," Juliette finished. "Is there any chance Oman would panic and have them executed anyway?"

"No, for they are now the only cards Oman holds to keep Aznan from his throat, and he knows it."

"But news of their deaths could be withheld for days, even months. And by that time, Oman may have an army large enough to protect the palace from an attack by Aznan," Juliette surmised.

Patak nodded at her. "It is as Aznan says. This woman knows much of the harem and of Oman's mind. Which brings me to Aznan's request." He looked to Deric. "He begs you to make all speed in this rescue. The Americans will not wait forever, and Aznan will not attack if his wife and son are not safe. He would not ask you to take unnecessary risks, but he loves his family very much and longs to have them safely at his side once again."

Juliette watched Deric anxiously, but his face was unreadable. She knew he disapproved of her going back into the harem. But the quickest way to effect Halide's escape was to have an inside contact. And that meant her. Would he see that?

"We will make all possible speed. Assure Aznan we will do all we can," Deric answered.

Patak stood and grabbed his bridle. "I will take your answer back to Aznan. May Allah guide and protect you." In a farewell sign, he touched the fingers of one hand to his forehead, his lips and then his chest before leaving.

They watched him ride off in silence, Juliette, Farouk and Deric, all lost in their own thoughts.

Juliette turned to Deric. He had barely said a word since

Patak's arrival. The knit of his brows and the drawn line of his mouth warned her he saw what she did—but felt differently.

"Deric, now will you admit I must go back inside the harem? How else will we learn if Halide is even alive or get her out quickly?"

"We can buy information."

"But not speed, and only speed may save her." She saw from the stubborn set of his jaw he was going to be difficult indeed.

"I am the one leading this rescue, and I am the one who will decide what risks we take," he said evenly.

"It's my risk," she flashed.

Farouk turned away, averting his eyes in embarrassment. "If you do not mind, I wish to return to my—"

"You'll stay right where you are, Farouk. You and I have much to discuss. Sit."

"And leave me out of the discussions? Are you so stubborn you won't even let the three of us talk about it?" Juliette asked incredulously.

"I've told you often enough I don't like it—"

"I'm not asking you to like it. I only ask that you admit when you're wrong."

Farouk stretched and made a move to leave. "I have so much to do before we break camp. I—"

"Stay where you are, Farouk."

"As you wish, Dahkir."

Deric stood only inches from her now, his nose nearly touching hers. "I . . . WAS . . . WRONG. Will you go back to your tent now so Farouk and I can decide what to do?"

"No, I will not," she stated stubbornly.

Deric drew himself up to his full height, fire flashing from his green eyes.

Farouk sat down and watched the two lovers face off. He was sure they would argue like two merchants over the price of a camel. But when the fighting was done, would they fall into bed like turtle doves? Only this morning, he'd been walking toward the tent they'd shared—at last!—and been startled to hear shouting. He'd turned quickly on his heel and gone back to join the men at the breakfast fire. And there they had stayed for the rest of the morning, a delay of many hours. He leaned back and, closing his eyes, pretended to fall asleep. Maybe if he could sneak off, this fight would end as their last one obviously had. Oh, well, it was a strange kind of love-play, but they seemed to enjoy it—arguing first, then settling their differences in bed.

"I will not go to my tent simply because Deric Raleigh commands me to do so. I will know why you disapprove of this plan. Especially, when you *know* it is the only plan that will succeed." Farouk heard the arguing go on above him.

There was no answer from Dahkir.

"Is it because I thought of it?"

"No. That's not it at all."

Farouk hid a smile. How often he'd been on the receiving end of that cold tone in the army. Any ordinary woman would be weeping. But Juli?

"Is it because I'm a woman?"

"That's part of it."

"And women are to be protected from danger?"

By Allah, for a woman so warm, her voice can ring with cold sarcasm, Farouk thought.

"Yes."

"And what right have you to protect me?"

"What do you mean by that?"

"You've told me often enough you want no responsibility where I'm concerned, so why won't you let me take my own risks? What difference does it make to you?"

"As long as you're under my care, I'm responsible for you—especially when you don't have the sense to be frightened when you should, like any proper woman would be."

"And I suppose I should shriek and faint at every turn. Is that your idea of a proper woman?"

"No. But if a lion opens its mouth, should you stick your head in it?"

"Not unless you're Deric Raleigh."

Farouk had to stifle a laugh.

"Don't try to be funny, Juli. This is no laughing matter. You heard Patak. They're executing spies right and left."

At the sound of boots being planted in the sand in front of him, Farouk opened his eyes with a sigh. Dahkir towered above him, glowering, fists on hips. "Talk some sense into this stubborn woman, Farouk! Tell her to listen to reason," he demanded, waving an arm in her direction. "Tell her only a madman would take such a risk!"

Before Farouk could even open his mouth, an angry Juliette was at Deric's side. *By the prophet's beard,* thought Farouk admiringly, *look at those eyes when she's angry! A woman of fire!* He settled in with enjoyment to hear what she would say next.

"Tell *him* it's my risk to take—to do this—and I'm no more mad than we all are!" she shouted.

His lips twitched. He wanted to agree with her, but Dahkir looked most dangerous just now. It would be safer to say nothing. Either of them looked capable of tearing him to pieces if he disagreed with them.

He raised his hands. "It does not take a Solomon to have the wisdom to stay out of this one. In fact, really, I must go, my friends, before one of you insists I take sides."

Farouk brought Juliette to her senses, and all at once she was deeply ashamed of the shouting they'd done—and in front of him.

"There's no need for you to leave, Farouk. I'll leave you—and Deric—to the plans *you* must make," she said with a single simmering glance at Deric. Damn him for acting like she had no place in their councils! And for so much more than just that!

She turned on her heel and strode away from the tent without so much as a backward glance.

Farouk sighed heavily, waiting for Deric to start after her. "You are letting her go?" he said at last.

"Yes, since that's what she wants," was the short reply.

"And you will sleep alone tonight?"

Deric gave him a sidelong glance that told Farouk he was treading on thin ice.

But Farouk wouldn't give in. "You and your woman play such games as I've never seen before. Your mating dance is even more bizarre than the peacock's."

"She's not my woman. And I don't wish to discuss this."

"Very well. Not a word more." But as if he hadn't heard his own words, Farouk continued, "Tell me, Dahkir, if the thought of her going back into the harem upsets you, why did you not forbid her part in it? You could have easily refused her."

Deric regarded his friend for a moment before answering, "She would never deny me the opportunity of helping a friend. I can't keep her from doing what she thinks is right, no matter how I feel. But I can damn well try to make her see reason—see how dangerous it is. She's angry now, yes. But this kind of anger passes. If I had refused to let her help Halide and Ismail—well, that sort of anger lasts forever, doesn't it, Farouk?"

"Yes, my friend, it does." Farouk shot a look at his friend, surprised at the insight of this remark. *Perhaps Dahkir is finally beginning to understand his woman.*

Juliette paced the small confines of her tent with a fury. Deric's clothes were scattered here and there, and the sight of them infuriated her even more. The argument had brought her to her senses, making her realize exactly how impossible being in love with Deric was.

A pair of his trousers hooked onto her foot as she strode angrily back and forth. She kicked them out of her way.

She could never win with him—not in an argument, not in love.

What his eyes and his body had told her, his lips simply refused to say.

She thought of the way only this morning he'd shouted at her he wasn't a marrying man and told her practically point-blank he only wanted her for her body.

And how willingly she'd given him just that!

She cringed as she remembered the brazen way she'd pulled the sheet from him.

So all he wants is a mistress?

She stumbled over one of his boots, then picked it up and flung it furiously out of her way.

She'd be damned if she'd settle for less than his love.

Why couldn't she hate him as she should? But no, one touch from him, and she lost all control.

Control.

That was the problem. She had to get her emotions under control and face the facts. She couldn't give of herself so freely without knowing he loved her.

But she couldn't give up, not when the last two days had been the most wonderful days she could remember. Nothing equaled being held in Deric's arms, waking to his kisses, loving him. Four months without him had shown her that. This time she would fight to win him if she had to—just like Farah had done to keep the sultan's attentions.

Farah! What would Farah do in a situation like this? She stopped her pacing again, struck. She thought of how the feisty concubine had withheld her favors from the sultan in order to get what she wanted.

Farah had been a distasteful woman, but she certainly knew how to win a man—and hold him.

Maybe—maybe Farah's methods, drastic as they were, would make Deric openly admit how he felt.

Juliette bent to pick up Deric's shirt. Thoughtfully, she shook it, then turned the sleeves right side out to fold it.

Suddenly, she smiled, a wicked smile. Perhaps a change of strategy was in order. If Deric wanted nothing more than an affair, she'd give it to him.

She placed his folded shirt on the bedroll and picked up his trousers.

And maybe that would bring him to his senses—make him realize that wasn't what he wanted at all.

She tossed the folded trousers on top of his shirt and bent to pick up his belt.

And if he didn't love her? Well, one way or another, she'd find out.

She let her hair down her back. Then she pulled off her clothes and began rummaging in her bags until she found what she was looking for: a sheer lacy chemise, so low-cut that it barely covered her breasts; a thin whisper of a petticoat that fell to her ankles. The garments were feminine, ribbon-trimmed, seductive—not like the boy's clothes she wore on their rides or the loose caftans.

She was tying the ribbons at her bodice when she heard his

footsteps outside the tent. Good. She wouldn't have to go looking for him. She straightened her shoulders and turned with a slanting smile, completely aware of the picture she would make when he came into the tent. Yes, Deric Raleigh would know what he would be missing.

And she wasn't disappointed by his reaction when he entered the tent. For a long moment, he just stood there, his eyes devouring her, and she felt such a rush of love for him she thought she might not have the nerve to go through with her plan. The sight of him filled her with desire—his tanned throat against his white shirt, his long hair with the golden streaks burnished by the lamplight, his strong dark brows.

Then her tall lover was crossing to her, his hands were cupping her breasts, his head bending so his lips could travel over their thrusting swell above the lacy edge of her chemise.

She almost forgot where she was, but she quickly gathered her wits and pulled away from him.

"Juli, I didn't mean to make you so angry. You're right—you have every right to decide what risks you'll take. Can you—"

She cut him off. "There's really no need to apologize, Deric. You were absolutely right. I shouldn't give a fig if you approve of what I do or not. How silly of me to even care what you think."

"Juli—"

"No, no. I've been thinking about this—not just tonight, but for a long time. And I think I've been confusing my *attraction* for you with other feelings. As much as I've *enjoyed* this little interlude we've shared, I think it's time it came to an end."

"To an end?" he repeated, stupefied. What could she mean, to an end?

"You're not the marrying type, as you're so fond of telling me. And we are almost to Tripoli. There we have a dangerous job to do, and when it's done, our ways will part. And though you've been a most satisfying lover, I do want to marry some day. You can't expect me to spend my life as your mistress."

She smiled as if the thought amused her, as if she expected him to see the funny side of it, to agree with her. She kept her voice light, hinting that the end of their "affair" was a matter of supreme indifference to her. She watched him closely as she spoke, delighting in the stunned disbelief she saw in his face. Maybe all she had to do was say this much! Maybe now, he'd tell her he'd be damned if she thought she was marrying someone else. She waited for his reply, hoping, almost holding her breath.

But her words hadn't had the effect on him she thought. Deric was struggling with disbelief—and dismay. At first, he couldn't credit it—Juli, talking like this? Like a light-moraled society woman who had amusing affairs? *For God's sake,* he thought angrily, *was that all this had been to her—a little interlude of passion to be forgotten when it was convenient?*

Juliette saw an enraged Deric draw himself up and growl, "Just what the hell do you mean by that?"

Not quite a declaration, but she definitely had his attention. Now for the finishing touch. "Let's not make this any more difficult by causing a scene. I would hate to end our affair on such a sour note." If this didn't get a rise out of him, then he was thick-headed and beyond all hope.

"But I won't end it."

Ah, it worked!

"And will you stop calling it an affair?" he snapped.

"What would you have me call it?" she mused coolly and waited for his reply. He was so close to an admission of his feelings, she was trembling. But how far could she push him?

He didn't answer. She bent and picked up his folded clothing from her bedroll, then turned and handed them to him. "There's no need for discussion. I think I've made myself clear." For all her cool tones, she was perspiring. If he didn't say he loved her, she would faint.

He ignored the clothing in her hands. His brows rushed together, and he looked as if he wanted to shake her. "So, this was just an affair to you. Well, you seem quite adept at calling it to an end."

There was a tone of accusation in his words that raised Juliette's hackles. What did he mean by "adept"? He should be telling her he couldn't live without her! Not calling her a trollop! "Why not—when it was never more than an affair to *you?* What's the matter? Are you shocked because I'm a woman and I admit I desired you? You may have forgotten, but you were the one who taught me how to feel desire!" she challenged.

"And did you also learn to take your pleasure where you can find it? Who else's bed have you warmed since I 'taught' you?"

She gasped at this outrageous comment. Oh, he was furious! Did anyone else's green eyes blaze like that? But she was furious, too—furious he would ever say such a thing to her. If she hadn't been sure she could harden her heart enough to stay out of his arms until he told her he loved her, she was sure she could now.

"No one's bed but yours, Deric Raleigh," she flashed. "But I'll warm it no longer, you can be sure of that!"

She stalked to the flap of the tent, flung it open and tossed his clothes outside. She stood in the opening, holding the flap back.

He crossed to her, but she stood, looking into the distance, regal and cold as a queen. And then he ducked his way out of her tent.

Outside he hesitated for a moment, looking down at his clothes now scattered by the desert wind. He was torn between outrage and disbelief.

But most of all, he was utterly confused. He spun around to take one last look at her.

What the *bloody hell* had just happened?

Chapter Thirty-Nine

The following afternoon, the caravan rode into the oasis of Homs Misurata. A short ride beyond was Tripoli. This time, they were not staying with Sheik Abd ul-Yazza, but in an inn—a *caravanseri.* Juliette gave a little smile as she thought of how she'd innocently asked Deric if he wasn't going to miss staying with Raneiri again. Her heart warmed as she thought of the way he'd replied shortly, "That snake-hearted witch? I think not."

But that had been before their fight. Since then, they'd said little enough. Deric had tried to corner her just before they left, obviously wanting to continue their argument, but she'd cut him short. Mounting her horse, she'd looked down at him and said, "Deric—please. I don't want to fight about it any more. I've said all I intend to say."

"But dammit, Juli—"

"Perhaps we can at least treat each other politely for the rest of the trip," she said coldly, and set spurs to her horse, but not before she'd seen the look of frustrated pain in his eyes and been glad for it.

It all went through her mind again as she sank gratefully into a steaming tub, sighing with pleasure as she felt the rose-scented water close over her tired muscles. Was she doing the right thing? Or . . . should she just go to his room right now, throw her pride to the winds, and tell him she loved him?

Wearily, she closed her eyes. She just didn't know what the right thing was any more. But this gamble was worth it. If she won, she'd have his love. If she lost . . . her pride.

Soon she was dressed and on her way down to dine. Deric and Farouk rose as she entered the private room where they were dining. They both bowed to her, but Deric avoided her gaze.

"How beautiful you are tonight, Juli," said Farouk, rolling his eyes to the sky as if begging for help from above at the sight of her. "Wouldn't you agree, Dahkir?"

Deric caught her eyes for only a moment, then seated himself at the table without saying a word.

His silence hung heavy in the air, and for a moment she didn't know what to do. This wasn't like him at all. Even at his angriest, Deric never ignored her. Then Farouk was at her elbow, holding her chair for her. She sat and tried to regain her composure. Taking a deep breath, she told herself she wouldn't let him ruin her evening.

"Thank you, Farouk. I feel wonderful," she said. "It's amazing what a little soap and water can do to one's attitude." She paused and leveled her gaze at Deric. "Apparently, some of us didn't use enough."

She sat back, smug, knowing he would rise to the bait. But he didn't. He just sat there, eating his meal as if he hadn't heard a word.

She looked at Farouk. "I see we're dining alone tonight."

Farouk's laugh was a trifle uncomfortable. But Deric's face was as impassive as a stone as he lifted another bite of the spicy stew into his mouth. Her own meal was getting cold. She hadn't eaten a bite since sitting down. This was too aggravating.

Deric finally looked up from his plate. He glanced at her as if noticing her for the first time tonight. Then he turned to Farouk. "Farouk, please pass the bread."

Juliette felt her anger drain away and a sick feeling rise to replace it. Normally, he would have glowered and returned her spiteful remarks, but he'd said nothing—not even a word to her since she'd entered the room. And then all at once, she felt childish. It was one thing to find herself in the middle of an argument with him, but to try to instigate one was another thing. She picked at her food, her appetite completely gone, and tried to answer Farouk's idle chatter, a conversation that he was trying to keep alive to cover the awkwardness between her and Deric.

When would dinner end so she could be alone? she wondered, depressed. It seemed like it never would, but at last, the last dish was cleared.

She rose. Forcing a smile, she said, "I think I'll go for a walk in the gardens. It's such a beautiful night." She left the room quickly.

Farouk looked at Deric inquiringly. "Something is troubling her."

"I'm not blind," growled Deric irritably. "I can see that."

"Maybe one of us should go find her."

"And maybe she wants to be alone! She has a lot to think over!"

Farouk shrugged expressively, saying nothing. Deric glowered at him for a few minutes.

"Pour me some more wine," he said at last. "Maybe later I'll go out after her, but for right now I'm just going to leave her alone."

"You know best, my friend," said Farouk, passing the wine bottle.

"And you know damn well I don't know best at all where women are concerned. I don't understand them! Or their moods! And I don't think I want to, either."

Deric cursed under his breath as Farouk settled down, a twinkle in his eyes, and replied, "Don't understand women, my friend? Why, you have come to the right place! If I may modestly make the claim, I am an expert on women. Let me explain them to you. . . ."

Juliette strolled along the graveled pathway in the inn's garden under trees fragrant with blossom. It was a balmy night, and she breathed deeply to clear her mind—to try to forget how cold Deric was at dinner. Well, could she blame him? She'd told him she wanted nothing more to do with him.

The path led to a stair set in the wall next to the inn. Curious, she climbed it and, after a twist, found it led to a rooftop garden. Up here, small trees grew in tubs, there were beds of flowers and herbs, and a small fountain splashed. She walked to the edge of the waist-high wall that enclosed the roof and leaned her elbows on it. Below, the lights of the oasis twinkled in the blue night, and noises drifted up from the inn, laughter, music and muted clatter. Above, soft stars clouded the sky, and the bright crescent moon had climbed high in the vault of the heavens. She listened to the strains of a zither playing an eerie, wailing melody.

A footstep on the stairs made her turn and she saw a black shape emerge from the staircase onto the roof. In a moment, by the walk and the breadth of the shoulders, she knew who it was.

Flustered, she quickly turned away and listened as his footsteps drew nearer.

"Here you are," he said, as he joined her and leaned on the wall next to her. "When I didn't find you in the gardens below, I was worried for a moment. I thought you might have taken it in your head to go wandering the streets, and they aren't really safe at this time of night."

"No, I wouldn't have done that," she answered, looking down at her hands. "About what happened in there—"

He shrugged, face impassive as he looked out over the gardens. "It was my fault, too."

For a few minutes they were silent, both leaning and looking out at the night. Finally Deric stirred and said softly, "On nights like these, I am glad I chose the kind of life I did and didn't settle down. There is so much of the world to see, and if I had stayed in England and lived a conventional life, I would never have seen any of it."

Juliette glanced at him uncertainly. He was talking intimately, as if they were friends, as if they'd never fought at all. She almost asked him what had caused the change, but then decided not to break the spell.

"That's how I feel," she answered. "I never wanted to stay in England. Even with everything that happened to me here. Of course, it could have turned out very differently. I often think of how strange fate's workings are."

"The dress you told me of?"

She was surprised that he remembered. "Yes—that dress. A strange thing to change a person's life."

"The Arabs are great believers in destiny. They would call it the will of Allah that you survived the ship's sinking when no one else did. They would say you were spared for a purpose."

"Perhaps I was saved so that in turn, I could save Halide?"

"Any Arab who was against the sultan would probably see you as a divine instrument of fate prepared for his downfall by the Prophet," he said, and she could hear the smile in his voice. "Yet who can say? Sometimes I think perhaps I have been out here too long, because I find comfort by just spreading my hands and saying, 'It will be as Allah wills.' Maybe it is a good way to live—trusting in destiny, not worrying over-much about the future."

Juliette laughed softly, staring up at the stars, wondering if Deric was beginning to realize he missed her. He certainly seemed to be calling a truce tonight. Aloud, she said, "Much easier said than done, I am afraid. I suppose I haven't been out here long enough to adopt a true Arab fatalism. I still worry about the future."

"About Tripoli—our getting caught? Going into the harem?"

"Then you've resigned yourself to my going back in?"

"If it's the only way. I still don't like it." Instead of his usual harsh rejection of this idea, he sounded reasonable.

"But that's a good example of how I feel, you see," she said. "I once was content to just let life happen to me. Now I want to be the one who shapes my future. I don't want anyone making decisions for me . . . and that includes whether or not I should take this risk."

Again she expected an argument but got none. Instead, he only said, "What is it you want from the future, Juli?" She glanced at his profile again, but it was impassive. She saw nothing she could read on his face.

You.

She almost said it aloud, but instead said only, "I don't know. Does anyone, really?" What else could she answer? The question deserved either a ten-minute answer or nothing.

"Perhaps the money we earn will help you lead the kind of life you would like to. A life where you make all your own decisions."

Was it irony in his voice? Oh, what was it he was feeling? For once, just to know. Maybe this was her chance to learn some of the things about him he'd never told her before. . . .

"What will you do with your part of the money, Deric? I

know money has always been important to you . . . but you've never really told me what it is you would do with it. Go back to England?"

"I used to think that I would . . . when I first left the army and Farouk and I started running our caravans. I used to dream of going back in my own coach-and-four, showing my family and all my neighbors that I had made good after all!" He laughed shortly. Juliette searched his face in the dark. She knew so little about him, really. What had caused him to turn his back on his family, to strike out on his own? She sensed that there was some hidden bitterness there.

"After all?" she inquired softly. "Did they doubt you so much?"

He looked down at her, eyes gleaming in the dark. "Doubt me? They thought I was mad," he said shortly. "None of them have ever struck out into the blue to try to earn fortunes carrying a rifle . . . worse yet, in *trade.*" There was mockery in his voice. "Soiling my hands with trade has been my greatest sin, I believe. They would have preferred me to make my fortune by marrying for money. And that kind of *mercenary* marriage would have been perfectly acceptable—even applauded by my family. And by most people."

The face of Amelia Williams rose briefly before his eyes. Once more he saw her blond curls, patrician beauty, her soft blue eyes. He had fancied himself in love with her when he was very young. And he knew she loved him back . . . or so he thought until he had asked her to marry him. How well he remembered her shocked dismay, her answer.

"But Deric, how could I marry you?" she'd said, her eyes round. "Why . . . you have no money! You are a younger son! My parents would never hear of it. They look for a great match for me, wealth and certainly a title. My family expects it of me." The tears had swum in her eyes, and his heart had gone out to her, thinking she was frightened of her family. What she had said next set him straight on that point.

"But I won't always be poor. I'll make a fortune, I swear it! Marry me anyway and forget what your family expects!" he'd said, sure her resistance was only token.

Instead, she'd stared at him as if he'd lost his mind. "But

Deric, marry you when you have no expectations? Live in poor lodgings? You just aren't thinking! What kind of a life would it be? Why, no one would invite us to parties . . . if I could even afford dresses to go to them! And how would you ever make enough to raise us to the social position we were born to? An estate . . . a house in London? Oh, Deric, you must be mad to even think I would consider marrying you! I . . . I am sorry." And as he'd stared in disbelief, the easy tears had rolled down her cheeks, and he'd seen suddenly past her beauty to her soul. Her love for him had never been deep, never been more than a thrilling flirtation. She had her eye squarely on the future, and on the place she would take in society some day. Nothing was worth risking that for . . . not even love, if she had ever felt it for him.

As he remembered, he half-smiled, half-winced at the humiliation this old memory still had the power to bring. How young he'd been then—how bitter when a month later he had read of her engagement in the society papers, to a viscount who would one day inherit an earldom. He had cursed and thrown the paper into the fire, watching it burn with a heart that burned, too. Women! They were shallow, fickle creatures who cared deeply about nothing, he thought, who had no integrity. He would never trust a woman with his heart again. Two weeks later, he had bought his commission in the army and come to the Mediterranean. It wasn't long before he was sure he had forgotten the deep wound Amelia had inflicted on his pride and his heart, but now he realized that for a long time, his dreams of making a fortune had all centered around her—on seeing her on the arm of her fat lord, her eyes widening as he entered a brilliant ballroom, the dismay on her face when she realized he had made his fortune after all and if she had just had faith . . .

He shook his head. He could barely remember her any more, and it had been many years since he'd dreamed of going back to England with a fortune. A little startled, he realized that now he no longer cared to prove his worth to his family. It just didn't seem important any more.

Juliette heard the bitterness in Deric's voice and was sure something had happened in England that caused it. But she sensed now was not the time to ask him. *I'll ask Farouk,* she thought. *Maybe he knows something about Deric's life in England.*

Aloud she said, "Not everyone thinks marrying for social position or fortune is important."

"No?" Deric laughed, and his laugh sounded ugly to her. "What about your wealthy Lord Ormsby? Would you be considering marrying him if he had no fortune?"

Juliette looked at him, hurt. "Why should you care who I marry—or why? But how can you accuse me of being mercenary, when really you know nothing about me or what I feel?" It was her turn to be bitter as she turned to go.

His words stopped her. "You're right. I don't know what you feel or think. In fact, though in some ways I know you so well, I find I really don't know you at all in other ways."

He was standing too near to her, and she was conscious of his body so close to hers, of his gaze holding hers.

"And I find I want to know everything about you," he added.

Fighting to remember her resolve, she managed to say, "Deric—you promised to accept my wishes that it's all over, and—" She was barely making sense, she knew it, but God help her, it was hard to think at all when he stood so close to her!

"I promised nothing," he said. His gaze left hers and fell to her lips, and his face changed in a way that sent a sudden terrifying thrill all through Juliette's body like a wave, making her draw in her breath. His voice roughened. "Though even if I did, how could you expect me to keep such a promise when I want you so much?"

Wanted her so much. His words were like a splash of ice water on her heated skin. So nothing had changed! He still spoke to her of his desire—not his love!

"Please—I must go inside now," she said coldly.

He stepped back, and the spell was broken.

"Goodnight, Juli," he said, and she glanced at him standing tall in the moonlight, his face unreadable in the dark. For a moment, she had a mad impulse to fling herself into his arms and lift her mouth to his, asking for his kisses, begging for his touch! But that was no way to make him realize he missed her—loved her. Instead, she took a deep breath and turned on her heel, saying goodnight over her shoulder, and left the garden without looking back.

Farouk, sitting alone at the table, saw Juliette cross the doorway and climb the stairs to her room, alone. The brief glimpse of her face that he saw showed him that she was unhappy, and he sighed heavily.

So, being in a moonlit garden had not brought them back together! He'd been so glad when at last they'd stayed in one tent. But now . . . he sighed again.

It looked like they would spend the night apart, both miserable if he was any judge. He couldn't understand what was causing their estrangement, but vowed that he would try no more schemes to get them alone together, as he had tonight. Obviously, it was making both of them unhappy.

Damn that Dahkir! he thought, wistfully. She was a beautiful woman, but more than that. She had courage and spirit as well. Could he not see her worth? Farouk shook his head. He would thank Allah if a woman like Juli wanted him. And he would certainly not waste a moonlit night alone in the garden with her, as Dahkir seemed to have done. There was no doubt about it . . . in some ways, Deric Raleigh was a fool.

Chapter Forty

Juliette sat on her mare, staring down at the city of Tripoli below. They had halted on a hill above the city, and it sprawled around the small harbor, just as she remembered it. City of dreams; city of nightmares.

Dominating everything was the palace.

It looked just as she remembered it, but she studied it with fresh eyes as a place she must now enter and then escape from. She could see part of the harem wing, high above the rest of the palace, dark barred windows above sheer walls. Inside those barred windows, Halide and her son were prisoners, prisoners without hope. Juliette stiffened her spine. It was worth the risk to help Halide get out of that hellish place!

Juliette couldn't suppress a shiver as they passed the city walls. They were heading for the home of Abu Ben Adzak, a Syrian trader whom Deric often dealt with. As the east gate opened for them and they entered the twisting streets of Tripoli, once again the city seemed sinister to her. She tried to remember how wonderful it had looked to her as she had galloped through its streets at Deric's side, away from the palace, and tried to focus on how it would feel to ride away again, this time with Halide and Ismail at her side. But it seemed like a dark cloud stood between her and that future moment. So many things could happen. . . .

Deric's voice broke into her thoughts. "If worse comes to worse and I am caught, I'll lie about what I'm doing—say I was spying for Aznan. They may just believe you weren't involved if they think you are nothing more than my slave still. So you'll have to start playing the part from the moment we enter the city. Even Abu Ben Adzak must believe it to be true."

She turned to look at him and caught him giving her a wry look, eyebrow lifted. There was a pregnant pause, then he said, "It means you will have to act deferential—like my slave. Think you can keep your temper and act the part convincingly?"

"If you don't act *your* part too well! Try not to enjoy humiliating me too obviously!"

He laughed. "I'll try, though the temptation will be very great. But you realize that you will have to . . . visit me in my bedroom?"

"In your bedroom? Why?" She pretended to be insulted, but inside she felt a small dart of triumph. So he was angling to get her alone—in his bedroom! Maybe missing her was beginning to be painful.

"Because Abu will expect it," he said with elaborate unconcern. Devil!

"I don't care *what* he expects! How can you—"

He threw back his head and laughed, startling her.

"What? What are you laughing at?"

"How else will you talk to me, once we're in his house? You'll have to come to my room to talk to me, because otherwise you will be confined to the women's quarters."

"Oh!" There was a smile on his lips that told her he was enjoying the way she'd risen to his bait . . . enjoying the chance to pay her back for her recent arm's-length stance.

Oh, Deric, if you only knew that visiting you in your room is exactly what I want. . . .

But aloud she said—still pretending she found the idea aggravating: "As long as that's *all* you expect me to visit your bedroom for—to talk!"

She was rewarded by seeing his lips tighten.

Abu Ben Adzak settled back on the divan's cushions, the long stem of a hookah in his hand, a contented smile on his face. A slave girl knelt, eyes downcast, face veiled, ready to serve the three men at a moment's notice.

"So, my friends, I am well satisfied with the goods you have brought me. The filigree work from Damascus is most unusual. And I am happy that we have agreed at last on a price, though as usual, you have almost broken me. You drive a hard bargain!"

Deric and Farouk caught each other's eye and laughed. "It is you who drives a hard bargain, Abu, as well you know. I am sure you are well pleased with today's work. You will earn three times on the market what you paid us for the goods—if not five! You are as sly an old fox as ever," Deric stated.

Abu lifted his hands in protest. "Three times? My friend, you horrify me! I give you the best prices in Tripoli, and this is my thanks? You almost have beggared me!"

Deric laughed again. "I know you must make a profit, so I don't begrudge it to you. And it is true—you offer me good prices, otherwise I would not deal with you. But now that our business has been concluded to all our satisfactions, I have a favor to ask of you, my old friend."

"A favor? Nothing easier! I shall be delighted! You have but to name it, my friend." Abu stroked his beard, his eyes narrowed. For all his generous protestations, he was secretly hoping the "favor" would not involve the loan of money.

"Farouk and I have business in Tripoli—business that will keep us here some weeks, perhaps," Deric began.

"And you wish to stay here? Nothing easier! My house is your house—as long as you wish!" cried the trader, much relieved that the request was so simple.

"We thank you for your offer, but before we accept it, you must know something. This business we are engaged in—it is business of a very delicate sort. It could be terribly risky for us . . . and for you. I wish I could tell you, but I don't want to put you in further jeopardy. Our staying here is dangerous enough, but if something were to go wrong—"

Abu Ben Adzak considered for a moment. "It is, perhaps, Aznan's business you are on?" Deric stared straightly at Abu without saying anything, and Abu nodded as if he had answered. "And involves danger from the sultan and his soldiers, I would hazard. I see. I will ask no more. By the beard of Allah,

I will be only too happy to have you here."

He lowered his voice and leaned forward confidentially. "I will be happy to help in any plan against the cursed Oman Kazamali! His war schemes ruin trade! They make it most precarious for a man to make a profit! Curse him, we can no longer trade with the Americans and the English because he is greedy and has declared a senseless war against them—a war which we must lose! By Allah, I believe he is mad. What will happen to us all when America brings its power to bear against us, which it certainly must one day? I have no wish to live under foreign rule—to be under the thumb of infidels! But this is what the mad sultan will bring down on all our heads!" He sat back and regarded them solemnly. "Your house is mine as long as you wish, my friends, and I wish to know nothing more!"

"Good—this is what I had hoped," said Deric. "We thank you, and I swear I will see to it that you do not regret it."

"Thank you, my friend," said Farouk warmly. "Let us drink to better times!"

Two hours later Deric and Farouk left Abu Ben Adzak's house, dressed in dark clothing, and faded down the dark streets of Tripoli, taking care to stay inconspicuous on their way to the palace. At last they stood below the outer walls of the huge, rambling structure. Deric put a hand on the wall and looked up.

"May Allah be with us, indeed, my friend," muttered Farouk. "How in the Prophet's name are we going to get on the roof without being seen?"

Deric turned and grinned at Farouk, his eyes gleaming in the dark. "I don't know, my friend! First I mean to go around this palace, inch by inch, and explore the layout. It could take us all night to find what we are looking for."

"And what are we looking for?" grumbled Farouk, following as Deric started along the wall. "This wall is too high to scale, and look—there is a guard! It looks very difficult!"

"Losing heart already? I will tell you what we are looking for—and we might find it on the south side of the palace. We are looking for a place where the city comes close to the palace walls, that's what."

"And what good will that do us if the walls are patrolled by guards?" muttered Farouk to himself, careful Deric did not hear him.

The palace, more like a small city, was built on a hill overlooking the harbor. It was enclosed by walls that varied in height as the ground rose and fell around the palace. Inside the walls were the jumbled piles of stables, living quarters that housed the sultan and his retinue, the harem, slaves' and servants' quarters, soldiers' quarters, kitchens, granaries and a veritable maze of buildings connected by passages, courtyards and tunnels. The outer walls were patrolled by guards pacing slowly along their perimeters, and now and again, a guard tower stuck up from the walls. Now that the sultan had declared war on America, the palace was more heavily guarded than ever, and the troops' quarters were full.

But in places, the city of Tripoli itself came right up to the palace walls, its leaning buildings and squalid, twisted streets under the palace's very shadow. It was in these areas Deric was hoping to find a place of access.

He and Farouk stood in an alleyway an hour later and studied the palace walls. The alley ran up a hill behind the palace, and was a narrow, dark, horrible-smelling place filled with rotting garbage and the rustlings of rats.

"There!" said Deric suddenly, pointing. "That building! It just might do." He was pointing to a tall, run-down-looking buiding that stood just a few paces from the palace wall. "From the roof of that building we could jump onto the wall. And see how the roof of those palace quarters comes so close to the wall? I think we could jump from the wall onto that roof."

"But what about the guards? And the harem is on the other side of the palace! It's too far! How will we get there?" demanded Farouk.

"First we get on the building's roof and watch the guards patrol tonight. When we know their routines, we pick a moment when they have passed to jump. Once we are on the palace roof, we see if we can find a way over the roofs to the harems. I would be surprised if the roofs are patrolled—just the outer walls is my guess. If we can stay out of sight of the walls once we are on the roof, I believe we can find our way to the harems. But we have to make no noise that can be heard from below."

"This might work for us . . . but what about when we have a child and two women with us? I cannot see the boy leaping from roof to wall! And the time it will take for three people to leap! The guards will surely see us."

"We'll bring a ladder on the night of the escape. We have only to lay it over the gap between the roof and the wall for everyone to cross quickly. Then a rope ladder down the wall. You'll be waiting there with horses, and we'll make for the gates."

"Even if this works, it's hopeless to try to get out the gates. They are locked at night! And even if they let us through, the gatekeeper will remember us and will be able to direct the pursuit, which will surely follow. We'll be ridden down before we are three miles from the palace!"

"You're right . . ." Deric rubbed his chin. "We'll have to think of another way to disappear once we are on the ground. But no matter. Right now we have to find out how often the guards patrol, if we can get on the roof at all, and once on the roof, whether we can even get to the harems. It's a tall order, my friend. If we get so far, perhaps your Allah will show us a way to disappear once we are on the ground!"

Farouk nodded, and they silently made their way to the tall building. It was a dwelling house with a noisy tavern on the first floor. The strains of music and laughter drifted out into the night as Deric and Farouk stood silently looking up at the three-story building.

They walked around to the back. The building was of mud bricks, old and crumbling. "We can climb this easily," Farouk said softly, "provided it does not give and send us sprawling into the street."

"We'll have to risk it," answered Deric, and grabbed the side of the building, finding handholds and footholds easily in the weathered brick. Farouk stood and kept watch as his dark shadowy shape slowly crept up the side of the building, and breathed a sigh of relief when, a few moments later, Deric made the roof, then turned and beckoned down at him.

With Deric keeping watch for passersby who might take them for thieves, Farouk slowly followed him to the top. When he reached there, he was sweating, his hands bruised from gripping the rough bricks. But the climb had been easy enough, the brick solid and in no danger of giving. As long as no one saw them, they could easily make the climb again when they needed to.

Stooping, they cautiously crossed the flat roof to the edge near the palace. A low wall perhaps three feet high enclosed the roof. They lay flat behind the wall and raised themselves until they could see over.

"There is a guard!" hissed Farouk.

They watched as the man slowly patrolled the wall, walking along its wide top, rifle gleaming in the moonlight, cutlass at his hip. They held their breath as he passed by, just a few feet below them, so close they could see the tassle on his fez and hear him breathing. He didn't look up to the roofs above him, his attention being focused on the ground below the palace wall. As he slowly reached the end of the palace wall, a good distance away, he turned, following the curve of the wall, and disappeared from sight behind the roofs.

Deric pulled out his watch. "Now we must time how long it is before another guard comes along, or before he comes back," he whispered.

It was nearly fifteen minutes before another guard—not the same man—appeared at the same end of the wall the first guard had come from. Deric and Farouk lay on the roof for nearly four hours, timing the appearance of the guards, talking softly in between their appearances to fight boredom. There seemed to be four guards patrolling the palace walls, spaced in about fifteen-minute intervals. "It takes them nearly an hour to walk all the way around the palace walls," Deric observed.

"I think we have watched long enough," said Farouk. "It is almost two in the morning. Are we going to try it tonight? Because we only have a couple of hours before dawn."

"Let's try it after the next guard passes. Even if we don't get to the harems tonight, we can at least start our exploration."

"Just make sure we don't get lost on the roofs, my friend. I would hate to have to spend all day tomorrow lying in hiding up there, waiting until dark! We have to get back here before dawn because I am getting hungry." Farouk laughed softly.

They watched as the next guard slowly walked down the length of the wall and disappeared. "Here we go," said Deric. "I'll go first since you are so scared."

Farouk swore at him softly as Deric stood. Looking both ways, he balanced for a moment on the small wall of the roof, measuring the distance. Then he leapt and, a moment later, landed light as a cat on the palace wall. He motioned to Farouk, who was already standing on the roof's wall, and Farouk leapt down, too. Without saying anything, they ran a few silent steps down the wall to where the outbuilding's roof came close, almost at an even height with the palace wall. It was a short jump, and once on the other side, they ducked low and ran softly across the roof to its other side, where they flung themselves full-length in some black shadows.

Breathing heavily with excitement and exertion, they lay there a few moments, listening breathlessly to the night. No one seemed to have marked their passage. There were no outcries, no running feet. They both wore soft moccasinlike goatskin shoes on their feet which were noiseless on the roof. They heard the distant bark of a dog, faint noises of voices and clatter from a nearby building, and soft music from the tavern. "We can be seen from the wall on this roof," whispered Deric after a moment, checking his watch. "We still have ten minutes before a guard comes. Let's get onto the next roof." They stood, half-crouched, and reconnoitered. Farouk's sharp eyes picked out landmarks. He was determined not to get lost.

It was an easy jump to the next roof, a long, low building from which light poured and voices could be heard. "I think we are over the barracks—and that is the stables," whispered Deric as they crouched on the next roof in a shadow. "If we can make it to that next building, we will be on the roof of the main palace. From there we should be able to get to the harem roof without having to go to ground at all. At least we are out of sight of the guards on the wall now—but keep a sharp eye out for guard towers! Come on!"

Farouk followed him up a sloping roof to its crest and down to the other side. They breathed a sigh of relief when they saw that the roof of a long, covered walkway connected the building they were on with the main palace.

As they started over the walkway, Farouk hissed, "Be careful! Some of these tiles may be loose! Go slowly!" They crept across the walkway without dislodging any tiles and sending them crashing to the pavement below, though once Deric had to grab a broken fragment to keep it from falling.

At last they were on the roof of the main palace. It stretched away, a wilderness of flat roofs at all levels, some overlooked by windows that they would have to avoid, keeping to the shadows. It was a maze. They would have to come here every night until they had discovered the fastest and safest route to the roof above the harems, and until they knew that route by heart.

They looked at the vast complex of roof, both dismayed and heartened. Dismayed because it was so huge—and heartened because its very complexity gave them plenty of hiding places in the shadows.

"This is no job for tonight, Dahkir," said Farouk, gazing at the moonlit tableau before them. "It is too late, and it could take hours to find a way across. Besides, we might get lost! I would feel better if we came back tomorrow night. I will bring something to mark our way."

Deric considered, again checking his watch. "You're right—the risk of getting lost is too great. That's a good idea to bring something to mark the route. Once we know the way, we should mark it with small spots of paint so there are no mistakes the night of the escape. Let's go back now. But a good night's work, my friend!"

Farouk grinned back at him. "Do not tempt Allah. We are not off this cursed roof yet!" Laughing softly, they turned to go.

When they reached the last roof before the wall, they lay in the patch of shadows again, watching for a guard. After what seemed an eternity, he appeared at the end of the wall, pacing out his route with the same deliberation. They watched until he passed, then stooping, ran across the roof.

In a moment, both had leapt onto the broad wall. Deric dropped down and let himself over the wall, dangling for a moment and hanging by his hands. It was a drop of about ten feet. He let go and landed in the dirt street below, rolling to break his fall. In a moment, Farouk landed beside him, and they stood, dusting themselves off.

They looked carefully to either side. Not a soul was around—no one had witnessed their drop into the street. "A good thing," whispered Farouk, "for I would have hated to have to kill them."

Deric laughed, his spirits high. They had done it! He looked toward the yellow square of light falling into the street from the tavern. The music and laughter rang out and suddenly seemed appealing. He needed a release from the breathless tension of the last few hours.

"Come on, my friend," he said, feeling good to be alive. "I'll buy you a drink!"

"Ten drinks! I need them!" Farouk laughed, and clapping Deric on the back, they walked to the tavern.

Chapter Forty-One

The sounds of a zither filled the rooms as Isla, Abu's plump, middle-aged wife, played softly and skillfully. Juliette knelt with downcast eyes to one side of the table, as she had knelt every night during the evening meal, waiting on Deric and Farouk. Under her face veil, her mouth formed in mutinous lines as Deric lazily lifted a hand without looking at her. She rose and fetched a plate of grapes and apricots that had been sitting not a foot from his elbow, and silently offered it to him. Absently, he helped himself as he listened intently to Abu's talk of business and trade in Tripoli.

As she offered the plate to Farouk, she was unwise enough to meet his eyes and see a merry twinkle there that almost startled her into laughing aloud. Oh, they were insufferable, both of them! Deric was playing the role of master to her slave to the hilt, treating her with as much unconcern as any good Arab man would. She admired his performance—but was galled by the obvious enjoyment he took from it!

She retired demurely to her place and listened to the talk of business. Though she couldn't speak, she enjoyed listening, because she was beginning to understand Deric's business as a trader.

At the end of the meal, Deric and Farouk rose and bowed politely.

"Tonight—you go again on your business? Or can I send one of my slave girls to your rooms?" asked Abu expansively.

"Not tonight." Deric smiled as Juliette narrowed her eyes at this offer. "We may be back late. I will have my slave, Juli, wait in my quarters for me in case I feel in need of . . . entertainment later."

Juliette fumed silently as she followed him out of the room, cheeks burning beneath her veil. Why did he have to make it so obvious, announcing it? As she made her way to the women's quarters, she vowed she'd find a way to get even for that one.

There, she would dress as expected in a more alluring dress—one to please her "master." Isla, Abu's wife, had insisted she borrow a sheer copper-colored caftan from her for tonight, throwing up her hands in horror at the thought of Juliette wearing the same green and silver dress for a third night in a row. When Juliette saw it, she smiled. The sheer robe left little to the imagination. It was a perfect piece of torture, she thought, imagining his reaction to it when he returned tonight. He could look, but not touch.

When she was dressed, she would go to Deric's room and pass the night trying to sleep as she waited for him to return. As always, she would be torn between worry, boredom and sometimes pique at the way he was enjoying playing her master in public. She almost wished it was time to go to the palace. This waiting was beginning to tell on her nerves.

"How alluring you look!" cried Isla, clapping her hands together when she had finished dressing Juliette. "Your master will never resist you tonight! He will be driven mad with desire, like a raging bull!" Juliette allowed herself a wicked smile at Isla's enthusiasm, pleased that she had been so successful in making her look alluring. She had done an expert job. Juliette's hair was loose down her back, brushed until it shone in soft bronze waves, and perfumed lightly with attar of roses. The sheer caftan fell loosely from a deep V-shaped neckline and was slit up the sides to the knees to display her legs as she walked. Underneath she wore nothing, just the perfumed musk oil Isla had massaged into her skin.

But instead of seeing his reaction, she was long asleep and the night almost gone before he got back. The perfumed hair was tangled, the caftan crumpled when the soft sound of the door opening and Deric's footstep brought her out of a light sleep. She sat up in his bed, watching his dark silhouette enter the room.

"You're back!" she said sleepily.

"Yes . . . though we almost ran into a little trouble tonight."

"Tell me!" she gasped, fully awake now. She searched his face as he lit a candle and sat down in a chair near the bed. In the candlelight, his face looked drawn and tired. All these nights awake, sleeping during the day, and tension were taking their toll on him, too, she suddenly saw, and felt ashamed of all her taunting games. They seemed petty in the light of the dangers that he was facing every night.

"On the tiled walkway on the way back, I slipped and a tile crashed onto the pavement. It's next to the soldiers' quarters, and it brought a soldier out into the courtyard to look. We were lying flat on the other side of the roof in the shadows . . . and we could hear him walk to the foot of the walkway. He must have seen the broken tile and looked up. He would have seen us, too, if he had crossed to the other side of the walkway, but one of his companions called something to him, and he went back inside. It was close."

She let out a long held breath. God, what if he'd been caught? Her heart was ice. Then a worse thought struck her. "What if the night we are escaping the same thing happens? How will we hide so many people from a guard?"

"It won't happen. We're going to make one last trip, and Farouk and I will go over every inch of that walkway, checking for loose tiles."

"So now—it will be soon," she said.

His eyes were grave. "Soon. We not only found the window, we perfected the route we must take across the roofs. Make sure everyone wears soft shoes that night—or if they can't for any reason—make sure they are all barefoot. We can't make a sound once we're out on the roof. Are you sure the boy will understand?"

"Yes—Ismail is old enough to understand the dangers." She chewed on her lip a moment. "Then we are almost ready," she said at last. "When will you go and see the slave master?"

"Probably tomorrow."

Tomorrow!

"And if he will not buy me back?"

"Why shouldn't he?"

Juliette looked away. "I didn't please the sultan when I was there. That's why he sold me to you."

"It's hard for me to believe he wouldn't want you back."

Juliette felt a tightening in her stomach at his low, caressing tone and the implication of his statement. She rose, sparked by his words. She knew where this was leading.

Deric rose swiftly, too. "Where are you going?"

"Back to the women's quarters . . . if we are done talking?"

"There are still some hours of night left. It would look strange if you went back now," he argued.

"But you let me leave before when we had finished talking," she stated innocently and moved toward the door.

"That was different. It was after dawn then. Tonight you'll have to stay and make the best of it." As he spoke, he walked—nonchalantly enough—to the door and closed it. His tone was flat, as if all that mattered to him was how it would look if she left.

But she wasn't fooled. It mattered to him. It must!

He turned his back on her, leaving her standing and staring at him. He began unbuttoning his shirt and then took it off, seemingly unconcerned at her presence. When he began undoing his trousers, Juliette deliberately turned away, looking out the window, not sure what to do next. The image of his broad shoulders, muscles rippling in the candlelight, long back and narrow waist, seemed to burn in her brain. Suddenly the room seemed breathless and hot. She twisted her hands, listening to his soft movements behind her, ready to jump out of her skin if he approached.

"Are you going to stand at the window all night?" came his voice from the bed.

She turned and saw him lounging in the bed, covered from the waist down by a sheet. She felt heat in her cheeks at the sight. It seemed a deliberate reminder of the last time they'd made love—when she'd pulled the sheet off him at his challenge. Her gaze flew to the chair, where his trousers were neatly folded with his other clothes. He was wearing nothing! What did he think he was up to?

"Suit yourself." He shrugged, a gleam of mockery in his eyes. "But I recommend you get in bed and try to get some sleep. God knows I need sleep! You'll have to trust me—or spend the night on the floor. It's up to you."

Juliette lifted her chin. He always challenged her this way—made her feel she was a coward not to take up his dare. "All right," she said, pretending to be coldly put out. "But blow out the candle."

He grinned at her and then blew it out, and in the darkness she walked to the bed and carefully climbed in her side. She pulled the sheet over her, staying as far as she could from him, glad there was a space between them.

"Goodnight, Juliette," he said softly, and she heard the amusement in his voice. She lay in the dark, staring at the shadows on the ceiling and listening to his breathing. He shifted slightly and she jumped, but he stayed on his side of the bed. In a few moments, she heard from the evenness of his breathing that he had fallen asleep.

Surprised, she turned her head to look at him. So—he wasn't even going to try? She was torn between regret . . . and relief. She was almost sure if he'd gathered her into his arms she wouldn't have been able to keep up this charade a moment longer. She wanted him too badly . . . she loved him too much.

In the faint light from the window, she could dimly make out his face and form. How quickly he had fallen asleep, she thought. He must be very tired . . . or else he did not desire her any more the way he once had. Feeling more than piqued at this thought, she studied him in the starlight, telling herself she was being ridiculous. Of course he still wanted her. That was the one constant between them. Covertly, her eyes traveled over his arms, noting the lean muscles under the smoothness of his skin. She listened to his breathing and then sighed. Turning on her side, she lay for a long time aware of the man next to her, remembering other times when she had slept curled next to him, her head pillowed on his broad chest, his arms encircling her. . . .

The sound of birds singing awoke her several hours later. She came slowly awake, full of a delicious sense of safety and well-being, not sure yet where she was. She felt a hand move slightly in her hair, felt the pressure of a leg thrown over hers, and suddenly came wide awake, remembering she was in Deric's bed in Abu Ben Adzak's house.

Startled, she turned her head. Deric had turned over during the night and now slept soundly with his hand coiled in her long hair, one leg thrown over hers. She felt his skin against her leg and realized he was completely naked! She stirred, trying to extricate herself from his all-too-intimate grasp, and he shifted and murmured groggily in his sleep, suddenly drawing her closer to him, his lips in her hair, his body pressed full-length along hers.

"Juli . . ." he murmured, his hands playing with her hair, his lips slowly finding her ear. She could feel the urgency of his desire as he pressed her closer to him, and she turned and met his half-closed green eyes staring into hers, heard her own indrawn breath. . . .

"Deric!" She twisted away from him, out of his grasp, and sat up. His eyes flew open, and he looked at her, astonished, his hand empty where a moment ago it had been filled with her silky hair.

Her face was on fire as she got up, looking away from his nakedness hardly covered by the twisted sheet. He looked at her from half-closed lids for a moment, then fell back on the pillow and grinned at her.

"Forgive me, Juli . . . I was having a dream," he said lazily.

"So I see," she said, avoiding his eyes, still disturbed by the intimate moment when he had pulled her so close along the length of his body and she'd felt his insistent manhood telling her just how much he desired her.

"I think it was about you. . . . Why don't you come back to bed?" he asked, low. "It seems I cannot hide the fact that I want you. And I believe you want me, too. . . ."

The truth of his words stopped her for a moment, and she had to gather her wits. She was supposed to be holding him at arm's length, but she was half-dazed by the ache she felt for him. "Deric—I told you it was over," she managed; then continued more strongly, "Why don't you get one of Abu's slave girls if you are in need of . . . servicing?"

His eyes narrowed, and a dangerous look replaced the lazy

one of a moment before. "Maybe I will," he said; then added sarcastically, "Sorry if I've insulted you. All I did was ask you if you wanted to share my bed. For a moment there I thought . . . but I see I was mistaken! And as for touching you in my sleep—it was hardly deliberate. I didn't even know it was you beside me at first."

"Oh! I'm sure that's true! You are so used to waking up with different women at your side! But I won't be one of them!" She turned, truly irked at this reminder that he had a habit of loving women and leaving them, and stalked from the room, slamming the door behind her.

Deric stared at the slammed door, fuming inside. Damn her! She was driving him crazy with her mercurial changes, pushing him away, then falling into his arms . . . and now, cold once again. And he understood none of it! But when he had pulled her to him this morning, half-asleep, kissing her hair and running his hands over her body, for a moment he thought he had felt her respond—had thought he had seen desire for him leap into her eyes.

"I must have been mad!" he said aloud, and picked up a boot and flung it at the closed door.

Chapter Forty-Two

A half-hour later, Juliette left the women's quarters, heading for Deric's room on the pretext of taking him a cup of coffee—but really hoping to talk to him.

She rounded a corner in the hall and stopped dead, her mouth dropping open, not able to believe what she saw.

One of Abu's slave girls, a young and pretty one named Lashi, was standing in front of Deric's door. She was wearing very little, and as Juliette watched, she gave a soft knock. The door swung open, and she murmured a few soft words Juliette couldn't catch, then disappeared inside.

With an angry gasp, Juliette turned and fled back to the women's quarters, her heart racing madly.

She reached the sanctuary of her room and slammed the door. It was unbelievable! He'd probably sent for her right after she'd declined to share his bed! All he wanted, obviously, was someone to cool his desires with—but to him, it didn't matter who it was!

Bitterly, she remembered seeing him kiss Raneiri. Why, he probably had a convenient *houri* in every city on the caravan route!

And to think I was tempted to share his bed!! Juliette thought furiously.

Tormented by conflicting emotions, she didn't hear the knock on her door at first. Finally the sound penetrated, and she jerked it open to find Farouk standing there.

From her white face and blazing eyes, he saw at once that

something was wrong.

"What is it, Farouk?"

"I just came to tell you that I am going to see the slave master," he said, wondering what it was now that had put her in a passion.

"I see," she said stiffly. "I suppose Deric is too *busy* to go himself?"

He drew his brows together at her sarcastic tone. "No—we just thought it would be best if I went first to arrange his visit."

"I'm sure," she said coldly.

"Juli—what is the matter?"

"Matter? What on earth could be the matter?"

"But I can see you are very angry about something. What is it? It must be something Dahkir has done."

"I don't give a damn what *Dahkir* does or does not do!" she burst out, and then to her surprise, tears spilled down her cheeks.

"But Juli—what is it? What has he done? Damn it, sometimes he can be a fool!"

She shook her head, too miserable to care what she was saying. "He doesn't give a damn how he humiliates me!"

"What did he say to you? Shall I go and beat some sense into him?" Farouk made a move as if to go.

"No—at least now now. You'd be interrupting him!"

Farouk drew his brows together. What was she talking about? "What do you mean? Interrupting what?"

"His tryst with a slave girl!" she burst out. "I saw the one called Lashi going into his room not a moment ago!"

Farouk's mouth dropped open in surprise. Of all things he'd expected to hear, it hadn't been this. Dahkir had rarely enough taken slaves to his bed in the past, and ever since he'd met Juli, he'd been living almost like a monk. "I see—I'm sorry, Juli," he said at last, not knowing what else to say. "This—hurts you."

She brushed angrily at her tears. "I know it shouldn't—I know I'm a fool to care for him when he doesn't care for me at all—but I can't help it."

"But—Dahkir does care for you, Juli," said Farouk softly. Juliette looked up startled, but he was walking away.

Somehow she got through the rest of the morning. She sat on the bed, again and again picturing the girl going into his room, and it was a long time before she could stop crying and think at all. As much as she dreaded it, she would have to wait on the men at the noon meal. Would he even *be* there? She felt sick every time she thought of what he was doing at this very moment.

She put on her black robes, glad that the veil would hide most of her face and her expressions. Only her eyes would show, and she could keep those cast down. She wouldn't give Deric the satisfaction of seeing what he'd done to her.

When she walked into the banqueting room, the two men were already there alone. Abu Ben Adzak was at the markets. For a moment, Deric's eyes met hers across the room, and seemed to burn into her. Then she lowered hers, feeling a jolt of anger so strong it shook her. She had to fight the impulse to stride across the room and slap him.

During the whole meal she kept her resolution and kept her eyes down, avoiding any contact with his. She knew that the fury she was feeling would show in her eyes if she looked at Deric again. And she wasn't going to let him see how angry he'd made her; she had more pride than that. But several times she stole glances at him when she knew he wasn't looking, and was glad to see that he looked tense. A muscle in his jaw was jumping.

When the meal was concluded, Juliette bowed deeply and made her way out of the room without a look at Deric or a backward glance. Farouk looked after her, a troubled look in his eyes.

"She is angry, my friend," he said at last, deciding to risk it.

Deric turned on him swiftly. "And what the hell is she angry about now?" he demanded. "I'd have had to be blind not to see something is wrong with her!"

"She saw the slave girl, Lashi, going into your room this morning," said Farouk.

"What?" Deric exploded. "And she thought—! But damn it, then she must have seen her come out again a moment later! She came to me on her own, and I sent her away after politely declining her . . . offer!"

"Then Juli must not have stayed long enough to see that Lashi left. I spoke to her this morning, and she thought—well, it seems she believes this is a habit of yours."

"Why would she think that?" Deric said irritably. "Damn it—I've been staying away from women so much I can hardly stand it. Because Juli—oh, hell!"

He didn't finish his sentence, but Farouk looked at him sympathetically. "There was something between you once. It's ended?"

Deric suddenly looked weary. "It's ended," he said flatly.

Farouk wanted to ask what had separated them, but the bleak look around his friend's mouth made him think better of it. Instead he said, "Well, even if it is all over, women are jealous." Farouk shrugged, spreading his hands to indicate that he understood women no better than Deric did. When Deric said nothing, just stared at the door, Farouk ventured, "Still, it would be a shame if things were clouded between you now. She is about to go into great danger, perhaps. I'm on my way to see the slave master to find when he will see you. It could happen soon, my friend. She should not have her wits clouded by anger at such a time."

Deric brooded. Farouk was right, and he knew it. Somehow, it was up to him to clear this up, even if it wasn't his fault that Lashi had come to his room. But because she had, there was hell to pay with Juli. He felt angry suddenly. It didn't seem fair! She didn't want him, she had made that clear, and yet she was jealous of other women.

"I'll have to try to explain to her, but I have an idea she isn't going to want to listen," he said gloomily.

Juliette was brooding, too, when the summons was brought by a slave girl. It was Lashi, and Juliette glared at her as she approached.

"Your master commands your presence in his quarters," she said softly, bowing to Juliette.

Juliette was fuming as she allowed the other women to help her dress. She felt bitter that she had to submit to being garbed in the green-and-silver dress before she could go to his room, her hair perfumed, her face painted. And she was furious that he dared to send for her! Well, she had nothing to say! She would listen to what he had to say and not say a word back to him—not one, she vowed.

Head high, she stalked down the hall that connected the women's quarters with the main house, to Deric's room.

She took a deep breath and opened the door to the room. One glance showed her Deric in a low chair near the window, his shirt loosened and open to the waist, a bottle of wine and two glasses on the table next to him. She lowered her eyes and advanced a few paces into the room, then stood silently, awaiting his orders.

Deric looked helplessly at her for a few moments. Damn it! So, she wasn't going to say a word—and he would have to start! It was awkward—damned awkward. Suddenly he had no idea what to say. Curse Farouk for suggesting he had to patch things up with her! As uncomfortable as he was, he knew Farouk was right. He had to set things to rights somehow . . . but he didn't know where to begin.

Finally he said stiffly, "Thank you for coming. Would you like some wine?" He paused. "Please, sit down."

Without meeting his eyes, she took a chair across the room and obediently sat on it. "Thank you, my lord," she answered softly. "I don't want any wine." Again she sat silent, waiting for him to talk.

"What do you mean, 'my lord?'" he exploded irritably. "You know there's no reason to call me that!"

Juliette hid a bitter smile at this explosion. So, her silent treatment was working! After a moment, she lifted her eyes innocently to him and said, "But you ordered me to come here, and I am merely obeying your orders. What was it you wanted, my lord?"

"Damn it—stop calling me 'my lord!' And I didn't *order* you to come here! You know you have to come here so we can talk about the plans!"

"All right . . . *Deric,*" she drawled deliberately. "Something new has happened you wanted to tell me about since last night?"

Deric was taken aback. Nothing *had* happened since last night. There was nothing they needed to discuss. He had called her here to clear the air between them, but she was making it damned hard to do!

He got up restlessly and ran his fingers through his long

hair. "Are you sure you won't have some wine?" he said.

"No thank you," she answered calmly.

"Damn it, Juli, have some wine!" he exploded again, pouring her a glass and roughly handing it to her.

She took it and took a small sip, her eyes fixed tauntingly on his. "Since my master so orders," she said.

"I'm not your master and you know it!" He rounded on her, eyes blazing.

He stood and regarded her for a moment, chest heaving. "You might as well say it!"

"Say what?" She pretended bewilderment.

"Say why you are treating me this way! Go ahead—scream at me if you want to. Farouk told me you saw that girl going into my room this morning!"

"Girl?" She lifted her brows delicately at him as if determined not to understand what he referred to.

"Yes, damn it! You're upset because you thought Lashi was—that I—"

She regarded him with what she hoped was an expression of innocent astonishment. At last she said, "What you do with your own time is no business of mine," in a chill voice.

He stared down at her, his mouth a compressed slash. "That's exactly what I told myself!" he said grimly. "And yet, it seems to have angered you from the way you're behaving. I can't afford to have you angry when we may leave any day now. Besides, nothing hap—" He didn't get the words out.

Juliette leapt to her feet, fists clenched at her sides.

"*You* can't afford to have me angry! Perhaps you should have thought of that before you sent for that slave girl to share your bed!" she gasped, and whirled on her heel to go.

His hand shot out and grabbed her wrist. "So you *are* angry about what you think you saw! Don't pretend you are not! You're jealous, when—"

He got no further. She whirled back to face him like an angry spitting cat, sparks in her eyes. "Jealous!" she cried. "How dare you accuse me of being *jealous* of you! I wouldn't have anything to do with you for . . . for the sultan's entire fortune. But you think no woman can resist you, don't you, Mr. Deric Raleigh?"

His face was close to hers as he stared down at her with eyes like the angry sea. "You've made it clear you want nothing to do with me, Juliette—don't fear I haven't gotten your message! But even though you won't have anything to do with me, you can't stand the thought that I look at another woman, can you!"

She stared up at him, panting. So many words wanted to rush out her lips they seemed to choke her. She was past caring what she said—too angry to care if truths tumbled out along with hurtful barbs. "If I couldn't stand the thought of you looking at another woman, I would have gone mad long ago, Deric Raleigh! That's all women are to you—playthings to enjoy until the next one catches your fancy! But I won't be just another plaything to you! Though that is what *you* are determined to make me! I can see you think there is nothing wrong with asking me to share your bed in the morning, and then taking another woman to share it an hour later!" She jerked her wrist violently, trying to free herself from his grasp; but his fingers tightened, and he held her easily.

"I think there would be nothing wrong with it when you keep me from your bed so determinedly," he raged at her. "Do you think I'm made of stone, Juli? Do you think I can see you every day—even sleep in the same bed with you—and not have it drive me mad? You accuse me of desiring women only as playthings—" His other arm suddenly grasped her other wrist, and he drew her close against him as she struggled. She turned her head away as his lips came close to her ear and he finished, his voice rough and low with desire, "But do you think I would even look at anyone else if I could have you?"

Juliette's heart began to race, and her knees felt weak in a way that was all too familiar to her. It seemed his arms around her and his body close to hers produced a wild reaction in her own body, a madness of the blood she couldn't fight. But she struggled weakly against him, fighting herself much more than she fought him, trying not to listen to the words he spoke against her ear.

"I've wanted you since the moment I first saw you, Juli, even though I fought against admitting it for as long as I could. I fought you because I didn't want a woman in my life, and I told myself I'd forget you—but God help me, I couldn't! And I try to keep away from you because you're too damned dangerous to my peace of mind, but when you're near me, it blinds me to everything else. . . . Nothing happened with that woman, though I know you won't believe me. If you'd stayed in the hall a moment, you would have seen her leaving! And do you know why I sent her away?" he demanded.

She couldn't answer.

"Because since I've known you, you've driven all other women out of my mind—so don't tell me I'm fickle." His voice was hoarse as he held her still, stopping her from running, but not caressing her or kissing her. Still she couldn't look at him, but could only stay imprisoned in his arms, frozen as the moments flew by because of what he was saying, by his arms around her . . .

"And I'm trying my best to believe you when you say it's over—trying my best not to touch you." There was a pause, and she felt his fingers tighten on her wrists; then he went on, "Don't be angry with me about that slave girl when for me she doesn't exist. No woman exists for me except you."

Juliette's head came up, and she slowly turned to look up into his eyes, a waterfall of her hair falling over his arm. His dark green eyes locked with hers for a few moments as his grip on her arms softened, then his hands began moving slowly up her arms. She caught her breath, able only to stare up at him electrified, but unable to move or speak.

He caressed her cheek, softly and delicately tracing its line until his fingertips brushed her mouth. She trembled in his arms and felt him tremble, too, as slowly he bent his head and his mouth gently closed over hers.

Never had he kissed her this way—with such soft tenderness that she felt dizzy. Yet beneath the tenderness, the softness of his mouth on hers, she could feel their passion burning, held in check only by the magic of this moment.

"Oh, Juli . . . my Juli . . . I can't fight you any more," he whispered against her mouth, and gathered her closer to him, his lips claiming hers, kissing her until the room spun—

A loud knock on the door startled both of them so much that they gasped, leaping apart as if the other's touch had burned. They stood staring at each other, stupefied, until the knock was repeated.

Without taking his eyes from hers, Deric called, "Who

is it?"

"Farouk," came the reply in urgent tones. "I come from the slave master. I have news!"

For a moment, it still didn't sink in to Juliette. All she could see were Deric's eyes, and she was still too lost in the world of their kisses to be able to think yet. Deric grimaced and said, "A moment, Farouk," before gathering her once again in his arms.

He tilted her chin up with a finger and softly kissed her mouth, then covered her face with tender kisses. Then he caught her close and hard against his chest while he stroked her hair. She could feel his breath in her hair, his chest rise and fall as he fought for control, the tenderness in the way he held her as if she was precious to him. She clung to him, not wanting the moment to end, she, too, fighting to come back to reality from a magic world. At last he released her and looked down into her wide eyes again and murmured, "This isn't finished between us, my Juli."

Juliette watched dazed as he strode to the door, looking once at her to check if she was ready to face Farouk, and then opened it. Farouk stood there, an impatient expression on his face, and at once stepped in.

He wasn't too preoccupied to notice the misty curve of Juliette's mouth and Deric's distracted look, and at once surmised what must have been happening. *By Allah, they are cursed!* he thought. *Always something keeps them apart!* And he rued that his errand could not have waited.

"What is it?" demanded Deric, none too cheerfully.

"I have just come from the slave master. He will grant you an audience in an hour."

Juliette's gaze flew to Deric.

An hour! So soon, she could be leaving for the palace!

Deric swallowed as he watched her, suddenly sick at heart that she would have to go, unwilling to let her face the dangers. "Juli—" he began, ready to call the whole thing off, but Farouk sat down near the table at the window and motioned to both of them.

"Come," he said. "Gather your wits. If it is now, we have much to do. We must perfect our plans, make sure the last detail is set." He looked from one to the other solemnly. "And may Allah watch over us all."

Chapter Forty-Three

Juliette stood alone in a dark hallway, lit only by two smoking torches. The floor was fitted stone paved in a square pattern and grimed with dirt. The walls were also stone, clammy to the touch and here and there glistening with moisture. On her right was an arch in the hallway with a heavy dark barred door. None of the elegance found everywhere else in the palace was evident here in this underground stronghold. She shivered as she looked around and tried to calm the beating of her heart.

She was back inside the palace at last.

And on the other side of that door were Farouk and Deric, talking to the slave master.

If all went well, they would perhaps leave her here. By tonight, she might be inside the harems again.

She would see Halide and Ismail.

She tried to focus on that thought to keep her spirits up, but this waiting was almost unbearable, not knowing her fate. A deep terror had descended on her when they left her alone in the hallway and went inside with the slave master. She remembered how Farouk, unseen by the slave master and the guards, had managed to squeeze her hand briefly before he followed them inside and they shut the door. His eyes had sparkled with courage, trying to will it to her.

Courage . . .

It was hard to find, here in the bowels of the palace. She glanced down at the silent guards far down the corridor and then glanced away again. If they were fortunate, those guards might lead her to the harem soon.

If they were fortunate, Deric might get her out again this very night. She shivered again and closed her eyes to pray. She caught her breath when at last the door opened and she was motioned inside.

On legs weak with fear, she walked through the door and saw Giza waiting for her. Although her heart was pumping furiously in her chest, she dropped to the floor and bowed low before the hated slave master, touching her forehead to the floor. She listened as his booted feet moved around her. *Everything depends on this meeting,* she thought. *Everything. He must not see how much I hate him in my eyes.*

Giza's voice came to her, dripping with the malice she remembered so well. "Rise, slave."

She rose to her feet, keeping her head bowed as she should. Again he circled her.

"As I recall, the sultan sold you this slave," he said.

"Yes, excellency," said Deric. "The same slave."

"You are unhappy with her?"

"No, she has been everything I could desire. Obedient, and most skilled in the arts of pleasure. Also most beautiful."

"Well I remember her beauty. The sultan was most taken by it. But I do not remember that she was particularly obedient . . . most rebellious in fact. And cold to his advances."

"Perhaps when I first bought her, but now she excels in both things, excellency," said Deric blandly.

"Ah! It is so?" Giza raised his eyebrows and tapped a finger to one shining cheek. "Then serving under you has improved her. I must inquire into your methods one day. But why do you come back here with the slave if she pleases you so well?"

Deric shrugged. "I find I am in a somewhat . . . delicate situation. I plan to leave these parts for several years. I will travel into the interior of Africa seeking trade goods. I am told I can find ivory and other unusual things."

"Your skills as a trader are well known to the sultan," said the slave master smoothly.

Deric inclined his head slightly, acknowledging the compliment. "But it puts me in a difficult position as regards this slave. I cannot take her with me on my travels."

"Why bring her here?"

"I would be glad to sell her back to the sultan . . . if that is his will in the matter. If he is not interested, I will find another buyer." Deric finished this speech with a note of indifference that Juliette inwardly applauded. It sounded as though he saw her as a mere inconvenience. She held her breath, looking at the floor. Had they fooled him? What would his answer be?

"I see." The slave master's voice was suspicious. "But you are English," he said. "Why did you not return this slave to your country? Give her her freedom?"

Deric sounded surprised. "If the sultan thought I would do that, I do not think he would have sold me the girl in the first place. Up until now I have not freed her because she has pleased me too well. There are few . . . perhaps none . . . who match her fire when making love." Inwardly he cursed the slave master and thought how true his words were.

"How much do you want for her?" Giza asked, and Juliette felt a dart of triumph mixed with fear. He was interested!

Deric named his price.

Giza considered, looking at the girl who stood so meekly, eyes downcast. Though strange, the Englishman's request did not seem unreasonable to him. It was true he could not take the girl with him if he were traveling into the interior of Africa. There were fierce deserts to cross, hostile tribes. Moving toward Juliette, he regarded Deric with a keen eye. He lifted a crooked finger and traced the neckline of Juliette's caftan slowly.

Deric started, then remembered his role. He smiled wickedly in Giza's direction. "It was not easy to tame her. She fought like a lion. I think the sultan will be pleased that I have offered him the first chance at her."

"I will consult the sultan as you ask," Giza said, face revealing nothing Deric could read. "It is convenient for you to wait until I have an answer as to the sultan's will?" At Deric's nod, he bowed his way out of the room.

As the slave master walked down the hall, he considered this strange development. The girl seemed to be obedient enough. He *would* have to ask the Englishman his methods of taming a slave, he decided. But first he would have to decide on his approach to the sultan.

Of course, Oman wouldn't want to buy her back. He'd been most anxious to get rid of her before. But she was an Englishwoman, and there was the war to consider. The situation with that cursed Aznan was most delicate just now. If they didn't buy her and she was sold elsewhere . . . and her tale of once being a slave in Oman's harem got back to the English governor . . . it could be the incident that brought the English firmly against the sultan.

I'll recommend he buy her back, then kill her, he thought. *She should have been poisoned long ago.*

Moments later, Giza found Oman Kazamali in his own chambers, a delicate slave girl bent at his feet, administering a pedicure. Another stroked his temples and cooed soothingly in his ear. He lay half-reclining on a low divan and allowed his women to see to his needs.

At sight of the bowing figure of his slave master, the sultan scowled and flicked an annoyed hand in signal for him to rise.

Giza approached the sultan, bowing again. "Your Supreme Highness."

"Why do you disturb me, slave master? Stop bowing and speak your mind," the sultan growled.

"Your majesty must certainly remember a certain slave girl who was sold to the trader, Dahkir?"

"Yes, what of it?" The sultan lifted his head, his interest piqued. He remembered the girl well—her silky white skin, her hair like fire.

"Dahkir wishes to sell her back to you."

"Does she not please him?"

"Dahkir speaks highly of her abilities. And I myself have seen her."

"Is she as tempting as she was before?" The sultan's tone held an eager note that took Giza aback.

He veiled his eyes, casting about for a way to dampen this enthusiasm. It was best she was bought and killed, for she was a danger as long as she lived. He must try to make the sultan see that. "As I recall she was not well-suited to slavery, nor was she warm beneath your touch. But Dahkir claims he has achieved the impossible. She is as docile and meek as a turtle dove. And he assures me that she is unsurpassed in her abilities to please a man." He paused. "I do not believe him for a moment. That one was a tigress. Obviously he lies because he wants to make a profit on the girl."

But he saw his words had only made the sultan more intrigued. "Dahkir said she's tamed? He is no man to lie—or to chase profits. And is she still beautiful?"

Giza's eyes closed, and he lifted his hands to the ceiling, resigned. He couldn't risk pushing the sultan further—too many had died lately for lesser things. And if she couldn't be dead, she'd be less of a danger back in the harem. "A true gift from Allah," he admitted.

The sultan waved the two women from his side. With bowed heads, they scurried quickly from the room, leaving Giza and the sultan alone.

He rose from the divan, Giza's eyes on him as he moved across the room to a low table and poured himself a goblet of wine. He drank off a large draught and turned back to the slave master.

"If she is as you describe, why then does Dahkir wish to rid himself of the girl?"

Giza shrugged. "He is traveling into the interior and cannot take the woman along. In friendship, he offers you the first opportunity to buy her back. If I may say so, your eminence, this is an opportunity that should not be passed by. Even if you don't want the girl, the English must not discover she lives and was once in your harems."

Oman Kazamali took another draught of the wine, mulling over what Giza had just told him. He remembered the Englishwoman well, all too well. He had been struck by her unique beauty and had desired her much that first night he visited her. But then there had been Farah's jealousies to contend with. She had forced him to get rid of the girl. Now—he wrinkled his nose in distaste as he thought of his once-favorite odalisque. Farah had grown fat with child, unbearably moody; he no longer visited her, nor wished to visit her, as he once had. The thought of the Englishwoman—docile and ready to please him—made his eyes gleam hungrily, and a slow smile spread across his face.

Giza noted it. "Shall I accept his offer?"

The sultan moved back to the divan and stretched full-length upon it. "Whatever his price, pay it."

Chapter Forty-Four

There was a clang of metal as the barred door to the harem opened, and the guards stood aside for Juliette to pass through its portal. She took a deep breath, trying her best to look calmer than she felt, and walked inside the door.

She was in the harem again. The door was closed behind her with a ringing finality, and there was nothing she could do except follow the guards down the long hallway that led to the main part of the harem.

Their final interview with Giza had been brief. She had stood with downcast eyes, hardly able to believe it when he said the sultan would buy her back. "He will give her another try. If she has learned obedience and skills to please a man as you claim, then she will be given a permanent place in his harems. If she does not please him, is disobedient, she will be sold."

Deric had nodded, signifying that he would accept these terms. "I would not like to see her sold on the block, because she has been a loyal slave who has pleased me. But I do not fear that will happen. I am sure the sultan will be most satisfied with her." His eyes had regarded her impassively, and she had bowed low to him, making a deep obeisance. "Farewell," he said. "Allah be with you, and see that you please your new master as well as you have pleased me."

"I will do your bidding, master," she said meekly. "May Allah bring you good fortune in your future endeavors." For a long moment, they held each other's gaze.

"Guards!" Giza clapped his hands. The business was

finished; it was time for her to go. Without looking at Deric again or saying another word, she had turned on her heel and followed the guards out of the slave master's quarters, down the hall that led to the barred door to the harems.

Now it was over, and she was on her own. The next time she would see Deric he would be holding a rope on the roof if all went well. But for this day and evening, she would have to play her role faultlessly; there could be no slips.

The harèms were just as she remembered them. The guards led her at once to the main courtyard, where a few women were lounging or bathing. Sitting in the shade of a palm, with two slaves fanning her with peacock-feather fans, was Lilla, the *valide-sultan,* the older woman who, along with the eunuch Giza, ruled the harem world. She looked like an ancient queen reposing in the great rattan chair that was almost like a throne with its high, round back. Her eyes were as hard and impassive as Juliette remembered them. She watched Juliette approach with the guards and waited until she stood before her. Then with a negligent wave of a wrinkled hand, she dismissed the guards, leaving Juliette to face her alone.

"So. You have returned," said Lilla after a moment, studying Juliette carefully. She didn't remember much about this English slave, except that she had not been properly deferential before.

"Yes, *effendi,*" answered Juliette, bowing low. "I have returned."

"So? Why has your master sold you back? You displeased him?" Her eyes were bright and sharp with malice. Juliette knew well that the *valide-sultan* would know exactly why she was back, but was ready to play a game of cat-and-mouse with her to test her.

"I hope not, *effendi.* He said I pleased him always. I did my best. But he leaves for—" she acted as if she were struggling with the words—"wild places. He could not take me. I am ready to please and obey my new master now."

Lilla's eyes narrowed as she considered this. The girl certainly seemed much meeker now than she had on her previous stay in the harems. Perhaps she had learned to accept the fate that Allah had decreed for her. But it was not wise to be too sure. She would have to be closely watched until Lilla was sure her obedience was more than lip deep.

"It is your task to please the sultan now. When you were here before you were most unwomanly in your behavior. Still, the sultan was intrigued by your beauty, and if you can please him in his bed this time, you will have a comfortable life here. If you do not please him—and obey me!—you will be sold. The matter of keeping you here could easily become tiresome. See that it does not." She clapped her hands, and a humble slave appeared and knelt before her, head touching the ground.

"Take this slave to her new quarters. See that she is fed, bathed and dressed for this evening. The sultan plans to visit her tonight."

Juliette smiled at the hateful old woman as if this news pleased her greatly.

Perhaps she has learned after all, thought Lilla, watching the smile. *She is a fool if she does not know that the sultan's favor is the only road to security and power inside these walls.*

Juliette made a deep reverence to the old woman and followed the slave to her quarters, searching covertly for a glimpse of Halide and Ismail. Where could they be? She *must* find a way to speak to Halide today. Everyone knew she and Halide had been friends. If she was not at the baths, Juliette could ask someone where she was and go visit her—unless Halide was confined. She was free for the rest of the afternoon and early evening. The sultan would not visit her until late—and by then, please God, she would have flown.

As soon as she could—more suitably garbed in a loose caftan, her hair unbound—she went down to the courtyard to bathe. She approached the bath, looking in vain for a sight of Halide. In the bath were three women, two of whom she recognized from her previous stay. Those two exchanged glances, and one was about to speak when Juliette forestalled her by saying, "Greetings. I remember you both. Do you remember me? I am Juli, the Englishwoman who was here many months ago."

"We remember you. Welcome," said one of the women. Her tone was friendly, and Juliette felt relieved. Maybe they would no longer be suspicious of her. "What brings you back?"

Juliette slipped off her caftan and descended into the bath, enjoying the feel of the warm waters closing over her. "My master went on a journey he could not take me on. He asked the sultan if he wanted to buy me back, and he did."

The three women giggled, eyes bright with interest as they looked over this fascinating red-haired Englishwoman. "He must remember that strange hair and white skin," said one. "You are lucky your master brought you back here to these beautiful harems. Was he a good master?"

"Oh, yes," answered Juliette. "Very good. But I am glad to be back here. It was a hard life with him. He was a trader and always traveling."

One of the women giggled and put her hand over her mouth. "He may be pleased you are back, but I bet Farah will not be. I remember she was always jealous of you."

Juliette smiled. "So she still has the sultan's favor?"

"Maybe," said one slyly. "But there are those who think her influence over him may not be as strong lately. She is with child now, and hopes for a son so that she may strengthen the sultan's love for her."

It was obvious from the malicious smiles they all exchanged that none of them loved Farah and were glad that her downfall might be near. She had ruled the sultan with an iron hand for a long time, but if he were losing interest, then the position of favorite could be seized by someone else. Each woman hoped secretly she would be the one to enchant the sultan—even if only for a brief period. His favor would bring them more security, more power, even if it was a passing fancy.

"You will have to beware of her jealousy," whispered one, glancing over her shoulder. "She hated you before, and who knows what she might do now that she feels threatened. She fears your unusual beauty will catch his interest."

Juliette threw the woman a grateful look but suppressed an inner sigh. Oh, it hadn't changed! She hadn't been back an hour, and already the air was full of intrigue. "My friend Halide," she said after a moment. "How does she fare? I cannot wait to see her again. How surprised she will be that I am back!"

"Oh, Halide is most well. She is with her son now, teaching

him, as she is every day at this time. You will find her in her rooms; they are the same ones. I am sure she will be happy to see you!" They all smiled, for Halide's gentleness had always made her popular with most of the harem women. And since she was the sultan's relative, they didn't need to fear her as a rival. All of them sympathized with her plight at being held hostage, kept from her husband, but felt she was lucky to have her son with her.

"I think I'll go see her now," said Juliette, rising casually from the bath and drying herself with a linen towel. "I will not have time later; the *valide-sultan* says he may visit me this evening!" She smiled as if the news pleased her, and the others giggled and remarked how lucky she was.

"I wouldn't be too sure if I were you!" rang out a harsh voice, and Juliette spun to find Farah standing at the edge of the pool, watching her, hands on her hips. It was the same Farah Juliette remembered so well—black eyes sparkling with malice, command in every haughty line of her body. But Farah's beauty, always lush, had grown heavy with her pregnancy. Juliette's eyes went swiftly over her body and judged she was too far along to be entertaining the sultan. That was probably why she was so frantic about her own position, Juliette speculated. She smiled at Farah.

"Why, greetings, Farah. It has been a long time. You are right. Of course I am not sure the sultan will visit me; it is only what the *valide-sultan* told me. But who he takes his pleasure with is his decision alone, is it not? If I am lucky and he does honor me with a visit, I hope to please him better this time than I did last time."

There! she thought, watching the effect of her words on Farah's face with satisfaction. *Now perhaps she will be so jealous she will try to keep the sultan from visiting me tonight—and I hope she succeeds, just in case something prevents us from escaping tonight!*

"You think a foreign devil like yourself could ever please him for long, once your novelty has worn off?" said Farah with tones that dripped scorn. "Never! You have not been trained since birth to be an odalisque. I am sure he will be amused by your lack of skill, but not for more than a night or two. He will turn back to women he knows can please him, as he always does!"

But I've learned a thing or two since I was here last—and some things from you yourself, Farah, she thought, thinking of Deric. Aloud, she shrugged and said, "Perhaps you are right, *effendi.* I have learned much in my time with my master; he was most skilled in the arts of love. But only time will tell whether I am fortunate enough to please the sultan." Her eyes challenged Farah's, the look in them saying that she believed she *would* be able to hold the sultan's interest once he had visited her.

Farah ground her teeth at the confidence she saw in the younger woman's eyes. Curse Allah, the woman was more beautiful than she remembered! She stood naked and unashamed before Farah, where once she would have cringed and tried to hide her body from modesty. Then, Farah had known that such modesty would only bore the sultan. But now that advantage was gone. And her body was magnificent. She had filled out—was not as thin as she had been last year. And she had lost that frightened, defiant look that had been so unattractive. Now she looked like a serene, beautiful woman secure in her own powers of attraction. And that unusual hair! Like a river of flowing copper, its shining molten waves fell in gleaming curls down nearly to her waist. Yes, she would be a formidable rival, one she must take seriously now that she was hampered by pregnancy and now that the sultan's interest was waning.

Farah had not reached her position of power by fooling herself. *He has not visited me in months,* she raged inwardly, *and until this child is born—may Allah see that it is a son!—he will have no interest in me. More than two more months! There is much this flame-haired witch could accomplish in that time! Why did she have to return now?*

"Perhaps you will please him . . . and perhaps harem life will not agree with you. The food here has been known to make foreigners sick . . . or worse!" Farah whirled on her heel and stalked off, and the three women in the bath gave Juliette worried looks.

"Oh, she is angry," said one. "She fears you. You must be very careful what you eat and drink! Always let a slave taste it.

Because she meant that as a threat."

Juliette nodded grimly and watched Farah's retreating back. She was perfectly suited for the sultan. They deserved one another, animals that they both were! Yet she had given Juliette the excuse she needed to allay suspicion when she talked to Halide alone. "I will go and see Halide. She will know how to help me against Farah." The three women nodded and murmured as she put on her caftan and left the baths, taking a route she remembered so well of old, to Halide's rooms. Thank God Halide was not being closely guarded because of the war.

And pray God nothing would stop them from escaping tonight! She had no intention, she thought, crossing her fingers superstitiously, of being there to receive Oman Kazamali's visit!

Chapter Forty-Five

"Juliette! It *is* you! Oh, someone just told me you were back, but I did not know if I could believe it!" Halide ran across her room to the door Juliette had just opened, a mixture of pleasure and concern battling on her face. She caught Juliette by the arms and looked into her face, then embraced her with emotion.

Juliette laughed and embraced Halide back, struggling with tears at the sight of her dear friend's face. Halide was as lovely as ever, her dark eyes still gentle, yet there seemed to Juliette to be new lines of worry and care in her face.

"Yes, Halide, it is me! Believe that I am back." She drew Halide inside the room and closed the door. Somehow they must talk . . . but it wasn't safe in Halide's rooms. Juliette was sure they were watched. After all, Halide was a valuable prisoner . . . a hostage. It would be dangerous and foolish to think they would not have some way of keeping an eye on her.

"But why are you back? What has been happening to you? Your master . . . where is he? I was so happy when you left . . . I thought you would be able to go back to England . . . to freedom . . . to your family and people."

"It was not the will of Allah," Juliette said carefully. "My master preferred to keep me. Then he was leaving on a long caravan trip to Africa and could not take me, so he sold me back to my first master. I am happy to be here now . . . I have changed, Halide."

Halide searched her face as if she could not believe what she was hearing. Juliette smiled at her but met her eyes steadily, trying to convey she had more to tell Halide.

"Oh, I am so happy to see you again, Halide. There is something I wish to talk to you about . . . Farah. I believe she is angry I am back. Will you walk in the gardens with me where we can talk privately?" Juliette knew that if there were any watchers or listeners, they would already know about her confrontation with Farah in the baths. They would think it natural that she would consult her friend Halide about it. There were places in the garden they could talk without being overheard, and this would give the watchers an explanation of why she wanted to be alone with Halide, of what they talked about.

"Yes, of course. I have some time before Ismail is brought to me. Shall we go now?" Juliette nodded and followed Halide out of the door, down the halls and into the gardens.

They walked along graveled paths until they were in the middle of a small lawn and sat on a stone bench. No one could approach them from any side without being seen. There were no trees nearby that could conceal a watcher.

"What of Farah?" asked Halide as they sat.

"Never mind Farah," said Juliette, quietly and swiftly. "I lied about my master and why I am here. I *did* gain my freedom. I have been living in Malta all these months. Listen carefully to me now. I am here to help you and Ismail escape. Deric . . . the man who once held me for Mulay, you remember?" Halide nodded. Juliette had told her everything before.

"He is a good man—not what I thought him. Trust me—there is no time to tell you the whole story." She took a deep breath and grasped Halide's hand. "He has been in touch with your husband Aznan. Together they have come up with a plan of escape. If you do just what I say, we will all be out of the harem tonight, and you will be with Aznan by this time tomorrow . . . you and Ismail will be free. It is a good plan, Halide. Will you trust us and try?"

Halide's face had paled as Juliette spoke, her lips going white. She crushed Juliette's hand in a grip that seemed like it would break bones.

"My husband knows of this plan . . . he helped with it?" she asked after a moment.

"Yes."

"Then I will do whatever you say. Tell me what I must do."

Juliette was both surprised and relieved at Halide's quick acceptance of the plan. She reflected that if it had been her, she would have had a thousand questions. Halide smiled as if she read her mind.

"We do not have time for my questions now. We must not be seen talking together too long if we do not want to create suspicion. So tell me what I must know and no more. If it succeeds, I will have time to ask everything I want to know."

Juliette swallowed and gathered her wits. "We escape tonight. Two hours after dark, take Ismail to the upstairs hallway between the harem rooms and the servants' rooms. There is a window that opens in the hallway. Deric will be on the roof. He will lower a rope, and we will escape over the roofs. He has been on the roof several nights . . . it is safe. Wear no shoes or soft shoes. Can you do this?"

"Yes. Ismail is sent to me every night before bed. I will get rid of my servants on a pretext. At exactly two hours after sunset?"

"Yes, *exactly*. I will be there waiting for you. If you have any other questions, ask them now. I will not see you the rest of the day. If anything goes wrong, send a servant to say you are indisposed. I will do the same if anything goes wrong for me."

"I have no more questions. We should go now."

They rose and linked arms, and Halide at once began telling Juliette amusing anecdotes of the harem that had happened in her absence. They strolled from the bench down the paths to the more populated areas of the garden, Juliette inwardly marveling at how relaxed and natural Halide seemed. She talked and laughed as if nothing more was on her mind than uncomplicated pleasure at seeing an old friend. Juliette squinted at the sun, seeing that it was beginning to wester. Oh, pray God, if everything went well, in only a few more hours she would be out of this accursed harem!

They passed a small group of women standing and chatting, and smiled and nodded at them. Halide went on, sure the women could hear them, "And so she is pregnant and hopes for a son. We all wait to see what sex the child will be; she will be angry if it is a daughter! Speaking of sons, you must come and see mine tonight or tomorrow. He will be so happy to see you! And he can practice English with you once again. . . ." They strolled out of earshot of the women, embraced fondly and parted, Juliette walking idly, looking at the flowers as if she had nothing better to do, nothing on her mind but filling time. Halide disappeared into the harem.

Finally Juliette went to her rooms, feeling exhausted. There were hours left before she would go to the hallway . . . hours where anything might go wrong. Her nerves felt stretched to the breaking point. *What if Deric is caught?* she found herself thinking, then tried hard to put all such thoughts out of her mind. *Now* was when she needed her courage, these empty hours alone, a spy with a dangerous secret, prey to every kind of fear and worry. Once the escape was under way, she knew that action would take the place of worry and she would not shake until it was all over.

She stretched out on the bed. She wished she could fall asleep . . . but she knew she was too keyed up to sleep. And besides . . . what if she fell asleep and slept through the rendezvous? She giggled nervously at the thought. She must think about something else . . . get her mind off tonight.

A picture of Deric's face rose unbidden before her. Deric. *My love . . .*

The memory of their interrupted kiss came to her, and a thrill strummed the pit of her stomach at the thought. Had he at last been about to tell her he loved her?

She sighed. Everything had happened so fast, they'd had no other moment alone. But for that moment, it had seemed as if he loved her, too. Was she fooling herself again?

For a few moments, she allowed herself the indulgence of wondering what it would be like to be married to Deric. He would always be restless for adventure; he would never live a conventional life. Would Deric even want children? A home? Or would he always roam the world, never wanting to settle down to one home . . . or one woman?

Once, she'd taken it for granted what she wanted was a settled home, a conventional husband . . . because that had been all she'd ever known. How far behind her, how long ago, her life in England seemed now. With a little smile, she remembered how excited she'd been to be leaving England . . . and how innocent she'd really been, thinking herself so worldly. That long-ago afternoon when she'd left Avery Ashburn without a stitch of clothing . . . it seemed like another lifetime.

And it was, in a way. That was before she'd met Deric, and before the sinking of the *Alexandria* had turned her life upside down and forced her to find out what she really wanted from life.

She sighed and turned on her side, pillowing her head on her arm. The truth was, she'd be happy if she lived in a tent forever, as long as it was Deric's tent.

No woman exists for me except you. . . . What a thrill even remembering his words gave her. He had said those words, but had he meant them?

A sharp rap on the door brought her to a sitting position, and after a moment's pause, the door was flung open.

Framed in the doorway was the malevolent face of Giza.

For a moment, he stood, looking her over with contempt, his eyes locked with hers. Then he swaggered inside the room as if he owned it.

"So . . . now you are back once more. It is twice now I have bought you," he said, and Juliette shuddered at the cruelty in his tone, the hateful voice she remembered so well. His dark eyes raked her, and he smiled as if he could see her fear of him and was enjoying it.

"So you have bought me twice," she answered, shrugging indifferently.

"Last time, because you did not please the sultan, he was angry with me. I have no intention of allowing you to endanger me a second time. This time, it is my business to see that you send him away satisfied. If you do not, I will see your naked body cowering from the lash of my *koorbash*. Seeing you suffer will be a revenge I will enjoy, in payment for the suffering you caused me last time because of the sultan's anger."

"Denying pleasure to you will make me very happy, so I shall be sure to be obedient in all things. I have changed, Giza.

I am ready to serve my master with my heart, soul . . . and body."

He smiled again, cruel and vicious. "So? We shall see. I have come to tell you that you will soon have a chance to prove your obedience. The sultan will visit you tonight. You must get ready. We will see if you please him this time."

Her heart sank, but she said with a smile, "This is not news. The *valide-sultan* has already told me to expect him. If that is all you came to say, you have wasted your time, Giza. I am sensible how fortunate I am. I can hardly wait for his presence. Last time he was too taken with Farah to visit my bed, so I never had the chance to delight him with my skills. Now that she is pregnant, perhaps I will have an opportunity to better please my master. What time will he come to me?"

Giza was watching her face closely. *She has changed,* he thought. *She seems happy he is coming . . . but was that fear I saw in her eyes for a moment? Perhaps she still fears him . . . as well she should. Or perhaps she fears all men and puts on a brave front to save her skin. If that is the case, I will know tomorrow, for she will not be able to fool the sultan.*

"Time?" he said aloud. "I do not know what time he will visit you. Be ready by dark, for he will come when it pleases him . . . or not at all. I will send in slaves to help you get ready."

He turned on his heel and left the room, banging the door behind him. Juliette sat staring at the closed door. The sultan was definitely going to visit her tonight. Should she postpone the escape? Or go—and risk him finding her gone when he came and raising the alarm?

But if she stayed, she would have to submit to him.

"I'm going tonight," she whispered.

Chapter Forty-Six

Juliette stood at the window watching the last fiery red of the sun disappear beneath the treetops. She checked her watch. In two hours, unless she sent a message that she was "indisposed," Halide and Ismail would meet her in the hall.

Whether they were there or not, Deric would be waiting on the roof tonight.

She could see him lying, looking over the edge for a white handkerchief to be waved out the window. He would wait all night, she knew. If they were not there by an hour before dawn, he would leave . . . and come back tomorrow night.

If they didn't come tonight . . . he would be frantic.

Every night they didn't come increased his chances of being caught, she knew. Every time he had to cross the roof, something could go wrong.

And if she stayed tonight . . . the sultan would visit her.

Juliette shivered at the thought. She never wanted to see his cruel face again. How could she allow him to touch her?

She couldn't.

But if she was gone when he came to her room . . . the alarm would be raised.

Would it matter? It would only take a few moments for them to get to the hall and climb to the roof, then a few moments more to cross the roof with luck. No . . . more than a few moments, Juliette corrected herself. The roofs were vast. It would take minutes, not moments.

But if he came to her room and she was missed . . . at first they wouldn't suspect escape. They would search the harem for her—think she was hiding—before they thought of escape.

Would they go to Halide's rooms first and find she was gone too? Then they would know it was an escape sooner.

But the sultan would dine first. Usually, he didn't come to a woman's room until later . . . perhaps midnight. By that time, they would all be long gone.

When Juliette left her room, she could tell her slave she was going for a walk in the gardens. The slave wouldn't stop her, even though she would be afraid since the sultan was expected tonight. But slaves were obedient, never questioning orders. That way, when he arrived and did not find her in her room, first they would search the dark gardens.

It would buy time.

Juliette turned from the window, her mouth setting in a grim line. The waiting was unendurable. She paced up and down like a caged animal, waiting for the hours to pass.

Every few moments she drew out her watch and looked at it. She had placed it on a gold chain around her neck. She grimaced, looking down at the clothes she was wearing: a pale yellow silk bodice and skirt trimmed with gleaming gold, bracelets on her wrists and ankles . . . veil over her hair. Please God, it would be the last time she had to dress in this degrading fashion, like a *houri* bent on a man's pleasure!

The minutes crawled. Juliette paced, trying to be calm, knowing that these would be the longest hours she would ever spend in her life.

"You have the horses hidden?" Deric whispered at the shadow who joined him in the black darkness at the foot of the palace wall, seeming to materialize out of the night itself without a sound.

"Yes . . . there is no problem. They are in a shed in the marketplace outside the walls." A flash of white teeth showed the speaker to be Farouk.

"Then say your prayers to Allah, my friend, it is time I go."

Farouk clasped Deric's hand hard in the darkness, and whispered, "I will be waiting for you. Allah be with you."

Farouk watched as Deric climbed the building to the roof,

slower than usual because of the ladder he held. Then Farouk slipped around the side of the building. He must hide in the darkness where he could see the palace wall, to be ready to lead them when they got there and climbed down. Pray Allah they could be trusted to be swift and silent when the time came! Farouk squatted on his heels in the darkness and settled down to wait, wishing he could smoke a pipe to pass the time, but knowing he could risk no match.

Deric crouched on the roof of the building in the dark, glad that tonight clouds obscured the moon. The night was dark as pitch as he waited for the guard to appear. He had blackened his face and hands, and wrapped a black turban around his head. His clothes were pitch black. He knew the sentry would not see him even if he happened to look at the building's roof as he passed.

In a few moments, the sentry appeared, and Deric watched his slow progress along the wall's top. He held his breath as the man approached and passed by, and watched with narrowed eyes as he walked down to the end of the wall and disappeared.

In a moment, he rose and balanced on the roof's edge, holding the ladder horizontally, then leapt silent as a panther onto the wall. He gained his balance and dropped onto the nearby roof of the palace, and ran in a crouch until he was out of sight of the palace walls. He stopped in the darkness to catch his breath and listen, setting the ladder down in the shadows. There it would wait until they returned.

Silence. It was quiet tonight, no night birds singing, perhaps because of the cloud cover and absolute darkness. He could hear a few faint noises from the palace and that was all.

Steady, he reminded himself silently. *Do everything with caution. Tonight of all nights, do not let excitement make you take any risks.*

Moving carefully, every sense alert, Deric crossed the roofs like a shade, flitting from cover to cover silently on the route he and Farouk had mapped out. At last, breathing hard, he reached the roof over the harems and went to the place he would wait above the window. He stretched flat on the ground and hung his head over slightly, looking down. All around him, the night was silent.

Now he, too, had only to wait.

As he lay there, a ferocious anxiety rose inside him . . . the same anxiety that had filled him all day, ever since Juliette had been led away by the guards into the harem.

I was mad! he thought for the hundredth time. *How could I have let her take this risk?*

He ground his teeth as he thought of the sultan. He had not taken her last time, though the thought of his hands pawing at Juliette caused him to become hot with rage. But if anything went wrong . . . nothing would stop him this time from taking her! He felt himself break into a sweat of helpless anger at the very thought.

Someone else touching my Juli! he fumed, amazed at the violence of his feelings. Not only could he not stand the thought of another man touching her . . . he couldn't stand the thought of her being frightened, or in danger. Bitterly he blamed himself again for letting her do this . . . take part in this mad scheme!

Deric shook his head, wondering what was wrong with him. How had one woman come to mean so much to him? She had twined her way around his heart before he knew it, stolen his feelings away when he wasn't looking. He had never been able to forget her after he had let her go in Tripoli. He couldn't stop wanting her—more than he wanted any other woman—no matter how hard he tried.

And it is more than just wanting her, he thought. *If that were all it was, it would be simple.* But no . . . it was so much more. It was the delight he took in talking to her . . . the sense and the courage she had, like no other woman he'd ever met! It was the way she made him laugh, the way she made him want to protect her, the way she made him feel so strangely tender one moment, so ragingly passionate the next.

His brows came together in a scowl, and he stared down into the night, in a fever of wondering where she was, what she was doing. "If I get you out of this safely, my girl, I'll never let you risk your pretty skin again," he growled softly, then shook his head. She had brought him to this state, talking aloud to himself, nearly out of his mind with worry for her!

"Damn it, Juli . . . I think I'm in love with you," he whispered aloud, struck to the core of his soul by the realization. He was nearly jolted off the roof. *Love Juliette?* It couldn't be possible. Wasn't falling in love the one thing he'd promised himself never to do again?

And then he thought of how discontent and restless he'd been those four months without her. How he hadn't known which way to turn, or what he wanted to do, wandering without purpose, all interest in his caravans—interest in just about everything—scattered to the winds. He had to face it. He'd been miserable without her, a walking dead man, a man without hope.

At least until Aznan approached him.

Aznan had finally given him back the hope he needed, the excuse he'd been looking for to go after her. He remembered how just the thought of seeing her again had been enough to breathe life back into his soul, to make him whole again.

No matter how many times he'd told himself it was the promise of fortune that had sent him to Malta, he had known it was Juli. It had been Juli all along. *Face it, old man, you can't stand being away from her. And do you know why?*

All at once it was as obvious as the sun rising in the morning.

Because, you stupid blind fool, you love her! You've loved her since she first tumbled down that hill and landed at your feet. And you've been fighting it ever since.

All the anger and frustration that had been building up inside him for so long was gone, and a completely new tide of emotions rushed through him. He loved her! He loved her, and it was the most wonderful feeling he'd ever known! He wanted to stand and shout it at the top of his lungs, wanted the whole world to know he was in love with Juliette Hawkins. And most of all, he wanted her to know it.

He thought of how she would react, and his mouth twisted in a bitter smile, his elation slowly fading. She didn't want him any more. Hadn't she told him so?

Maybe . . . maybe once she had, he thought, remembering the happy sparkle in her deep blue eyes during the first week they spent together . . . remembering the pain in her eyes when he'd been fool enough to let her leave with Lionel.

And you never said a word to stop her.

The realization of how he'd treated her wrenched his gut.

Maybe once she'd loved him; but now she said it was all over, and who could blame her?

He clenched his fists as the thought tied his stomach in knots. This was the very reason why he'd vowed never to love a woman again, never to give away his heart. It could only cause pain.

It's too late, he told himself. The damage was already done. He couldn't take back all the hurtful things he'd said and done to her—and he'd done plenty. She'd asked for nothing, and he'd given her exactly that. She had offered him her love, and like a fool he'd pushed it away. It was far too late.

You selfish bastard, he cursed himself. *You've thrown away the greatest fortune any man could ever possess. If she doesn't hate you by now, she should.*

He checked his watch. It was getting late, and he wondered how long he would have to wait. They had to come tonight! Otherwise, he knew he would have to find a way into the harem himself to make sure Juli was safe from the sultan. Even if he had to kill every guard in the place, he couldn't leave her inside. . . .

"She had better come tonight," he whispered, and settled down to wait for what he knew would be the longest night of his life.

Juliette checked her watch again. Only a half an hour left until she must leave! The minutes had crawled by slowly, each one seeming like an hour. But now the end was in sight. By now Deric would be waiting on the roof. There had been no message from Halide. At every moment, she had listened for a knock on the door, fearing a servant who would tell her Halide was indisposed and the escape put off.

There was a soft knock on the door.

Juliette froze in mid-stride, staring at the door in horror. She felt her pulse beat madly in her throat three times, and she swallowed with a mouth suddenly dry.

"C-come in," she managed after a frozen moment.

The door opened.

It was not one of Halide's servants that she saw framed in the doorway.

It was the sultan himself.

He was magnificently dressed in a white shirt and full, raw-

trying to feign passion at his touch.

Suddenly he pulled her onto his lap on the divan, his mouth still brutally searching hers, his arms around her like iron bands. She shifted her weight and put her arms around his shoulders, feeling the world melt into a red rage that their plans were foiled . . . that he would dare kiss her . . . that he thought he could take her to his bed! With a will of its own, as she kissed him back passionately, one hand found and gripped the wine bottle on the table, and before she knew consciously what she was doing, she brought it up and, with a violent movement that used all her strength, crashed it down on the back of his head.

It shattered, and she sat back, horrified and shaking at what she had done. He was slumped on the divan under her, his head wet with wine and with—her hand felt the back of his head and came back covered with blood. In horror, she listened to his faint breathing and then jumped up.

She had hit the sultan over the head with a wine bottle. Perhaps he was dying! But what if he woke up any moment? She had never hit anyone over the head before; she did not know how long he would be out.

Hands shaking, she picked up her veil and bound it around his mouth as a tight gag, leaving his nose uncovered so he could breathe. Then she raced to her coffer and rummaged in it for some strong cords which were used as belts for her caftans and raced back to him, binding his hands and feet as tightly as she could. It would keep him, perhaps, from raising the alarm a little longer when he awoke.

Shaking and staring at the slumped man she had gagged and bound, she straightened and listened with terror for a moment to his low, labored breaths.

Then Juliette whirled and fled to the door, opening it a crack and peering out into the hallway.

It was empty.

If he didn't wake for a long time—an hour . . . never—Juliette knew it would be long before anyone entered her chambers. The sultan was given utter privacy when he was with his women.

Uttering a fervent prayer for luck, she opened the door and slipped into the hallway.

Chapter Forty-Seven

Juliette ran down the empty hall, her heart pounding in her throat, breath short. She slowed her steps with an effort, realizing suddenly that if someone saw her running, they would be suspicious. The hall seemed endless as her soft steps fell on the tiles.

Reaching the end of the hall, she passed through an arched doorway to the stairs to the upper hall. She climbed them two at a time, trying hard not to feel frantic, praying every moment that Halide and Ismail would be there.

When she reached the upper hall, she stopped and looked around. It was deserted as always. She ran swiftly down the hall around a corner, and to her great relief, Halide and Ismail stood by the window, waiting for her.

"Halide!" she whispered, running up to her. "We must not lose a moment. The sultan came to me; I hit him over the head. He is unconscious, but I do not know how long it will be before he wakes up."

Halide's eyes widened, and she drew Ismail close to her. Juliette noted that they both wore dark clothes and were barefoot. She went to the window and opened it swiftly, leaning out and pulling a white scarf from her belt as she did so.

She leaned into the darkness and waved the scarf up and down.

"Coming, Juli," came a soft voice from above. Deric! A moment later, a rope snaked down, and Juliette caught it.

"Quickly," she whispered, turning to Halide. "Ismail first."

Ismail stepped forward silently, his dark eyes sparkling with excitement. "Hold the rope," Juliette whispered. "It is a short way. Deric will pull you up."

They set the boy on the windowsill and tied the rope around his waist. He held tightly as Juliette picked him up and held him out the window. At once, Deric began hauling the rope hand over hand upward, and the boy was raised swiftly up to the roof.

Juliette felt her palms sweating with anxiety. Even though only moments were passing, it seemed to her impossible that they would not be discovered at any second.

At last the rope descended again.

"Go, Halide—do not argue with me," Juliette whispered fiercely, seeing her friend was about to protest that Juliette should go first. She pushed Halide to the window. "We are too heavy for Deric to lift. Can you help by climbing while he pulls?"

Halide nodded, and taking the rope between her hands, hung for a moment before with supreme effort, she began to raise herself hand over hand. Juliette watched anxiously as she cleared the window and gained the wall above, finding footholds to help her balance and push upward. Deric was hauling on the rope, too, and as Juliette held her breath, leaning out the window, she saw Deric's dark shape lean over and grasp Halide under the arms, pulling her onto the roof.

The rope descended again, and Juliette climbed onto the window ledge, ready to duplicate Halide's climb. She swung out and hung for a moment, feeling the rough rope grate on her palms, feeling as if her body was an impossible weight that she could never lift. Just as she began to raise herself, hand by hand, past the window to the wall, her blood ran cold. There was a shout in the hallway.

"We are discovered!" she gasped as adrenaline surged through her and she swarmed upward.

"Climb, Juli!" Deric cried, hauling on the rope. She reached the wall as a shout at the window made her look down. Giza was leaning out the window, a terrible snarl on his face. He leaned out and reached upward, grabbing her ankle.

"You try to escape!" he shouted. "I will never let you!"

Juliette kicked frantically, trying to free her ankle from his iron grasp. She felt the rope abrade her palms as Deric pulled from above. Her grip started to slip, Giza's strength pulling her downward. In a moment she would fall—fall to her death on the rocks below!

Giza leaned far out the window, his other hand reaching for her other kicking ankle. He grabbed wildly, and just at that moment, Juliette, fueled by a tremendous burst of adrenaline as she felt her grip giving, kicked the ankle he held with all her might outward.

For a moment, he flailed in the air, still holding her ankle, then she felt his fingers open as he lost his balance. She hung, watching in horror as his arms pinwheeled and he tried to save himself. But he was too far out the window. Suddenly he fell, spiraling into the darkness below, a long scream coming up through the air that ended sharply as they heard a thud where his body hit the rocks.

Hanging with her arms over her head, Juliette felt herself being pulled swiftly upward, and in a moment, Deric's arms were lifting her onto the roof and depositing her in a shaking bundle next to Halide, who put her arms around Juliette and held her.

Deric looked into her face for a moment, then said, "I'll be right back. I have to see if there is anyone else in the hallway and, if there is, kill them."

Before Juliette could protest, he had lowered himself over the side on the rope, and went swiftly hand over hand down to the window. He peered in and, to Juliette's bewildered mind, was swiftly back up over the roof at her side.

"He was alone, but someone will have heard his scream. We have to go!" He grabbed her hand and Halide's while Halide grasped Ismail's hand in hers. "Follow me and don't make a sound."

It seemed like a nightmare to Juliette as they all crossed the dark roofs, following Deric's crouching run from shadow to shadow. She was still in shock from the grasp of Giza's hand on her ankle, from hitting the sultan over the head, from Giza's horrible fall to his death. But there was no time now to give in to the hysterics she could feel just under the surface. That would come later. Now every sense was painfully alert as they ran like fugitives over the dark roofs, following Deric's lead.

They reached the place where they had to cross the roofed walkway between two roofs. Deric crouched for a moment in the dark, seeing that all was clear, listening for sounds. "We must be silent here if we are not to be discovered," he commanded in a whisper. "You have all been brave. Ismail, your father will be proud. We will see him soon. Now, do not hurry. Go slowly and quietly. When you get to the other side, crouch down. Then when we are across, we can all run again." His quiet words calmed them all, giving them confidence and strength.

One by one, they slowly crawled over the walkway roof. They could hear faint talking from below, and again, Juliette found herself thinking it was impossible they would not be discovered at any moment. But finally Deric, the last to cross, joined them on the other side, and their crouching run from shadow to shadow started again. Deric swerved and snatched up the ladder.

"We are almost there!" gasped Deric at last, over his shoulder. "Just this last roof to cross and we are at the wall."

As they began to run across the roof, they heard faint shouts far behind them. Turning in terror, they saw the shapes of perhaps ten guards far behind them on the roofs, outlined against the night, running after them. Juliette could make out cutlasses being waved and hear blood-curdling yells. A moment later there was a shot.

"We are discovered! Run!" shouted Deric, dropping behind them and pulling out his pistol, which gleamed dully in the faint light. He shoved the ladder into Juliette's hands, and she took it, staring behind her at the pursuing soldiers.

Terror lent wings to their feet as they crossed the roof. Juliette threw the ladder down, and they scrambled across, Deric last. He knocked the ladder down, and it fell with a clatter to the cobblestones beneath. They all stood on the wall, looking at Deric.

"Over the side!" shouted Deric. "There isn't time for a rope—Halide—go first. Hang and then drop. Juliette will hand Ismail down to you."

Quick as thought, Halide obeyed him, and Deric stood watchfully as Juliette lifted Ismail by the arms, laid down and dangled him over the side, then dropped him a short distance into Halide's arms. A dark shape appeared at Halide's side, and Juliette knew it was Farouk.

"Here comes a guard—quickly! I'll hold him off," said Deric grimly.

Juliette had been trying not to listen to the sounds of shouting pursuit and gunshots on the roof getting closer as she lifted the boy over the wall, but once he was safely down, she looked up in fear and saw a guard running along the wall toward Deric, sword raised.

She jumped up in horror and saw Deric and the guard grappling on the wall, rolling in a desperate fight. The guard's cutlass flashed, Deric's arm jerked and suddenly the guard slumped in a heap as Deric's knife found him.

"Go, Juli!" Deric shouted.

"Deric—" she cried.

"They are almost here. Go! I'll hold them off. Go, damn you!" Deric's face was fierce beneath the black as he took her by the shoulders and shook her. A sob escaped her throat as she climbed over the wall and hung. Deric's face was above her for a moment. "I'll hold them off for a few moments and then join you. Save Halide and Ismail and get away, Juli! Now go!"

She dropped and rolled when she hit the ground. Farouk picked her up.

"Dahkir?" he panted.

"He won't come!" she cried. "He is going to try to hold off the soldiers, then come!"

Farouk glanced swiftly up at the wall, battling the instinct to stay with his comrade. Shots rang out from above. "He is buying us time. We make his bravery in vain if we do not take it!" he cried suddenly and seized her hand. Halide and she grabbed the boy's hands and followed Farouk at a run down a dark alley, while sounds of a fight exploded in the night behind them.

They ran through dark streets, feeling their breath catching in their throats, down twisting alleys and flights of steps that caught at their feet in the dark, making them stumble. Farouk picked up Ismail and swung him to his chest as he ran.

"Only speed can save us now," he gasped. "Not far now—run for your lives!"

When Juliette thought her lungs would burst, they came out of an alley to the foot of a dark wall. A rope ladder hung over the ten-foot wall.

"Climb!" ordered Farouk, setting Ismail on the ladder. "This is the outer wall of the city. Climb—everyone!"

They followed each other closely up the ladder to the top, then down the other side. They stood waiting, their breath coming in ragged gasps, as Farouk climbed down, leaving the ladder on the wall in case Deric was somewhere behind them.

"To that shed," he gasped, pointing to a low dark building close by in the dark.

They ran the few steps. Inside the building were four saddled horses. Swiftly, Halide, Farouk and Juliette mounted three of them, Farouk lifting Ismail in front of him.

"Deric?" cried Juliette desperately as they swung the horses' heads toward the door and rode out of the shed.

"We can do nothing for him now. Allah willing, he will get here and get to his horse. We must ride now like the devil himself was after us!"

They spurred their horses into the night and rode at a gallop away from the city walls. Juliette turned as she rode and looked back at the dark bulk of the city against the night. There was no sign of pursuit—and no sign of Deric.

Deric! Was he dead? Captured? Or had he managed to escape? And they—could they outride the pursuit that was soon to follow and reach safety?

Juliette felt the night wind whipping the tears that fell from her eyes backward into the night as she set her spurs to her horse again and rode for her life.

Chapter Forty-Eight

At last their exhausted horses emerged from the hills onto a small strip of deserted beach. Juliette felt like crying with relief at the sight of the ship anchored at the head of the bay—Aznan's ship! They were safe. But Deric—? She threw a despairing glance behind her but saw nothing but dark night.

"Thank Allah, thank Allah, we are here!" cried Halide in a voice that throbbed with emotion and exhaustion.

As they reined their blowing, stumbling horses, four men appeared from a place of concealment behind some rocks and came running down the shore toward them. Juliette slid numbly from her horse.

She stumbled over to Halide, her legs feeling as if they would not hold her up, and the two women fell into each other's arms.

"Oh, Halide, thank God we are here—safe!"

"Yes—but I am so worried—your Deric! I tremble to think!"

Halide's dark eyes looked with sorrow into Juliette's frightened ones.

"I tremble to think, too, Halide," she whispered.

She bent her head and prayed with all her heart and soul that Deric was safe, had somehow escaped the swarm of guards on the roof. But the dread in her heart told her there was little hope, and that perhaps a bullet had found him as they raced away from the wall.

"Dear God," she prayed, "just give me a chance to see him one more time. Please let me see him one more time—let him be safe!"

A tall shape appeared at their side, turning Halide around. With a cry, Halide let Juliette go and fell into his arms. Juliette stared at the handsome man who embraced Halide, watching their tears of joy mingle. It was Aznan.

"Father! Father!" Ismail shouted, and Aznan turned and caught Ismail in his arms. Then the three of them clung together, and Aznan covered their faces with kisses and tears. Juliette felt her heart twist with pain and pleasure as she watched. A sob escaped her throat as she thought of how happy this moment would be if only Deric were at her side—

An arm encircled her, and she looked up into Farouk's grave dark eyes. "Do not cry, Juli," he said, trying to comfort her. "Perhaps he escaped. We must not believe the worst until we know. Trust Allah and ask him for strength if you can. Already you have shown more strength than any woman I have ever known. Allah gave you a warrior's heart. Try to keep up that courage I know you have now. If there is any way on earth, I will find him."

He looked down into her tear-stained face, her blue eyes and lashes sparkling. Then he said quietly, "You love him, don't you?"

She let out a ragged sigh. "Yes, I love him. Even though I know he does not love me—may never love *one* woman—but instead gives his heart to many. I know he is an adventurer. But somehow, my heart won't listen to my head and doesn't care that we can never be together."

Farouk looked out to sea, and his arm tightened around her shoulder. "I know he cares about you more than he has ever cared about any woman."

At that moment Aznan walked up to them, followed closely by his wife and son. He bowed deeply to them, his eyes alive with emotion, then took their hands.

"My friends—Farouk, Miss Hawkins—I should have thanked you first before I did anything else, but seeing my wife and son drove it out of my mind. How can I thank you enough? A lifetime would not be adequate to express gratitude for what you have done. Because of you, they are safe—and my endless days and nights of worry and anguish over them are at an end. I will never, never find words to express to you what this means to me—to my family. Anything you want in life, you have only to ask me, as long as I draw breath."

Farouk smiled. "We are happy that we were able to help you. And I wish I could stay to rejoice with you. But Deric has been left behind, perhaps captured. Every moment is precious to me now. I must get back to Tripoli and find out what has become of him."

"I know—this distresses me to no end. What will you need? Money for bribes? Fresh horses? Soldiers? Whatever you ask will be yours. I will do anything in my power to free him if he has been captured."

"I will not be sure what I will need until I get back to Tripoli and find out what has happened to him. I will need a fast horse now to ride back, and yes, perhaps some money for bribes. Is there a contact of yours in Tripoli I can get word to in case I need more assistance, soldiers, once I know what has happened?"

"Of course." Aznan's face was grave and businesslike. "But you cannot ride alone, my friend. You must have at least a few trained soldiers with you, disguised. You may run into the sultan's soldiers. They will be searching for you. And how do you propose to get inside the city gates?"

"I have a plan for that," Farouk said. "But yes, perhaps two men to accompany me in case of trouble will be good. And I must be armed."

"Can you not rest for a short time first?"

"I fear to lose even a moment. Perhaps I can rest once I find out what has happened."

"Then I will keep you no longer." Aznan held up a commanding hand that made Juliette see why he was a leader of men, and turned to his waiting men. "Ready fresh horses." He turned back to Farouk. "May Allah be with you, my friend, giving you every blessing for the great good you have already done. May He preserve our friend from harm." Aznan strode away to see to the horses, his cloak billowing in the wind. Juliette turned to Farouk.

"Farouk . . . I am going with you," she said.

He looked up, startled. "Going with me? No, you are not,"

he said, almost angrily.

"Yes, I am . . . and you cannot stop me. Aznan will give me a horse if I ask. If you do not take me, I will ride back to Tripoli alone."

"You're mad! It is too dangerous! The sultan's soldiers will be searching everywhere for us! And if they find you, it will be death."

"It will be death for you, too, if they find you . . . not just for me. Farouk, I *must* go! I cannot just stay here and wait! I have faced worse dangers in the past few days, and you let me face them. I tell you, you cannot stop me from coming!"

Farouk's face hardened. "If Dahkir is alive," he said brutally, "then he would never forgive me if I took you along and exposed you to more danger. I will not let you! Don't you see, Juli—you must face facts. Dahkir is probably dead. I go without hope to hear the news of his death. And if by some miracle he is alive, then he cannot have escaped. He will be a prisoner. What good would your coming do except put us all in more danger?"

"I don't care—I will go!"

Farouk scowled at her, looking like a pirate missing nothing but the knife between his teeth.

The sound of pounding hooves made both of their heads whip up. The black shape of a rider could be seen back at the entrance to the beach.

"Is it—" Juliette gasped.

Farouk was already running toward the rider, and in a moment, Juliette's own feet were flying across the sand. She saw the horse stumble to a stop as the rider slumped in the saddle. As she ran up, he slowly crumpled and slid onto the ground in a heap.

Farouk was beside him, kneeling. She flung herself on the ground next to him. "Is he—"

"Still breathing—but wounded," Farouk said, his hands busy at Deric's chest. She gasped when she saw them come away dark with glistening blood. She heard running footsteps, and Aznan came up beside them.

Farouk picked up Deric, who was limp in his arms. "We must get him on that ship!"

They all began running along the sand to where the waiting longboats were pulled up. Juliette could hardly breathe. Deric was alive—but he was hurt! Oh, God, could he be dying?

In a few moments, they were in the boat, Aznan and Farouk gently lifting Deric in. "There is a doctor on the ship," she heard Aznan say.

"Thank God," she breathed as they laid Deric's head in her lap.

As the men rowed out to the dark silhouette of the waiting ship, Juliette stroked Deric's hair and stared at his unconscious face. He'd gotten away. Surely—surely God would not desert them now! Surely Deric could not die now!

Chapter Forty-Nine

Juliette stood in front of the small mirror on her cabin wall, vainly trying to subdue her wayward hair into a French twist and pin it. The pins escaped from her tired fingers, and a strand of curls fell over her eyes. She shook her head in frustration and tried again impatiently.

"Oh—damn this hair!" she cried, almost ready to weep with frustration. Finally, she pinned down the last unruly curl and stared at the face reflected in the mirror. She almost didn't recognize herself. There were blue shadows under her eyes, and her face was pale with lack of sleep and worry.

She shook her head and bit her lip, turning to leave her cabin and go back to Deric's.

For three days and nights now, she had hardly left Deric's side. The ship had sailed down the coast, and they were anchored at Derna to care for Deric. He was burning up with a high fever, and they all feared for his life. His wound was truly dreadful. He'd been shot through the shoulder, and it was badly inflamed.

She entered his dimly lit cabin and crossed swiftly to a chair by his bed, taking the place she had barely left these last few days. She leaned forward and placed a hand on his forehead. It was still hot and dry.

Deric shifted restlessly in his sleep, drawing ragged breaths and muttering to himself. At least his delirium seemed to have passed, she thought thankfully, staring worriedly at his white, drawn features. For two days he had tossed and raved like a madman, in a jumbled mixture of Arabic and English that they could hardly understand.

And other times, he had shouted, "Juli! Juli!" over and over again, not able to hear when she leaned over him and softly repeated that she was beside him—that she was safe. She knew he worried in his delirium that she was still in the sultan's clutches, and wished there were some way she could let him know she was at his side.

She rose and sopped a linen cloth in a basin of cool water and wrung it out, putting it on his forehead and holding it there. Again, he moved restlessly under her touch and groaned in his sleep.

An hour later, after she had made him drink broth and water, holding up his head and patiently spooning the liquids down him, and then washed him, she dropped exhausted into the chair and took his hand. He had fallen into a deep, calm sleep with none of the restlessness of before, and for a few minutes, she sat looking at him as he slept.

Even when he was ill, how handsome he was to her! His golden brown hair fell over his pale face and sharp cheekbones, and the lines around his mouth had deepened. But when he was asleep or ill, there was a vulnerability about his face that she loved to watch, for it reminded her almost of the boy he must have once been. As she watched him, her heart ached with love for him, and she willed him with her entire being to get better, to be well!

She woke with a start in the dim cabin. Without realizing it, she had fallen asleep while she sat with Deric. The hand that was gripping hers was wet with sweat. She sat up and felt his forehead. His hair was damp; his fever had broken! He felt cooler to the touch!

Juliette said a quick prayer of thanks that came from the bottom of her heart, then loosened her hand from his clasp and got up. She opened the curtain of the cabin's porthole and let in the early morning light. Then she fetched a fresh basin of cool water to bathe him with, and fresh clothes.

She was pouring a glass of water for him to drink and one for herself when behind her, his voice said weakly, "Juli—it *is* you. It was you all along."

She whirled, setting down the water. "Deric!" she exclaimed, her voice vibrant. "You're awake! Oh, thank God!" She went to the chair by the bed and sat down, taking his hand again, struggling with tears that threatened to fall.

"I thought I saw you beside me sometimes—but I thought it was a dream. Oh, Juli—" He stopped for a moment, exhausted. "I thought maybe you were a vision—a mirage. Are you really here?"

"Yes, Deric, I've been here all along. You've been very ill. You mustn't tire yourself with too much talking now."

"Where—where am I?"

"You don't remember? You're aboard Aznan's ship now, far from Tripoli."

Deric's brows knitted as he tried to remember. "Halide—the boy?" he asked at last.

"All safe, and all on board this ship, too. Everything is fine—you succeeded. Because of you we are all safe, and now you're safe too." A few tears spilled over Juliette's lashes and rolled down her cheeks.

He closed his eyes, clearly exhausted. "Riding—like the wind. I remember a little, I think."

Juliette fetched the glass of water. "Here—drink this now, then sleep. You must rest, Deric; you've been wounded. We have all the time in the world to talk later, and when you're feeling stronger, I'm sure you'll remember everything." She held the glass to his lips, and he drank, never taking his eyes from her face. When he had drunk it all, he lay back weakly on the pillows, but he smiled at her.

"Juli—don't leave," he said, taking her hand and closing his eyes.

She smiled through her tears of joy. "I won't leave. I promise I'll be right here when you wake up." She watched as he fell into a healing sleep, his breathing even, so much different from the troubled delirium he had fought for so many days. It wasn't a few moments before her own eyes closed and her head dropped on her chest, and she slept an untroubled sleep, too, for the first time in days.

Deric awoke, feeling much more clear-headed than before, to find Farouk at his side.

"Where is Juli?" he asked, after a look around the tiny cabin showed him she was nowhere in sight.

Farouk grinned tauntingly at Deric. "So that is all the thanks I get! Not even a 'hello'—just 'Where's Juli?' as a reward for my pains!"

Deric laughed weakly. "Hello, Farouk—I *am* glad to see you. Now tell me where she is!"

"You *are* persistent, my friend! I sent her away to eat and get some sleep. She has been at your side practically without sleep for four days. I can tell you I had a hell of a time getting her to leave, too. She said she'd promised you to stay by your side. I almost had to pick her up and carry her out of here to get her to go. I think it was my threat to do just that that made her see reason."

Deric smiled again. "Headstrong as always, I see."

Farouk nodded. "Headstrong? Someday I will tell you how I tried to leave her behind when I thought I had to go back to rescue you! You will have your hands full if you marry that one, by Allah!"

Deric's face darkened, his eyes troubled for a moment. Farouk frowned, watching him. Then Deric shook his head slightly and demanded, "Tell me everything that happened! I can't seem to remember things except in fits and flashes, and it is driving me mad not to know!"

"Very well—on one condition. You must eat this food I've brought you while I talk. The ship's doctor has seen you and says we must not tire you with too much talk or excitement yet. But you have to stay awake to eat, and I know how tough you are. It would take more than a story to kill you, so I think it's safe."

Deric laughed again. He still felt weak, but much better. And he was surprised to find he was hungry. With Farouk's help, he sat up and Farouk put a tray on the bed. Deric started on some beef broth while Farouk sat down at his ease.

"First tell me—how badly am I wounded?" asked Deric. "This arm feels like merry hell."

"Not so badly. It is a bullet wound—you must have taken it on the roof. Clean through the shoulder. But were it not for the ship's doctor and Juli's devoted nursing, I think it would have finished you."

Deric's eyes darkened with memory. "Yes," he said shortly.

"Eat your soup or I will tell you no more," threatened Farouk, getting another smile from Deric. As Deric ate, Farouk took up the tale, allowing no interruptions. "When you are stronger, you can ask me all the questions you want," he warned, "but for now that is all you'll get, so be content with it!"

When he had finished, Farouk said, "Now tell me—how did you escape from the wall? I thought you were done for, my friend."

"The soldiers hid behind a wall when I started shooting at them, and started firing at me. I was trying to buy time—" He stopped. "Then I took that bullet, and it spun me off the wall. When I hit the ground, I got up and ran. I could hear them after me, but I lost them in the alleys. Somehow I made it to the horse."

"You were very brave, my friend," Farouk said softly. "Now you must sleep again or that doctor will kill me. And I will not answer for your own health if you refuse."

"Juli is very brave, Farouk. Going back into that harem was harder than facing an enemy's bullet," said Deric.

"Yes, she is. As brave as any man I know. Now sleep—or I swear I'll go fetch that doctor and he'll give you something to force you to!"

Deric smiled lazily at Farouk. "If you do that I'll thrash you as soon as I can stand. Don't worry—if you stop all this chattering, I'll sleep again, I promise you!" The two men smiled at each other, than clasped hands before Farouk walked out.

The next morning, Juliette stood in the passageway outside Deric's door, hesitating. She had slept around the clock and eaten a huge meal when at last she awoke, and she felt like a new person. Farouk told her Deric was much better after more food and sleep, and his memory of everything that happened was fast coming back to him. His arm was still sore, but the doctor had seen him again and pronounced him on the mend.

Juliette still hesitated before knocking on the door, suddenly feeling strangely shy. For several days and nights now, she had barely left his side, praying every moment for his recovery, feeding him and bathing him as if he were a tiny child. Even though he had been unconscious, she had felt closely bound to him during his struggle to live. And now she was standing out here, afraid for some reason to knock on his door—as if he were a total stranger!

She shook her head and smiled at herself, then lifted her hand and knocked on the door.

"Come in," he called. She took a deep breath and opened the door.

He was sitting up in bed, wearing a fresh white shirt, she saw. And he had shaved. He still looked pale and rather drawn, but his green eyes had the animation of returning health as he smiled at her.

"Juli! I was hoping it would be you and not Farouk," he said. "Please, come in—sit down!"

"Oh, thank God—you *are* better!" She smiled, crossing the room and sitting down on the chair at his side.

"Thanks to you," he said, his eyes searching hers.

Juliette shook her head, still smiling. "Thanks to your own strength, I believe."

"But you have nursed me. Farouk told me. I owe you my life, and I can never thank you for what you have done . . . or forget that."

Juliette was silent for a moment, then said, "But Deric—Halide and her son owe *you* everything. We all do. If it had not been for your bravery on the wall—holding them off—none of us would have escaped. You faced certain death—and worse, risked capture—to save us. There can be no talk of debts. We all owe each other too much for that. I only thank God every moment that we are all safe now. That is all that matters."

Deric smiled ruefully. "So . . . our adventures are over. I imagine you will run a mile if anyone ever suggests another dangerous adventure to you again."

Juliette rose and walked to the porthole, fighting a sudden rush of emotion she didn't want him to see in her face. *If you were at my side, I would face anything*, were the words that rose to her lips, the words she fought down. It was enough that Deric had lived. It was what she had prayed for. He would never love her the way she loved him; she was wise enough to know it. *And I won't burden him with my love,* she thought firmly. After a moment, she turned back to him and smiled.

"I imagine you're right. Right at this moment, all I want is a peaceful life. No danger . . . no surprises. Nothing to worry about except what to have for breakfast," she said lightly.

Deric was watching her with puzzled eyes. He had seen the dart of pain on her face when he had teased her about future adventures, her agitation. He had watched her straight back as she stood at the porthole, wondering what it was she was thinking. He frowned slightly when she turned and made her remark about a "peaceful life," trying to ignore the stab in his heart the words gave him. *Of course she wants a peaceful life—a life like that damned Lord Ormsby can give her,* he thought, and forced himself to smile back at her.

"We are headed back to Malta, are we not? You will be . . . going back to live with the governor? Or will it be something completely different? Our adventures have made you a woman of independent means."

Juliette suppressed a stab at her heart in turn. So he didn't even care if she went back to Malta—and out of his life! She realized she had been hoping against hope that somehow, during his illness, he might have come to feel something for her . . . to at least regret that they would have to part. But he spoke so lightly! It obviously didn't matter to him that he might never see her again.

She smiled at him brightly again, as artificial a smile as she had ever flashed at a dancing partner in a ballroom. "I'm afraid I haven't thought what I will do yet. Though it *is* comforting to know that whatever I decide, I will not have to worry about money."

Deric concealed gritted teeth under his equally false smile. He wanted to fling himself out of the bed and take her into his arms, shout at her that he loved her, damn it! And how dare she think of a future that didn't include *him?* Then he would kiss her until she was dizzy, until she told him she loved him, too.

But she had done so much for him. His Juli. *I owe her my life,* he thought. *I owe it to her to act like a gentleman for once—just for once—even if it means I must watch her marry someone else!*

"I'm glad . . . I hope you will find whatever it is that makes you happy, Juli. You deserve it so much . . ." He couldn't go on. He didn't trust his voice.

You would make me happy, Deric, she thought wildly, feeling tears rise in her throat. Before they showed in her face, she said quickly, "The . . . the doctor says I must not tire you yet. I am so glad you are better, Deric. I must go now. I'll come back . . . later." And she turned before he could say anything else and fled the room.

Deric stared at the slammed door. There had been pain in her face. Pain? Wasn't she happy? Everything was over, Halide and Ismail were safe, she had a small fortune coming from Aznan, and she was on her way back to Malta, where she could marry her lord and live a respectable, comfortable life. He shook his head angrily. And then, somewhere inside his heart, the memory of the expression on her face just before she left the room raised a faint flicker of hope in his heart.

Could it be . . . ?

He sat up straighter in bed.

"Farouk!" he bellowed, as loudly as he could.

Chapter Fifty

"So, what is it that could not wait, my friend, that you have to shout like a madman?" Farouk grinned as he settled in the chair next to Deric's bedside. There was a determined look on Deric's face.

"I wanted to talk to you about something," said Deric.

"So talk," said Farouk, lifting an eyebrow. He had a feeling he knew what the subject would be . . . but he wouldn't make it any easier.

"About Juli," said Deric irritably, watching Farouk's face closely.

"So? I thought so. It's about time," said Farouk, his face bland.

"What do you mean, about time?" demanded Deric.

"Dahkir, sometimes I think you are blind. It is obvious to me that you and Juli are eating your hearts out . . . and always have been."

"Juli . . . eating her heart out?" said Deric so eagerly that Farouk threw back his head and laughed.

Deric scowled. "And I suppose the way I feel about her—that's been obvious to you, too, from the first?"

Farouk regarded Deric, amused. "Completely obvious. I have seen you with many women, my friend—but never have I seen one affect you the way she does. Why won't you admit your feelings for her? Why do you fight against it so much?"

"Because at first, I didn't know how I felt. It may have been obvious to you, my very wise friend, but it wasn't obvious to me. I thought . . . well, never mind what I thought. I know now that—" Deric looked accusingly at Farouk. "What the devil do you mean by saying Juli is eating her heart out?"

"Just what I said. I am sure she feels about you as you feel about her."

"It's impossible!" Deric exploded, past all patience. "She wants nothing to do with me! And why should she? What can I offer her? I don't lead a settled life! You know I've been thinking of going to America . . . taking the money we've made and starting a plantation. But it's a wilderness. Why would she even consider that when there are men like that Lord Ormsby who want to marry her?"

Farouk considered gravely, stroking his moustache. "That's all true, no doubt. Juli *could* marry this lord . . . or another like him. Live a life of ease. Be a lady with a title, have security. But how do you know that's what she wants? Have you asked her . . . or are you just guessing?"

"Isn't it obvious?" replied Deric bitterly. "No, I haven't asked her . . . but what woman wouldn't want all those things? Don't they all?"

"Juli is not Amelia," Farouk said quietly. "All women are *not* the same. I would think that after everything we've been through, you would know that Juli especially is different than most women."

Deric's brows came together when Farouk mentioned Amelia. "No, she is *not* like other women. She is better than any of them. So how could I ask her to give up the kind of life she deserves and live the kind of life I can offer her?"

"You are being stubborn, my friend." Farouk smiled, amused again. "It is really *her* choice, not yours, is it not? All you can do is ask. She may say no."

"Will say no, you mean. You've forgotten the biggest problem of all. She doesn't want me." But Deric's eyes were searching Farouk's face as if he hoped Farouk would deny it.

Farouk did. "I think you are wrong again. I was with her every moment after we escaped from the harem and while you were ill. I know she feels strongly for you. Where her feelings go from here is perhaps up to you. If you let her leave your life again without even trying, will you not regret it forever?"

Deric stared at Farouk for a long moment. "Yes," he said at last.

Farouk grinned at him. "I'm glad to see you coming to your senses at last. I thought you never would." He rose and walked to the door. "Rest now. You're going to need all your strength." He laughed at Deric's curse and dodged a pillow flung at him before sauntering out the door, a wicked gleam of amusement in his eyes.

A knock sounded on Juliette's cabin door.

"Come in," she called.

The door swung open, and there stood Farouk, practically concealed by an enormous armload of cascading silks and laces. He walked in, a huge smile on his face.

"Farouk, what is all this?" She laughed.

"All this is for you," he said, throwing the welter of silks on the bed.

"But these are dresses!" She snatched up a gown and held it before her. It was an evening gown trimmed with point lace and velvet ribbons. With a squeal, she dug through the rest of the clothing. There were day dresses, ribbons, dainty lace-trimmed chemises and petticoats, even stockings. She whirled back to Farouk.

"Where did you get these?"

He grinned, pleased by her reaction. "But from the markets, of course."

"You bought these for me?"

"I did the purchasing—on Dahkir's instructions. You had better be pleased or Dahkir will have my head."

"He told you to buy these things for me?" Juliette asked disbelievingly.

"Yes, he knew you had nothing to wear and wanted to surprise you. Are you pleased with them?"

Juliette held the ball dress to her shoulders and twirled in front of her mirror. "They're beautiful! Did you pick them all out?" She flung the dress back onto the bed, picked up a filmy chemise and said teasingly, "Farouk, where did you get such intimate knowledge of women's fashions?"

He laughed. "You should be glad Dahkir was still too weak to make the shopping trip and had to send me." Modestly, he added, "Buying clothing for women is not new to me."

"Farouk, you devil. I never knew you were such a ladykiller!"

"The rewards are great when a man can make a woman happy."

She looked at him. "Deric bought these for me—to make me happy?"

"He wished to make you angry! What do you think, silly woman?"

She smiled and hugged the chemise to her breast. "Farouk—what did you mean when you told me he cares for me more than any other woman you have known about?" she asked softly.

"Just what I said."

His answer was inadequate. She wanted to know more. "Have there been many other women?"

"Not so many as you imagine, Juli. There was one once, back in England, who mattered to him. Since then, no woman has caught his attention for long."

Juliette remembered the bitterness in his voice when he had spoken of his home that night they'd talked in the garden. She'd wanted to ask Farouk then about Deric's past. Now was her chance. "He seems bitter about his life in England. Is it because of this woman?"

"Maybe at one time he was bitter. This English girl, Amelia, would not marry him because he had no money. Her scorn made him want to earn a fortune to prove to her his worth. He was very young then. But he is changed now."

"How has he changed?" It hurt Juliette to hear he had once wanted to marry someone else.

"When Dahkir realized this woman cared more for money than him, his love for her melted like snow in the sun. But it was a long time before the wound to his pride was healed. Perhaps it still pains him, because he still believes all women would choose to marry a rich man instead of a poor man."

"Some women would choose to marry for love," she said wistfully.

Farouk looked sympathetically at her averted face. "I hope you will marry for love, Juli," he said quietly, and left, closing the door behind him.

That evening, everyone gathered for dinner in the captain's

cabin. Farouk, Aznan and Halide all complimented the new dress Juliette wore until she laughingly told them to compliment Farouk instead. She smoothed the dark green velvet skirts, wishing Deric was there to see the new dress. But he still was too weak to leave his cabin.

Halide giggled. "I'll have to send Farouk to the bazaars to choose a new wardrobe for me! He has quite an eye for fabrics—and even sizes, it seems!"

"Halide, you would not believe it, but he is even an expert at buying women's undergarments!"

For once Farouk looked embarrassed as they all laughed. He looked to Aznan and said hastily, "Don't worry—I have no intention of picking out—such things!—for your wife!"

Aznan said blandly, "This is good, because I would hate to have to kill you after everything you've done for me."

Farouk hastened to change the subject. "So—we should reach Malta in two days." The ship had left Derna this morning and was now making way under a stiff wind for Malta.

"I think I embarrassed Farouk." Juliette laughed. "Look how he rushes to drop the subject of his expertise on women's clothes!"

"Pour me some wine. I think I'm going to need it," growled Farouk.

"Don't let him get his hands on the bottle or there will be none left for me, and I've a mind for a glass of wine."

They all turned to find Deric standing in the doorway. Juliette's heart skipped a beat. He looked healthy. His skin had regained its bronze tone, and he'd lost that haggard look that had haunted her. He was startlingly handsome as he stood smiling at them all.

"What has embarrassed Farouk?" he inquired, walking in.

"Dahkir! What are you doing up?" asked Farouk.

"You should not be out of bed yet," reproved Halide.

"I feel fine. The only thing that would make me ill would be spending another minute in bed alone." His eyes met Juliette's. "Hello, Juli," he said.

"Hello," she replied, feeling suddenly shy.

Aznan handed Deric a glass of wine. "It does my heart good to see you on the road to health. Your timing is excellent. We are just about to sit down to dinner."

Deric's eyes danced. "I hope beef broth isn't on the menu tonight."

As Juliette walked to the table, she found Deric at her elbow. With a courtly gesture, he pulled out her chair and seated her. She looked up at him in surprise, remembering the early days on the caravan when he had mocked her dainty manners. Now here he was, playing the gentleman!

He sat down across from her. As if reading her mind, he looked at her and said, "It's been a long time since I sat at a real table and used a knife and fork."

Farouk put in, "Dahkir has become quite the desert nomad, always in a tent and avoiding cities. I will have to refresh his memory on civilized behavior, I see."

"You teach me civilized behavior! Why, you should have seen him the last time I had to carry him out of a tavern . . ."

Juliette joined in the laughter and sat listening to their friendly bantering, happy to see Deric so recovered. She looked at Aznan and Halide. They were sitting so close their shoulders touched, hands clasped, a glow of happiness about them. They kept glancing at each other as if to make sure the other was really there. She sighed. She envied their great love for each other. It was what she'd always wished for herself.

Aznan lifted his wineglass. "I would like to make a toast to my beautiful wife Halide. For her bravery, her steadfastness in suffering, for her tender care of my son, and for her faith that Allah would one day reunite us." He looked at her tenderly, his dark eyes shining. "I pledge to her my undying love, and I swear that I will never let us be separated again."

They all lifted their glasses and drank, their eyes misty. Juliette felt Deric's gaze on her.

"You are a wise man, Aznan. A man should never let the woman he loves go," said Deric.

Juliette could not look away. Could he mean—?

Then to her disappointment, Deric turned and began talking to Farouk. His voice was matter-of-fact, and she cast her eyes down and stared at the table.

No, of course he couldn't mean anything. As usual, she was taking his slightest words too seriously.

Chapter Fifty-One

Night had fallen, and the full moon rose above a calm sea. The ship was nearing Malta. They would make port in the morning, and the voyage would end. Juliette sighed as she got dressed for dinner, dreading their arrival. Deric's face rose before her eyes.

The face she might never see again after tomorrow.

Her heart ached as she thought how kind he had been these last few days—polite, smiling, joking with her—a complete gentleman. She smiled ruefully. She never thought she would regret that Deric would act like a gentleman . . . but she did. Once, she remembered all too well, he was no gentleman at all where she was concerned. Once it had only taken him moments to have her clothes in a heap, and she in his arms. Now he treated her as if she were made of porcelain, never touching her. How she wished he would take her in his arms! Yes, he was finally treating her with respect.

And how she hated it!

She walked to the mirror. She had dressed with extra care tonight. Her gown was of deep burnished silver, almost pewter, trimmed with black velvet ribbons and frothing falls of white lace. The square-cut neckline was daringly low, and the tight sleeves hugged her arms to the elbow, where they were tied with black ribbons above a spilling waterfall of lace.

Her mouth tightened as she stared at her image. "Do I look pretty enough to make him want to kiss me?" she wondered. "Or has he forgotten? I'll *make* him remember. I can't let him go without at least kissing him once more!"

The night before she'd gone back into the harem, she believed he'd been about to tell her he loved her. This was their last night together, and still he hadn't spoken. If a kiss didn't lead him to speak . . . then she would have to speak herself. She couldn't let him leave her life again without knowing how he really felt.

She thought of those four months without him in Malta, and a chill struck her heart. Oh God, if he was going to let her go again . . . if she had to live without Deric . . .

She straightened her shoulders and walked to the door, fighting the fear that after tomorrow she might never see him again. There was tonight. And tonight there was still hope.

Climbing to the deck, she walked to the rail. She could hear voices faintly from the captain's cabin, where everyone was already gathered. She stood staring out at the sea, at the dark velvety Mediterranean sea, the waves tipped with gleams of silver from the moon high in the sky. It swam in a cloudy haze of light that seemed breathtakingly beautiful and mysterious to Juliette, and her eyes swept the stars, taking in their humbling loveliness.

At the sound of a soft step on the deck, she turned. A dark shape loomed behind her—an unmistakable male outline of broad shoulders and narrow waist.

"Deric," she breathed.

He stood still, watching her in the moonlight. She could see the gleam of his eyes under dark brows, but could not tell the expression on his face.

"You look . . . beautiful," he said after a moment.

She drew in her breath at something in his voice.

"After I left you in Tripoli, I would lie in my tent and remember how you looked that night I pulled you out of the well. I couldn't forget," he went on, his voice low and soft. "From the very beginning, you had a hold on me whether I wanted you to or not. When I first found you in a faint at my feet, I remember I expected you to scream and cry when you woke up. Instead you fought me. And I in turn fought you. But Juli—I fought you in vain. You'd won since the very moment I looked into your eyes and realized I'd never met a woman like you."

There was a pause, and she could barely breathe at the way her heart was feeling.

"I've never been able to forget anything about you. The nights we spent together were hardest of all to forget," he said.

"I couldn't forget them, either," she whispered.

Their eyes locked, hers widening, his darkening. The moonlight poured down around them in luminous enchantment, making the night look as wild and magic as what they saw in each other's eyes.

"Let me remember how it feels to kiss you."

And then he was taking her into his arms, his mouth coming down to cover hers, and she was reaching up to pull him closer while the world spun around her, vanishing. . . .

Farouk opened the door to the captain's cabin and called back, "I will see what is keeping them," with a laugh. He emerged on deck and stood for a moment looking at the moonlight. Then his gaze fell on the outline of two figures entwined at the rail, a tall silhouette with broad shoulders, and a slender shape that clung to the tall one as if for life.

He smiled, then said under his breath softly, "This time, my friends, I will *not* interrupt you . . . but leave you to the night together."

He turned and walked back to the captain's cabin, whistling softly, and went inside. He held up his hands to the inquiring faces turned toward him, and said, "I am sorry, but Dahkir feels too weak to join us. His wound, I am afraid."

Halide at once rose and offered to go to him. "That is terrible! Poor Mr. Raleigh!" she said, concerned.

Farouk held up his hand again. "Juli is with him. She said for all of you to enjoy your dinners, and promises she will try to join us presently." Smoothly, he took Halide's arm and guided her back to her seat. "Now, how about a glass of wine for me?" He laughed. Finding Aznan's eyes fixed on him, one eyebrow inquiringly lifted, Farouk swiftly winked at him. He raised his glass. "To love! There is such a moon tonight, that I would drink to lovers everywhere!"

Halide suddenly smiled, too, catching something in her husband's face, and they all laughed at once. "To love," agreed Aznan.

"I've waited too long for this," said Deric at last, lifting his head and looking down at her. She was a glorious vision, her eyes half closed in the moonlight, her curls tumbling on her shoulders, her skin glowing luminously.

"I wanted you to kiss me one more time . . . before we reach Malta tomorrow, and—"

"And?" She saw his face darken as his grip on her shoulders tightened. "Say what you mean."

"And—and we may never see each other again," she continued softly, hardly able to meet his eyes.

His grasp left her shoulders, and he turned abruptly to the rail, gripping it. Startled, she searched his face. It looked hard in the moonlight, its planes carved of stone, his eyes shadowed under his brows.

"No," he said, his voice controlled. "We may never see each other again. You still haven't told me what you mean to do."

Juliette stiffened. She heard the coolness in his voice, and her heart sank. He was pushing her away again!

"I still haven't decided," she said quietly, trying to find the courage to tell him the truth—tell him how she felt. "I suppose I will have to wait until I get there and see . . . how things are."

"I suppose you will marry," he said through clenched teeth. "That . . . Lord Ormsby who asked for your hand, he would offer you a comfortable life."

"A comfortable life! I remember once you told me you thought that is what every woman wants. You think women are all the same—you made up your mind about them long ago—and you never bother to find out if you are right or not!"

He searched her face. "I once thought that, it's true," he said. "But I was wrong. You're not like any woman I have ever met—and now I'm asking you. Aren't those things important to you? A settled home? A place in society—the place that is rightfully yours?"

Juliette stared at the silver moon and felt bewitched. It was a night of wild beauty, a lovers' night, warm and soft. And it was time to throw caution to the winds . . . tell the truth . . . even at the cost of her pride.

"Those things don't matter to me at all," she whispered, her exquisite profile tilted up toward the moon, away from Deric. "All that matters to me is being with the man I love."

His eyes were riveted to her face. Passion and love and hope leapt in his heart like a flame at her words.

"Juli." She turned slowly and looked up at him. His mouth tightened and his gaze slowly dropped to linger on her mouth. "I know what it is that *I* want," he said, his voice rough with desire. His arms came around her again, and he tilted her chin up to his face. "I want you."

Juliette surrendered to the tide of feeling rushing through her as his mouth claimed hers. Her arms came up around his neck and twined in his hair as she felt the passion leap between them, and she was lost in the world of his kiss. The earth vanished; nothing else existed, nothing else except her love for him.

"Juli . . . you want me, too," he was whispering as his lips traveled across her cheek to her ear. "Tell me—say it," he demanded.

She felt the color flood her cheeks at his bold words, but tonight was a magic night . . . her last magic night with Deric. What was the use of pretending?

"Yes, this is what I want," she whispered back shyly. "To have your arms around me like this. Nothing else matters."

Deric straightened, clasping her close to his chest, holding her tightly for a moment. She could feel his heart hammering against her ear, feel his long, strong body pressed breathlessly against hers.

"But I want more than just desire from you" came the unbelievable words from above her ear. She felt him take a deep breath. "I want love from you."

"Love?" she repeated, dazed. Before she could say another word, he was speaking again, saying the words she'd never thought to hear.

"Because I love you. I love you! I love you like I've never loved any woman. Before I met you I thought once I'd loved and lost love, but God help me, I didn't know what it was to lose the woman I love until the day I left you in Tripoli. I let you leave me once, and it was the biggest mistake I ever made. I knew I could never offer you the kind of life I thought you wanted . . . the security you deserve. But now I can't let you go again without telling you how I feel, even though I know you don't feel the same way," he finished.

"Oh, Deric," she cried, feeling tears start, but laughing up into his face, her heart about to burst with joy too great to contain, with love for him too large for her heart to hold. "There you go again—making up your mind before you ask me what I think." She was laughing and crying as he captured her face in his hands, searching her eyes with an eager look she would never forget, a look that told her his love was as great as her own.

"I love you, Deric Raleigh! I've loved you since the beginning, but I was so afraid you didn't care about me—!"

"Didn't care about you—" He swore, and she caught her breath at the relief in his eyes—and the love she saw there.

Again his mouth claimed hers, in a kiss of surpassing tenderness and passion. As he felt her melting in his arms, he breathed in suddenly, unable to resist her a moment longer, and swept her up in his arms, his mouth never leaving hers.

He strode with her through the moonlight down the deck to his cabin, where he paused a moment. His darkly shadowed eyes looked down into her loving ones.

"You love me?" he asked, almost roughly. "You really love me?"

"I love you," she sighed, and he kicked open the door and carried her inside.

Chapter Fifty-Two

Moonlight poured into the cabin through the porthole, turning everything to black and silver shadows and pools of light. The ship swayed on the waves, but the two lying twined on the bed were aware of nothing but each other. Juliette lay in a tumble of long silken legs, her hair streaming over her back, her arms around Deric and her head resting on his broad chest. His hand slowly moved up and down her back, and gradually, their breathing slowed, returning to normal.

Juliette lay in a daze of happiness that she had never felt. Deric loved her! She was slowly descending from a whirling world of feeling that had carried her to heights she had never suspected existed. Tonight, there had been an added tenderness to their lovemaking—a depth of feeling that was new for both of them. She heard Deric sigh and felt his arms tighten as he drew her even closer to him.

She stirred in his arms, smiling. "Deric—we missed the dinner," she said, laughing softly.

He chuckled, too. "Well worth missing, wouldn't you say? I think I would gladly miss anything for a night like this with you."

She smiled against his chest and raised herself to look down at him. Her eyes sparkled with a wicked slant, her mouth curved.

"Anything?" she teased. "Anything in the whole world—even a wild adventure?"

"Even a wild adventure," he answered firmly, reaching up a

hand to stroke her hair.

Suddenly Juliette's eyes filled with mischief. "I suppose it will be an adventure being your mistress."

"Mistress?" He sat up, the scowl she'd come to love darkening his features, and she had to stifle a giggle.

"You've told me often enough you're not a marrying man."

"And you've told me often enough you wouldn't marry me if I was the last man on earth!"

She burst out laughing, and after a moment, he laughed, too.

He threw her a wicked smile, one brow lifted. "You also told me you wanted to marry for love—and that you loved me. But I'm not the last man on earth."

She threw her arms around him. "You know you're the only man on earth for me, you rogue!"

Suddenly his eyes were serious. "But I don't know what your answer would be—because I haven't asked you yet, have I?" He stopped, and she felt her heart speed up at the love she saw in his eyes. "Juli, I love you—I could never live without you." Again he stopped, and she waited, barely able to breathe.

"Will you marry me?"

"Oh, Deric—yes!" Joy flooded every corner of her being like dazzling light. "Of course I will marry you—I love you—I could never be happy, either, unless I was at your side!"

His mouth found hers in the moonlight, and they merged in a kiss of joy, a kiss that seemed to seal them together, forging a silver chain of love for the future.

After a moment, Juliette broke away, laughing, shaking her head. "Oh, Deric," she said, tears filling her eyes, "we have never understood each other from the first, have we? I thought you still didn't want to marry—even if you did love me! And you thought—you thought I wouldn't want to marry you because of your life! Oh, it frightens me to think what would have happened if somehow, neither of us had spoken—if somehow, we had walked away from each other!"

"I never could have walked away from you, Juli. I let you go once, and it was the biggest mistake I ever made. I'm not going to let you go ever again."

She clasped him close, not wanting to lose him. "Deric, how could you think I wouldn't marry you—go anywhere with you?" There was a catch in her voice, and she looked at him mistily for a long moment. Then a thought struck her, and a spark lit her eyes. Teasingly, she added, "By the way, where *are* we going to go?"

He looked at her. Her eyes flashed with mischief, her mouth curved with merriment, and there was still a mist of tears on her lower lashes. He thought he had never seen a woman so beautiful—so glorious. He drew in his breath and smiled back at her.

"Wherever you want on the earth, Juli. I swear, at this moment, I would give you anything you asked!"

She laughed and tossed her hair. "Anywhere on earth? What if I said London or Paris?" She giggled deliciously. "Don't worry, my love, I won't ask it! I'm too used to a life of adventure—and as long as I'm at your side, I don't care where we go. But you can't tell me you don't have a single idea where you want to go."

He folded his arms and sat back, feigning exasperation. "You know me far too well, I can see. Yes . . . I had an idea. The Americas. I thought I would like to sail there . . . to the Indies . . . to Virginia . . . the Carolinas . . . Jamaica . . . and see what it is like. Then, if we found a place we liked, perhaps we could make a home in the New World. Help to carve out the new land. It should be an adventure." Deric's voice became serious. "And there would be some dangers and hardships, I fear. But it would also be a settled life. We could have a home someday . . . one we would build ourselves, together. A home for ourselves—for our children."

"Oh, Deric," said Juliette softly, overcome with emotion. "It sounds wonderful. When do we leave?" She flung her arms around his neck, showering him with kisses.

"I think we should get married first," he said presently, in a lazy drawl.

Juliette lay in the moonlit cabin, dissolved in bliss, feeling Deric's chest rise and fall under her cheek. She thought again of how they might have walked away from each other without telling their feelings . . . and then been lonely all their lives. How slender was the thread that a life's destiny and happiness could hang on! She knew that Deric was her fate . . . and that fate had brought them together, meant for each other.

Fate. The narrow thread. She looked at the silver and black moonlight, and was reminded of the rose-and-silver brocade dress—the dress that had really started it all. The dress that had stopped the pirate's sword, so that she lived, so that she was taken to Mulay . . . to Deric. The dress that had, in the end, brought them together.

She stirred in the dark.

"Deric . . . you said you would give me anything in the world before. Did you mean it?"

"Of course I meant it," he said, his hand in her hair. She could hear a smile in his voice. "Why—what great and impossible thing is it that you want? What are you about to ask of me?"

"No great and impossible thing," she said softly, smiling too. "Just a dress."

"That's easy enough, my love. Is that all?"

"Yes," she said. "That's all I want you to give me. Just a dress. A rose-and-silver brocade dress to be married in."